More Praise for *The Travelling Hornplayer*

"The brilliant [Trapido] . . . is one of the better-kept secrets of contemporary letters . . . In its wisdom, in its genius for the dance of character and story, in its inexhaustible mastery of the funny and painful details of everyday middle-class life, above all in its acceptance of tragedy, *The Travelling Hornplayer* will surely outlast most of the books being touted and enjoyed today. Trapido is a great novelist; sooner or later the whole reading world will know it." —*San Francisco Chronicle*

"A wrenching ride . . . There are points in the book when you don't know whether to laugh or cry." —*USA Today*

"Barbara Trapido deserves to be better known on this side of the Atlantic." —*Newsday*

"Quietly poignant, *The Travelling Hornplayer* is notable not only for its tragic moments, but for its . . . penetrating humor and biting sarcasm." —*Milwaukee–Wisconsin Journal Sentinel*

"A significant accomplishment of literary cunningness." —*The Seattle Times*

"Rollicking, bitter-sweet . . . No one will identify more readily with this novel than those who feel their lives are also like a deflating balloon hissing, darting, and then collapsing in an unreachable corner. But they'll take comfort from Trapido's very real concern for her characters, and the fact that she always has enough breath to blow hope back into their dizzy lives and ours." —*Christian Science Monitor*

"Her fans might be forgiven for thinking this writer couldn't get any better. She just has." —*The Guardian*

"A rare combination of a good, fun read with more serious literature." —*The Virginia Quarterly Review*

"The woman is brilliant. She deserves to be up there, topping the bestseller lists and winning all the prizes. And she actually makes you laugh . . . I enjoyed every page of this book." —*The Daily Mail*

"Reading Barbara Trapido is sheer pleasure. Afterwards, I went out and bought everything else she has written—and am only disappointed I didn't do it earlier." —*The Independent on Sunday*

"[A] mischievous social comedy . . . Enchanting . . . Romantic and sexual complications are worked out with almost Shakespearean finesse and unpredictability . . . Trapido blithely analyzes her people's sometimes disastrous comings and goings in a bittersweet, often very sexy romance reminiscent of the fiction of Muriel Spark, Beryl Bainbridge and perhaps Rose Macaulay. But she is triumphantly her own woman, and this is one of her most entertaining books." —*Kirkus Reviews*

"Deliciously subversive . . . As Trapido's characters experience love, loss, grief and plucky survival, the narrative twists are accomplished with a sleight of hand so subtle that the reader is often stunned." —*Publishers Weekly* (starred review)

"With tenderness and wit, Trapido weaves together a huge cast of characters in contemporary England and tells a story of family love and grief, passionate sex and betrayal, and bleak coincidence . . . Wry . . . and hilarious." —*Booklist*

The Travelling Hornplayer

BARBARA TRAPIDO

BLOOMSBURY
NEW YORK • LONDON • OXFORD • NEW DELHI • SYDNEY

For Alexandra Pringle and Charles van Onselen

Bloomsbury USA
An imprint of Bloomsbury Publishing Plc

1385 Broadway
New York
NY 10018
USA

50 Bedford Square
London
WC1B 3DP
UK

www.bloomsbury.com

First published by Hamish Hamilton in 1998
This paperback edition first published by Bloomsbury in 2009
First U.S. edition published 2016

ISBN: TPB: 978-1-62040-873-5
ePub: 978-1-62040-879-7

Library of Congress Cataloging-in-Publication Data is available.

2 4 6 8 10 9 7 5 3 1

Typeset by Hewer Text UK Ltd, Edinburgh
Printed and bound in the U.S.A. by Berryville Graphics Inc., Berryville, Virginia

Foreword

I first discovered Barbara Trapido's writing the old-fashioned way, in a local bookstore. It was last summer, and I had been on tour with my own book for a few months, teaching, speaking, on another planet basically. At last a small vacation with my family approached, and I was desperate to read something that would make me laugh. In South Brooklyn I had lunch with a friend, and decided to drop in on Community Bookstore, a gem of the neighborhood. Stephanie, the owner, greeted me as I walked in, and I said, "I'm here for some summer reading." She looked at me off-kilter. It was nearly September. I had missed the entire thing and hadn't realized it.

I told her I wanted something funny. She held up *The Dud Avocado*. "I've read it but that's exactly what I want," I said. "Give me another that." Then she handed me Barbara Trapido's first novel, *Brother of the More Famous Jack*, and I said, "What else you got?" (I can never just take the first suggestion. That takes all the fun out of it.) She suggested a Ferrante, because everyone should read Ferrante if they haven't yet, but of course Ferrante isn't very funny, at least not in the way I was thinking.

Eventually she passed me off to another bookseller and I said, "I want something funny," and he said, "Have you ever read him?" And then he pointed to a long row of every Phillip Roth novel ever written in paperback, and I said, "Uh yeah, I've read him," and then he said, "What about Shalom Auslander," and I said, "Yeah," and he said, "What about Sam Lipsyte," and I said, "Yeah," and then Stephanie, overhearing all of this, came back to me and handed me the Trapido book again and said, "Trust me, you want this."

Which is how I came to read and love Barbara Trapido on my one vacation that summer, and discover her fresh, human, spritely characters, and her vibrant, witty prose. "Now *that's* how to write a book," I said to myself. And it's also how I came to post a picture of her book with an admiring remark on my Instagram account, which happens to be followed by a publicist at Bloomsbury, who then told an editor there that I was reading Trapido, who then contacted me and asked me if I'd be interested in reading her fifth book, *The Travelling Hornplayer*, all of which is obviously an extremely modern way to be introduced to a book.

Anyway this book—no spoilers, I know—is a delight. You know a book is good when you want to steal everything. The way Trapido glides from tragedy to joy on a shimmering light wave of prose. Her effortless switch of perspectives, both between characters and within those characters themselves. All the angles of each person, like a glittering jewel being turned from facet to facet. And yes, it's funny. Such sharp little monsters she's created: Stella, the difficult, dyslexic, silky-red-haired musician whose "flecked pussycat eyes always veer sideways; always slightly off target"; her wise friend Ellen, haunted by a tragic death and a devastated family, "a person who—as her stepmother put it—had experienced amputation"; and the people that surround them: philandering fathers, whip-smart mothers, manipulative lovers, and more. It's just a very pure, vivid tale, full of loud, intelligent voices, where some people get the happy endings, and some people are cursed never to be happy.

And there's a certain moral center to it, as well, which I take comfort in these days, more than ever, looking for guidance in literature. How to be, how not to be. Trapido has actual grown-up opinions on this! All of this she offers us within the confines of one beautiful little book. I found it deeply satisfying.

I end this foreword with a marker for myself. I write this as a reminder and an admonishment to take the books handed to me. I think I can say—after living a life as a contemporary writer which, when promoting oneself, can often feel like being a traveling salesman/sideshow act/toot-your-own-hornplayer—that we should take the valuable recommendations wherever they come from, and treasure them when they do. And I've never met Barbara Trapido myself but I suspect she's exactly the kind of person who'll insist you read something, absolutely insist on it, put a book in your hand and say, "Trust me, this is the one you want."

March 2016

'I ask no flower,
I ask no star;
. . .
. . .
I am no gardener,
And the stars are too high.'

WILHELM MÜLLER (1794–1827), *Seventy-Seven Poems from the Posthumous Papers of a Travelling Hornplayer*

Contents

The chapter subtitles are from Schubert's *Die schöne Müllerin*, words by Wilhelm Müller.

1. Des Müllers Blumen

Ellen

EARLY ON THE morning of my interview, I woke up and saw my dead sister. I had not seen her for three years. She came into my bedroom, opening and closing the door without a sound. Her hair was bobbed short and she was dressed in plain white cotton T-shirt and knickers. Nothing else. I watched her cross the room on bare feet, and pause to touch the somewhat staid interview clothes that I had laid out on a chair the night before: navy calflength skirt, navy lambswool jumper, cream silk shirt, paisley silk scarf, best polished boots. She paused again to stroke the foot-end of my duvet. Then she walked on towards the window, where the curtains were drawn shut. While her facial expression in life had been characteristically animated, it was now serene and fixed, like that of a person sleep-walking.

Though she made no sound, she left a five-word sentence behind her in the room. The words were in German. I heard them in her voice but, at the same time, I was aware that the voice was audible only inside my own head: '*Die Sterne stehn zu hoch.*' I should explain here that I don't really speak German – that is, not beyond the level of GCSE Grade C – though I knew that I had come across the phrase before, and I knew enough to be able to translate it: 'The stars are too high.'

As soon as she had disappeared behind the curtain, I jumped out of bed and went to the window. Nothing was there; only the cold glass panes and, beyond them, the gleaming monochrome of the garden in the minutes before the dawn. Of one thing I am completely certain. I was not asleep. I remember that the vision of her filled me with a terrible longing, and that my lack of fear surprised me. I remember that I felt honoured by her being there, and that afterwards I felt pain. I felt the loss of her, once again, like an ugly lump of flesh twisting inside my own chest.

When my sister was killed by a car in north London, her small leather backpack was thrown clear of her body. It contained nothing except a return train ticket between King's Cross and Royston in Hertfordshire, where she was still at school, her Young Person's Railcard and the extended essay she had just then had returned to her that she had written for her A level German course.

Since she had not filled in the address section of the railcard, it was the essay that had made the job of identifying her such an easy one for the police. The front cover of the essay's binder had a large adhesive label with the name of her examination board and that of her school. It also gave her name and candidate number, and the title of her essay. It was called *Love and Death at the Mill: Twenty Poems from the Posthumous Papers of a Travelling Hornplayer*.

I was in Edinburgh when she died – I was coming to the end of my first year at the university – but no one at home had any idea why Lydia had gone into London that day, though within the week, while going through her things, my father and the Stepmother had come upon the draft of a letter written to the middle-aged writer son of one of my sister's godmother's friends; a person whom neither I nor my parents had ever met though we were all aware that he had written a novel some years earlier entitled *Have Horn; Will Travel*. The place where my sister died was directly in front of his London flat.

The letter, which was long and jaunty, was one in which she had sought his advice over the essay, but it was not difficult to tell that, in its childish, girly way, the letter was a bit of a come-on. Some months after the date of it, she had submitted the essay and had been awarded an A, along with special words of praise from both teacher and moderator. The speculation was that, on having the essay returned to her, she had simply decided, on the spur of the moment, to take it into London and show it to him, her unofficial adviser. She hadn't made any arrangement to do so, and had evidently found the writer away from his flat, since he had gone home two days earlier than usual that week, to be with his wife and family somewhere in the Cotswolds, where they lived. The place in London was merely a small bolt-hole where he went during the week to work.

Though the driver had been travelling too fast, the accident was ruled not to have been his fault. A witness confirmed that, for some reason, my sister had run at speed straight out in front of the car without looking to left or to right. It was said that she had seemed distressed.

The force of contact had been such that she had been thrown clear of the road onto the grass of park. Near to where her body had landed, there was a small man-made lake bordered with periwinkles and forget-me-nots. *Vergissmeinnicht.* It is difficult, in retrospect, to avoid the crude symbolism of this too blatant coincidence, since the same blue flowers – the *blaue Blümelein* – are associated with the mill girl's eyes in the cycle of German Romantic poems to which her essay relates. They grow by water and they come to deck the grave of the miller who dies, of course, of unrequited love. They are a repeating and prevalent feature of my sister's extended essay; the essay which my father has had bound in leather and which he keeps on his study desk.

After that early morning visitation, I went downstairs to the tall bookshelves in the hall where, at the top near the ceiling, are stacked some dark green box files that contain those of my sister's papers that my father chose to keep. I felt impelled right then to re-read the letter, and it brought vividly back to me all that schoolgirl bubble and silliness that she and I had shared in our capacity as each other's best friend. Once my sister was gone, these were qualities that I either suppressed or lost. Not having Lydia to bounce off, I became somebody else. When you are young enough – and I was eighteen to her seventeen when she died – you still, perhaps, have options about the kind of person you will become. I became, because of her dying, a more earnest, more straight-faced, more directed person. It may be that I became a bit of a bore.

It surprises me now to remember that my father – our father – had used to call us 'Gigglers One and Two'; that he was always inclined to treat us as if we were two halves of the same pantomime horse. He has treated me very seriously ever since. People in the past were often unable to tell us one from the other. This was not only because we looked alike, but because our speech and other mannerisms were similar. It is only very rarely now that a person will call me by her name. The Lydia that once lived is dead in both of us.

My sister's letter went like this:

Dear Mr Goldman,

I don't expect you will remember me, but I met you in my Godmother Vanessa's house in Worcestershire last summer. You had driven down to drop your mother. However, you may remember that Godmother was a concert soprano in her day and that she made you sing. You sang songs from Schubert's Die schöne Müllerin *and your mother played the piano. Although, as you must know, you sing very well, I confess that, had my sister Ellie not left an hour before your arrival, we would have giggled throughout your performance. As it was, I merely yawned and played with the cat, and ate far too much of the carrot cake that Godmother had made in your honour. Godmother Vanessa is your greatest fan, and she always calls you 'The Novelist'.*

'My dears,' she'd said to Ellie and me, 'do you know that "The Novelist" is coming to tea? I think we will make him a carrot cake.'

My point now is that when I got home I recollected your singing. After I got back I began to think about some of the things I'd half overheard you say to Godmother. You said that water was the metaphor that bound the poems together and you made some joke about its 'convenient fluidity'. You said that the water, while it encouraged and sanctioned the idea of male restlessness and male wanderings, then became quite cruelly deceitful, detached and inscrutable. You said something about sex and fluids and suicide. You said what a useful thing it was for the German Romantics that the word Herz *rhymed with* Schmerz. *(I hope you enjoy being paraphrased like this.)*

To tell you the truth, I went out the next day and I bought the song cycle on CD. I bought it twice, once being sung by Dietrich Fischer-Dieskau, who sings beautifully but he has irritating nursery sibilants, and once, somewhat shriekishly, by a woman called Birgitte Something. I wanted to see if the songs could cross gender, but I expect they can't.

I decided then and there to abandon my previous resolution to Improve my Mind by reading my way through the Encyclopaedia Britannica, *starting with the letter A. I have opted for A level German, though my sister thinks I must be off my head. We both did GCSE German, you see, because our mother said we had to. That's because she's French and she'd always made us speak French with her at home, so we could do that quite well already. Naturally, we'd wanted to sign up for GCSE French, thinking it would be a good skive, but the tyrant matriarch wouldn't allow it. After that, Ellie thought two years of German had been quite enough. Two years of:*

'Was hast du gern?'

'Ich habe Popmusik gern.'

'Und hast du eine Lieblingsgruppe?'

'Ja. Abba ist meine Lieblingsgruppe.'

She'd also had a Bad Experience during the German exchange, while I'd had the most adorable dentist's family in Munich who took me on lovely jaunts and offered to put braces on my teeth. Ellie's family swept her off over the border into the country somewhere outside Vienna. She was stuck with these two pigmentless boys in lederhosen called Hubert-und-Norbert, *who looked exactly like white mice and had not an eyebrow between them. One of them played a squeeze-box and the other one blew on this brasswind item at all hours, right under her window. On Easter morning she'd woken up to a blast, only to find that* Herr Vater *White Mouse was looming over her bed, clothed from head to foot in a yellow fur-fabric bunny suit with polka-dot bow-tie and handy pull-down zip.*

The only outing she'd been taken on was once to the cathedral in Vienna, where Frau Mutti *White Mouse had been so odiously smug about the Defeated Infidel at the Siege of Vienna that Ellie was moved to observe (in English) that if only the Infidel had not been repulsed at the gates of Vienna then perhaps* Hubert-und-Norbert *would be sporting sexy black eyebrows and even sexier black moustaches. The episode has left my sister with leanings towards dark men called Ishmael and Quoresh, especially in djellabahs. She thinks it no accident that the word 'pasha' should sound so much like 'passion'.*

Anyway, the upshot is that I have decided to write my A level long essay on the poet Wilhelm Müller, who, as you will of course know, wrote the poems on which Die schöne Müllerin *was based. The trouble is, I knew very little about German poetry – or poetry in general, since I see now that I have Misspent My Youth reading Quite the Wrong Sort of Book. I only know German poetry if it's hymns. I know* 'Ein feste Burg ist Unser Gott' *and I know 'Praise the Lord, Ye Heavens Adore Him', which is really* Deutschland über Alles. *So I wonder now if you could bear it if I were to come in on the train to see you and talk to you about German poetry, and German Romanticism, and* Herz, *and* Schmerz, *and especially about Wilhelm Müller? And would you mind if I were to take down absolutely every word you utter? And if I were then to submit these utterings, word for word, as my extended essay?*

This letter is getting far too long. Ade. Ade. *Please reply to me.*

Yours sincerely,

Lydia Dent

My sister had added the obligatory adolescent postscript. It said:

> *P.S. I have translated one line in the poems as 'Better you should have stayed in the woods'* – 'Doch besser du bliebest im Walde dazu' *– but it sounds too much like the punchline of a Jewish joke. (As in 'Better he should have been a doctor.') Is German a dialect of Yiddish, do you know, or could it be the other way round?*
>
> *Yours again*
> *Lydia Dent*

As Lydia has mentioned in her letter, I was no longer with her when she met The Novelist. I had missed him by one hour, having left in order to accompany our paternal grandmother on a trip to Derbyshire which she had offered me as an eighteenth birthday treat. When I returned, Lydia reported, rather casually, that he was tall and dark, and wore a white linen shirt and steel-rimmed glasses and deck shoes, which she estimated as approximately European size 46. She said nothing about him singing.

The Novelist's mother had been at school with Liddie's godmother before and during the War. Both women were very musical. Both had married and were now widowed, though – while her friend had had six children – Liddie's godmother had remained childless. Liddie was completely right in her letter about Godmother's enthusiasm for The Novelist. She was a regular guest at all his launch parties and she liked to attend his readings. She was always in possession of his most recent hardback, signed and dated by the author.

I do remember that the making of the carrot cake had provoked in Lydia and me all our usual gigglings and foolings. Lydia's godmother had set us to grate the carrots while she had busied herself with the kitchen scales.

'Godmother,' Liddie said, 'will The Novelist like his carrots grated finer than this?' We wrestled enjoyably for turns with the grater.

'Godmother,' Liddie said, 'will The Novelist mind bits of blood and grated bones in his carrot cake?'

'Give over, Liddie,' I said, as the grater fell to the floor. 'Now look what you've gone and made me do.'

'Godmother?' Liddie said. 'Will The Novelist mind floor scrapings in his carrot cake?'

Lydia's godmother had merely continued to regret that I was going to miss The Novelist's visit and had expressed the hope that my grandmother would be just a teeny bit late. In the event, Grandmother was punctual to the minute, and I believe that The Novelist and his mother were late. I have been told that he was somewhere in the background at Lydia's funeral.

Just as she flattered us with assumptions of consensus in the matter of The Novelist's work, so Lydia's godmother had always behaved as if we were in agreement generally upon matters of high culture. She took us to recitals and theatres and poetry readings and to exhibitions of paintings. On the whole, she affected not to notice that we tittered and fidgeted our way through all of them. If a soprano had the merest hint of moustache, or a poet a tendency to gather saliva at the corners of his mouth, or a painter appeared to us over-keen on lilac-tinted depictions of female crotch and nipple, then these would be things to set us off on our gigglers' course. If, on the other hand, the tenor were young enough or handsome enough, then Lydia would adopt a policy of staring at him fixedly with huge goose-eyes, until the poor man would resort to singing all of 'On Wenlock Edge' or 'Have You Seen But a White Lily Grow?' with his eyes glued to the ceiling.

Once, when Lydia's godmother had taken us to a production of *Waiting for Godot*, we had begun quite early on to wonder how long it would be before Godot came.

'When does Godot come?' Lydia whispered to me. I shrugged, having no idea, of course. 'Godmother,' she said. 'When does Godot come?'

'Oh,' said Lydia's godmother. 'Oh, my darlings, he doesn't *come*, you see. Or perhaps he has come already. That is really the point.' After that, Lydia fell asleep.

From the start, GCSE German had made us giggle, along with more or less everything else. We giggled while testing each other's vocabulary – and it is obvious that, for any English schoolchild bent upon rudimentary satire, a language in which the word for one's male parent coincides so rewardingly with the word in one's own language for a person given to anal expulsions of gas has blatant possibilities. We had already been disposed to it through the history class, which had offered us Martin Luther and his done-to-death Diet of Worms. Lydia informed us one weekend that a certain girl in her history class had been labouring under the misapprehension that Martin Luther had nailed, not his 'theses', but his 'faeces' to the church door in Wittenburg. Yet, to us, even theses had seemed bizarre enough.

'Theses,' Lydia said, 'are what graduate students write. They come in huge books, about four hundred pages long. Martin Luther wrote ninety-five of them. And then he nailed them all to the door of the church in Wittenburg. The door must have been "pitted with holes the size of a sixpence".'

'Pitted with holes the size of a sixpence' was one of our automatic giggle-phrases. 'It must have given the vicar "fair gyp",' I said, which was another.

One of our father's elderly one-time colleagues, now dead, had suffered a leg injury during the war. His left thigh had been peppered with bullet-holes that had never ceased, periodically, to suppurate – a gruesome detail that his wife, an old-style staff nurse, had liked to dwell upon in detail.

'Will's leg is giving him gyp,' she'd say, 'fair gyp. Pitted with holes, it is, the size of a sixpence, and each one filled with pus.'

All Lydia or I had to say when the couple came to visit was, 'How's Mr Kethley's leg, Mrs Kethley?' and the response was always delightful. Even the idea of a sixpence was agreeably archaic to the two of us.

'Did you know,' Lydia said to her once, after one of her more extended septic set pieces, 'Nietzsche oozed a pint of pus every day?'

'Every day?' Mrs Kethley said crossly, as if resentful of such up-staging of Will's capacity for festering.

'Syphilis,' Lydia said. 'Our Sex Ed teacher told us.'

Whenever we stayed with Lydia's godmother, she would place one or other of The Novelist's books on our shared bedside table, though these were definitely not the sort of novels that Lydia and I ever read. And to confirm us in our reluctance was the fact that The Novelist had won a prize. Throughout our childhoods Lydia and I distrusted any prize-winning book because we knew it would be worthy; and for worthy, we read boring.

While our mother, before she left us all for her lover, had been inclined to abhor our philistinism in tones of despising innuendo, our father would cheerfully dish us out tenpences, chapter by chapter, as inducements to make us cast our eyes over the occasional improving volume. Or he would slip the odd superior book in amongst our Christmas and birthday presents, labelled in bold marker-pen, 'This Book is NOT Literature.' Though we dismissed most of his offerings as 'boys' books', he did, in this way, expose us to some shorter works of decent fiction and, just once, to an anthology of verse, containing Matthew Arnold's 'Dover Beach'.

Occasionally, as we sniggered and shrieked our way through shared readings of dog-eared school stories, or through easy pulp romance, our father would oblige us by stopping to take an interest.

'What on earth goes on in these frightful books you read?' he'd say, and that was all the invitation we needed.

'Oh, but they're brilliant,' Lydia would say. 'This one's completely brilliant. You see, all the teachers are lesbians. They're all kinky and butch.'

'All of them?' Father said. Our father was, and still is, the headmaster of a public school. We had lived in some stone splendour in the headmaster's house for most of our lives.

'They all believe in sensible haircuts and sensible shoes,' Lydia said, as though that clinched her assertions.

'And punishment,' I said.

'Oh, lots of punishment,' Lydia said. 'Well, that's except for the French teacher. She's a weed, of course. And she's always got her hair in "curl papers". What are curl papers, Father dear? Are they like cigarette papers?'

'Search me,' Father said, who claimed never to have encountered a curl paper in his life.

'Anyway,' Lydia said, 'she's always got them. Not in class but at night, when she's woken up by a mouse coming into her bedroom. The French teachers are always terrified of mice. I expect you'd call the rat-catcher if your school had mice, wouldn't you?'

'Dear me,' was all Father said.

'And the American girls,' I pitched in. 'They come to English schools so that they can learn to speak properly.'

'And their fathers are called "Pops", and they drive huge cars, and they're all road hogs,' Lydia said.

'And they never ever get out of their cars at all,' I said. 'They're surgically attached to them, we think.'

'And if there's a Spanish girl,' Lydia said, 'then she always swings upside down from trees, sort of like a primate, and her parents work in the circus.'

'Big top,' I said, 'it's brill. And the French girls are always cheats.'

'They have to come to English schools to learn a Sense of Honour, but they never do, they can't,' Lydia said.

'Why can't they?' our father said.

'Because they're French,' Lydia said, 'of course.'

'And the teacher's job is to make everyone into "ordinary little schoolgirls",' I said. 'The teachers are all bombed on ordinariness.'

'There's this girl,' Lydia said, 'and she wants to be an opera singer, so she runs away to an audition because she's not allowed to go. But then it pours with rain and she loses her voice and she gets very ill and then she can't sing any more, and Matron says' – here we both chanted gloatingly in unison – ' "Mavis can't sing at all. She can only croak." '

'After that,' Lydia said, 'Mavis becomes an "ordinary little schoolgirl". She has pigtails and she croaks "Play up!" at the school hockey matches.'

'Do you two learn these books off by heart?' Father said.

'No,' Lydia said. 'It's just that they're so good they stick in our minds.'

'They're fantastic,' I said. 'There's this other girl, who wants to be an Olympic swimmer but she's not allowed to train, you see, so she strikes out—'

'In the rain?' father ventured, half rising to go.

'Well, yes,' I said. 'There's a storm and she's dashed against the rocks and she's paralysed.'

'You see, it's all right to swim for your school,' Lydia said, 'but the Olympics is a bit too ambitious – for an ordinary little schoolgirl.'

'Tell me,' Father said, 'aren't you two getting a bit too old for this sort of stuff?'

'Never,' Lydia said. 'You can never be too old. Anyway, there's lots of sex and bondage. We're probably far too young for it.' Father raised an eyebrow.

'No, truly,' I said. 'There's this bit when this girl who's bombed on horses keeps sneaking out to see this horse that's sick. But then there's this horrible teacher that captures her and keeps on punishing her.'

'She's not horrible. She's strict-but-fair,' Lydia said.

I ignored her. 'She keeps on gating her and giving her lines and stuff,' I said. 'But she still goes on sneaking out.'

'In the rain?' Father said.

'Yes,' Lydia said, 'that's right.'

'I really don't think I can take any more of this,' Father said. 'So if you will excuse me—'

'Anyway,' Lydia said quickly, 'she sneaks out in the middle of the night in the pouring rain, and suddenly while she's there the teacher is right there behind her – because the teacher is really a Good Sort and she likes horses too.'

'That's the bond,' I said.

'Bond-age,' Lydia said. 'See, they stand all huddled together in the pouring rain and the teacher says—' We did the next bit again in unison, dropping our voices an octave and putting on Marlene Dietrich voices – ' "I zink I vill never haff to punish you again." '

'So you see,' Lydia said, 'it's all about SM and rubber macs. We need these books, Father. They're sex manuals for us.'

'*And* our mother's not here to tell us anything,' I said.

'And you thought they were just school stories for "ordinary little schoolgirls", didn't you, Father?' Lydia said.

Our father laughed. 'Spare me,' he said. He made attempts to leave. 'I really have things I must attend to,' he said.

'Well, I think you should punish us more,' Lydia said, getting up and standing in his path. 'Go on, punish us. Punish us now.'

'My dear girls,' he said. He held up his hands in mock surrender. 'My dear girls.' And so we let him go.

* * *

I remember just a little bit later how hard we tried to embarrass him in front of the Stepmother, who was, at that time, not yet the Stepmother. She was Father's new woman. It was during a Sunday lunch. Father had bought the lunch entirely in Marks & Spencer's food department, because he was unable to do any sort of cooking except for what you did over camp-fires, and Liddie and I could only do jam tarts and cheese straws and convalescent diets and the sort of useless rubbish they'd taught us to make at school.

Liddie and I had been reading a trash romance about the Regency period.

'We've read this historical novel,' Liddie said to the new woman. 'It's educational. It's all about this French convent girl.'

'She's not French,' I said, 'she's an English convent girl. Her fiancé's French, that's all.'

'OK,' Liddie said. 'Sorry. She's English, but she's supposed to marry this Frenchman, you see. Arranged Marriage. He's kind of experienced and wicked and all that. Well, he would be. He's a French *comte*.'

'But this girl,' I said, 'she doesn't want to marry him because she's in love with someone else, so her friend says she'll marry the *comte* instead, in disguise.'

'So she does,' Lydia said, 'and the *comte* doesn't even notice.'

'Why doesn't he notice?' said Father's new woman, while Father helped her to a carefully calculated twenty-five per cent of the M & S salmon *en croute* that he'd somewhat high-roasted in the oven.

'Oh, veils and stuff,' Lydia said vaguely. 'You know. Anyway, he doesn't notice and then after the ceremony they go gallop-a-gallop all the way to Dover. And then they go on a boat. But he reads his book all the way and—'

'What does he read?' asked Father's new woman.

'Oh, well, never mind,' Lydia said. 'Some Black Lace number, I expect. But anyway, she's too sea-sick to raise her head and he orders his manservant to see to all her needs.'

'Not quite *all* her needs, I hope,' the new woman said, a little saucily.

'And then they go all through France,' I said, 'bumpety bumpety in a golden coach, until at last they get to his *château*.' Father's *croute* had become so papery-dry, it was hard not to puff it about the room as one spoke. It was like those amaretto papers that used to make floaty angels in the air when you set them alight.

'And still he hasn't noticed,' Lydia said. 'It's so exciting.'

'One of the maids meets them in the hall,' I said. 'And she does lots of curtseying and bowing and scraping. And then she takes the convent girl up vast flights of stairs, and bathes her, and brushes her hair with a hundred strokes, and anoints her with perfumed oils, and puts her in a silk nightie, and tucks her up in a four-poster bed hung all around with tapestries.'

'And then,' Lydia said, 'after a few tankards of brandy, the wicked, experienced *comte* turns up and they do the business, and—'

'I beg your pardon?' Father said.

'They do it,' I said, 'and all is Confessed and Revealed.'

Father was attending to his new woman's wine glass.

'And next morning I suppose she's got cystitis?' ventured the new woman.

'No, of course not,' Lydia said confidently, though I don't think either of us had heard of cystitis at that point in our lives. 'He forgives her because he's wild about her. Because she's so snowy-white and inexperienced. You see, men always love virgins.'

'Broccoli for you, my dear?' Father said, offering his new woman the M & S veg *au gratin* that he had decanted from the oval-shaped foil dish into one of our mother's oval-shaped

Alsatian ceramics, thus causing the *gratin* to present itself upside down.

'You can tell she's inexperienced because she always speaks in dots when she's in bed,' I said.

'You mean she speaks in Morse code?' Father said.

'Oh, don't be silly,' Lydia said. 'It's sort of like this. Like she'll say—' and here Lydia clutched her bosom and talked in a higher, girlier voice than usual '– "Oh," dot, dot, dot. "My dearest *comte*," dot, dot. "My beloved husband," dot, dot, dot, dot, dot. "Take me," dot, "all the way up to heaven *again*," dot, dot, dot.'

'The *comte* is terrifically lechy and sexy,' I said, perhaps extraneously.

'Please can we have arranged marriages, Father, with sexy Frenchmen?' Lydia said.

'Oh yes, please,' I said, 'with wild, bad, experienced *comtes*. And then we can swap. Liddie can have my *comte* and I can have hers.'

'That happens in a Mozart opera,' Father's new woman said – a remark which we instantly found more deeply embarrassing than she had found any of our prattlings. 'The men come back in disguise,' she said, 'and the women don't recognize them.'

'Pudding,' Father said firmly and he got up and was away for some minutes. He had bought four tea-cup-sized M & S Treacle Puddings and a half-litre carton of M & S English Custard. He had heated the puddings, two by two, in the microwave and had inverted them onto Grandmother's Crown Derby pudding plates. The custard was still inexplicably in the carton, wrenched open at the side that said 'Open Other Side'.

'Bravo,' said the new woman, who had grown up in America. 'Oh, I just love these little boarding-school puddings.'

It was not long afterwards that the new woman became the Stepmother.

* * *

Lydia and I were fond of the Stepmother and pleased to see our father become so happy. A lot of our knockabout clowning had been our clumsy, unwitting attempts to cheer him up, I think, because he'd been so shut in and grave in the two years since our mother had left. We had each other, we reasoned, while he had only himself, now that we were away at school.

Our father, by necessity, often ate in the school dining-hall, enduring, maybe even enjoying, the pomp and the gowns and the Latin grace – *Omo Lux Domestos Brobat*, as Liddie and I had sometimes chanted – but we tried, when we came home to him, during our half-terms and holidays, to do our best over the catering for his sake. We were, I think, unique in being able to make lumps even in instant mashed potatoes and gravy mix and powdered custard. Usually we gave up and opened tins of beans and soup and delicious Patak's Kashmiri Lamb Curry. We saved our creativity for making him fudge and cocoa and peppermint creams.

Liddie had a project for us to work our way through all the 'serving suggestions' that we saw on the tins and boxes from the supermarket. The cracker boxes had illustrations labelled 'serving suggestions' that showed a row of four savoury biscuits, the first with a sliver of cheese, topped with a small stick of celery.

'Now that's a good idea,' Lydia said. The next picture depicted an identical biscuit decorated with a small, half-moon shrimp on a blodge of cottage cheese. Once we found a box of Tesco's Coconut Cakes where the 'serving suggestion' invited us to place the cakes on a silver platter daintily laid with a doily.

'Let's do it, Ellie,' Lydia said. 'Only we don't know how to make doilies.'

'Yes we do,' I said. 'You fold up a sheet of paper into quarters and cut bits out of the sides. It's like making snowflakes at playschool.'

'Brilliant,' Liddie said. 'Get the scissors there, Ellie.'

If we weren't floating on 'serving suggestions' we immersed ourselves in the 'perfection recipe' that adorned the label of an old cocoa tin we had found at the back of the larder. I expect our mother had banished it there in her time. It not only told you how to make cocoa boringly everyday wise, but it offered a de luxe alternative; it offered perfection. For this, one mixed the cocoa with a modicum of cold milk, then turned the blend of both into a saucepan containing the bulk of the milk before heating through. The method was intended to produce the sort of cocoa that didn't leave your teeth on edge, and it allowed Liddie and me to feel like connoisseurs for having chosen it – though Father, who is from an old army family, is always happy to eat and drink almost anything, including the sort of cocoa in which the spoon will stand up in a half-inch of silt on the bottom of the mug.

Only once did we have a go at a seriously ambitious pudding: an Austrian *torte*, which we tried to make shortly after my return from the *Hubert-und-Norbert* experience. The recipe called for fifteen eggs and a whole pint of cream. There were only two eggs in the larder, but Lydia had once read, in a wartime cookbook of her godmother's, that a tablespoon of vinegar could deputize for an egg, so we made the Austrian *torte* with two eggs and thirteen spoons of vinegar. I must admit that not even our father could be prevailed upon to believe that the resulting mess was how the Viennese liked their cakes.

During term-time weekends, when we were swept off to stay with our mother and her new man in Cambridge – and where we were expected to pull our weight in the kitchen with regard to a daunting range of distinctly unskilled chores – our sessions never took on this dotty, *Blue Peter*-ish quality. We were always much too subdued to fool about in the male usurper's house and we felt not a little like Cinderella girls, or perhaps like sorcerer's apprentices, left to peel potatoes and wash down surfaces, as we watched our mother, through the wide glass door, with her Garbo-like aura and her distinctly more townish clothes, making languid eyes at the incumbent.

My mother's new husband was one Hugo Campbell, a person who, to Liddie's eyes and mine, was a somewhat precious and foppish scholar, not notable for his emotional warmth or easy humanity. He and my mother had fallen precipitously in love – or had, at least, been precipitously enchanted by each other's air of calm, egotistical detachment. From that moment on, her life with us in the Worcestershire countryside had simply become a closed chapter; a thing that ceased to exist.

Her going had occurred when Liddie and I were twelve and thirteen, a time when one tends to change schools, and our father – perhaps typically of him – arranged, in response to this distressing new development, for us to be placed in a boarding school some ten miles from our mother's new domicile. His action was, I think, built on the assumption that girl children had a greater need of their mothers, though, at the same time, he was adamant that he would not have us as day-to-day residents in Hugo Campbell's house. My mother had us for weekends only and, during the holidays, we returned home to him.

The arrangement did not suit any of us terribly well. Lydia and I missed our home at a time when our lives had been turned upside down, and we resented the way we were coerced into spending weekends in Hugo's house when what we wanted, if we couldn't be at home, was to party with our new schoolfriends. And our mother, who had, I think, never really adjusted to life in the country after her life in Paris, had by now returned to work with gusto. Her mindset had reverted to that of a full-time professional woman, and Lydia and I sensed her impatience at the weekly prospect of having to play mother to us on her precious days off.

Meanwhile, for us, it was positively unnerving to watch her negotiate a different kitchen in order to serve up our food on different plates. It was as though we'd landed ourselves in some ghoulish self-catering holiday house where, by horrible oversight, the landlord was permanently in residence as part of the package. And I think it was in order to reassure Hugo that she did not come trailing two great parasitical appendages, that our mother went in for such a rigorous show of delegation and insisted on our exhibiting company manners, especially at mealtimes.

Hugo was evidently quite freaked by children and engaged with us only to fire the same round of dead-end questions at us across the table about our 'O level' subjects – an examination system that was, by then, already two years defunct.

'Speak clearly, Ellen. Don't mumble,' Mother would say and she'd pull us up for not eating with sufficient enthusiasm. She was going in for a different style of cuisine, now that she was no longer in the house in which we had started out as little girls. The message we read from this was that she was cooking, not for us, but for Hugo, who evidently had a more sophisticated and adventurous palate than our father. I admit that we were probably silly and bigoted, but our altered situation made us wish to regress at weekends, not advance, and what we longed for, in place of all the monkfish and okra and whiffy foreign cheeses, was roast chicken and gravy, and apple crumble for pudding.

In front of Hugo, our mother always referred to our father as 'the Headmaster' – a mannerism that we found both belittling and weird. And, when we balked at eating anything we'd deemed a touch wayout, she'd say to him, 'You see. The Headmaster's children.'

It was shortly before the advent of the Stepmother that Lydia and I had conceived the idea that Father needed a dog. The truth is that, having gone to the dog rescue bent upon any sort of puppy just as long as it was fluffy, we had quickly been persuaded that what our father needed was a retired racing greyhound. It was our good luck that, in the event, Father and the greyhound bitch fell in love at first sight – though, of the two, Father was the less demonstrative.

'Dear girls,' he said, 'you bad, unforgivable girls. How could you have taken a decision like this without consulting me?' The greyhound merely watched him fixedly. Every time he opened his mouth to speak she dived in with her tongue and gave him sexy, wet French kisses.

'Her name's Dilly,' we lied, because her registered name was Lady and we didn't like it. It lifted our hearts to watch Father take off across the fields in his green wellies with the greyhound running in huge wide circles as though programmed by the racetrack to proceed in spiral movements. Sometimes, as she got scent of a rabbit, she would break her pattern and zigzag wildly, bringing all four feet together in the air.

The following year we chanced our arm still further and found the greyhound a husband. The result was eight greyhound puppies, most of whose infancy I missed through my being away at university, but Lydia told me that they made it their business to bite the heads off all the wallflowers and to see to it that not a lupin was left standing. After that, she said, they had uprooted all the climbing plants and piddled on the grass until it yellowed. Our grandmother had then recommended the placing of a notice in the pages of *Horse and Hound*, which had resulted in queues of sensible country types – exactly Father's sort of people – who turned up in Range Rovers and talked with Father about the escalating price of gundogs.

And then the puppies were gone – all but one, whose home had fallen through in the last minute. Another home was found, but the delay, in the event, proved vital. Four weeks passed before the family concerned were scheduled to return from a holiday and collect her. This meant that the puppy was still at home on the evening I was suddenly summoned from Edinburgh. It meant that the puppy never left us. It meant that the puppy was still with us on the day that my sister died.

* * *

When Lydia died, my father and the Stepmother had been married for only twenty-five months. They were in many ways an incongruous couple. She was tiny and more than twenty years his junior, and, to us countrified, boarding-school types, she seemed quite a radical progressive. Having got herself a degree and a teacher's qualification, the Stepmother had pointedly acquired her first teaching job in a large urban comprehensive school in an area of social disadvantage.

Every morning, before anyone else got up, the Stepmother, sluiced, dressed and ready for work, would leave the house with its tall chimneys and its two wide staircases, its inlaid clocks and polished brass and whatnots and tallboys, and she would tiptoe through the vines of the kitchen garden to where she kept her rusty little VW Beetle. Then she would head out for what Father, somewhat archaically, called 'the Smoke'.

Nonetheless, because, as was evident to Lydia and me, she loved him dearly, she had very soon got pregnant, at a time that must have been most inconvenient to her as a determined and energetic young teacher wanting to make a career for herself. Father's somewhat fuddy-duddy reasoning was that he did not wish to deny her the experience of motherhood, even if at her age the matter did not seem pressing. By the time she had reached an age to be afflicted with maternal longings, he argued, he would be so advanced in years that the child would have an old age pensioner for a male parent.

When Father said 'the child', Lydia and I were fairly sure that, in his heart, he meant boy child. He meant a person who would depend upon him to assist with the construction of model aeroplanes and to guide his bowler's arm. Admittedly, he has a stepson, Peter, who is the child of Liddie's and my mother by her first marriage – a boy who was four years old when our parents met and who is almost six years my senior.

But Peter does not exactly meet my father's case. Peter is a strange, dreamy type of whom, throughout our early childhood, Lydia and I made nothing, but we gradually came to admire and love him devotedly. He is a small, blond, balding homosexual who runs a dog rescue centre in Sussex. He runs it with his beautiful, crop-haired French lover, who is an undisputed *Übermensch*. The Übermensch is almost perpetually in waistcoat and designer stubble and grandad shirt. He stands six foot two in his socks and has alluring dimples that play around his mouth. Sometimes, if he wears braces or dungarees, and if he leans on a baling fork, he looks exactly like one of those hunky, dancing wife-abductors in *Seven Brides for Seven Brothers*. And how fervently Liddie and I longed to be abducted by the Übermensch.

Once, when Peter and the Übermensch had first asked us to spend a half-term holiday, Lydia and I had come upon an unexpected barrage of resistance from both our parents; on Father's part, a po-faced, unexplained reluctance that I see, with hindsight, had to do with our half-brother's sexual orientation and, on our mother's, with an unambiguously expressed sniffy conviction that we would come back flea-ridden and probably afflicted with rabies, tick-bite fever and mange.

In the event, they let us go: two little girls and a quorum of love-starved canines. The holiday was bliss. Our best thing, however, and one we never disclosed, was that from our bedroom, adjoining the men's, we were able to lend an ear to the sounds of our half-brother's sexual activities. These were nothing like the smoochy gasps and groanings we had occasionally overheard from adult heteros – noises that we always found embarrassing and invasive. These were far more like the noises of two boys fighting. Not gutter stuff; not flick-knife and broken bottle stuff; just the sort of thumping and wrestling entanglements that schoolboys enter into among friends and that always look so alarmingly physical and violent to uninitiated members of the female sex. Peter and the Übermensch made those POW! BASH! BAM! noises that emanate from Asterix and Obelix in uppercase balloons. (Or, as they say in the original French, TCHAC! PAFF! CLONC!) To us, with our background in a boys' school, these were undisturbing and manly sounds; not groping but jousting. They were easier on the ear than the hetero stuff.

It was Peter whom Lydia and I had approached in the matter of Father's 'puppy', and Peter who had instead steered us towards the greyhound bitch. She was a dog in a million, Peter said, and if our father didn't like her, he would personally eat his hat. Peter's hat was one of those panamas that you can roll up and put in a tube. He had even been able to piece together bits of the greyhound's biography, since she had been quite a winner in her day, before she – and presumably her owner – had fallen on hard times. All Peter knew was that, at some point, the greyhound had fallen into the hands of a party of New Age travellers, because she'd been reported, abandoned and tethered among the burnt-out debris of a summer camp in Hove, where all she had found to eat were plastic bags that had blown her way in the wind. For her first days in Peter's care she had passed sections of soiled plastic bag bearing vestiges of the exhortation to 'Collect a Sainsbury's Reward Card from the Homestore in Truro'. Yet here she was – confident, elegant, sociable and infinitely capable of love.

'I run the dog rescue,' Peter once said to the Stepmother in my hearing, 'because every day I'm reminded that characters like me can land with their bums in the butter.' By then I was just old enough to understand that dearest Peter might not have been speaking exclusively in metaphor.

As my sister and I had left to return to school after that glorious half-term holiday, Lydia had extracted a promise from the Übermensch.

'When you and Peter get married,' she said, 'can Ellie and I please be your bridesmaids?'

'*Mais oui*,' said the Übermensch. 'One of you the bridesmaid and one the best woman.' He had declared Lydia and me to be the finest entertainment in England; better than those stupid comedy shows on the television. He slung our bags into the car and settled us inside. Then he blew us several saucy kisses as Peter drove us off.

And then my life, our lives, everything, went black. Not black like not remembering. Black like being lost in a dark place very far from home. I regret bitterly that I never saw my sister dead, but when my father left to identify her body, I was not at home. At the time I felt relieved. I was struggling to blink away an image that had kept recurring as my friend Pen had driven with me to the airport that night so that I could board the last plane out of Edinburgh; an image of Lydia's face, like that of a cat she and I had once seen, struck by a car and lying dead in a gutter. All the planes of its face had been pushed sideways into stiff, ghoulish parallelograms.

At home, I pleaded for my sister not to be cremated and I begged to be allowed to take the greyhounds to her funeral. Strange priorities, perhaps, but Father conceded both. Lydia and I, having all too recently attended the funeral service of poor old Mr Kethley in the chapel of what was locally known as 'the Crem', had watched the box containing the remains of Mr Kethley slide – presumably at the touch of an invisible button under the clergyman's foot – through a chute in the apse behind where the altar ought to have been.

The building had appeared to us until that moment much like any other rather boringly modern church, but there, where one might have expected a depiction of Christ in Glory, was a dumb waiter's hatch, an automated conveyor belt, a railway line for the ghost train to the burning fiery furnace. We thought it a *trompe l'œil* of bad taste; the ultimate last laugh. So I could not cope with the idea of Lydia entering that furnace – and yet in the event, I think that the grave was just as difficult.

The Stepmother reacted differently. She was disproportionately upset by the hideousness of all the coffins that the undertaker had on offer and thought them a violation. In these ways – while my father appeared bleakly, miserably undemonstrative – did we two women process the first stages of our shock and grief. We wept and screamed about cremations and coffins.

'It's an outrage,' the Stepmother said. 'An *OUTRAGE*! I don't believe it. They're all plastic mahogany veneer. They're like those horrible seventies kitchen units.' Lydia, she said, could not possibly be nailed up in any monstrosity of formica and polished brass like that.

The Stepmother threw herself into a frenzy of specialist consumer activity, until she discovered the Green Burial Service, which provided my sister with a beautiful, understated, manila cardboard coffin, its shape mercifully cuboid, like a large croquet box. It came with undyed hemp ropes made by a fair-trade collective in the Philippines and, with these ropes, my father and Peter performed the appalling task of lowering Lydia into the ground.

It feels to me still as if that lowering happened in slow motion. So too the throwing of earth and flowers. And all the time I felt myself drawn to the idea of jumping into the grave. I wanted the inexorable event to stop rolling. Had I been brave enough and expressive enough – had I perhaps been more genuinely like Lydia – I might have done what I felt impelled to do. Instead, I stood there, staring and staring into the hole, with the greyhounds beside me on their leads. Curious how, until that time, *Hamlet* had seemed to the two of us such a melodrama. In the event, jumping into the grave was exactly what I most wanted to do. Would I or would I not have gone crashing through the sturdy manila card to clutch at my sister in a last embrace? Would I have raised her? Would I at least have seen her face?

Instead, I began to shiver and scratch my arms. Then I left. I turned silently from the graveside and took the path through the churchyard to the lych-gate and I walked up through the village.

As I arrived at the crossing opposite the pub, a decrepit-looking wino whom I had never seen before began to yell something at me, from the other side of the street. He was calling me 'lady' and waving his arms. I could tell that Dilly was becoming restless and I knew that Lydia's burial had distressed her. Greyhounds have small narrow heads and easily slip their collars. Dilly, at this moment, chose to slip her collar. She bounded hazardously across the street and leapt at the wino. I remember screaming and screaming her name, as a small bus narrowly missed her and swerved in to pull up at the bus-stop. For a moment there was a van blocking my view and it was only when it moved forward that I realized the wino and Dilly had made a pact. I saw the two of them simply moving off towards the bus and all I could do was stand and scream. I suppose I was hysterical. Just then, a man who had emerged from the phone-box alongside the pub made a grab for Dilly and held her until I and the puppy had crossed the street. I tried to fit her collar, but my hands were shaking so violently that my rescuer was obliged to take it over.

Meanwhile the old wino merely hovered and gabbled. He was still calling me 'lady'. 'Lady, you're a fine one,' he said. 'Aye, you're a fine one. Isn't she a fine one?'

I was not in a frame of mind to give him my attention. I didn't even look at him. 'But lady, you're a fine one,' he said. 'Aye, but you're all right.'

'Are you OK?' said the phone-call man. I think I nodded ungraciously before I fled.

Once at home, I kept on shivering and scratching. I'd developed a sort of psoriasis which still plagues me from time to time. The skin on my arms and legs became a meshwork of goosebumps and then of red weals. I had disfiguring patches on the right side of my face.

Recollecting Lydia's funeral in the weeks that followed, I became aware of strange, disturbing things. It occurred to me, but only after the event, that my mother had almost totally ignored me. I suppose this is called disengagement. She had also ignored Peter. Yet we two were so much preoccupied with loss and grief that we didn't immediately take her rejection on board. Conversely, she seemed once more to be powerfully drawn towards my father; drawn, no doubt, by the torment of the shared dead child. There she was, pale, beautiful and alone, since, perhaps understandably, her new husband had not accompanied her. Her grey eyes were huge and haunted as she clung to Father's arm.

My mother has ignored me ever since. I have become the expendable half of something that once was whole. From that day all semblance of her custodial role in me has lapsed. I have since then heard newly single people say that after separation all invitations cease; that friends, accustomed to a couple, are not able to take on board the singularity of their oneness. This is something I am able, from experience, to understand.

At the funeral, while Father behaved supportively with my mother, I and the Stepmother had both of us clung to Peter. The Übermensch had hung back, weeping copiously, wetting the front of his shirt. He, too, has since then found me something of an affront. He does not care for me without Lydia since I do not entertain him. Our value for him was as a double-act and now I am minus my partner. I tend to wear a February face, for which he has no use.

It was months, too, before it dawned on me that the old wino for whom Dilly had displayed such enthusiasm had not been addressing me, but the dog. He had been calling 'Lady', not 'lady' and she – as dogs will – had entirely failed to judge him for having reduced her to the ingestion of supermarket plastic bags on an abandoned camp-site.

Within the month, just as I had at last begun to stop shivering, the poor little Stepmother miscarried. She did so at a time when the space for grief was consumed by the greater loss of Lydia. The worst of it was that she miscarried, not once, but twice within five days. The first miscarriage happened at home over a weekend, when the Stepmother passed a perfect four-month-old male foetus, which she buried at nightfall, wrapped in a scrap of blanket, under an oak tree in the garden. For this purpose, my father, at her request, dug a deep hole. Afterwards, as the two of us women watched, he dragged a weighty stone paving slab over the grave.

The second miscarriage happened suddenly during the following week, when the Stepmother was taken acutely ill during an end-of-term theatrical performance at her school. This time she was rushed into whichever down-at-heel female surgical ward 'the Smoke' still had on offer, and there it was that she passed a foetid brown object, a poor wizened reptile of a thing, a hapless twin, who had evidently lain dead and undiagnosed within her for some days before the first miscarriage. According to the doctors, it was this, the second twin, whose dying had caused the toxins that had proved fatal to that more amiable foetus that now lay beneath the slab under the oak tree.

After that, a silence enveloped the subject of the Stepmother's maternal needs and she became quite as besotted as I was with the greyhound and the puppy – though the latter was an apprehensive little thing, who always piddled on the hall rugs in deference to the Stepmother's daily return from 'the Smoke'.

I don't suppose that Lydia's dying could have done much for the Stepmother's newly-wed sex life. They were, in themselves, so very different, my father and the Stepmother. Now, after my four years away at university, I can see that my father is conservative by nature. He honours, more than is fashionable, the traditions of family, church, state and monarchy in which he was, perhaps anachronistically, reared. The Stepmother is by nature an iconoclast. She is against religion, perhaps because her parents were practising Catholics. She is against eating meat, perhaps because her father was a gourmet carnivore. She is a rigorous egalitarian, perhaps because her parents are very comfortable.

Some months after Lydia's dying, the Stepmother announced, towards the end of one of the horrible, plate-scrapingly silent meals we went in for through that summer, that she had been exploring the possibility of us going to Italy for a break.

'Just the three of us,' she said. 'Come on, it couldn't hurt, could it? It couldn't make us feel any worse.'

'What about the dogs?' was all that Father said. He forked up some limp, waterlogged cauliflower as he spoke, because the Stepmother couldn't cook either. It was giving off that unpleasant armpit odour.

'There's Peter,' said the Stepmother. 'I've already asked him, and he's game.'

'Yes,' said Father, 'that's true. There's Peter.'

The Stepmother would doubtless have appreciated a more committed response. She has a married sister who lives with her family in Fiesole. Furthermore, the Stepmother speaks a more than adequate Italian through her paternal connection with ethnically conscientious Italian Americans. The sister had expressed a wish – had positively pleaded with the Stepmother – to have us come as guests for a week, and had already followed up this suggestion by procuring a flat for us thereafter, rent free, in Rome. Not any old flat, but a beautiful apartment belonging to a friend in the Via Sistina. It lay between the Quattro Fontane and the Spanish Steps, the Stepmother said. Pearls before swine. To our shame, this coup meant nothing to Father and me. We had neither of us ever been to Rome and we simply continued to stare into our plates.

'So?' said the Stepmother after a moment, when she ought to have thrown the cauliflower mush at us. 'So, is it yes?'

'My dear,' Father began, 'my dear Christina—'

'Yes?' said the Stepmother.

Father sighed. 'Very well,' he said. Perhaps it was that neither he nor I wanted to put the sea between ourselves and Lydia's grave. The poor woman might have been proposing a trip to the chiropodist, for all the enthusiasm she provoked. 'That,' said Father, 'is if Ellen has no objection.'

'I don't mind,' I said, and I continued to stare into my plate.

The Stepmother took us first to stay with her sister's family in Fiesole, the most magical of old towns, from which the boy Fra Angelico would have been able to see the skyline of Florence as the golden beckoning cupolas of the heavenly city. The dear couple could not have been kinder to us, nor more solicitous. They laid tables before us on their little roof terrace under a vine and, unlike the Stepmother, they could cook. They sat with us in the shell of the ancient Roman theatre while their two small children, Bruno and Cosima, romped happily on the grass against a backdrop of the Etruscan city wall. They led us through ancient cypress trees, past a tiny chapel in an orchard, to an extraordinary old convent where a friar, dressed in sackcloth and sucking upon Tic-tacs, led us past a dimpled della Robbia madonna and several terracotta saints. They ascended with us into a steep, strange woodland, featuring the cells and grottoes of long-dead hermits.

In Florence, they steered us skilfully away from the summer crowds around the Uffizi, to the quiet of the Brancacci Chapel and the monastery of San Marco. Yet of the latter I have a single memory: that of my father, sitting glumly in the courtyard beside the great bell that rang out the execution of

Savonarola. And, in the former, I remember that the Stepmother took hold of Father's arm and planted him four-square in front of Masaccio's *The Tribute Money*.

'There,' she said, as brightly as she could. 'The best Sunday-school picture ever painted. Admire it, please.' She pointed its stages for him. 'See,' she said. 'Here are the Lord and his disciples with the taxman. But, look, they have no money to pay him. Here Jesus tells Peter, "Go to the lake and pluck out a little silver fish. In its belly you will find a coin." ' With her hand she echoed the gesture of the Christly indicating arm. 'Now,' she said, 'here is Peter, crouching by the lake. And, bingo, he has the fish. See him, with his little slippery silver fish? And here they are, handing the coin to the taxman. Now they can enter the city.'

I stared at the taxman, who, with his back to us, was exhibiting Nureyev legs and the sort of shell-pink blouson that male Florentines of the time evidently went in for. Father was nodding and nodding, saying nothing.

'There's no such story in the Bible,' I said. I saw the Stepmother and the sister's husband exchange slightly arch looks.

'But there are plenty of fish stories in the Bible,' said the husband. 'One more, one less. What the hell, Ellen? There is a noble family in this country,' he added, hoping to amuse me, 'which claims descent from the sexual union of Our Lord and Mary Magdalene.'

'Lighten up, Ellen,' said the Stepmother, showing a moment's irritation with me. 'It's a propaganda piece for tax gathering. God pays his taxes, and so must all good citizens. Now you can't say there aren't any tax gatherers in the Bible.' Then, to curry my favour, she said, 'But look at the beauty of St John, Ellen. Isn't he a gorgeous man?'

I stared sternly at St John, with his corkscrew blond curls, and his profile, and his clear, sea-green eyes. I thought he looked like a celebrity footballer, with a styled perm and highlights.

'I don't like blond men,' I said. As we left, we all walked past the expelled Adam and Eve, pretending not to register the howling, inconsolable depths of their loss.

The Stepmother's sister had taken two days off to guide us round Pisa and Lucca, where we walked through a maze of moonbright squares, their strangely Moorish white lace buildings like mirages. It was like dream-wanderings choreographed by Peter Greenaway, but Father and I, having established, ploddingly, that the Leaning Tower leaned, unwrapped our crusty sandwiches glumly on the grass outside the great Duomo, and longed for Allinson's pre-sliced stoneground. Bread wi' nowt tekken owt.

Finally, poor things, the sister and her family put us on the train for Rome, with a bag of star-shaped bread rolls, and a whole salami, and a paper carton of nectarines, and a bottle of Brunello di Montalcino.

'Skip the churches,' said the sister's husband astutely into the ear of the Stepmother. 'Take Himself straight to the Forum.'

There were kisses and hugs on parting; there were tears in the Stepmother's eyes – but, once at the Forum, Father stared out over that awesome vista of tall palm trees and colossal broken columns, and sighed, and said nothing. It was evident that what the columns confirmed for him was that all good things had passed away from the earth.

For the next few days we stared at several fountains, as directed by the Stepmother. We remarked upon the thickness of the Pantheon's walls. We observed that the buses and the taxis were bumpier because the streets were cobbled. We were impatient with the crowds near the apartment.

After a week we were all agreed that we were still missing the greyhounds. None of us dared quite to say out loud that we were most of all missing Lydia. Then the Stepmother surprised us.

'Look,' she said. She spoke bravely but with several pauses and gulps. 'I know I ought not to, but I feel that I'm an intruder. I'm the gatecrasher on your grief.'

'Christina, please,' Father said.

'It's a fact,' she said. 'I know this is my own marriage. I know this isn't what I ought to be feeling, but that's the way it is. Lydia was a honey. Lydia was the sweetest thing. I don't say I don't miss her. I don't say it doesn't hurt. But there's no way I'm going to feel about her the way you guys feel. It's not like having a part of my body lopped off. It's not like amputation . . .' She was evidently holding back tears. She stopped and reformulated: 'I feel that I owe it to the miscarriages,' she said, 'that I have any rights here at all.'

'But this is appalling,' Father said. The Stepmother sniffed and wiped her nose and her eyes with her hand.

'I know that the dead babies are not comparable,' she said. She held out her hand to prevent any approach or expression of sympathy. 'But I need to go away and be sad about them someplace where that doesn't make me feel so unworthy.'

'We've failed you,' Father said miserably.

'Please,' she said. 'I'm going back to my sister's. I'm packed. The thing's all fixed. I'll stay there just as long as I feel I need to.'

Father and I looked helplessly at each other. I sensed that alarm bells were ringing in his brain.

'See out the fortnight here without me,' she said. 'You'll manage. There's really no sense in us bouncing our miseries off each other.' There was nothing more to be said. She went into the bedroom and got her bag. 'I'll see you guys back in England,' she said. She kissed us both once and walked over to the door. 'I will come back,' she said. 'You needn't doubt me.' Then she was gone.

Without the Stepmother, things were suddenly easier. The two of us stopped feeling the need to put on faces for each other. On our own, we just mooched. We mooched for days. And, all around us, the privacy of the alien language soothed us like a balm. It is the closest I have ever been to my father; the closeness during that time, when we developed our own half-life rhythm. We became more like siblings. In the absence of Lydia, I became my father's older sister. This is perhaps not surprising, since he is the youngest in a family of sisters and I am the elder of what was once two.

Some days we didn't go out at all; some days we did no more than find the nearest supermarket and throw food into a basket, and pass without words through the checkout. One day we sat at the very top of the Spanish Steps near the apartment, staring far down at the ant-sized tourists clustered around the ice-cream vans. We sat with our heads propped in our hands, our elbows on our knees.

'Ellen,' Father said eventually, 'I must tell you that I am really rather at sea.'

I stared at the stones between my feet. Then I remembered 'Dover Beach'. It came back to me, wearing a label that said, 'This Book is NOT Literature' from a Christmas morning many years earlier. Off the top of my head, I began to recite the poem with its exhortation that we be true to one another, because the world that lies about us like a world of dreams is, in reality, nothing; null and void, a darkling plain. I recited it deadpan, having always shared with Lydia a horror of poetry recited 'with expression'.

'There,' I said when I'd finished. 'Perhaps you paid me to learn that off by heart.' Father put his arm around me. 'Does it bother you that I look so much like her?' I said.

He turned his head and stared at me. 'You don't look like her,' he said. 'Strangers always thought that you looked alike. You never did to me.'

Then we kept on sitting there until our buttocks were numb and cold. We must have sat there for well over an hour. The Fiats and taxis way down below us had gradually leached their colour into the encroaching dusk.

'Ellie,' Father said, 'your mother has an extraordinary notion. She wants to come back to me.'

'To you, maybe,' I said, a little bitterly, 'but certainly not to me.' I spoke before I had quite assimilated what he was saying.

'It's nonsense, of course,' he said, 'but we must go carefully. Liddie's death has unlocked something alarming. I must tell you that she writes to me and telephones constantly.'

I got up. 'Well, she can't come back,' I said. I surprised myself with my own anger. 'How dare she even suggest it?'

'No, of course not,' Father said. 'Water under the bridge. It's absolutely not on. It's distressing, that's all. I have told her that the calls must stop.' Then he said, 'She's always been so controlled, Ellen. I wonder now if you could possibly think of going to see her?'

'*Me?*' I said, '*I'm* not going to see her. I'm not. She doesn't even like me. She probably wishes it was me that was dead.'

Father paused. Then he said, 'You must understand that she is not at all herself at the moment.'

'Good,' I said. 'And what about Christina? How dare she do this when Christina is your wife now? Does she have the faintest clue about what has happened to Christina?'

'She knew that Christina was pregnant,' Father said. 'I dare say she has come by the rest of it somehow, through the ether.'

'Well then,' I said.

'Yes,' Father said. 'Ellen, depressed people can become quite incapable of seeing beyond themselves.'

'She never could,' I said and I started to cry.

'I take your point,' Father said. 'Look, dearest. Don't worry about visiting. Not if the prospect is too upsetting.'

'It *is* too upsetting,' I said. I thought about my mother; about with what apparent ease she had left him and moved on. Now she had entirely moved on from Peter and me. So let her, if that was how she wanted it.

Then I thought about what Lydia and I had seen of the brief, but quite different interaction our father had had with the Stepmother – before bereavement had got in the way.

'But you love Christina,' I said. 'You don't even love her.'

'Yes,' he said.

'You don't love her,' I said again.

'Ellie,' he said. 'Don't belittle the past. It's your past as well as mine. And it's Lydia's. I ought not to be talking to you like this. I'm sorry.'

'Yes you ought,' I said. 'Because I'll tell you why Liddie and I were so giggly over that M & S lunch. Do you remember? We could tell that you loved Christina. I mean *loved* her. We could tell by the way you took her coat. We could tell by the way you filled her glass. It embarrassed us, don't you see?'

Father got up and joined me as I made ready to go. Then, on the way back, I said, 'Are you sad about the twin babies?'

He was a long time in answering. 'Ellen,' he said, 'it has come to me recently that you and I have been trying so hard not to feel the loss of Lydia, that we have ended up scarcely able to feel anything at all.'

'Phone her,' I said. 'Tell her to come back. Tell her to join us – just for the weekend.'

'Do I have the right, I wonder?' he said.

'Phone her,' I said, still in my big sister mode, but I had been feeling very unlike a child of late, and certainly not young. It is odd that the death of my sister should have had this effect upon me, because while Lydia lived, I think we were always far more like twins.

The three of us spent that last weekend in Rome together. The Stepmother met us among the Saturday morning crowd in the Piazza Navona. She had had a very short haircut and she wore stylish new jeans that stopped six inches above her ankles. On her ridiculous size two feet she had new shoes – tiny red shoes like ballet pumps. She wore a red spotted snuff handkerchief tied around her throat. She looked unburdened and very much happier. She looked very *Roman Holiday*.

The Stepmother mimicked the flamboyant gestures of the men on the Bernini fountain as we passed it on our way to the café. She was buoyant from a week with her sister's small children. Her head was full of Dr Seuss books. She and I could bounce them off each other as we walked.

'This one has a little star.'
'This one has a little car.'
'Say! what a lot of fish there are.'

She kissed Father smoochily, jumping up at his jaw. 'Sit down, Roland,' she said. 'I can't kiss you if you stand up. You know that. Have pity on the vertically challenged.'

Then, after the café, we made our way back to the apartment. At the entrance, I changed my mind. I employed an adult's tact.

'I'll go for a walk,' I said.

Once back in the piazza, I took note of a small severe church – quite different from the extravagance of its surroundings – and I entered the graveyard, finding it quite by chance. I discovered this to have a series of underground chapels decoratively laid out with the bones of dead monks. It brought home to me how much Father and I were lacking in any assuaging flair for the theatre of death.

When I got back, the Stepmother was making bathroom noises in the shower. My father was jauntily whistling 'The Battle Hymn of the Republic' in the kitchen, where he had made a pot of tea and laid a tray. That is to say, he had made a pot of tea in a saucepan because the kitchen had no teapot. Neither did the cups have any saucers.

'Alas, poor foreigners,' I said. 'What do they know about tea?'

He smiled at me. 'Thank you, Ellen,' he said. He did not say what for. 'You are a wise and wonderful girl,' he said. On our last day we did the corny thing. The Stepmother coerced us. We went to St Peter's where she made us light candles for Lydia and also for the dead babies. The approach was an avenue of outrageous kitsch where I observed that the tourist shops were selling indulgences. It brought to mind Martin Luther: ninety-five faeces nailed to the door of the church in Wittenburg. Faeces, theses, bones and pus. Will's leg is giving him gyp. Fair gyp.

'Did you know,' I said, 'that Nietzsche oozed a pint of pus every day?' Father and the Stepmother looked at me, then they looked at each other. 'Syphilis,' I said. 'Lydia told me that.'

A little later, I thought of the Übermensch while staring at the gorgeous naked boys on the ceiling of the Sistine Chapel; boys bursting acorns from horns of plenty; boys with curls falling into their eyes; boys with sweatbands and bedroom glances, their accoutrements the colours of mango and pistachio ice-cream.

'Now why do I think of Peter?' said the Stepmother, as the crowd jostled us forward. I glanced back towards the altar where I saw that my father was staring hard at the great painting of the Last Judgement. Fire and Sleet and Candlelight. And cardboard. And bones. And hemp rope.

'What did you bury her in?' I said, as we left. 'I mean, what was she wearing?'

'Oh,' Father said. 'Oh—'

'White T-shirt and knickers,' the Stepmother said. 'I thought you'd never ask.'

After that, Ellen's stepmother went back to her sister's in Fiesole, while Ellen and her father returned home, where the greyhounds were very pleased to see them. In the autumn, just as the Stepmother returned, Ellen went back to her student digs in Edinburgh and entered the second year. In the circumstances, she occasionally wished herself closer to home. Yet the city, as it had done through her first year, enchanted her and sustained her with its cold and stony grandeur; with its clear and crystal light. No one would have called her a frothy person. She was no longer a particularly sociable person. She was a person who – as her stepmother had put it – had experienced amputation. But, of course, that didn't show.

She began to work very hard. She had a few sedate, strictly ungiggly friends. There was nobody there for her like Peregrine Massingham, the great friend of her first year, or even like Izzy, or Stella, her housemates of the previous year. They had all gone. Peregrine, her favourite companion and indispensable cooking person, had graduated and left. Izzy Tench, the painter boy, likewise – though, to her annoyance, he had left her one of his drawings in place of a cheque, as his contribution to the previous quarter's electricity bill. The drawing had been done in red chalk on grey paper and was of his beautiful girlfriend Stella; she of the cello and the mass of orange hair.

What puzzled Ellen was that Stella had not come back either, though she had only completed two of her four years. Someone else was due to take occupancy of the room that Stella and Izzy had shared. Yet all Stella's stuff had been left in the storeroom as if she'd meant to come back. It was bagged up in black plastic dustbin sacks and marked with her name. And on what had been Izzy's cruddy bedside chair, Stella had left her copy of *Heart of Darkness*, which Ellen took up, on that first night back, and read until four in the morning. And when she'd finished it, she read it again. And again.

2. Das Wandern

Jonathan

ON THE DAY I get back to find Lydia Dent's letter about her German essay, I've been lunching with my sister-in-law. For years now we've been meeting like this, Sally and I, roughly once every three months. It's an arrangement she initiates and more or less coerces me into, but on the whole I'm not unwilling.

Recently we've been meeting at a place called Oliveto near Victoria Coach Station which, for all that it spells its name with a final 'o', reminds me pleasantly of the old portable typewriter that I bashed to death twenty years ago in the process of typing my first novel. That was an experience of passionate and youthful excitement, equalled only by my experience, shortly thereafter, of meeting Katherine again – Katherine, who then became my wife.

My sister-in-law lives with my brother in Oxford, but comes into London for her profession, about which I am agreeably hazy. It's educational think-tank stuff; consultancy stuff; exam stuff; quango stuff. Not my stuff at all. Sally has a talent for committees. My sister-in-law does not have original thoughts. She has management skills. Were it not for these, I do not believe that she and my brother would ever have got married. He would not have got the thing together. Sally will have managed him into the marriage, just as she managed the catering, the florist, the music, the hairdresser and the wedding list at Peter Jones. Sally spooks Katherine by being bossy and snoopy, but I am merely entertained by it. Sally is, after all, a decent sort. My brother is lucky to have her.

Over the years I have become quite fond of my sister-in-law – the more so because she is so emphatically not the sort of woman who could possibly ring my bells. Though she flirts with me in her rather headgirl way, I can always trust myself with her completely. And I never give anything away. We have been enjoying each other's company now for a little over two decades, though the balance of power between us has shifted. It is not bragging to say that, for Sally, I have always offered vicarious excitement as a sort of Danger Man, because Sally plays so safe that it is not strenuous to appear a little dangerous before her.

My brother – older brother – will, I think, have married Sally for the echoes he found in her of our mother. We have a charming but very demanding mother, to whose tune my brother always danced. Being highly intelligent, academically inclined and musically gifted, he was always bright enough to oblige her. He brought home golden reports from school for her. He played first violin in the National Youth Orchestra for her and he went on, clutching his first in mathematics from Oxford, to become the youngest college fellow for her in fifteen years. As a bonus – and as an effective disguise for his multiple emotional inadequacies – my brother is also very handsome. Roger has the sort of delicate, dark good looks that used to cause teenage girls to ambush him on his way home from school; a form of tribute that gave him no pleasure, but merely added to his torments of self-consciousness. In short, he was a beautiful, bright, sulky, Oedipal boy. He was snobbish, precious, arrogant, insecure and chockful of anxieties that he could not confront.

He and Sally met at Oxford, married early and the sun shone down upon them. They set up a conspicuously grade A show.

Handsome, musical young maths don gets hitched to English Rose. Wedding in the college chapel. House in the leafy environs of north Oxford. Three nice little daughters, Claire, Sheila and Fiona. Tree-house in the garden. Edwardian rocking-horse in the nursery window. William Morris wall-paper in the hall. Magnetic letters on the door of the fridge-freezer. High-tech kitchen with rustic implications – old pine dresser and table stripped and waxed from a superior barn-like outfit somewhere near Chipping Norton. Stalwart Mrs Thing from a smallholding in Wolvercote who, with regulation perm and headscarf, came three times a week to keep the place nice and to offer her elevating folk wisdoms to smooth over any ensuing difficulties of relative privilege.

All this time I suppose I struck dear Sally as a bit of a perennial dosser. That is to say, I lived in a bedsit in un-smart north London, owned two shirts, collected my dole money once a week and showed no sign of wishing to change my life. Having finished at university some years earlier, I had wandered round Europe in a somewhat aimless manner, and had returned to London on the rebound from an unwise, short-lived marriage.

In fact, the bedsit was a nice little pad, a satisfactorily uncluttered and rudimentary affair, somewhat icy in winter, with patterned fifties lino on the floor and a kitchenette en suite containing stone sink, mesh-fronted meat safe and small electric cooker on cabriole legs – all things that now feature as desirable finds on the pages of *Elle Decoration.* (I know this because *Elle Decoration* has become Katherine's only adult reading matter.) The lavatory, ditto, across the landing, had a WC with fixed wooden seat and overhead wooden cistern, with mortice and tenon joints. It was called 'The Jakpak'.

My landlady, a nice old Bavarian Quaker person with swollen legs, lived in a modest flat on the ground floor and had me in from time to time for bowls of lentil and potato soup. She enjoyed my company because I could speak to her in

German and she believed in me as a worthy cause because, unlike almost anyone else, she had become party to the fact that I was typing up a novel in her attic, dressed in two overcoats and wearing those fingerless gloves that you see on market traders. She thought it exciting that I should be doing such a thing in her house. Sometimes, to encourage me when I had dates with women, she went so far as to lend me her funny little front-loading bubble car, which operated not so much as an accessory to my virility but as an invariable conversation-starter.

All this time Sally presented her place as a sort of home from home for me. She liked to imagine that I was her indigent supplicant and, as Roger lunched in college, and as she plied me with her home-made pâtés and quiches in that vast, flash kitchen full of pings and clicks, she liked to lecture me about 'finding a nice girl' and settling down. I should explain here that these were the days when women like Sally found it acceptable to talk about unattached female persons as 'girls'.

The truth is that Sally preferred me unsettled, and invited me a lot less often once Katherine had become a fixture in my life. Admittedly, Katherine's instinct against head girls didn't help, and she and I were, in any case, very self-contained, very smoochily rocks-and-stars in love, and we went almost nowhere, though Katherine did venture out reluctantly to her job.

For half a year we made a passionate love-nest of the icy bedsit, snuggling under a de luxe duckdown duvet that a previous woman in my life had given me as an unsolicited Christmas present, having first gone to the trouble of stealing it for me from Heal's. Before my air of shopsoiled middle age invades my purpose, I ought to establish right away that Katherine was, and still is, the nicest thing that has ever happened to me.

At that time we stayed indoors, occupied with marvelling at the commonplace differences in our bodies. I experienced it as a daily miracle that her body was so very unlike mine; that it was white and smooth and hairless except for the three small clumps of light brown fuzz that had touched down so moderately upon her crotch and armpits. It was a marvel to me that what grew from her head came pale and straight, where my head grew tight spirals of black wire.

Meanwhile, the book did well. That is, it got terrific reviews and a book club deal and several foreign sales and a film option, albeit an option on a film that never actually got made. Then, six months after its publication, my maternal grandmother died, leaving me a tiny, wonderfully isolated cottage in the west of Ireland which Katherine and I promptly set out to inhabit. I had in mind for us to go there and live out that Rosie O'Grady lifestyle that Stephen Daedalus's friend Cranly epitomizes so charmingly towards the end of *A Portrait of the Artist as a Young Man*:

> 'For I love sweet Rosie O'Grady
> And Rosie O'Grady loves me.'

Katherine was pregnant with our daughter when we left. The pregnancy was not easy and she was still vulnerable and ever close to tears given the newness, at that time, of her return to Britain after a bruising love affair in Italy and the cot death of her one-month-old Italian baby. I considered it my priority, my privilege, my joy, to restore Katherine with all the kid glove treatment I could muster, and it may be that, for ever after, I have made a habit of behaving with her as though she might break in two, were I to confront her with my more usual, stroppy-bugger tendencies in matters of interlocution. My sweet Katie, always in need of my restoring broth and bandages.

Ironically, it frustrates me that Katherine adopts these protective assumptions writ large in her handling of our daughter Stella. Stella, alias the Nuisance Chip, since – as potluck determines these things – our daughter; only daughter; only child; Precious Girl – comes bearing a nuisance chip in the brain.

Hailing, as I do, from a family of six, I find it difficult to explain why Stella is quite such a full-time job. Stella is omnipresent. Stella is Katherine's career. OK, so she's conceived by miracle and born by Caesarean, since Katherine's first experience of childbirth has left her reproductive equipment impaired. We start off knowing that Stella will be our only child. But, from the beginning, Stella is as if programmed for maximum nuisance capacity. She appears to have an allergy to milk – her own mother's breast milk. She vomits after every feed and fails to thrive. Her skin erupts in such immoderately violent rashes in response to contact with her own urine that her bum becomes a proud case study in the *BMJ*. She appears to be allergic to water, or to whatever is in the water. She frequently develops soaring body temperatures and collapses with febrile convulsions, her eyes open, pupils fixed upon nothing. She is hyperactive, asthmatic and nasally congested to such a degree that friends visiting at night mistake the sound of Stella's deep-sleep infant breathing for a ten-ton lorry idling in the yard.

Before she is two years old, Stella has been rushed to hospital some twelve or thirteen times, usually with her lips turning blue. Once there, she is injected, X-rayed and placed under an all-night oxygen tent. She is dragged through lumbar punctures and a tonsillectomy. She is stuffed with so much penicillin that she not only becomes allergic to it, but develops chronic oral and vaginal thrush.

Nonetheless, she is a bright, restless little thing and her mobility is extremely precocious. So are her incessantly employed verbal skills. By nine months she is walking and can scale the henhouse roof. By twenty months she can speak in perfect sentences, knows all her Puffins off by heart and delivers us short lectures on the

Long March and the Sword Excalibur. Her singing voice is captivating. She combines these talents with remarkably retarded sphincter control and pees on people's carpets, and on the floors of grocery shops and bookshops, until she's four.

When Katherine's mother arrives to visit Stella at two, she comes bearing a canary yellow potty as inducement. Stella sits on it immediately and scuffs it around the floor.

'Are you doing a nice wee-wee?' Kath's mother says.

'As a matter of fact,' says the Nuisance Chip, with that exquisite, provoking toddler articulation, 'as a matter of fact, I'm *ack*-shully sculling to Brighton.' Stella has never been to Brighton. For her it is a literary concept.

By the age of seven, the Nuisance Chip has already been firmly labelled dyslexic. She scrambles letters and numbers. Two years later, she can still neither read nor write. With regard to any practical task she has two left hands and half a brain. In school she seems incapable of learning anything. Katherine and I sneak anxious, eavesdropped glances at her in the playground, where she stands on her own near the fence, shuffling her feet and sucking on her left thumb.

Katherine is so accommodated to the business of giving over her life to making the Nuisance Chip viable that the learning difficulties are, by now, merely an additional chapter. As the years pass, I watch Katherine teach herself everything that Stella is required to know. She becomes the child's sole conduit of knowledge. Stella grows and the scholastic demands become more complex. So does Katherine's commitment. She rises from my bed at five and acquaints herself with the mysteries of matrices and binomial equations. She masters molar mass. She reads the child's every examination set book onto audiotape, either in English or, where necessary, in French or German. She becomes Stella's bottomless resource.

Katherine, who was running a small designer knitwear and weaving business from home up to the time of Stella's birth, very soon packs it in. She has envisaged herself dyeing and spinning her yarns with an infant peacefully cooing in a Moses basket at her feet, but the Nuisance Chip soon disabuses her of this fantasy. She unravels the yarns, swallows the dyes and gets rushed off to Casualty. Plus she has frantic screaming fits if Katherine turns away from her for a moment. Katherine, who is a literate woman, simply gives up reading. She reads not a single line of newsprint for over four years. Stella understands that the printed page is a rival for Katherine's attention. Her insecurities cannot co-exist with it.

Let it be said that Stella is, and was, enchanting. She charms us. She charms our friends. She has the gift of the gab. Her looks are astonishing. Stella, perhaps to underline her status as our miracle child, has flecked pussycat eyes and orange crêpe hair which is always kept long. Heaven knows where the hair comes from. Nobody in either of our families is in possession of such an attribute. It belongs, uniquely, to Stella. Could it be a gift from some unidentified Celtic ancestor – the illegitimate issue of my mother's Anglo-Irish antecedents? Or from the intricacies of my dear dead father's part Sephardic DNA? God knows.

As a young child, Stella enjoys hearing Katherine tell her that, as she sat sewing on a snowy day, she pricked her finger on a needle and wished for a little girl with skin as white as snow and hair as orange as marmalade. But, as the years advance, Stella learns to complain about her hair. Schoolteachers pick on her because of it, she says. A hundred mouse heads can be chattering in assembly and it will be, 'You there! You with the red hair. Report to my office at once!'

And boys, she complains – teenage boys – will always go for blondes.

'Even,' Stella says, 'when they've got faces like horses. All blokes see is the hair. Well, you know what I mean, don't you? Mum's blonde, isn't she?' This is not a thing I can deny.

At thirteen, a ranting chemistry teacher denounces Stella's hair as 'unhygienic', though the hair is washed unremittingly and frequently clogs the shower. It is worn drawn away from the brow and temples and held by two stout grips. Admittedly, then, two feet of hair cascade down Stella's back.

'Do you come to school on the BUS?!' rages the creature, as she looms over her test tubes. Stella says that she takes the train.

'Only think of the GERMS you're spreading!' says the creature. 'Keep it plaited or CUT IT OFF!'

It is Katherine who passes on the details of this episode to me.

'Orange hair; orange bush,' I say. I have not, in fact, seen my post-pubertal daughter in the nude, but she has telling, orange underarm hair.

'Jonathan!' Katherine says.

'Sexual jealousy,' I say. 'The old bat is obviously jealous.'

'And what if she's a young bat?' Katherine says, changing sides. 'Don't be such a bloke.'

The upshot is that Katherine makes plaits in Stella's hair until the child's head is as if painted by Botticelli. The unfortunate chemistry teacher is required to suffer the ignominy of having one of the Three Graces invade her laboratory. No ordinary plaits for the Precious Girl.

'For Christ's sake, Kath,' I say. 'That takes you forever.'

'It's fun,' Katherine says. 'Fun' is a word that she and Stella use a lot – and I can see that Katherine's willing slavery makes for all sorts of happy bonds between them. They shop, gad, giggle, dress up and generally bounce off each other like the best of bosom buddies. Only my mother is sceptical.

'Oh, my dear ones,' she says on one occasion. 'Katherine, my sweetheart, this is going to end in tears.'

When the Nuisance Chip is eight – and very much for her sake; and very much at Katherine's pleading – we abandon the rural Irish idyll and we return to England. I drag my feet all the way.

Katherine is certain that Stella's educational needs can be better served in a context of greater intellectual sophistication. Both grandmothers are ecstatic at the prospect of having Stella and Katherine closer – 'and you too, my darling,' as my mother observes to me in afterthought. We buy a stone cottage in a Cotswold village – a grander sort of cottage on a commuter line to Paddington – with a kitchen not unlike a smaller version of my sister-in-law's, containing a dishwasher, an automatic washing-machine and various other gadgets that pip, rumble and squeak.

Katherine, intimidated by Sally, who is now within striking distance, makes efforts to acquire us a cleaner, but, unlike Sally, we do not have it in us quite to master the servant relationship. I find it particularly irksome, since Katherine always escapes the cleaner by going off to work as a voluntary helper in Stella's new school and leaves me at home to face the intruder.

We make our way in quick succession through a scornful young Swede, who despises us for being in possession of a string mop and zinc bucket instead of a squeezy sponge on a plastic stick, and an adorable but wholly unreliable school-leaver – a bright, bookish little thing whom Katherine ends up tutoring for free through A level English and Art History. Finally, we acquire a monstrous, cone-shaped matron, weighing twenty stone, whose tiny face is close-gathered at the pinnacle end of the cone. She has a Betty Boop voice and wears her hair in two pre-teen bunches tied with ribbons and novelty bobble grips. This person's zeal for cleanliness is so extreme that after three hours in the house she has not only removed all the varnish from the work-boards but has also dismantled the cafetière into a gleaming Meccano-set assortment of nuts, wheels, mesh disc and axle shaft. In addition, she is inconveniently phobic about a range of household pets, including, I suspect, stay-at-home husbands. I sense that she is a fundamentalist crusader in some personal gender jihad for which I am a major focus.

'I had to leave one of my other jobs today,' she says warningly, as I venture out of my room for a cup of coffee, 'because the tortoise kept on staring at me. I don't like to be stared at, thank you very much.'

'Oh really?' I say. 'You'd think a tortoise would be hibernating by now.'

'He can't hibernate,' she says. 'He's far too small. He needs his hormone injections before he can hibernate.'

Hormone injections are a recurring theme with her. I begin to fantasize about the cone-shaped cleaning person keeping a syringe at the ready for me in her capacious patchwork handbag. By Christmas, Katherine is twisting her arm to stay, because it appears that I have been staring at her, along with the tortoise and the neighbour's tabby cat.

'Well,' I point out, 'it's difficult not to stare at a person who comes cone-shaped. Especially one who insists on wearing bunny-rabbit bobble grips in her hair.'

'Oh, for Christ's sake, Jonathan,' Katherine says, 'the poor thing's terribly shy. Plus she's a man. Surely even you can suss that?'

'You're kidding,' I say.

'Trust you to victimize a transvestite,' she says.

'What?' I say.

'Rambo,' she says. Then she says, 'You're such a pussycat, Jonathan. Why do you always pretend to be such a swine?'

We can, I suppose, be regarded as having upgraded our lifestyle since the Rosie O'Grady period. We have an idiotic emasculating address: Cottage-on-the-Green, Ashford-on-the-Heath, Bourton-in-the-Marsh. I spend my days anticipating that some wag will start addressing me as Toad-in-the-Hole.

For all sorts of reasons – not the least among them the ever more complex demands of the Nuisance Chip – I find it increasingly difficult to work there. Katherine now gives all the creative energy she has left after nurturing Stella to making the place nice. Or nice enough to pass muster with a new, improved class of local dropper-in. She makes calico Roman blinds and rag-rolls the walls. She does cut-and-stick. She stencils tasteful twiddles on the dresser. She talks about 'dragging' and 'liming'. She becomes addicted to auction sales and car boot sales and comes home with little spinner's chairs, or with art deco clocks – or, on one occasion, with a whole set of Marcel Breuer dining-chairs that now live permanently in the outhouse because they won't fit anywhere else. Parcels arrive in the porch from Designers Guild and from Osborne & Little. Within the year, the house is so pleasing to the eye that I spend the whole time staring at the walls while eating too many biscuits.

Which brings me to the socio-culinary dimension. The house has a context. It has neighbours who keep on asking us to dinner, and Katherine keeps on asking the neighbours back. For these unspeakable occasions there are apparently no limits to the lengths of dedication required of the host victim. Whole days are spent marinating salmon into gravadlax – preferably salmon caught by oneself the previous weekend in the Scottish Highlands – or cleaving the intractable stones of peaches prior to steeping in marsala. Busy, high-earning career persons take time out to make their own olive bread, to grow their own coriander, and to pick their own wild mushrooms in the nearby woods.

The company is moreover so indescribably dire that my customary defence against it is one that drives poor Katherine to shame and fury. I drink myself either into a premature sleep or, more usually, into a confrontational mindset. Katherine insists that I have insulted both of our immediate neighbours – to the right, the bikist solicitor and his wife, the fraggle-haired sociologist, and, to the left, the merchant banker twerp and his wife, the parliamentary private secretary. The bikist is a

Neighbourhood Watch man whose other vehicle is a Porsche. He is the sort of cyclist who cannot set forth five paces to the corner shop without clothing himself from head to foot in black Lycra, safety helmet and a full deck of illuminated sparklers. The twerp, by contrast, possesses not even this alleviating eccentricity.

'OK, so you think he's a twerp,' Katherine says. 'But at least he's got decent manners.'

'Oh, Kath, for Christ's sake,' I say, my voice soggy with reproach. I mean to imply that time was when nothing mattered to us but necking and fishing and boiling eggs and pulling off each other's clothes.

'*And*,' she says, 'even after I had bloody *dragged* you from the table, and the poor man had *offered* to shake your hand, you *still* had to insult him, didn't you? You *still* had to have the last word.'

Our host, the merchant banker twerp, has, in point of fact, spent the night bending my ear with his opinions; has referred to me no less than three times as 'you writer chappies'; has argued with me, in the face of all reasonable evidence to the contrary, that everyone in America is 'rich' – this because he sees a good quality of luggage in the foyer of his Manhattan hotel – and finally, in unison with the bikist, has lobbied forcefully to sign me up for Neighbourhood Watch. I am a sitting duck here, being a homebound worker, and they see no reason at all why I should not take control of the 'Telephone Cascade' until I tell them I consider Neighbourhood Watch to be a bourgeois vigilante organization; a smuggies' club for people with too much stuff.

'You were shouting at him,' Katherine says. 'You looked as though you were going to hit him.'

She says she had to 'drag' me away and that when the twerp had thrust his right hand at me on parting and had said, 'No hard feelings, old man. Will you shake me by the hand?' I had behaved really badly.

'Well, I shook him by the hand, didn't I?' I say.

'Plus,' Katherine says, spitting the words, 'plus, you said, "Sure I'll shake you by the hand. I've shaken hands with all sorts of arseholes in my time."'

I confess I am rather pleased with this reminder. I laugh a smug, ill-timed laugh.

'Well, I'm glad you think it's so funny,' Katherine says. 'I have to go.'

'Don't go,' I say.

'I have to,' she says. 'It's time to collect Stella.'

Stella is at the local school on the green – quite literally on the green. She can see our garden gate from the school playground. But Katie collects her because she likes chatting with the other mothers. I have no idea, until the move, what a one my Katie is for the gaggle. Also, she collects Stella because her mind is full of child abductors and hooded axemen. They lurk round every corner in Katherine's mind, in every country lane. They haunt the village shop, waiting to pounce on Stella, who is, admittedly, an absolute sweetheart.

In her absence, and knowing she'll be forever, I rustle up a batch of scones and set the kitchen table for tea with jampot and napkins and little china plates and bone-handled knives.

When they come we are four to tea, not three, because Stella has brought a friend. The friend can be any one of four or five young persons of the moment, but current favourites are the Princess and the Tart. Today it is the Tart, who enters wearing shiny skinfit aerobics clobber, clackety, backless high heels and a necklace of boiled sweets that she sucks on, but will not share. She comes from 'the estate'. The Tart is three months older than Stella and is an expert manipulator.

'If you don't say I can draw Woo-pert Bear better than you,' says the Tart, 'then you can't come to my burfday.' Stella is brought to heel by this transparent gamesmanship, even though she knows the Tart's birthday celebration will encompass no more than a car ride to McDonald's. It won't be in the class of five-hour banquet that Katherine lays on in our house for Stella's natal anniversaries. These come along with personalized loot bags, ballerina cakes, treasure hunts requiring labyrinths of multicoloured ribbons running up and down the stairwell, sacks full of superior prizes and an epilogue of chilled sparkling wine for collecting parents.

A little later the Tart rips up Stella's drawing, tacitly conceding, I suppose, that the Nuisance Chip's draughtsmanship has some merit.

'Anyway,' says the Tart, 'I can wide a torilla.' She means that she can ride a two-wheeler; a bicycle. '*You* can't,' she says. This is true: Stella still has the stabilizers on her bicycle. Katie and I break our backs all day, bending over and running along behind, clutching the back of the saddle while Stella screams at us, 'Don't let go! I said, "Don't let go!" ' Us she can tyrannize. Not the Tart.

Towards evening, as Katie and I are reading Stella her nightly quota of nine to twelve bedtime stories, the Tart is astride the torilla. She rides the winding country lanes after dark, weaving perilously all over the road. Katherine and I are convinced that the Tart will come to a sticky end, but she bears a charmed life. That is, she survives long enough to get pregnant at sixteen and qualify, two years later, for her own flat on 'the estate'. This is just as Katie is hot-housing Stella through her A levels and Stella is playing the cello all day, because she has set her heart on getting a place at the School of Music at Edinburgh University. The class system in this country stinks. The education system likewise. I have to hand it to the Tart: she was a bright, sparky girl. She deserved better. She could multiply hundreds tens and units in her head before the Nuisance Chip could add two and three.

That night after our quarrel, Katherine and I make our peace. First I make a policy statement, while lying flat on my back on our bed under the stolen duvet. Katherine is pottering at her dressing-table. She is dabbling with her Under-Eye Cream and her High-Colour Treatment Cream. My behaviour over the last twenty-four hours has presumably provoked the high colour. She is lingering at the dressing-table too long, but she is wearing special pyjamas, not her usual old rags. They are cream satin pyjamas with splashes of red poppies and red poppy-coloured binding. They were a present from my mother, who adores Katherine and accuses me constantly of doing her down. I hope, now, that she is wearing them for me.

'Kath,' I say, 'I care about the two of us more than my life.' She says nothing. She still has her back to me. 'I care about you and Stella and me,' I say. 'I care about having breakfast with you, and fucking you, and loving you, and all of us being together.' Still she says nothing. I say, 'Look, I don't want all that other stuff in my life. I hate it. All the bloody socializing and crap. I can't deal with it, and I won't have it.'

'The point is,' Katherine says, still not turning round. 'The point is, you're brilliant at it. They ask us because of you. Even the twerp as you call him. He's flattered to have you insult him.'

'Well, I can't deal with it,' I say again. 'I don't exist to flatter and insult twerps. I'm saying it has to stop. Just promise me it will stop. Don't keep saying yes to these people. Or tell them your husband won't come. Tell them he's a bastard, all right?'

'All right,' Katherine says, after a very long silence.

'I mean it,' I say. 'Katie, I'm serious.' Katherine says nothing. She still sits with her back to me.

'Do you love me?' I say.

She says nothing for a long time. She sighs. 'Yes,' she says crossly. Then she says, 'It's not always easy for me.'

Oh shit, I think, irritably. Oh yeah? And how easy is it for any of us? Bloody women, I think. Then I feel ashamed. I change my tack. I am encouraged by the poppy-splashed pyjamas.

'Come here and commit oral sex with me,' I say. I say it to provoke her, but she comes. Katherine is great at sex but oral sex is not a big thing with her. She doesn't like the gloop in her mouth, to quote her. But she agrees, as usual, to some initial mammalian sucklings and nibblings, before the gloop becomes an issue, so to speak.

I emit a range of gorilla groans until I can bear what she does no longer. Then I bed her in the mattress and heave myself on top of her like the big needy primate that I am, and we hump until we judder together, feeling, as always, ecstatic about our unfailing cleverness at making it so brilliantly in unison.

'That was nice,' Katherine says and she laughs a little at her own understatement. I promptly flatten her, groping across her breasts for the Kleenex so that the dear thing won't have to sleep on my splat as it goes cold on the sheet under her thighs. 'Don't worry about it,' she says. 'I'm already using your socks.'

Great, I think. My very own intractable oyster-globs on my wool-rich navy ribbed hosiery. Then I think – Oh Jesus – how extraordinary is my love for this woman. Trout fishing and having sex are my only serious hobbies, now that I have given up even intermittently playing the flute. I fall, as I always do, into a heavy, ungracious sleep, even as I shift myself from Katherine's body. When I stir, briefly, thereafter, it is to find that she is planting kisses on my bum. I quiz her about this in a mumbly sort of way.

'You don't jump me when you're asleep,' she says. Very Katie. Very put-down.

The next day I take the bull by the horns. I contact the Bavarian Quaker landlady who, now almost wholly immobile, is nonetheless once again happy to have me rent her attic. The plan is not to abandon my family, though I cannot pretend that I'm not abandoning my weekday timeshare in the Nuisance Chip. I am constructing a system which will allow me to get on with my work. From the following week, I go there, Monday to Friday, enjoying the solitude and the unchanged lino on the floor and the fraying donkey-brown blanket that I hang up over the window at night and my own blissfully un-fussed catering. I eat chorizos out of the bag and chunks of Galician cheese. I eat hard-boiled eggs with blobs of Hellmann's and packets of Mini-Cheddars. I eat those delicious polystyrene caterpillars rolled in orange granules, called Wotsits.

And I write. Sometimes I write all day. Sometimes I write between two and five in the morning. The system works really well and, within the year, I've written my fifth novel – *Have Horn; Will Travel* – easier than all the others, both to read and to write. It gains me a new kind of audience and is subsequently filmed. It sparks itself into existence one night as I sit at a Lieder recital with my mother and Katherine, contemplating the stock characters and rustic stereotyping of those somewhat so-so lyrics of Wilhelm Müller's upon which Lydia Dent now wishes to write her A level essay – and which Schubert, under the cloud of his own recently diagnosed syphilis, managed so brilliantly to layer and elevate into a profound, bombarding symbiosis of love and death.

Basically, the novel asks whether we ever die of love. It brings tears to the eyes of schoolgirls who write to me on lined pages ripped from school exercise books – though none has thus far written to me quite as charmingly as Lydia Dent.

My return to London is something that Sally cottons on to pretty soon and we re-adopt the habit of lunching together, though now we always do so in the neutral space of restaurants. By the time we begin our Oliveto phase, Sally's children are twenty, eighteen and sixteen, while even my little Stella is coming up seventeen.

Twenty years on from her early marriage, I am no longer in need of Sally's pâtés and quiches, while she, on the other hand, has a need of me. She is not given to therapists. She believes in pulling herself together. Plus, she unloads on me – almost always about the oddities of her husband. I am bound to say that this has made her a less rewarding companion, so that our meetings, from my point of view, are now more duty than pleasure. God knows, I cannot claim to have found the running of my own life a hazard-free process. I have never claimed the blueprint for getting it right, but I don't spill the beans like Sally. I am cagier, perhaps. I am discreet. I am satisfied that Sally, after all these years, knows precious little about me.

My brother, predictably enough, since he was always a premature eccentric for those with eyes to see beyond the prettiness of his face, has become increasingly peculiar with age. He has developed some ingenious techniques, of late, which have made him an increasingly slippery customer for efficient Sally to control. He has discovered oblique forms of obstruction. He has become a saboteur.

And the home computer has helped to do for him, since it has allowed him to commune less with his colleagues and more with his electronic subordinate. Roger has an addictive relationship with the subordinate which keeps him permanently in bondage. He cannot produce his next great work because he will only be able to do so when he and the machine have achieved nirvana. And the laptop is an innovation which has significantly reduced the circumstances in which Roger need ever get out of bed – his and Sally's bed, that is. The marriage bed.

Roger, all through childhood, was a monumental slob but, oddly enough, this has come as a recent surprise to Sally, who, throughout all the years of her marriage, has managed to have him mime the habits of a tidy person. Now, in his middle age, Roger has reverted to type. He will no longer dance to Sally's tune. The Master Bedroom, Sally tells me, has become a health hazard. What she describes is what I remember as Roger's routine stockpile of old newspapers, sheet music and specialist journals rolled round with mouldering coffee cups and apple cores, brown and festering, growing into the rugs. Roger, she tells me, has taken to chewing a brand of sugar-free spearmint gum which glues itself permanently to the carpet nap.

The bedroom has become a no-go area for Mrs Thing, who is now almost seventy-eight. Yet for Sally to gather up Roger's laundry – the balled socks stuck down the foot-end of the duvet cover, the underpants abandoned in the grate along with old envelopes and oily food wrappings and (just once, she says) a packet of wild bird food – has become a form of mortification. It is a thing she takes amiss, given her status as a busy commuting worker with three nearly grown-up daughters. Then there are Roger's recent nutritional theories.

'He's got this really funny diet,' she says to me one day. 'His bedside table is stuffed with these quack pills' – pills that spill, capless of course, all over the floor, where they mingle with the ooze of the festering apple cores. Since Roger these days likes to work at home, he has no particular reason to get dressed and wanders, naked, into the kitchen to make himself plates of snack food. Or he wears an egg-stained pullover that stops short of his genitals.

'So he's not wearing any trousers?' I say.

'Oh, no,' Sally says. 'After all, one doesn't wear trousers in bed, does one?'

Old Mrs Thing has begun to treat my brother as if he were a recalcitrant two-year-old grandson. 'One day, the ducks will have that,' she says, speaking of what she calls Roger's 'winkle'.

Roger, Sally says, allows himself a single brand of coffee and a single cup, once a day – after which he dumps the soggy grounds straight from his Moka gadget onto whatever happens to be already in the sink, thus coating it all with a layer of fine brown grit.

'I've asked him not to,' Sally says, querulously, as I eagerly consult the menu and urge her to make her choice. Sally is a conventional woman, the child of an East Anglian vicarage. 'I've tried to tell him it makes everything gritty,' she says.

Roger's reply to this particular complaint, she says, is to observe that what is 'soggy' cannot also be 'gritty'; a dubious quip, perhaps, when one's wife is telling one to leave it out in no uncertain terms. In short, Roger has decided to re-launch himself as a disobliging nutcase with a set of unlikeable habits. He has devised a system for ruling his family where, in the past, Sally has always had the upper hand. He has become an underground worker.

I observe to my sister-in-law – hoping to woo her into a more mellow generality – that Roger sounds not unlike one of those rural Irish dowagers that Katherine and I occasionally encountered years back, who had 'taken to the bed' with strongbox and chamber-pot, from thence to call all the shots. Sally is neither diverted nor particularly interested. She peremptorily makes her menu choice. Then she returns to her theme.

'Talking of chamber-pots,' she says, 'Roger pees in all my Kilner jars. He gets them out of the shed. They stand in a row along the bedroom fender. He never empties them, of course, and I need hardly tell you that they stink.'

The quack pills have come concurrently with Roger's new dietary beliefs, which have, I suspect, been constructed for Sally's maximum inconvenience. These have entrenched and extended themselves over the months and, for a mathematician, Roger is making what sound like rather simplistic connections between cause and effect. If he has a headache, for example, he will attribute it quite arbitrarily to his having eaten chestnut purée in the previous evening's meal. If his hands show patches of dry skin, then it is because Sally, contrary to his explicit instructions, has added a half-teaspoon of sugar to her home-made tomato sauce.

These days, Roger's eating habits feature somewhat obsessionally in Sally's hierarchy of grumbles. From being a person who was once fond of cooking – albeit she is one of those vicarage English women for whom Coronation Chicken and Summer Pudding hold ominous attractions – poor Sal now finds it a penance, as my brother interrogates her about the content of every cup and plateful. Roger's diet, she says, requires her to cook without sugar, without wheat, without yeast, without dairy produce, without vinegar, without fruit peel, without fruit juice, without raisins, without grapes, without chocolate, without alcohol and without tinned food.

'He's found this doctor in Basingstoke,' Sally says. 'He's a born-again Southern Baptist with hair replacements. I've seen him. He relays charismatic hymns over a tannoy.' The Southern Baptist healer, she says, has disconcerting, hirsute implants that sprout gridwise from his pate in tufts arranged at intervals of exactly one centimetre.

'It's not that I haven't tried,' Sally says, and she promptly kills the Oliveto inkfish pasta stone dead for me, running through the demise of all her sensible, cheap, family dishes. She has struggled, poor Sal, to make soups without cream, stews without wine, salads without vinegar, pasta without cheese and puddings without fruit, sugar, chocolate, custard or pastry. She has baked loaves of wheat-free, yeast-free bread, using cornmeal and rice flour and millet. It all tastes foul, she says, and the girls have begun to rebel. Sally is worried because her two younger daughters swipe money from her purse and stuff themselves, night after night, at the doner kebab van. She is especially worried about Sheila, the sparkiest of my nieces, who has begun to stay away all night. Naturally, she blames my brother.

My advice to Sally has not always been of the best. I tell her to make Roger cook for himself but, on our next meeting, Sally reveals that this has merely given Roger the opening to commandeer the kitchen at moments of peak inconvenience for the preparation of his own brand of Fungus the Bogeyman cuisine.

'It's driving me round the bend,' she says. 'He does these high-protein breakfasts. He does offal and smoked fish.'

Since Roger has never related to food in any sensual way – he has related to nothing, I believe, in any properly sensual way, except perhaps to the violin and to our mother – he has no way of understanding that his productions are unacceptable. In no time at all, he has burnt his way through all the superior, last-a-lifetime cookware that came Sally's way via the wedding list at Peter Jones.

'If all he's cooking is one tiny little scrap of lamb's liver,' Sally says to me, 'then why does he need to use a frying-pan that's fifteen inches in diameter?'

Roger's method is to pour enough oil into the pan to drown a stack of chapattis. Then he will pitch in his morsel of liver and leave it on maximum heat to smoke and stink until it looks like a small dried turd. Meanwhile, the entire extraneously lubricated surface of the pan is blackened to no purpose.

'Unless,' Sally says viciously, 'he scrambles an egg into the smoke.' Sometimes, she says, he likes to scramble an egg into the blood instead, thus turning his egg from yellow to pink.

'Washed in the Blood of the Lamb,' I say, to annoy her high church sensibilities. We are eating tender medallions of venison as we speak, but Sally is too far gone to try enjoying them.

'Or he scrambles eggs into his fried kipper ooze,' she says. 'Normal people poach kippers.' She begins to play with her fork. Roger fries his kippers into a bakelite carapace, she says. Then he eats them with his fingers – bones, skin, eye sockets and all.

'The girls say he looks like a giant eating a cockroach,' she says.

Roger, thanks to my advice, has now become a demon with the family pressure cooker, which he uses for the preparation of his daily ration of scorched pulses.

'That's if he gets round to cooking them,' she says. 'Sometimes they just stand around in smelly water, going fizzy.'

I have a sudden, unpleasant vision of Sally's bedroom as a vaporous Fuseli witch-landscape where chickpeas steep and bubble in outsize Kilner jars brim-full of stale pee. I abandon the remains of my venison and promptly decline the sorbet. I take a swig of red wine. So Roger has slipped away from her, I muse, perhaps a little smugly, after all those years of Sally's rhetoric of rotas and role flexibility.

Next thing, Sally is doing a postscript on Roger's clothes. He wears his evening shoes on muddy walks, 'Deliberately,' she says, sounding like a prefect giving out order marks, 'in the hour before the college feast.'

I call for the bill. 'Do you have sex?' I say. Unfortunately I say it just as the waiter comes. I pull out my Visa card and chuck it into the saucer along with the bill.

Sally is rattled. She starts to pull rank on me in matters of marital deportment.

'I don't intend to leave him,' she says. 'We both believe in marriage, Jonathan. We both believe in loyalty. Don't think I'd ever be unfaithful to him.' I wonder, for a moment, whether Sally could possibly be offering me her body. Does she offer anyone her body? 'I don't philander, Jonathan,' she says, 'and neither does your brother. I will say that for him.'

'Heave him out, Sal,' I say. 'Give yourself a break. Pack his bag and leave it for him at the college lodge.' As a piece of advice, I consider this to have more future than the cooking suggestion. Roger is driving them crazy. Plus Sheila, Sally tells me, has now upped and left school. Perhaps to her credit, she has refused to apply for any of that array of hire-and-fire skivvy jobs with which our leaders have so effectively replaced proper work. Sheila refuses to sell hot dogs from a cart or scrape food off plates for two pounds fifty an hour. She has fixed her hair into dusty ropes with superglue and has made several holes along her earlobes. I admire her for having thus rendered herself unemployable, but I don't say so to Sally. To do so would be to drive her into an extended, moralizing frenzy.

'Sal,' I say. 'I've got to go.' This is true. I have to go, but when I look up, I see that Sally has tears in her eyes. Oh Christ.

'Jonathan,' she says, 'he has this photograph of me beside the bed. It's from when I was – you know – young and pretty.' Sally was, and still is, very pretty. Admittedly she has begun to get that formidable, WI look; that sort of look that, I imagine, would make old colonels call her 'a fine figure of a woman'.

'For Christ's sake, Sal,' I say, 'you're pretty.'

'Jonathan,' she says, 'it ought to be in a frame. *He* ought to have put it in a frame.'

'Do yourself a favour, lovey,' I say. 'Swipe it back or put it in a frame yourself.' I say this because expecting Roger to frame a photograph is like expecting a cat to walk on its hind legs.

'If it was Katherine,' she says, 'you'd have put it in a frame.'

Things are getting heavy here. Heavy but true. I may desert my wife all week in order to tread ancient lino underfoot, but I keep my photograph of Katherine in a small, leaf-patterned pewter frame beside my bed in north London, where its presence is irksome to Sonia. Sonia is a clandestine presence in my life about whom Sally, of course, knows nothing. Sonia is the woman who isn't my wife, with whom I have sex on a regular basis.

'Sal,' I say again, 'I have to go.' The same Sonia will be on her way to me and will not appreciate being kept waiting on the Quaker landlady's doorstep. She is a highly paid professional woman who believes that her time is money.

My first meeting with Sonia is at a party in London on the top floor of a high-rise glass box off Euston Road. It does me no credit to say that we are drawn together by strong mutual dislike. I dislike everything about her appearance, for a start. I dislike the hint of childhood about the in-turned toes. I dislike her hollow thighs. I dislike the Mabel Lucie Attwell face, framed in dark brown toddler curls. I know, without having to hear her voice, that the speech will come with a lisp. I dislike her self-satisfied pekinesey smirk and the hint of puppy fat disposed about her chest that deputizes for breasts.

I catch her eye while staring at her hard from the other end of the room. I'm staring in order to work out why a woman about whom I know absolutely nothing is capable of irritating the hell out of me. Just as she begins to cross the room towards me, I decode the cause of my irritation: it has to do with conflicting messages and I take these to indicate duplicity.

The tight strapless Lycra tank top (worn under a wisp of what Sonia calls 'dévoré') says, 'I'm explicit, I'm sexy,' but the flat chest and the cutey-pie, turned-in toes say, 'I'm still a girlie.' The yellow bleached streak to the front of her hair says, 'I'm adventurous, try me,' but the fact that she intermittently sucks on the end of it says, 'Baby me, I'm little.' The narrow shoulders say, 'I'm fragile. Be rough with me and I'll get asthma.' The kohl-work around the eyes says, 'I'm easy,' but the smudges say, 'Someone has blacked my eye. Maybe it's Daddy. Maybe it's you. It's men. Join the crowd. Abuse me.' The skin, from a distance, is peaches and cream, but from close up the patches of rosiness on the cheeks look like areas of slight irritation. A wine rash, perhaps. They say, 'I'm sensitive. I am allergic to one hundred substances. Pamper me. Buy me my own special soap.' The shoes are Shirley Temple, but the get-up, including the jewellery, says, 'My annual income is seriously grown-up and I spend it on nobody but myself.'

Sonia is a development economist at a college of London University. She has recently been elevated to Reader. She has also made it fairly big in the media, through a by-line in a mass market Sunday tabloid, and from there she has invaded various glossies, specialist publications and broadsheets. She also appears on television. In short, Sonia has become one of that clutch of female style-gurus that I hardly need describe. She peddles fellatio and knicker-sniffing with a sociological slant. It is, most of it, a sort of look-at-me consumerism in the guise of the cutting edge. It concentrates on matters relating to sex, gender, bishops, gender, celebrity divorce, gender, and personal lifestyle: style holidays, style food, style art, style clothing and style feminism. It may be tomorrow's kindling but, in Sonia's case, it has the effect of doubling her academic salary for an additional five hours' work a week. In between, Sonia collects air miles attending Third World conferences. She has been known, in my experience, to climb into her designer tart's kit for a beanfest called a Poverty Banquet.

In matters of pick-up, Sonia works fast. We leave the party early. I help her into her coat, which is made from the pelts of dead animals. Sonia tells me, when I comment on this, that she has had the bad luck the previous week to run into a brigade of pickets on her way back from a gallery where she has recorded her thoughts on the recent work of Sir Eduardo Paolozzi. By the time we are in the lift together descending to the street, Sonia turns and says to me, 'Your place or mine?' She is no slouch, is Sonia. She employs a cliché with aplomb.

It is because I find her place so gruesome at this, our first seduction event, so rigorously interior-designed – her furniture like great splintery lumps of driftwood and railway sleeper, all banged together with nails exhibiting large, pyramidal heads; her huge bed as if constructed from unreconstituted builder's pallets; her bathroom full of ersatz verdigris and distressed wood – that I make the mistake of inviting her to my place three days later and I give her the address.

I hurry from my lunch with Sally, but Sonia is not on the doorstep. She is inside the house, sitting, fully clothed, under The Jakpak, on the wooden seat of the lavatory on my upper landing. The landlady has let her in. She has her feet splayed, toes as usual turned inward, her feet clothed in one of the fifty-odd pairs of designer bondage shoes that her wardrobe can yield up. Sonia's shoes come in categories. That is to say, I have categorized them. They come as bondage, Minnie Mouse, Ginger Rogers and Prince Valiant.

She is immersed in reading the day's letters – my letters – and doesn't bother to look up.

'So what the hell do you think you're doing?' I say. The only post that comes to me at the bedsit is that re-directed by my publisher.

'There's a bloke here from the Buddhist clappies,' Sonia says. 'He says that you are a manifestation of grace in his life.'

'Sonia,' I say extraneously, 'are those my letters?'

'He writes to you on saffron paper,' she says, 'to match his robes.' She waves the sheet of cheap, pumpkin-yellow photocopy paper briefly in the air before putting it to the bottom of the pile and proceeding to the next. 'And here's this other bloke,' she says. 'He says you write that Yeovil is in Dorset (see page 73, line 49) when you ought to know that it's in Somerset.'

'So it's on the bloody border, for Christ's sake,' I say.

'On the bloody border,' Sonia says, 'but nonetheless in Somerset.'

'As any fule kno,' I say, sarcastically. 'Sonia, just what exactly do you think that you're doing?'

'Also, he says that you say "fit" (see page 86, line 12) when what you ought to say is "seizure".'

'Sonia—' I say.

'Seizure,' she says, 'is more correct. In fact, he's amazed that they gave you a prize for it, and frankly so am I.'

'Look,' I say irritably, 'just go fuck yourself, will you?'

'I didn't come here to "fuck myself",' Sonia says, and she pauses to look up at me before planting my letters in a careless sprawl on the floor. 'And you'd better get your skates on, lover boy,' she says. 'I've an interview in Amsterdam this evening.' Involuntarily, I look at my watch. 'I'm on television,' she says, 'so you've got less than an hour before my cab arrives to take me to the airport.'

Sonia has recently become a minor cultural icon for what I confess I still think of as the International Femintern.

'Your third letter,' she says, 'is from St Austin's College, Oxford. They're offering you a three-year fellowship – a writer's fellowship.'

'Sonia—' I say.

'And your fourth letter,' she says, 'is from a girlie.' She nods again towards the pile on the floor. 'She met you last summer in her godmother's house. She wants help with an essay and she fancies you something rotten.'

I reach down, pick up the letters and stuff them into the pocket of my greatcoat, along with their ravaged envelopes. I am wearing the coat unbuttoned and hanging open to the floor. Katherine made the greatcoat. She has these prodigious tailoring skills which she learnt in some terrible private girls' school in Hendon. Along with the tailoring skills, she can still remember all five verses of the school song. Katherine, who has a degree in philosophy, will still occasionally turn her hand to an epauletted, virtuoso *Good Soldier Schweik* number like this – lined, panelled, placketed, double-breasted and all.

I yank Sonia irritably across the hall, unlock my front door and, leaving the keys impatiently dangling in the lock, propel her swiftly through it. Given that time is at a premium, we short-circuit the bed and confront each other standing upright, Sonia with her back against the door. Sonia is instantly accessible, thanks to her preference for tart's underclothing, though I believe the marketing word is lingerie. Sheer stockings, with lacy tops, that hold themselves up, and one of those all-in-one stretch babygro things with poppers in the crotch.

Katherine's undergarments, which might once have rivalled Sonia's, before the advent of the Nuisance Chip, are something else altogether. She wears the same white cotton knickers decade upon decade, until they drop in rags, their elastic swagged and sagging. She says that anything more glamorous will only be swiped off her by Stella. Sometimes she has a safety-pin at the hip to keep them from falling off. My Katie is a great believer in safety-pins, and pounces with joy in old haberdashers upon those obsolete nappy pins that come with pastel blue or pink safety hoods fitted over the clasps. Eventually, when even she admits that her knickers are done for, they will end up behind the lavatories or the washbasins, or in the shoe-polish cupboard, as cleaning rags, hacked into rough squares, their fabric striated with ladders. In the winter, she goes bra-less under a demure little singlet of unisex construction and encases her nether regions in quality Wolford tights. But I digress.

Our passion spent, Sonia does some preliminary feminine abluting with her travel pack of hypo-allergenic wet wipes, before proceeding to her usual method of squatting with splayed crotch over my plastic wash-up basin, which she fills with warm water at the sink, before placing it on my floor. She always brings her own soap. She looks almost appealing, like an infant caught short on a car journey and obliged to pee in a layby, her female parts sweetly unassailed by childbirth. I watch, slumped in a chair, still in the unbuttoned greatcoat with the letters jutting from the pocket.

It is only once she is doing up the poppers of the babygro that I notice she has that duo of much-travestied Raphael child-angels distorting in Lycra across her pubic mound. Trust Sonia, I think irritably, to wear the Sistine Madonna's accessories on her twat and think that by doing so she is striking a blow against two thousand years of patriarchal Christianity. I wonder where the hell she bought such a thing. In the National Gallery shop?

Sonia is quite knowledgeable in a lumpen sort of way. That is to say she knows a little about a wide range of things and she will spread this knowledge confidently among a great multitude. Fine Art is an area she has begun to colonize quite recently and she has just completed a piece for a popular art magazine explaining that Mantegna's *Christ Entering the Mouth of Hell* is, in reality, a paranoid male nightmare about being sucked into a giant vagina. Sonia is the White Goddess's answer to all those blokes who see, in the Chrysler Building, a monument to their own phallic potency.

Sonia watches me watching her. 'Do you like what you see, lover boy?' she says. Dark pubic hairs are exposing themselves between the poppers of the babygro and curling round the edges of its angel gusset.

'Bleach it,' I say, just for the hell of it, because Sonia's greed for tribute always invites put-down. I envisage that this will be done by her beautician, as she lies on a day-bed, planning one of her Third World lectures with cucumbers on her eyelids and Nile mud all over where her tits ought to be.

Sonia pulls down her skinny-rib skirt, adjusts her scarf and draws on her silk jersey gloves. With a gloved hand, she smooths her hair, which, in deference to the Amsterdam TV interview, she has had styled into what she calls 'Marcel waves'. She looks, around the head, like an illustration in an Angela Brazil school story. The Marcel waves, she has explained to me, are achieved by her hairdresser, who employs purpose-built bulldog clips which he clamps in horizontal tiers around her head, to produce an effect like contour ploughing. Having smoothed her hair, she gives me the *noblesse oblige* Windsor wave from four to five yards off.

'*À bientôt*,' she says. 'Think about the writer's fellowship, Jonathan. It's a feather in your cap and money for jam.' Then she says, 'And please have fun with the girlie.'

For reasons best known to herself, Sonia playfully locks my door from the outside and pockets the keys, so that I have to telephone down to the poor old landlady, who heaves herself, puffing and blowing, up the stairs to relieve me and to provide me with her spare keys, which I immediately go out and have copied before I get on with my day.

First thing is, I skim all my letters. I separate Lydia's letter and the letter from the Oxford college. Then I read Lydia's properly and even draft a reply. This is unusual, because I have a system with mail that is perhaps not all it should be.

First, I isolate all necessary and pressing communications and place them on a spike. The rest I throw into a plastic intray. Then, when the intray is full, I empty its contents into a cardboard box. When the cardboard box is full, I stuff it into a cupboard. Then I start a new box. Once the cupboard is full, I ship the boxes down to the landlady's cellar, where their contents swiftly become so damp that to handle them is disagreeable. Only then do I concede that the letters will remain unanswered.

Lydia's letter charms me, coming with all its bubble, after the Buddhist and the geographer. Something about its youthfulness, in the immediate wake of Sally and Sonia; something about my knowing that the writer is a person who has never opened a bank account, never visited the family planning clinic, never filled in a tax return, never endured the horrors of a parent-teacher association meeting, never grown coriander to impress a dinner party. There is something purifying about it.

I suggest in my reply that she meet me at Fortnum & Mason, and that she do so during her half-term holiday, after arranging it with me by telephone. Two factors govern this suggestion: one, I like to make appointments as far away as possible from the bedsit and, two, the venue is one to which I have occasionally taken my daughter Stella who is of roughly similar age.

I need not have bothered with my letter. The very next day, at 3 p.m., the girl is on my doorstep.

'I hope I'm not too early,' she says, but my surprise is difficult to disguise. 'You were expecting me? Your PA did assure me that she'd put it in your diary.'

At this I can't help laughing. 'PA?' I say. Bloody Sonia! She will have taken down Lydia's particulars from the letter before I got back from lunching with Sally. Then she will have taken the trouble to make a call to Lydia from Heathrow – just for what? To be capricious? Is she a mad-woman? I mean, what for, for Christ's sake?

'I'm embarrassed,' Lydia says. 'It's terribly inconvenient.'

'No,' I say. 'No, not in the least. It's fine.' I sit her on the carpeted bottom step while I return upstairs for my jacket and my wallet. Then I come back.

'OK,' I say, 'let's go.' We step out and begin to look out for a cab.

And I do remember her from that day at her godmother's, when she had been dressed in sweatshirt and jeans. Now she has dressed up. She wears a jersey-knit mini dress in broad horizontal bands of pink and grey, with crazy bright pink tights and clumpy black lace-ups. It's exactly the kind of dress that causes my snotty little Stella to mouth 'Topshop', but Lydia looks terrific in it; Lydia looks great. With none of Stella's strange, fragile beauty, she is robustly pretty. She has the pleasing air of one who plans to pass easily through this life, collecting admirers at tennis parties. Lydia strikes me as the Miss Joan Hunter-Dunn of the upper sixth. I admire her already.

'I've borrowed a dictaphone,' she says, once we've settled in a quiet corner. 'You're not going to mind, I hope?' I laugh. I don't mind a bit. If the child has a value for my off-the-cuff remarks, well, good luck to her, I think.

Assisting with the construction of A level essays is Katherine's cabbage patch, not mine. I am a novice here. However, the first thing I confront is Lydia's subject matter. I tell her it's far too wide and I suggest that we reformulate her title as: *Love and Death at the Mill: Twenty Poems from the Posthumous Papers of a Travelling Hornplayer* – this being a combination of Müller's anthology title and the number of his *Müllerin* poems that Schubert saw fit to set.

Lydia looks aghast. 'Four thousand words on twenty poems?' she says. 'But that's about two hundred words on each. I can't write two hundred words on a poem!'

From this I deduce that Lydia's number concept is well in place, even if her lit. crit. is dodgy. I suggest that she begin with an introductory page on German Romanticism – and I tell her what to write. Then I say she must place Müller's poems in this context – and I tell her what to write. Lydia, meanwhile, pours tea and smiles and eats one of her dainty little sandwiches.

'This is fun,' she says. 'This is really interesting.'

'Now,' I say. 'If I were you, I'd tell the story. Can you do that? Just tell me the story.'

Lydia begins on another little sandwich. 'You don't mean now?' she says. 'You don't mean *out loud?*' Then she smiles at me again and says nothing.

Perhaps it is not inappropriate, at this point, for me to tell you the story of Müller's poetic sequence. It is parlour-game romanticism. Müller wrote it as part of a Sunday afternoon role play exercise for a small group of intellectuals and artists of which he was one. Another was the young man soon to become Fanie Mendelssohn's husband. Participants were allotted the roles of miller, huntsman and gardener and required to play their parts as aspirant lovers of the beautiful mill-maid, who was, in real life, the pretty seventeen-year-old daughter of their salon host – a girl exactly of an age with Lydia.

The miller, the 'white' man, is struck by wanderlust. The stream, with its constant rushing movement, eggs him on.

Nothing stands still – not the water, not the mill blades, not the wheel, not the heavy millstones themselves. Everything exists in a dance of restlessness. Everything spins, churns, rotates, lifts and grinds. The poem that describes this is rather good.

The miller, for whom the stream has become friend and confidante, follows the water's winding path until he comes upon a mill-house whose windows wink at him in welcome. Windows are eyes and eyes are windows. Eyes are the windows of the soul. He falls in love at once, with the blue-eyed mill-girl who lives within, and he decides to put down roots. The girl is represented by the small blue flowers – the *blaue Blümelein* – that grow around her cottage and border the water. She is the constant focus of his urgent, passionate need.

It is not long, of course, before the miller's rival appears, in the form of the huntsman, the boar-scourging predator, the 'green' man who emerges from the woods to trample the vegetable patch and to steal the mill-girl's heart. The miller, who has previously made her a present of the green ribbon that fixed his lute to the wall, now sees the mill-girl wear it as a pennant for her newer, wilder love. His response, though he plays with some nice literary conceits, is instant defeatism. He, too, will become a hunter, but the beast he will hunt is Death. He sinks down into a watery grave and dies on a hope that the blue flowers will reappear after the winter, to border the water and to remind his beloved of the man who loved her so well.

I must admit that I, too, am a romantic. The rustic idyll and the exchange of eyes are ideas that work on me. In the hands of better poets than Wilhelm Müller they are capable of increasing my pulse rate.

> 'I did but see her passing by,
> Yet will I love her till I die.'

This is, in truth, exactly how I fell in love with Katherine and, while I may diversify, I do not waver.

> 'Change she earth and change she sky,
> Yet will I love her till I die.'

I too have planted bean-rows and lived in a bee-loud glade.

But Lydia is made of sterner stuff. 'It's too silly,' she says. 'I can't tell you the story. Not out loud.'

Next, I suggest that she choose six poems to analyse in detail – the ones she thinks most significant. Lydia blobs jam and cream onto her scone and raises it to her mouth.

'Oh yum,' she says. 'This is the best tea ever.'

'Just pick your six favourites,' I say.

Lydia dimples and bites her lip. 'You choose,' she says. 'I don't know which.'

'Oh come on,' I say. 'Give me one. There must be one that's special.'

After a while she says, 'I like the one that says the stars are too high: "*Die Sterne stehn zu hoch*",' but she can't tell me why. 'It's just the stars, I suppose,' she says. 'You know. "Star light; star bright, Would I may, would I might . . ." All that.'

I tell her why I think she likes it. Lydia eats a little boat-shaped cake. She makes pretty eyes at me.

'I'd love to be brainy,' she says.

'Ever read Goethe?' I say. I begin to mark pages in her anthology with torn-up strips of A4. 'Just read these,' I say.

'Goethe *as well*?' she says.

And so it goes. Finally, she's used up both sides of her tape. When I get up to go, Lydia says, 'Mr Goldman, do people ever really die of love?'

The mister business is often irritating to me. 'Jonathan,' I say. 'Just call me Jonathan, OK?'

'Well, do they?' she says.

I brush her off with flippancy. 'Only if they get syphilis,' I say. 'Like Schubert.'

'Or AIDS,' she says. 'Well, I know that *sex* can make you die. They used to be forever telling us that in Sex Ed. Are sex and love the same?'

I refuse to commit myself here. 'I'm too old to be giving you an answer to that question,' I say. 'Come on, Lydia. Time's up.'

Lydia gets up and we walk towards the exit. 'I wish you weren't,' she says.

'Weren't what?' I say.

'Too old,' she says. 'Thank you so much, Jonathan.'

Within the week, Lydia is back on the phone.

'Done it,' she says.

This does rather take me by surprise. 'Already?' I say.

'Oh yes,' she says. 'Can I please show it to you? I'd love your opinion.'

Lydia has a winning manner. She is the girl who features in madrigals. 'OK, post it to me,' I say.

'The thing is,' Lydia says, 'I happen to be in London, and I've got it with me.'

Long pause. 'OK, I'll meet you,' I say. 'Same place?'

'The thing is,' Lydia says, 'the thing is, I'm in the call-box at the end of your street.'

Then there is bloody Sonia, who comes back from Amsterdam and gets a big buzz from quizzing me about 'the girlie'. Having set me up to waste my time, she then takes exception to what I tell her.

'I practically wrote the bloody thing for her,' I say. 'She recorded my every word on tape. She brought a dictaphone with her to Fortnum's.'

'Come again?' Sonia says, sounding indignant.

'Dictaphone?' I say.

'No, the other thing.'

'Fortnum's?' I say.

'So when do you take me out to Fortnum's for tea?' Sonia says.

I stare at her in amazement. 'Don't be so bloody ridiculous,' I say. We're grown-ups. We're busy. We don't "go out" together, Sonia. For Christ's sake, we stay in and fuck.' But it's a theme she returns to again and again. And again.

3. Morgengruss

Stella

I'M STELLA. Mad, bad Stella. Demanding Stella; deeply ungrateful Stella. Difficult Stella, who had such kind, long-suffering parents. Weren't they paragons? Especially my mother, a sainted angel, giving me her life like that. All that input; all that expense. I was so patently not the daughter she wanted and yet no effort was spared. Well, that's life. Kids nowadays. I didn't ask to get born. The truth is I had made every effort against it. There was a precursor in the womb, you see – an Italian half-sister – who had made things difficult for me. Little Simonetta, who was born after a bodged high-tech labour and who then died of cot death four weeks later. Simonetta, named by my mother after Botticelli's voguey, braided lady-love with all that voluminous blonde hair. Well, I got the hair, didn't I? But then I had to subvert it. Typical Stella. Always perverse. Always at loggerheads with life. My hair, as you will know, is red. Carrot-tops, ginger-nuts, Orlando the Marmalade Cat – 'Pre-Raphaelite', as the pretentious among us will have it.

Perhaps if my mother had not spent twenty years diverting me from the edginess and anger that buzzed in my child's brain; had not endlessly neutralized conflict, smoothed every difficulty; had not played best friend along with saint, tutor and angel – well, then, I might have been illiterate, but better able to fight for myself along the way. I might even have been able to fight with her. As it was, she gave me skills and thereby robbed me of others. The parental double-edged sword. So I waited till her job on me was done. I grew up, I took advantage and then I gave her the brush-off. Shook the dust from my feet. How could I have been so cruel? I venture that bossy Aunt Sally and her husband are suitably scandalized.

Perhaps I can begin with music, though you may expect me to wander from the subject. I don't hold onto a thread too well; don't concentrate for long. I didn't as a child and I do not now – now that I am once again 'unwell'. I have this uncle. Let's call him the Fiddle Anorak. Maths dork with violin. Father's older brother. Bossy wife Aunt Sally. They have three daughters, my girl cousins, all three striving as hell. An obscene greed for achievement that drives them hell-bent through their childhoods. They all play the violin – Claire, Sheila and Fiona. The String Trio. They talk whenever I meet them in a babble of goals achieved and striven for.

'I can do French verbs – *je suis, tu es, il est.* Can you do French verbs? I can tell the time. I can hop twelve metres, I'm doing Grade 3. I'm doing Grade 5. What grade's Stella doing? But Stella ain't doin' no grades because Stella is all thumbs. At an age when Stella's own dear mother was sweetly knitting moss-stitch matinée jackets for the neighbour's new baby or making her own little papier mâché Christmas tree decorations – 'Such a quiet child, such a good child, always so imaginative, she'd play on her own for hours'; this, my maternal grandmother; not quite our class, dear; a monstrous but kindly practitioner of the suburban cliché; a person whose favourite painting is that Chinese woman with the green face – Stella, at nine, can't thread a needle. She can't wash her own hair. She can't read a clock-face. She can't do proper bows in shoe laces. She holds a pencil as if it were a javelin. She puts jigsaw puzzle pieces curly side out around the edges and she still can't see why that's wrong.

The String Trio and their mother are astonished by her incompetence. All through Stella's childhood, Aunt Sally, whenever she gets the chance, bears down upon Stella like the Playschool lady, zealous to transmit clock-reading skills: 'The big hand is pointing straight up, so it's something o'clock. The little hand is pointing to the. . .?'

In random panic Stella grasps at numbers from the air. 'It's four o'clock,' she says, guessing by the sun. 'No. No, I mean it's five. I forgot, I meant five o'clock.' The time is, of course, three o'clock.

While the String Trio write in neat, laboured joined-up, Stella writes her name from right to left, and usually with the letters reversed:

10119+2

What she writes looks to normal people like 10,119 + 2, but the initial 10 is merely the way I write lower-case 'a' – a ball with a stick, you see, only here the stick has come adrift from the ball and it's on the wrong side, that's all. The '9' is lower-case 'e' – a simple case of reversal. I make the ciphers huge, like buttons. Numbers, letters, they're all hieroglyphics to me, dafty Stella. Stella's cuneiform. Plus until she's eight, Stella speaks with an Irish accent. This gives joy to the String Trio, who regale her with Irish jokes; the cack-handed logic of what Paddy says to Mick. Suits me. It's conversant with my abilities.

The String Trio do Suzuki violin. Aunt Sally drives them to their lessons near the baker's shop. When I stay with them I go along in the car. I hate their snotty little violins but I love the smell of the bakery, and sometimes Aunt Sally buys buns. At home the String Trio play rounds on the recorder; Carl Dolmetsch around the Bechstein in the music room.

'Don't you "do" recorders at your school?' they say. Their grade certificates from the Royal College of Music adorn the music-room walls. I make a fool of myself on one occasion because I think some of these must be for me. I think the italically inscribed 'Sheila' says 'Stella'. Sheila Goldman; Stella Goldman. Both names start with 'S' and end with 'a'; both have six letters; two of the intervening letters are the same, 'e' and 'l'; of the remaining dissimilar letters, the 'i' and the 'l' – well – an 'i' is nearly like an 'l' only it's not so tall. The 'h' is tall like the 't' and with a similar curly foot.

'This one says Stella,' I say, proudly pointing. The String Trio are amused. They fall about.

They try then to teach me the recorder, but after an hour I am still putting my right hand above my left hand instead of the other way round. I don't know which is which.

'Just think which hand your watch goes on,' Claire says helpfully.

'Just think which hand does treble,' Sheila says, going, as she does, for overkill. She means treble on the piano. 'Oh, I forgot,' she says. 'You don't "do" piano, do you?'

Stella did have a watch but wearing it got embarrassing when people kept asking her the time. 'I knew yesterday. I knew how to tell the time yesterday, but I've forgotten.'

The String Trio play a round that goes 'Life is but a melancholy flower'. Life is butter; butter; melon. Life is butter; melon; cauliflower. It puns to my infinite puzzlement. Back home with Mum and Dad, I ask them, 'What is a butter melon?' but I don't say why. I think of it as a sort of pumpkin.

'Oh, dearest,' Mummy says. 'My angel-pie.'

'Darling Butter Melon,' Daddy says. He puts me on his shoulders. He lets me come fishing with him. Along the way he tells me the story of the Magic Halibut and the Greedy Fisherman's Wife.

'But your wife isn't greedy,' I say. 'Mummy isn't greedy.'

He laughs. 'No,' he says. 'Mummy is an angel.'

* * *

At school in Ireland my teacher is the Dragon Lady. She breathes fire and smoke. On Friday afternoons we do 'Craft'. Sometimes Craft is knitting. Though my mother has managed her own knitwear design and textile business before I appeared to sabotage it; has supplied shops in the King's Road and in Manhattan, I, of course, can't knit. Stella can't knit. For all her efforts, I don't get the hang of it at all. Eventually, to protect me from the Dragon Lady, my mother, every Thursday evening, knits up six rows of the most irregular, lumpy-looking garter stitch she can manage and advises me to spend the half-hour pushing the stitches from one needle to the other, in the hope that the Dragon Lady will not notice.

On this particular Friday the Dragon Lady does. She pauses beside me during her *passeggiata* along the aisles. I freeze. Seconds later the world implodes on the Dragon Lady's wrath at my left ear.

'Show me how you knit!' she yells. I can't, of course. Poor Stella. She can't. 'You can't?' she booms.

'Please, Miss, I forgot,' I say. Moron Stella's parrot-babble. 'I did know, I did know yesterday, but I've forgotten.'

'Forgotten?' she booms. 'Shall we remind her, class? In!' she barks. I am paralysed. 'Round!' she yells. I am paralysed. 'Through!' she booms. I gawp, I cannot move. 'Out!' she yells. She raises her hands like the conductor of an orchestra, encouraging class participation. 'In – round – through – out,' she says.

They all begin to chant. The refrain gathers pace like a train picking up speed. 'In – round – through – out. In – round – through – out.' I begin to cry. Thanks to the Dragon Lady I have by now learnt to cry without making the slightest sound or movement. No hiccups, no juddering shoulders, no sniff. Just the well of tears that brim over and splash into my lap. The Dragon Lady snatches up my needles and my knitting. She unravels the lot. She dumps it on my desk – two short needles thick as pencils and a bird's nest of pretty, twiddled wool. My wool is soft and beautiful; sky-blue with pale flecks like birds' eggs. I can't knit but I have the prettiest wool in the class. Of course. Stella always has the prettiest things. Stella has smocked dresses, Stella has silky ribbons, Stella has pretty shoes, Stella is spoilt, Stella is rich – richer than the other children anyway, whose parents milk cows and dig potatoes.

The Dragon Lady hears us read every morning before assembly, two by two, one in each ear; a paragon of the old school. We stand in two lines, paired with people of roughly equivalent ability. I read last, of course, with Joyce O'Dowd, whose family is the poorest of conspicuously non-coping rural poor. With hindsight I see that Joyce is genetically debilitated, possibly through generations of incest, who knows? What is certain is that neither of us has a single clue about what the Little Red Hen is saying to her friends on the subject of the ear of wheat that she holds in her beak. We stick forever on the books that have yellow adhesive tape fixed to their spines. When you've done yellow then you move on to blue, then to green, then to red. Some people have passed red and they are reading 'unclassified'. Stella has stopped even dreaming about being on 'unclassified'.

But Mummy and Daddy read to her lots and lots at home. Sometimes Mum lets her play hookey when things get too bad. Mum is very good at writing mendacious notes. She is always on Stella's side. They are Best Friends; full-time best friends. Stella is very demanding.

At home occasional adult visitors admire Stella's chat. She is often alone with adults and speaks precociously on matters of international affairs and on aspects of the arts. She can recite *The Pied Piper of Hamelin.* She knows quite a bit about Italian food and about the Mountain Kingdom of Bhutan. She knows who has won the Irish Times Aer Lingus prize. She can tell early Mozart from Haydn. She can tell early Beethoven from Mozart. These are not accomplishments that pass muster with the Dragon Lady.

* * *

My mother's notes are a treat: never the old 'Stella has had a slight head cold'. It is always something original, something utterly convincing; anything from the orthodontist to suppurating verrucas. I love her, my Mummy. I love being at home, where she gives me all her time. If she turns away from me, even for one minute, to read a book, to read the paper, I panic. 'Mummeee!'

One day when I return to school after one of my not infrequent spells of genuine illness, a week of running a temperature of 104 at bedtime; a week punctuated by spoonsful of sweet antibiotic syrup prescribed by the GP along with a precautionary dose of my anti-convulsive medicine, I return to school and present my note to the Dragon Lady. This time she refuses to read it. She rips it up and rains the pieces theatrically over her desk. She is possessed by an inexplicable rage.

'What's been the matter with you *this* time?' she booms.

'I had fever,' I say in a small, scared voice.

'Fever?' she says. 'And what sort of fever did you have?'

I stand quaking alongside her. 'Just fever,' I say.

'Scarlet fever?' she says. 'Rheumatic fever? Yellow fever?' People in the class begin to titter quietly.

'Just fever,' I say, in a smaller, quieter voice.

The mad-woman tugs at my earlobes. 'Did you have fever in your ears?' she says.

I shake my head. 'No, just fever,' I say. By now I am scarcely audible.

She tweaks my nose. 'Did you have fever in your nose?' she says.

In my nasal passages snot squeaks against cartilage. 'No, just fever.'

Then the mad-woman yanks at my hair. She grabs a foot-long orange tassel in each hand and tugs so that the hair roots ache like bruises on my skull. She stamps, one by one, on each of my feet.

'Did you have fever in your hair?' she says. 'Did you have fever in your feet?'

Once again, tears well silently in my eyes. I shake my head. 'No,' I say. 'Just fever.' I am audible only to myself.

'Go to your place and sit down,' she booms. 'Cry-baby.'

I spend the day weeping quietly. Tactfully, everyone leaves me alone. I squint through tears at my neighbour's sums and try to adjust my answers, as I usually do, erasing them by rubbing smudgy holes in the page with a damp thumb.

After that I don't go to school for three weeks. My parents let me stay at home. I love it, though in the evening, after I have gone to bed, I hear my Mum crying over my Dad. In the mornings Mum makes long paper-chains for me of little girls all in a row holding hands. We give them smiling faces and different hair, yellow and brown, black and orange, curly and straight. She shows me how to make them for myself, but mine never come joined together. They always come in groups of two and a half little girls, the halved girl spliced lengthways, usually with one leg or arm severed at knee or elbow. I cannot grasp the principle of leaving the figures joined at the fold. I have no spatial sense. I seem to have no sense at all, except that I can sing. Is that intuition, perhaps, not sense? I have a nice resonance and clarity and I sing with confidence. I can sing in harmony. I never lose a tune. I sing rounds. My pitch is true. My tone is pleasing.

By now it is December. We go to England and spend Christmas with my paternal grandmother in London. This involves touching down upon the String Trio on Boxing Day. Even the String Trio stop dead in their tracks when my dad and I sing 'The Angel Gabriel from Heaven Came' in two parts, unaccompanied. Then I sing 'The Cherry Tree Carol' all by myself. In the car I sing 'Hey Down, Hoe Down'.

'She amazing,' says the Uncle Fiddle Anorak to my dad. 'Say, Jon, you do realize that she's unusual?'

'Can she sight-read?' say the String Trio in some alarm and agitation, jumping up and down in the back. Sight-read! Poor old Stella, give her a break. She can't so much as read *Peter and Jane* Book 1a. She can't read page one of *The Blue Pirate.*

'No she can't,' says Dad.

'Pity,' says Aunt Sally. 'You'd get her a place in the choir school like a shot with that voice, Jonathan. But she would have to pass the entrance exam.'

'Can she do middle C?' says Sheila, always the most persistently murderous of the String Trio, but the aunt continues, oblivious.

'She'd get her fees paid in toto,' she says with a sigh. 'They *are* rather demanding academically,' she says. 'Unfortunately.'

When we get back to Ireland I go to see a specialist in Dublin. He puts a patch over my left eye and sends me home with lots of phonetic exercises, but I still don't learn to read. When I go back to school the Dragon Lady lays off. Unbeknown to me, some adult negotiations have taken place between the head and the Dragon Lady and my parents. I believe the teachers' union may have been involved as well. The Dragon Lady hates me more than ever but she has found subtler ways of transmitting this. She has certainly transmitted it to the class because I have become Number One Class Pariah. The Untouchable. Not even Joyce O'Dowd likes to be paired with me.

At break I play on my own in a grassy corner of the playground. I teach myself to turn somersaults, then I teach myself to do the same thing backwards – forwards, backwards – it's all the same to dafty Stella, who writes her name from right to left. When the bell goes I have leaves and twigs in my beautiful Rapunzel hair. My luck is in that week. A young supply teacher does PE with us and we do forward rolls on the mat.

She says, 'Can anyone do a backward roll?'

I can and I do. Stella can do backward rolls! Then she gets us to do headstands. I'm the best in the class by a mile. She claps her hands for attention. 'Everyone watch Stella,' she says. 'Well done, Stella.' Suddenly, I am assimilated.

'Stella can do headstands. Stella can do backward rolls,' the children tell the Dragon Lady when we return to the classroom in our knickers and slip-on gym shoes to reclaim our folded clothes.

I go home in triumph but my success has come too late. The parents have decided to ship out back to England where the Precious Girl won't be harassed and troubled by the likes of the Dragon Lady. Plans have been afoot during the visit over Christmas – estate agents consulted, houses considered for purchase and we move to a pretty cottage in the Cotswolds, right on the village green but with a stone wall and farmland behind it, where patient cows munch and stare. Some of the cows have red hair.

I go to a new school with no desks and no exercise books. The teacher has no special table and no blackboard. She is very advanced. We sit at little café tables and chat. We do almost no work at all. I feel instantly at home. I am very good at chatting. This time the teacher likes my chat lines about the Deutschmark and the Oktober Revolution and the *Well-Tempered Clavier* and the Scottish Impressionists. She does not seem to notice that I cannot tell the time, or that when I add 103 and 64 it becomes 130 plus 46, or that my answer, either way, is always wrong.

I am now, on the whole, among members of my own social class, though the village does have a council estate and one of my favourites, Michelle – a pushy little brain-box with beautiful handwriting and blonde hair and the latest in child fashion – lives there. Her mother is our dinner lady. The children in my village school are in the main the children of lawyers, antique dealers and furniture restorers, bankers, civil servants, artists, potters and academics. Not one of them milks cows. Some of them dig potatoes, but only for fun in their kitchen gardens. The farmer, the only person who does milk cows, has a daughter who is not in my school at all. She gets driven to a private school in Oxford, which is attended by Sheila and Fiona.

Nobody hears us read before assembly. Almost nobody hears us read at all. There isn't assembly except in the afternoons, once a week, on Fridays. There certainly is no knitting – knitting is for Celtic peasants; knitting for Filipino sweatshops. We accomplish something like one and a half lines of writing a week. We do this on scrap paper and afterwards we crumple it up and then we throw it at each other or we lose it. We do lots of cooking and trips and treats. We do drama and singing. We blow whistles and little trumpets in *The Toy Symphony* in the village hall.

And, once a week, we do Sex Education. In the hall we watch a film of people playing tennis without their clothes on. Mixed doubles. We all giggle because their boobs and willies bounce up and down with every thwack. Then we watch a video of puberty speeded up. Hips thicken and boobs swell; testicles drop and clumps of hair sprout like mustard and cress, all to a count of five. 'The main difference between Tessa and Harry,' says the voice-over, 'is between the legs.' We all giggle like anything – especially me and Michelle.

Afterwards the teacher calls us in for a private chat. She says she understands that we giggled because we were embarrassed, but sex is nothing to get embarrassed about. We try hard not to giggle until she's let us go. Then we chortle and skip and roll about on the grass.

'Well, I was laughing because it was funny,' Michelle says. 'I wasn't embarrassed.'

Three-quarters of the children have been taught to read by their mothers. Then there is me, though my mother, God knows, has tried. Then there are some of the children from the council estate who don't have clued-up mothers. Some of the mothers can't read either. The two best readers in the class, not counting Michelle, have recently come respectively from the British Council school in Abu Dhabi and from a primary school in New Zealand; both can spell and punctuate, both can do fractions, both are streets ahead; both have their work frequently pinned up in the school entrance hall to show what can be achieved by café society methods. The quarter of the class who can't read are delicately said to 'lack coping skills'. Nobody says we can't read.

I have abandoned the eye patch on coming to England but I am drawn out of class once a week, because my parents agitate, and I am taught by a special teacher. I accomplish very little with the teacher, but the good news is that my school has a gym club and that I have a shiny, mint-green leotard which is soon covered in badges, all sewn onto the fabric by my mother with the finest little stitches. I walk on my hands on the horse and on the bar. Parents gasp when I turn cartwheels across the green, my orange hair flying.

I sign up for piano lessons when the idea is mooted. Two of my friends have done likewise. They are the two friends that my parents call the Tart and the Princess behind my back. The Tart is Michelle. The Princess is Sarah. Dad buys a piano at once, in consultation with my paternal grandmother, and the Tart and the Princess have their lessons at my house. This is an inducement to encourage me to play – and to integrate. My mother has always tried to ensure that my social life runs smooth. She is always at the school gate at home time, ready to welcome potential visitors and to give me a leg-up in the popularity stakes.

'Your mother always has double-choc chip cookies,' says the Princess admiringly, who has a sweet tooth. 'Your mother is the nicest mother of all the mothers in our school.'

The Tart makes rapid strides and is much beloved of the piano teacher, who is a sweet young man. It is open house now for Michelle, who visits all the time but spends most of it at the piano doing her practice. Sarah and I are pretty well useless. We don't practise much, but the teacher puts us in for Preliminary Grade, thinking this will be a spur.

I make my mother sit through every minute of my practice. She has to sit alongside me on the same stool or else I screech and fuss. She has never played the piano before, though she learns along with me. Learn-along-with-Stella is her watchword in all things. The piano is my enemy but I must conquer it. I can't read the music. I can't remember about the crosses and the wiggles denoting sharps and flats, but I grit my teeth and rush at it like a cat crossing a busy road. Mum, who secretly practises but only when I am out so as not to intimidate me with her budding proficiency, can already play her way through little Bach and Telemann minuets. She sits besides me anticipating that I will play F natural where I need to play F sharp.

'F sharp,' she says, trying to sound casual, just before I get there.

I stop and stamp and sigh. 'I know,' I say. 'I know.' And I toss my orange hair. 'Don't tell me!'

I start all over again. She says nothing. She sits on her hands, willing me in silence to get it right. I play F natural instead of sharp. Of course. Dwang. Dwoing. I thump my hands down on the piano. I slam down the lid.

Tentatively, over tea, Mum says, 'Wouldn't you like to give it up, my sweetheart?'

'No!' I scream. I stamp. The piano is torture. I fail the Preliminary Grade, of course. The Princess, like a traitor, scrapes through. The Tart gets a distinction. The piano sits there lifeless. Mum doesn't dare to play it for fear of appearing one up on me. Dad, who was made to play it in childhood, hates it and seldom does. Ultimately it is removed to Michelle's house – a present from the Green to the Close.

The year I turn eleven is a good one. It is a miracle year for me. Not only do I sing female solo lead in the school production of *Oliver*, but – Miracle Number One – I teach myself to read. I do this very suddenly. Instead of miming what others do; that is, holding the book still and moving my eyes along the rows – my eyes that invariably jump and scramble and reverse – I open my eyes very wide and fix them rigidly on a spot on the wall and stare unblinking till they water. I move the book to and fro in front of this fixed spot, to and fro like the roller of an old-fashioned typewriter, zoom, ting, zoom, ting.

Before I know it, I am reading. I am reading *Rosie's Walk*. I am reading all the *Monster* books. By the end of the day I have a hideous headache, but the next day, in the same way, I read *Are You My Mother?* My eyeballs ache. They feel like giant marbles about to roll from out of my head and clunk onto the floor. I feel the pain in my optic nerves like the severed stalks of flowers inside my head, but I carry on. I read aloud on an endless monotone. ' "The-kitten-and-the-hen-were-not-his-mother-the-dog-and-the-cow-were-not-his-mother-did-he-have-a-mother? I-did-have-a-mother-said-the-baby-bird." '

That night I vomit the paracetamol my mother gives me to ease the pain. I whimper in the dark. I cannot bear the light. The next day, in the same fashion, I read *Mr Rabbit and the Lovely Present*. I read *The Sign on Rosie's Door*, which was given to me three years earlier as a leaving present when I departed from the Dragon Lady's class. (Now what shall we give to the non-reading Stella? Why, we'll give her a book. Of course.) That night I groan feebly. I can speak only in whispers. The bone of the eye socket above my right eye pulses and burns like fire. By the next day I have developed a nervous tic, a rapid eye blink from fatigue.

Over the next five days I read two books without pictures. They have chapters. I read *The Diddakoi.* I read *The Railway Children.* The following week I read Noel Streatfeild's *Ballet Shoes*. I read *The Ghost of Thomas Kempe*. I read *Sweet Valley High.* Am I the only ten-year-old dyslexic who reads *The Magic Toyshop* in one day? After eleven days I have stopped talking the words out loud. After thirteen days I have stopped zapping the book to and fro. For a while my lips move silently. Then they stop.

All this while the saintly parents have said nothing. They have watched in silent terror, hoping that I will not stop. When I fall silent for long enough, Dad addresses me with a careful casualness.

'You've gone very quiet, Mrs Mouse,' he says. It is a Sunday evening.

'That's just because the words can talk inside my head,' I say to him.

Mummy makes us a specially nice dinner, which we eat by candlelight. Dad has a little place in London where he goes on Mondays to work, but I skip school that Monday and go with him. We have Big Treat Day, during which he buys me a new leotard and special acrobat's shoes. He buys me new boots and a very grown-up swagger coat. He buys me a stash of new clothes for my Sindy Doll, and then he takes me for tea at Fortnum & Mason, which is like being inside a brilliant kaleidoscope. He waits forever outside the Ladies' Room while I play at the marble washbasins and smile at the hundred glowing, literate Stellas in the glass, all of them wearing the same beautiful new coat. In Hatchards he buys me a hardback edition of *The Rhyme of the Ancient Mariner* with engraved illustrations by Gustave Doré. Finally he puts me on the train which Mummy is due to meet at the other end.

'Your mother can say you had verrucas,' he says. 'Get her to knit you a pair of verruca socks.' Then he kisses me and waves me off. I laugh and laugh as I collapse into my seat, because there has been a plague of verrucas at my school. They are no longer outlandish excuses; no longer original. And everybody knows that you do not knit verruca socks. They are made of rubber, like old bathing caps, and they do not come in pairs.

Miracle Number Two. I take to playing the cello. My grandmother (paternal) comes to stay. One day we drive out to fetch the String Trio. She is taking the four of us to a chamber music concert in the Holywell Music Room. She and I get on well. As we drive she tells me a story, talking all the way. She tells me about my Aunt Rosie and the cello. It's a story I have never heard before. My grandmother had six children. The first is the Uncle Fiddle Anorak, and the second is my dad. The third is Aunt Rosie, the first girl. There are three of each, three boys, three girls. After the two boy brain-boxes, Aunt Rosie came as a bit of a surprise.

'She was always very good at PE and flirting,' Grandma says. I think perhaps I will be good at flirting one day, but in the event this proves not to be quite the case. Aunt Rosie is beautiful and has had three husbands, but it is probably not her beauty that has attracted them, though it certainly has not been a hindrance. It is something to do with her smell and I do not mean her perfume. I mean that there is a mysterious chemical that certain women give off. Must be – though none of us is aware of it. It exists to give men the come-on.

Grandma is a firm, decisive sort of person; she possesses a quiet, upper-class confidence. She resolved, she tells me, to make all her children play two musical instruments, the piano and one other. The Fiddle Anorak does piano and violin; my dad does piano and flute; Rosie does piano and cello. But very quickly, in the face of Rosie's musical limitations, Grandma drops her standards and insists only on the cello. Aunt Rosie throws herself around and contrives to fall off chairs during her practice. She pokes the bow in Grandma's eye. She spikes the end pin through the floor. She cracks the back putting her foot through it in rage – an assault that necessitates a horrendously expensive and skilled repair that mercifully, for Aunt Rosie, takes almost two months.

After a year Aunt Rosie has just about grasped that the outer two strings are C and A, and the inner two are G and D. After eighteen months she can struggle her way through to the end of three little tunes: 'Michael Row Your Boat Ashore, Alleluiah' and 'Marco Polo Sailed for a Day, Caught Six Fish, Went Home for his Pay'. Grandma is laughing at herself through this story. She sings the songs aloud for me through her laughter. I am laughing too – perhaps with relief that Aunt Rosie should so remind me of myself. Perhaps I am not, after all, an inept, orange-haired changeling displaced into a family of high-flyers.

The last tune Aunt Rosie played was 'Grandpa's Birthday, Let's Play Bridge. Grandpa's Birthday, Beer's in the Fridge'.

'She could only play it,' Grandma says, 'because it had no sharps, you see.'

'And then,' Grandma says, 'one day, I learnt my lesson. Your daddy, who was always rather too full of good ideas – he took it into his head to bury Rosie's cello. In an unmarked grave, of course.' I gasp and giggle and bite my lower lip. 'He came to me at nightfall,' Grandma says, 'after I'd searched high and low for hours. "I've buried the bloody thing," he said, "and I'll only tell you where it is if you promise, *in writing*, that Rosie won't ever have to play it again."' She pauses. 'Well,' she says, 'I refused, of course. I wasn't going to be held to ransom like that by a cocky sixteen-year-old boy. I lectured him on how valuable it was and I demanded to see Rosie. "Rosie hasn't a clue where it is," he said, "so you leave her out of this, you witch." I'm afraid to say, Stella dear, that your daddy was always a very impertinent boy.' This, as it's intended to, causes me to giggle with pride.

'Actually, it was true that Rosie had no idea,' Grandma goes on. 'Only it took me ages to believe them both. All this time I must say I was worried sick about the instrument.'

Grandma had then called her husband and tried to make him get my dad to say where the cello was buried, but my grandfather had just laughed at her and had clapped my dad on the shoulder and told him, 'Well done, boy. I should have thought of that myself.'

'They were always thick as thieves, those two,' Grandma says, with feeling. 'Your dear Grandpa and your dad.' I sit in a glow listening to her. I know that this is true. My dad adored his father, while Grandma, whom Mum and I love to bits, almost invariably gets on his nerves.

'And then?' I say.

'Well,' Grandma says, 'I was naturally quite frantic about the cello. Finally I signed a promise that Rosie need never play the thing again and then your dad went out with a spirit lamp into the woods and dug it up. I still thank God that it hadn't started to rain.'

'Have you still got it?' I say, excitedly.

'Most certainly,' Grandma says, 'I couldn't possibly have got rid of it. It's a very beautiful old cello, you know. It belonged to your great-great-grandfather.'

We pick up the String Trio and proceed to the concert. I sit transfixed, staring at the cellist, who incidentally is female and pregnant. I say nothing on the way home until we have dropped off the String Trio. Then, when we are alone in the car, I say to Grandma, 'Can I try and play it, Grandma?'

'What's that, my dearest?' she says.

'The cello,' I say.

Grandma looks really pleased. 'Do you know,' she says, 'I'd absolutely adore you to play it. Tell you what. Why don't you come and stay with me, and we'll get you some lessons with a friend of mine. And we'll keep it a secret, shall we?'

Grandma is good at little conspiracies. She has lived alone in Hampstead since her husband died, which happened just after I was born. She is surrounded by musicians of calibre. She herself plays the piano and the harpsichord. When she isn't playing, she's gardening. I love to stay with her, especially without the String Trio. She has that firm, headmistressy style that my mother absolutely lacks. She has a penetrating *grande dame* voice that always gives my dad the heebies in public places.

The cello doesn't have a case like a modern cello, made of moulded fibreglass. The case is a huge matt black wooden box, like a coffin, that stands upright on the floor. It's about as big as I am, maybe bigger. It has two brass bolts and a slightly pocked purple baize lining. The bow lives alone in an engraved glass tankard that stands on Grandma's writing desk.

'Now the bow is not to go in the box, Stella,' Grandma says. 'Unfortunately, the case has a weevil that likes to eat the horsehair. It won't do the cello any harm.' I like to believe that the weevil has entered the box as a result of my dad's burial procedures.

The cello itself is beautiful. It is slightly smaller than the one at the concert and it has a different sort of end pin. This one isn't detachable and it isn't as clumpy. It's a smooth chrome shaft like a shiny nail that slides out from the cello's insides when you loosen a small nut at the base. It has a beautiful gleaming fingerboard made of ebony. It has fine tuners on the tailpiece.

'That's because, in its time, some very good cellists have played it,' Grandma says. 'Most of us don't actually need the fine tuners.' I resolve, recklessly, that one day I will need the fine tuners.

The cellist neighbour has agreed to give me lessons. He is a sweet old Dutch recitalist, now retired, called Joonas, who has lived in Frognal Lane these fifty years, ever since he left The Hague as a young music student fleeing the Occupation. He is bent into a question mark with osteoporosis. He wears his trousers almost under his arms. First he tunes the cello, banging on individual piano keys and twiddling with the pegs. Then he sits me on a pretty upright chair and puts the cello against my chest so that the C peg is tickling my left ear. I am feverish with excitement. ('Do you have fever in your left ear, Stella?')

Though he puts my left hand on the strings and my right on the heel of the bow, he does not say a word about left and right. Perhaps Grandma has forewarned him about my dafty brain. Then he asks me to sing to him, so I sing bravely with the cello between my knees. Thinking of Aunt Rosie, I sing 'Michael Row Your Boat Ashore, Alleluiah.'

'Excellent,' he says. 'This cello will be happy with you. You will sing together. You will be friends.'

Then he tells me a story. He says that long ago – 'perhaps seven hundert, eight hundert years' – people already had a sort of violin, and they sang in strange, high-pitched, nasal voices. He pauses and, to my surprise, he sings an extended twelfth-century whine that strikes my ear like the soundtrack of *Mother India*. A little old man like a bag of bones in worsted and Viyella. His shoes are shiny brown with perforations. He has jaunty yellow socks with Prince of Wales diamond patterns. 'Now,' he says, 'when they once began to sing like you, Stella, so beautiful, so deep with open throat –' he stops '– for this, of course, they needed soon the cello.'

I sit taller on my pretty chair, feeling that, but for the likes of me, the cello might never have been invented. As I do so, and lest I think he has been dismissive of the violin, he tells me that long ago, 'not quite seven hundert, eight hundert years', when he was a boy in The Hague, his next-door neighbour had had the honour to billet Yehudi Menuhin, the boy wonder, the touring virtuoso in short pants, and that he and the little violinist had played with spinning tops together in the street, crouching together on the paving stones.

'So, in the street. With spinning tops,' he says.

The man is magic: I walk on air all the way back to my grandmother's house – I and my new friend in the big wooden box. The box has a homely, scoop-shaped carry-handle made of brass, just like the ones on our kitchen dresser drawers at home. Aunt Rosie's cello and I are in love.

Music-wallahs are often crushing bores, as I know better than most, perhaps, from my years of contact with the String Trio. I have various explanations for why the cello suited me; for why it so quickly became my friend and remained so when the piano was always so much my enemy. But I won't unload them on you, if only because my reasons would sound like extracts from 'Pseuds Corner'. I will say that there is a particular way, because of the stance and the instrument's size, in which the music becomes a part of you; the music runs up and down your left arm. It leaves you so much freedom and yet it binds you so much with form. Form was good for me. It changed my life. It bound me to something. Perhaps it is extravagant to say that it gave me vision. God knows. I was in all other respects so completely all over the place; a person still so lacking in 'the coping skills'. The cello protected me from the *angst* and *drang* of the GCSE and the A level exams – those routine demands for which I had remained so peculiarly ill-equipped emotionally, neurologically, conceptually; demands which made me cling all the more to my mother, who made a full-time job of seeing me through. 'Mummeee!' My mother, who became my own personal tugboat, always there to guide me into harbour. Oh, Christ. I do not wish to belittle her achievement. I was her one, onerous, unlikely work of art.

Yet it was never with her, only with the cello, that I experienced glimpses of what Yeats so divinely calls 'the cold and rook-delighting heaven'. Only with the cello, and perhaps while turning cartwheels. I had found a higher, colder and more exquisite interaction. I had found a way, at last – at last – of playing on my own.

And I was lucky with my teacher. In the last letters we gave and received before he died, Joonas and I had some jokey little exchange about bowings. He'd sent me a pair of two-bar transcriptions from Bach's Cello Suite in D. The first, that he had copied from the hand of Anna Magdalena Bach, looked like this:

The second, from a modern published version of the same passage, looked like this:

'But this,' he wrote, 'is the mindless modern mentality, dear Stella. It is like paint-by-numbers. It is like reading words without sense.' Then he wrote out his last sentence again in plodding, regular spacing, letters in clusters of four, to mock the even groupings: 'Itis like read ingw ords with outs ense.' I wrote back to him as follows: 'Dear estJ oona sbef oreI mety ouIu seda lway stor eadw itho utse nsel ovey ouSt ella.' 'Dearest Joonas, before I met you I used always to read without sense. Love you, Stella.'

When I turn seventeen, my mother lets me down – my omnipresent mother, who has personally tutored me through every coursework essay; who has acquainted herself with every syllabus; who has recommended improvements to my syntax, corrected my spelling and advised upon rearrangements of, and extensions to, my paragraphs. My mother, who has always been available to 'test' me on every conceivable subject, no matter how mind-numbingly boring – my mother has failed to notice that, in order to enter the music department of Edinburgh University, a candidate needs not only to demonstrate proficiency in his or her major instrument, but has also to submit evidence of competence upon a keyboard instrument up to, or equivalent to, Grade VII.

My heart is set on Edinburgh University, I don't really know why. At fifteen, I go there with my father, when he gives a talk at the Festival. We stay for one night in the George Hotel and I love the miniature jars of honey and marmalade that come with the room service breakfast. We spend the next night in a nice, cheap little B and B that is awash with pink nylon flounces. Before we check out, Dad and I sign the visitors' book where the two parties above us on the page have filled in the 'comment' space. 'Very nice 'n' quite,' the first party has written. The next party has written, 'Peaceful 'n' quite.' I watch Dad write, 'Quiet nice 'n' quite.' Then we leave, sniggering gleefully. My joy lies in the realization that I can at last be counted among the élite who can spell both 'quiet' and 'quite'.

In the evening, just before we go back home on the sleeper, we go to see a troupe of Romanian acrobats – a show Dad chooses in deference to my gymnastical accomplishments. I fall, not only for the acrobats, but for all the student bustle in the cobbled courtyard of the Pleasance Theatre and for the views of Salisbury Crags.

Naturally, I say nothing to my mother about the keyboard requirement, which suddenly jumps out at me from the prospectus, but my heart falls with a thump into my boots, and stays there all week.

And my despondency is exacerbated that Saturday evening when I happen to coincide with my cousin Sheila in the Oxford High Street. One of my circle has already told me that Sheila is co-habiting in a dug-out on Port Meadow with a drug dealer who was expelled from public school. They share the dug-out,

I'm told, with a litter of puppies who aren't yet potty-trained. The friend has actually penetrated the dug-out in the hope of retrieving a garment illicitly borrowed from her mother and loaned on to Sheila, who can't or won't give it back. She is particularly graphic about the effect of the puppies' bowel actions on the earth floor of the dug-out.

By contrast, I have not seen Sheila for nearly two years and to do so leaves me startled and discomposed. She and her man-friend are touching passers-by for money. I watch in disbelief, as Sheila burbles beggars' catchphrases about the price of a cup of tea. She says 'mate' and 'cheers' to people. Then she approaches me without knowing who I am and I fork out a quid with shaking hand. Suddenly, once I have moved off with my friends, she calls out after me in her Oxford High School accent.

'Hey,' she says, 'aren't you my cousin or something?'

'That's right,' I say.

'Aren't you the one that's thick?' she says. The unreconstituted overkill.

'That's right,' I say again.

On the way to the pub and through half the evening I wrestle with the discomfort of finding myself Sheila's donor when history has so firmly cast me as her supplicant. In the event, I can't quite handle this reversal in our fortunes.

A bit of me admires Sheila for baling out. She seems suddenly more acceptable to me than her older sister Claire, who, having taken a degree in maths like both her parents, is now making a pile of money in the City. An unnerving clone of Aunt Sally, Claire has become her mother's terrible twin. They use the same hairdresser. They have monthly facials in the same beautician's parlour. They dress in different sizes of the same Karen Millen suits.

To buoy my spirits and entertain my company, who are curious about the connection, I tell the story of how I once thought Sheila's music certificates were mine.

'Sheila Goldman, Stella Goldman – well, they are nearly the same,' I say.

It's only on the train going home that it occurs to me how I can right the balance between us and place myself once again in Sheila's debt; how Sheila can be restored to her position as donor, and I to mine of supplicant. I need to steal that certificate – the one stating that Sheila Goldman has satisfied the examiners of her proficiency upon the pianoforte to Grade VII – and, having stolen it, I need to get it doctored by the only person I know, other than my mother, whose handwriting is good enough. In short, I need the dinner lady's daughter. I need Michelle.

In the event, the theft is easy. At sixteen, my parents had got me into the lower sixth of a comprehensive school in Oxford, just a stone's throw from the String Trio's house in Charlbury Road. So every weekday morning I put my bicycle on the train and bike to school from the railway station. It is with ease, therefore, that I proceed to the house in my lunch hour the following Monday and lean my bicycle against the String Trio's garden wall. The front door is unlocked and the aged cleaner is managing so busily with a vacuum cleaner on the stairs that she doesn't hear a thing.

I slip the certificate, clip frame and all, into my schoolbag, leaving behind me a telltale hook and four grubby right angles patterned in dust on the wall. Then, flush with my success, I make my way to the office supply shop in the Banbury Road, where I match the cream-coloured parchment from a range of pastel-tinted Tippex and I buy a nice, broad-nibbed, italic pen. After that, I colour-photocopy the certificate, trim the copy and shove it into the clip frame. I return promptly to the music room and hang the copy on the wall, where I decide it looks pretty damn good.

Then, on the way out, I run straight into the Uncle Fiddle Anorak in the hall. He is dressed to go out, in faded beige baggies and a really nice old jacket that looks as if he's made it himself out of weevilly pool-table cloth. It reminds me of the inside of my cello case. I also notice, for the first time in my life, that he's good-looking.

'I came by to see if I could borrow a copy of *Heart of Darkness*,' I say. Thanks to a childhood spent covering myself against every form of incompetence, I seldom have a problem with inventing excuses on the spot – though I must admit that, where Aunt Sally would have inspected my person for bulges, unnerved me with eye contact, and routed out my true purpose within seconds, the uncle merely flings open the door to the downstairs study and indicates the shelves.

'Novels are somewhere about,' he says. 'Sally's got them all classified. Please help yourself.' And with that he is gone. I watch him through the low sash windows of the study as he proceeds down the path and flings his left leg over the crossbar of my bicycle. It's a much-coveted old policeman's bicycle – one with an all-encasing chain-guard and a Brooks leather saddle and a bell – yet I have to let it go. I take *Heart of Darkness* for the sake of authenticity, and then I return to school on foot.

That night I go and see Michelle. Having got pregnant at sixteen, Michelle had then opted to have the baby and to leave school, though she had just then got four As and three Bs at GCSE. At eighteen she left her mum's place and moved into a real dump of a B and B with syringes all over the bathroom, thus rendering herself homeless. Now she's just been housed in a little flat of her own on her mum's estate.

Michelle seems much older since the baby and she isn't quite so much fun. She's never skimped on her exercises and, right now, she looks pretty slinky in shiny leggings with patterns of citrus-fruit segments which she wears with one of those little tops that shows your belly button. It's made of tangerine cotton shagpile.

'Could've made it out of my mum's bathmat, I suppose,' she says, when I admire it. 'Excuse the feet.' She's got her feet in huge quilted slippers with toucan beaks at the toes. I covet them immediately. Somehow, Michelle has always had the art of making me covet her goods.

I notice that she has the piano in the flat and that it's standing open, with sheet music on the stand; also that she's got an Apple Mac on which she's making herself computer literate with the aid of a manual. The babe is plumply asleep, breathing evenly. His name is Max.

Michelle makes me a cup of coffee as I explain my purpose. 'Bloody hell,' she says. 'Stell-a!'

'It's only the "i" needs lengthening,' I say, apologetically. 'And there's an extra little leg on the "h". It's just that I wouldn't trust myself with a bottle of Tippex.'

'Me neither,' Michelle says. 'You always did have two left hands, didn't you?'

I watch her respectfully as, after a few test runs with the brush on scrap paper, she Tippexes out the tiny vertical downstroke of the 'h'. Then she crosses its tall stem with a flourish. After that, having waited for these little tamperings to dry, she deftly extends the lower-case 'i', making a perfect 'l'. I stare at the finesse of her handiwork.

'It says Stella,' I say in wonder. 'My God, it really does say Stella.'

'You could have had my Grade VII, I suppose,' Michelle says, 'but you'd've had to change your name by deed-poll.'

'Yes,' I say. 'Look. Thanks a million, Michelle.'

'You're welcome,' she says. 'You've got the certificate and I've got the piano. Fair exchange.'

On the doorstep I hover awkwardly. 'Perhaps we could start playing together, Michelle?' I say. 'We could work up a few little sonatas. We could play them to Max.'

'Get off,' she says, slightly as though she's putting down a child. 'I'm much too busy. Have fun in Scotland.'

'If they have me,' I say.

'I expect you'll fall in love with the MacLeod of MacLeod,' she says.

'Not likely,' I say, pulling a face.

'Send me an invite to the wedding,' she says. 'Bye now.'

I do get in. And I do fall in love, though not with the MacLeod of MacLeod. About the interview I remember almost nothing except that everyone is nice to me. And that somebody shakes my hand on parting, admires my cello and says, 'Given your name, Miss Goldman, we might have expected you to play the horn.' Joke. My dad's got quite well-known through a book he wrote that got made into a film. It's called *Have Horn; Will Travel.*

I fall in love with a boy; a boy I meet unexpectedly in Ellen Dent's digs. It happens on the morning after I run away from my flatmate. I won't bother you too long with the story, but the fact is that, after an unhappy, misfit first year, I arrange to share with a girl called Grania – though what draws us to each other is little more than that we admire each other's clothes. I have beautiful expensive clothes because my mother spoils me rotten, and Grania has beautiful expensive clothes because her family has serious money.

In due course, we bodge our letting arrangement, by forgetting to confirm it with the landlady, so we find ourselves facing a term with nowhere to lay our heads. Then, instead of letting us kip on people's floors until some doss comes our way, my mother, of course, comes to the rescue. She tramps herself flat-footed visiting agent after agent, while Grania and I are off vacationing abroad and, finally, she signs the lease herself on a much too mod-cons flat in Stockbridge – a shiny pine 'executive' number, with central heating and newly fitted kitchen and a pile of brand new, squeaky clean, shop floor stuff. It's all there is, she says. By doing so, she extends my dependence on her all through that year and stacks the cards against me with Grania and her friends.

Grania materializes in no time as a super-confident party-girl. She fills the flat every evening with revelling public school-boys, and it's not long before *The Rake's Progress* is happening in our living-room. And there am I, Miss Goody Two Shoes, plucking by the sleeve these confident creatures and asking them, please, to be careful. Please be careful because my mum has signed an inventory for the ready-to-hang polyester-and-cotton-mix curtains, for the naff but pristine cane-and-glass coffee table with handy magazine-rack below.

Not unnaturally, the champagne set think of me as major creep and spoilsport. They see no reason to be careful with supermarket wine glasses when their parents drink out of Waterford crystal. They see no reason not to have fork-bending contests when the forks are hardly heirloom, after all, they are high street stainless steel.

There is one particular favourite of mine. He's called Simon Baxendale. 'What's up, angel?' he says to me one day. 'Is it Louis Quatorze?' I've been trying to stop him stubbing out his cigarettes on a self-assemblage, roll-top desk.

Always omnipresent in my relationship with Grania is the plastic bucket factor. Because, on my first day, my mother and I arrive early and Mum promptly makes a list of all the things the flat still requires, in her opinion – a laundry basket, a doormat, a clothes-line, a dustpan and brush, etcetera – Grania is able at once to typecast me as the partner with responsibility in the Bissell Mop department, while she becomes guardian of the higher aesthetic of the household. It is her family photographs that soon grace the chimneypiece. It is her exhibition posters that hang framed on the walls. Everything about me is quickly marginalized, until I become effectively invisible.

It may be difficult for anyone to believe that I, with two foot of orange hair that looks acrylic in sunlight, can become invisible, but in the right conditions it's possible. I know this because I've been there. Some evenings, other people are sleeping in my bed. Some days I watch, without protest, as people leave the flat in my clothes – but even I can't fail to see that the partnership is bad for my state of mind.

The night I decide to leave, it's because I realize that I'm watching in silence as Grania is giving away my toaster to Simon Baxendale right in front of me.

'Here,' she says, 'take this. I think it's surplus to requirements.'

Within the half-hour, I flee. I flee with nothing except my winter pyjamas and my toiletries and my wallet in a Kenyan basket. And, of course, I take my cello. I make my way down Glenogle Road and cross the bridge. I flag down a cab in Raeburn Place.

'Where to?' says the cabbie. It's only then that the necessity of fixing upon an address begins to impinge. Where to? The address I fix on is Ellen's. Ellen is a person whom I do not know well, but then I really haven't got to know anybody well. I've never found my niche in student circles and I've become a bit of a recluse. I can't explain how or why this has happened, but all through my first year I just watch other people making alliances around me. I'm like the intruder in the joke about the jokers' convention. Remember that joke? The delegates merely refer to jokes by number and everybody laughs – except that when the newcomer offers a number, none of the delegates laugh. He doesn't tell them proper, as the punchline goes. Then I team up with Grania, whose friends do not like me, while the rest of the student body doesn't like Grania's friends. Something like that. Or, more succinctly, I have great potential as social cripple.

Ellen is a first-year student who manages to be a mainstream, popular, joining sort of girl, and one who – unusually – does not fill me with revulsion. This is the best I can do. Something about Ellen's manner must suggest to me she has it in her to take on the walking wounded.

Ellen lives in an averagely down-at-heel student apartment with rather inadequate heating, but with the usual compensating loftiness of Edinburgh's stately structures. The apartment has three bedrooms and a shared living-room. She looks surprised to see me, especially given the hour, but she takes me in and puts me up on the sofa. Having found me two blankets, she goes into the kitchen and returns with a hot water bottle and a mug of cocoa.

'God,' I say, with my hands around the mug. 'Isn't this obsolete? Isn't this delicious?' I've never before tasted cocoa, only those little sachets of drinking chocolate.

'"Perfection Recipe",' she says briskly. 'My sister and I learnt it from the back of an old tin. Drink up and you'll stop shivering.'

I begin to tell her my story, with my bare feet on the hot water bottle, but Ellen cuts me short.

'Frankly, Stella, it's late,' she says. 'I've always thought that Grania was completely round the bend. As for lending her my toaster, I wouldn't lend her a matchbox in hell. Not if I wanted it back.' Then she goes to bed.

Being in need of extra warmth, I climb out of my day clothes and into my porridge-coloured pyjamas. These are my miracle pyjamas, bought, of course, by my mother. The top is a thick, outsize version of a grandad vest, bum length and fleece-lined. The bottoms are soft ribbed long johns with optional built-in feet that join at the ankles with Velcro. God knows where Mum bought them, but on this night they certainly prove to be the goods. When I wake just before nine, slightly stiff-necked in the unheated air, I am still nicely insulated all the way from my shoulders to my toddler's felt feet. I tiptoe into the kitchen and make a cup of Nescafé. Then I do what I always do. I begin to practise the cello.

I have been doing so for no more than ten minutes before a boy barges into the room, presumably from across the hall. He brings with him the stink of white spirit mixed with cigarette smoke, which has been faintly on the air all night. He is wearing nothing but a pair of saggy threadbare Y-fronts made of white cotton that have gone dishcloth grey after years of launderette bagwash, I expect.

'Fuck's sake, will you fuckin' stop this fuckin' racket?' he says. 'There's folks here need some sleep.'

I make no serious attempt from henceforth to represent his accent, but suffice it to say that he uses the word 'folk', not to be folksy, but merely as a synonym for 'people'. He does the same, as I discover, with words like 'lassies' and 'bairns'. The boy is nothing but bones and skin – strangely dark olive skin, for a Scot, and jutting bones.

'There's folk have been working through the night,' he says. His small, pointed, rodent face is pushed self-righteously forward, his eyes dark and large. Having fired off this volley, he turns and heads for the door, his shoulder-blades showing prominent, like wings of bone on either side of his spine. Then, in the doorway, I watch him stop for a count of four seconds. He turns back to me and stares.

'Fuck's sake,' he says, his tone mollifying. He looks me up and down from the hair to the toddler's feet. He gropes crabwise for a chair and sits down without taking his eyes off me. 'Carry on,' he says. 'Just keep on playing that thing.'

Somewhat mesmerized by his presence, I continue with my practice. For more than half an hour he sits there and stares intently, his arms clutched about his knees, his legs drawn up against his washboard chest, hugging himself against the cold. His testicles, delicately pouched in the threadbare cotton, make an outline under the cloth like two hen's eggs nestling side by side. Finally I stop. I lay the cello carefully on its side and put the bow beside it on the floor. Then I stare back at him. My heart, for some reason, is pounding in my chest.

'D'ye fuck?' he says. He does not blink or turn away. Though I have never yet in my nineteen years done such a thing, I nod mutely with downcast eyes, indicating, I suppose, not so much a willingness as a curious inability to deny him.

The boy gets up. He takes my wrist and leads me to the door.

'But you're freezing,' I say, feeling the touch of his hand on my skin.

'Don't blather,' he says as he pulls me across the hall and through the doorway of his room.

His bed linen, upon which I soon thereafter place my white nakedness, is a tumble of grubby layers, more like the stuff you'd get in a dog's kennel. The room stinks quite strongly of turps and old ashtrays. The walls are stacked with canvases, cardboard sheets and drawing boards. Capless and twisted tubes of student oils lie in clusters on every available surface. Two large, makeshift palettes are on the floor, one made from what appears to be the glass front window of a motorcar. There are beer cans and brimming saucers of fag-ends. In the centre of the room, an easel stands on rumpled newspaper, its face turned away from me, the canvas blasted by the room's only source of light, which comes from two precariously rigged-up Anglepoise lamps fitted with ghoulish blue bulbs.

I lie obligingly still for him among the muddle and crushed beer cans, my long orange hair spilling over the pillow, my bloodless whiteness in the blue light like the corpse of drowned Ophelia. The boy makes an abrupt attempt upon my crotch but, finding me as one in rigor mortis, desists and addresses me instead.

'You a lesbian?' he says. I say nothing, I shake my head slightly. 'Christ's sakes,' he says. 'How old are you?' I do not answer. I watch him suck on his right middle finger, blodged as it is with titanium white. Then he shoves it high into my chalk-dry virgin orifice.

Afterwards he dispatches me, still naked, stunned and dribbling down one inside leg, to go and fetch my cello. He scoops the clutter from the chair alongside his bed and instructs me to sit on it and play. Naked, I continue with my practice. I watch him climb into my pyjama bottoms. He substitutes the canvas on the easel for another and scratches at it with a brush. He looks up irritably if ever I stop playing.

'Just keep on playing the bastard, will you?' he says. When I need to pee, he follows me to the lavatory. I play until those silent tears learnt at the feet of the Dragon Lady begin to fill my eyes.

'I'm hungry,' I say. 'I'm cold. I can't go on.' The whole thing is very strange. He agrees that we should take a break. It's mid-morning and I've missed all my classes. We get dressed and go to a café where he stipples his omelette with ketchup and slurps his tea. I pay. Before I agree to return, I say that we have to buy some coal and firelighters and kindling. We pay for it all with my money. The boy is quite weedy out in the street. He staggers and grumbles under the weight of the coal. He coughs his smoker's cough. I almost offer to take it from him, but I don't.

Once back in the room, I scrape the grot from the fireplace. I lay three firelighters in the iron basket and on these I place six rosettes of rolled-up newspaper gathered from the floor. I make a neat gridwork of kindling, just as my dad always does. The boy does nothing. He sits and stares at me and smokes.

'You can deal with the coal,' I say. 'I don't want coal dust on my cello.'

'Wear that plastic bag over your hand,' he says. 'Just wear it like a glove. I'm busy.' I turn to him for a moment to see if he is being serious, but I do already appreciate that staring is a form of being busy in his book.

Then I turn back to the fire. In my innocence it has not occurred to me that I am on all fours with my bum end pointing in his direction – an Allen Jones coffee table presenting from the rear. The boy comes up behind me and drags at my leggings, pulling me back a foot or so from the grate, exposing my little moon-white buttocks in their cotton piqué knickers. Spoilt girl knickers; Mummy's pet knickers. Stella always has the prettiest things.

He is so skinny that when he unbuckles his belt his jeans fall to the floor.

'Varoom,' he says. 'Voom, varoom.' Boys' comic-book lingo, as I gasp and almost pass out, trapped between revelation and nausea. The nausea is being exacerbated because the boy keeps two fingers of his right hand pressed against my anus almost throughout. He removes them only to pass his hand over my nipples, while I feel myself compromised that my breasts, for all their merciful smallness, are hanging downwards. Then he forces his right index finger between my teeth so that I taste the remnants of oil paint and nicotine and ketchup along with the faint odour of my own anal sweat.

When the boy removes his finger from my mouth, I find that I am dribbling. He leans back, apparently relaxing. He makes ironic hobbledehoy movements, shambling casually from one knee to the other. It makes my insides go haywire. The boy pauses and watches me. In panic, I think that he will turn from me and take a drag on his cigarette, which lies nearby in a saucer.

'No—' I say, because I want him to shape and structure the hopeless meltdown that is taking place in my abdomen. He does. Varoom.

Afterwards I lie down on the floor among his mangled paint tubes and unwashed, cheesy socks. It is remarkable to me to discover that through what feels like shame and compromise and total loss of dignity, I also feel more adult, less clueless, more poised. His room has a sink. He pees down it, leaving the cold tap running. Then he gets dressed and makes the fire. When I am not playing the cello, he plays hip-hop on the tape recorder. Once the fire is going, he switches off the tape and he returns to the easel.

'Play,' he says.

By six o'clock in the evening I am dead with exhaustion. By eight, the perennial cello player's calluses on my right finger-ends are burning and itching like chilblains. The boy has had no sleep for twenty-four hours, but he is still on his feet at the easel.

'I'm sorry,' I say, 'I'd like to have a bath.' The boy nods. He wipes his brush on a rag and flings it into one of his old pickle jars filled with turps.

'Do you have a towel?' I say. The towel is one he picks up from the floor. It has Snoopy on it, sleeping flat on his back on top of his dog-house, his ears hanging downwards. The under-side has no nap.

'Thanks,' I say.

He comes with me to the bathroom and sits on the lav seat while I run the water, which, thank God, is brilliantly hot and copious. I take a giant grip from my Kenyan basket and hold it open in my teeth while I bunch up my hair. Then I clip the hair into a bathtime topknot.

'I'm not likely to run away, you know,' I say. I climb into the water. I slide down and watch my white thighs develop tide-marks of pink in the marvellous heat. 'I wouldn't go off without my cello.'

'I need to watch you,' he says. That's all he says. Once I have soaped and rinsed myself, he throws off his clothes and joins me. He sits folded small at the tap end with his back to me. After a while I sit up and begin to soap him. I explore the surfaces of his brown washboard thin body with my callused right hand. I feel tenderness for him begin to flower like pain. Rinsed and stretched out we lie, our arms intertwined. We let in more and more hot water until it almost reaches the rim of the tub. I turn the tap on and off with my left foot. Finally we fall asleep.

When we wake the water feels like melted jelly, blood-heat. The room is almost dark. Ellen is knocking on the door.

'Stella!' she says. 'Are you in there? Are you all right?'

I start in some confusion. 'Yes,' I say, 'yes, I'm fine.'

'Why are you in the dark?' she says.

'Oh,' I say, 'I think I fell asleep.' There is a pause.

'Have you got Izzy in there,' she says, 'by any chance?'

'Izzy?' I say. The boy has his head on my shoulder. His strange beautiful eyes are closed. He has incredible long dark lashes. His awesome genital equipment is now wafting innocuous on the ebb of the water like a small toy bird. I am all at once quite certain that I love him, that he is absolutely precious to me, that he is everything.

'Izzy the painter boy,' Ellen says. Then she adds pointedly, 'The Guttersnipe.' The boy opens his eyes and laughs. He kisses me noisily, ostentatiously, on the mouth.

'For heaven's sake,' Ellen says. 'First Grania and now this. You really know how to pick them, Stella, don't you?' Then, when I say nothing, she says, addressing both of us, 'Look, Pen has made some soup. Why don't you both come out and eat?' Then she goes away.

'Stella,' the boy says. He licks my face and laughs.

'Izzy,' I say. His name is Ishmael Valentine Tench: brilliant name, brilliant boy. He is from Dundee or, as he says, 'frae Dundee'. He says it like Fray Bentos. Brother Bentos, Brother Dundee. His mother works in a cake shop. His father, once a Lebanese engineering student in Scotland, was deported soon after his visa expired. The neighbours reported on him. He was carted off in the night and locked up at the airport. The boy was three at the time. His mother has never heard from his father again, nor received any child support. Valentine is because his mother liked Val Doonican. She doesn't know it's a saint's name and neither does the boy. They think it has to do with pink hearts and quilted greeting cards.

Stella draws a heart in the steam on the bath tiles. 'Do you love me?' she says.

He kisses her, leaving her mouth like a sucked boiled sweet. He has an erection. He looks like a stick insect with one absurd Dalek antenna.

'D'ye fuck?' he says. Then he says, 'Who's Grania?'

Pen is not a girl called Penelope. He is a final-year engineering student called Peregrine Massingham and he has a room in the flat. He has made a very decent carrot soup, which he and Ellen serve with chunks of crusty bread and butter. Stella assesses that he either is, or would like to be, Ellen's consort. Ellen is pretty. She's the ultimate girl-next-door. Pen speaks the King's English and wears a necktie like a cravat. Stella assumes that he is one of those upper-class Scots who gets sent to school in England and who wears a kilt at the hunt ball – a sort of tartan Hooray Henry. But he is from Northumberland.

'He's named after a bird,' Izzy says rudely, slurping his soup.

'He's named after a pilgrim, you idiot,' Ellen says.

When they have finished, Izzy says, 'Come on, Stella, back to work.'

'You don't have to go, you know,' Ellen says, but Stella goes. She tries to play the cello but she can't. She collapses onto Izzy's bed and falls asleep. For the first time in her life she leaves the cello out of its case. The boy paints through the night with his hip-hop on the tape recorder. He takes occasional cat-naps on the floor. He is undoubtedly something extraordinary. He almost never sleeps. He smokes. His productivity is phenomenal. Though he is the most talented student at the Art School, he prefers to eschew the bright lofty studios and work in the clutter of his bedsitting room, especially now, with Stella.

Stella has become his project, his obsession. Stella will be his degree show. He paints her and draws her day and night. The work stacks up against the walls. He has an extraordinary visual memory. His draughtsmanship is exhilarating. He draws her in every possible attitude: Stella asleep, Stella having a pee, Stella having a bath, Stella laying the fire, Stella playing the cello, Stella fucking. Above all, Stella fucks. She is almost always, but not invariably, naked.

He draws on pale manila cardboard, or on faded grey or blue paper. He draws with black, red or white chalk, sometimes with all three. Sometimes he uses the chalk with grey colour-washes. And he paints. He paints with oils on canvas – canvas nailed untidily to the frame. He paints quickly, aggressively, using the paint very thick. He trowels, he incises and gouges. Where the drawings have an extraordinary tenderness, the paintings look harsh, cruel, obsessive, dissecting. Stella is the subject, she and her cello. She is dissected, exposed. Red hair, red bush, white legs, white breasts, cello. She is gouged onto the canvas. The paintings are like nothing except themselves, though at moments Stella thinks they are maybe just a bit like Auerbach; maybe just slightly like Auerbach crossed with Egon Schiele. 'Who's Auerbach?' Izzy says. He is mind-bogglingly ignorant, she thinks; mind-bogglingly indifferent to what anybody else does.

Stella and Izzy are an item. She moves permanently into the muddly room that smells of turps and tobacco. Fearing the return of her childhood asthma, she takes the doggy bedding to the laundry. She goes to the doctor and gets herself a prescription for oral contraceptive pills. She and he go together in a taxi to beard Grania and collect her things; her clothes, her lovely duvet in its undyed calico cover, kingsize with tog rating 14.5. Curiously, among the books she gathers up she finds that she still has the Uncle Fiddle Anorak's *Heart of Darkness*.

* * *

Stella is riding high. She has managed to persuade the department that her voice will be her second instrument for examination purposes. She has been having voice lessons as well as cello lessons all along. She argues that she could not afford piano lessons as well, and that, in consequence, her keyboard skills have 'lapsed'. She makes her case with her fingers crossed, but all goes well. Recently she has sung solo in St John's Church on Princes Street; a Bach cantata – '*Gott soll allein mein Herze haben*' – though in truth it is Izzy who alone has her heart.

Izzy doesn't come to hear her, though Ellen and Pen do. He doesn't like church, he says. He doesn't like the sound of her singing either. He prefers the sound of hip-hop. When she practises in the bedsit he tells her to be quiet.

Then Izzy has his degree show. He is older than Stella, older than he looks. The work is mounted or framed. She and Izzy go into the Art School, past the rows of classical statues and the friezes along the wide, noble corridors. They work all night for three nights running at making window mounts in mounting card with Stanley knives. Stella has paid for the mounting card and the Stanley knives. Some of the drawings are wall-mounted, others are presented stacked in a cradle.

The paintings are no longer hoarded against the walls in the bedsit. They are hung on the vast, white, bright walls of the Art School studios; Stella incised and gouged; Stella fucking; Stella asleep; Stella with cello. Stella. Red hair. Red bush. White legs. The paintings cause quite a stir. Gallery owners won't leave Izzy alone.

Stella's parents come up to Edinburgh and take the young people out to lunch. They go to a French restaurant with pink tablecloths called La Bagatelle. They are so glad that Stella is happy, that she is in love, that she has put the Grania business behind her. And they are amazed by Izzy's paintings. They are amazed by his talent. They are urbane, emancipated people. They display no obvious unease at the memory of their daughter depicted in red chalk with splayed thighs; their daughter depicted on the job with little Brother Dundee. The restaurant bill comes to just over a hundred pounds, which surprises nobody except Izzy.

When the summer vacation comes along, Izzy and Stella pack their stuff into large black bin-bags and shove it into the lock-up in the basement area, marking it all with sticky labels. Izzy's artwork has been boxed and sent for exhibition, first to Napier Street in Edinburgh and then on to London. He and Stella have a plan to spend a week with her parents in the Cotswolds. Then they hope to travel. They don't yet know where. Izzy favours Israel, Egypt, the Middle East. Stella thinks France or Spain. She has an overwhelming desire to plant Izzy in the middle of a room full of paintings by Rubens; vast canvases, floor to ceiling; vast women, all with orange hair, orange pubes; all for Izzy.

She is becoming towards him the way her mother is with her – constant treats and stimuli, never saying no. She dedicates herself to the contemplation of what Izzy would like best. It does not cross her mind that Izzy is beginning to perceive her with the same degree of callousness as she perceives her mother; as something of an endless resource.

They take the train to Euston, each with a backpack, plus Stella has her cello and her Kenyan basket. Izzy has a plastic bag, from the bookseller James Thin, with a small sketchbook and pencils.

At Euston, Stella has a plan. Instead of heading straight for Paddington and the Cotswolds, she suggests that she and Izzy make use of the left luggage and that they trawl the galleries around Cork Street. Then she will take him to tea at Fortnum's. They will have Big Treat Day.

The galleries on the whole do not excite him. Izzy won't even enter one that has Dubuffet in the window – turd-coloured doodles, he says. It is nothing to do with him. He consents to enter a small gallery exhibiting the work of a young Spaniard whose predominant colour is like that of old rubies, or perhaps of old blood. His partially obscured figures, like fractured icons, perhaps ghosts, perhaps torture victims, all eyes and no mouths, are seen as if through dark glass.

Then they go to Fortnum's. They move through the jewelled halls to find a table in the corner of the tea-room far away from the door. Stella is excited and happy, her love for Izzy brims over. They order Darjeeling and the waitress brings tea with sandwiches. Then she brings scones and jam and cream, then cakes. Each time the waitress brings something new, Izzy and Stella say yes, yes please. They each choose a glazed French tart with summer berries and segments of tangerine. Izzy has a chocolate wedge as well. They eat and eat. Then Izzy needs to pee. He places the James Thin carrier bag carefully on the table and goes in search of the Gents.

When he has gone, Stella reaches for the sketchbook and draws it out of the bag. The sketches are done in soft graphite on pale grey paper with a faint pin-stripe. The sketches are all of Grania: Grania naked but for her boots; Grania naked but for her hat. Grania removing her bra; Grania sprawled on a bed; Grania asleep; Grania naked but for a man's tie; Grania putting on her stockings.

Stella believes that Izzy has willed her to look. She understands that the sketches are more than merely life drawings. They are a message for her. She reads them as betrayal. She reads them as rejection. Grania, she can see, is not a good artist's model, though she may well be a good fuck. She is too inescapably *Harper's & Queen*, even without her clothes on.

Stella replaces the book in the James Thin plastic bag, though her hand shakes. Her eyes swim with tears. She gropes for twenty pounds from her purse and leaves it on the table. She turns to go, but stops. Through the blur of her tearful eyes she sees what has to be a mirage, but it is not. At a table near the door her father and a woman are making ready to leave. The woman is glamorous. She has a slash of red lipstick and shapely hair. She wears a sage-green buttoned sheath dress with a Chinese collar. She has white button earrings and white sling-back shoes with heels.

Even as they gather their things to go, they are explicitly sexual in their interaction. The woman is all over him. She kisses him across the table. As they leave she is literally licking his cheek. She makes kissy mouths and darting movements at his face at which he laughs. She is a bright, shiny, exciting bird. Her arm is clutched around his sleeve. The sleeve is that of the greatcoat that her mother once made for him – a real labour of love. Stella remembers the paper pattern stretched out on the kitchen table, and the chalk and the tailor's tacks, like funny white butterflies, on the dark grey cloth. Her whole being surges with anger, against Izzy, against herself, against her mother, who is a sucker, a sacrifice.

She darts out of the side door with her basket until she sees Izzy come back to the table. Then she turns the corner and re-enters by the front, taking the lift to the Ladies' Room where, having had a quick pee, she sees that a hundred Stellas are shaking slightly in the glass, their faces chalk-white, framed in a cloud of orange crêpe hair. Then she leaves. She takes the underground to her father's flat. She has to speak to him; she is frantic to attack him; challenge him; rage at him; cry over him. She knows that he will be there, since he is always there on Wednesdays. She knows he will eventually return there.

There is no reply to the speaky thing, so she lets herself in with her key and climbs the stairs. At the top she knocks. No reply. Inside is nobody. She waits, she looks around. On the desk, alongside her father's keyboard, are two silly plastic champagne flutes and a bottle of Rémy Martin. Plus there is a bunch of poncy-looking flowers, just dumped there, alongside, still in their wrapping. Then she rips the duvet angrily from the bed, where she stares at a severed, flesh-pink suspender on the sheet. Stella hates it. She finds it disgusting. She herself would never wear such a thing. Yet, most of all, she hates herself. She weeps for Izzy – her lovely, vicious, brilliant, selfish boy who doesn't want her any more. Without him she has no wish to be alive. She throws herself onto the bed and cries.

Then the doorbell rings and the grille from the intercom speaks. 'Jonathan,' says the woman's voice, all breathlessly sweet and starstruck. Stella stiffens with hatred as she listens. She gets goosebumps on her arms. 'Jonathan, it's Lydia,' says the voice. 'Can you let me in? I'm so happy and it's all thanks to you.'

Stella storms to the grille, her face blousy with weeping. 'Bugger off, do you hear me?' she says. 'And don't you ever dare come here again. Don't you *dare*, you stupid bitch, or the police will have you for harassment. Just you leave my family alone.'

She does not wait to hear the girlish, strangulated gasp that follows her outburst. She throws herself onto the bed and cries herself to sleep.

When she wakes it is two hours later. The answerphone is speaking to her. It's her father, sounding terrible.

'Stella, it's Dad. For Christ's sake, if you're there, sweetie, please respond. Izzy is here with us. He's just come. He says he lost you somewhere in a café.'

Stella ignores it. She gets up, straightens the bed and leaves promptly. At the front door she heads briskly for the underground. She can see that, on the far side of the road, the police have erected bollards and plastic tape, but she pays it no attention. At the left luggage she finds that Izzy has taken her stuff with him on the train to the Cotswolds, but she's past caring. All she has is the Kenyan basket.

She uses her return ticket on the night train back to Edinburgh. She cries to herself, on and off, pretty well all night, though she falls asleep somewhere near Newcastle. In the morning she heads straight for Ellen's flat and makes herself some coffee. There is a message in Pen's writing, left from the previous night. The message asks her to phone home.

Half an hour later Pen comes in. His hair is damp.

'Is it raining?' Stella says.

'Stella,' he says. 'Good God. Have you telephoned home? There was a message. I think it's urgent.' He looks pretty terrible too. Everyone is terrible.

'Where's Ellen?' Stella says. 'Is she asleep?'

'Ellen's gone,' he says. 'I took her to the airport late last night. Her sister's been killed in a road accident. In London.' Then he says, 'She's distraught. They were terribly close. She was beside herself.'

'Oh, Jesus,' Stella says, going cold all over. She bursts into tears. 'Oh, for Christ's sake.' She cries and cries. She can hardly believe that life can be so horrible, so malicious, to her and to Ellen. And all in a single day.

She begins to tell him about Izzy and Grania, and about her father and the woman in Fortnum's. She tells him as she watches him pack. His stuff is already folded on the bed, his trunk open on the floor, his things folded sleeves to middles in neat, flat, square parcels, classified in groups. They look like items in an old-fashioned gentlemen's outfitters. He puts dirty things in a linen drawstring bag marked 'Linen'. He has special cloth bags for his shoes. He has a wooden box with shoe polish. Putting the things into his trunk takes him five minutes. Then he folds his duvet carefully and puts it on top of everything.

'Stella,' he says, 'telephone home.' He clicks shut the clasps of the trunk.

'I haven't even got my cello any more,' she says, 'but I don't care.'

'Stella,' Pen says, 'you must telephone your parents.'

'No,' Stella says. 'No, I can't, and I can't go home either. It's not possible. Really, I'd rather die.'

'Stella,' he says, 'they'll have the police out by now. Frankly, I'm very surprised that you weren't stopped at the station.' Finally he says, 'Look, Stella, I'll phone them. I'll say you're coming home with me.'

'But,' she says, 'but I . . .'

'Oh, for heaven's sake,' he says. 'I'll call them.'

The call is brief. Pen tells her father that various things have happened to change Stella's plans. He says that she'll call home when she's ready.

'Look,' Pen says, in response to what Stella assumes is a degree of pressure from her father. 'Here is my parents' telephone number in Northumberland. I'm afraid that's the best I can do.'

When he has put the phone down, he says to her, 'They have reported you missing, as a matter of fact. I think we might avoid a pep talk from the constabulary if we make our departure pretty quick.' Then he phones his parents. He calls his mother 'Old Thing'.

'Listen, Old Thing,' he says. 'Small complication. I'll have a guest, all right? Yes,' he says, 'a girl. No,' he says, 'not Ellen.' He says yes and no to a couple more questions that Stella does not hear. The matter is resolved.

They step out and hail a cab. Pen gets the driver to stop near MacSween's haggis shop so that he can buy things for his mother. The shop is full of tartan.

'Do Scots like tartan, do you suppose?' Stella asks Pen. 'Or do they just think they have to have it?' Then she remembers something. 'There's a thing I need to buy as well,' Stella says. She darts round the corner to the chemist's. She makes her purchase quickly and flings it into the Kenyan basket before joining Pen in the taxi, but it falls out onto the floor, when the driver lurches at a traffic light. She has, at last, bought the pregnancy testing kit she's been meaning to buy for weeks. Pen picks it up and hands it to her.

'Keep that under wraps, there's a dear,' he says, 'or the Old Thing just might go ballistic. We're awfully Catholic, I'm afraid.'

Stella stuffs it back in her basket but, on the next lurch, and the next, it falls out again. And again.

4. Wohin?

Stella

THE JOURNEY FROM Edinburgh to Pen's house is nowhere near as long as the journey I have just undertaken through the night. But for me, right now, its shortness has no advantage. I'd prefer to be contained indefinitely. I yearn for a distance between nowhere and nowhere. And then a steward in the dining-car places an omelette before me on the starched cloth, along with a pot of tea and a four-slice rack of toast.

'Marmalade, Madam?' he says. This is not railway cuisine as I have ever experienced it, and I have never been called 'Madam' before. It has to do with Pen, who carries the air of adulthood and knows how to tip with aplomb.

'Comfort food,' Pen says. 'Eat up, Stella dear.' Perhaps there is, after all, something a bit reassuring about the heavy, battered cutlery showing patches of brass. It calls to mind Grandma's bathtaps.

Pen has elected for us to occupy the ninety minutes between Edinburgh and Newcastle consuming the full breakfast. He imagines that this will lift my spirits. He is convivial as he spends his money on me and plays mother over the teapot. I might as well admit right away that Pen has always puzzled me. For one, I find him sexually unfathomable, and I suspect him of professional virginity. His relationship with Ellen is impossible to decode. On one level, they behave like newly-weds, laughing together as they busy themselves at the sink and at the chopping board, and exchanging what look like friendly conjugal kisses. Yet Ellen has lots of boyfriends and Pen, in the evenings, goes out without her, to do I know not what.

His courteous air of old-world posh has the effect of embarrassing me in public. He has just used the word 'splendid' to the railway steward. He sounds as though he has stepped from the cast of *Brief Encounter*. Or perhaps he has come to earth in a telephone-box from forty-five years ago?

Yet he is the only one of my peers who genuinely understands the workings of modern life. He has no trouble getting his brain round the electronic revolution and part of the reason for his many phone-calls and visitors is that he is the person everyone comes to when their dissertations have gone missing in the word processor. He can fix outboard motors. He can explain the Stock Exchange. He understands those wiggly lines on the weather report.

Pen seems so much older than he is, that for months I took him for a person whose adolescence had been eaten up while he convalesced from some mysterious long-term illness. I believed he must have made it late to the undergraduate life from which he has, just this week, graduated without the slightest perceptible fuss or flap. The simple fact is that he is just more boringly sensible than the rest of us. Pen is twenty-three. Yet he has such certainty, such apparently relentless stability. He treats all matters short of premature death with a degree of detached jollity, and somewhere he has learned the business of cooking and household management – this while the rest of us have yet to discover that bath-tubs don't clean themselves. Pen knows about things like *bains-marie* and French polish. He knows that Swarfega will remove candle-wax from Ellen's raw silk shirt without leaving a mark. Why is it he comports himself as if he's been apprenticed at 'Le Manoir Aux Quat' Saisons', or as if he's done time as a junior trainee at Sotheby's?

His fine blond hair, already receding at the temples, disguises its ominous thinness by having a pleasing natural lift and a hint of curl. Even through the Edinburgh winter, Pen's hair looks as if touched by sunlight. It has that greenish patina that settles on the hair of blond professional swimmers. While his features come with an almost pre-pubertal, choirboy delicacy, he has the physical development of a well-nourished male person who takes regular exercise. He is not by any means a bag of bones like Izzy; my little ruthless Izzy, the contemplation of whose narrow gawkiness and sexual magic now bring a wave of nausea to my throat that completely does in the chance of my eating Pen's prescribed breakfast. I push away the plate and gnaw, like a spoilsport, on a piece of dry toast, which I wash down with a gulp of milkless tea.

The Old Thing is there to meet us at the station in a vehicle the size of a small bus. Its name makes it sound like a Samurai warrior and it has four rows of seats. The Old Thing looks more advanced in years than my mother, but it may be that, like Pen, she is younger than she seems. She is shy and unassertive which, along with her air of distracted tiredness, makes her wholly unintimidating. Like Pen, the Old Thing is slim and tall, with prominent cheekbones and that same skimpy blonde hair that shampoo bottles used to call 'flyaway'. She wears it uncoiffed and tied up under a scarf. Her clothes are terrible. She has on a sort of shoebag dirndl skirt, which sits disconcertingly on top of a protruding middle-aged tummy, and a little cap-sleeved blouse showing her housemaid's elbows and vaccination scars. I observe all this with pity, since I'm inclined to make character assessments of people on the basis of their clothes. To wit Grania. So I am in the midst of thinking patronizingly about Pen's Old Thing when she flashes me the sweetest smile – one of those smiles that shows lots of top gum – and she holds out her hand to me.

'I'm Felicity,' she says. Then she looks round a little vaguely for my luggage. Nothing about her prepares me for how incredibly rich Pen's family is.

In the Samurai warrior, she has Pen's two youngest siblings – two little girls, both blonde, both screwing up their eyes against the brightness of the sun. Their names are Helen and Agatha. Helen is eight and bossy. Agatha is five and a sweetie-pie. They unbuckle themselves and fall over Pen with enthusiasm. He, having stowed his trunk, seats himself between them in the second row, directly behind where he has placed me, alongside his mother.

The girls are in checked cotton school uniforms and white ankle socks and button-over black school shoes. They are not in school, as they begin to tell Pen, amidst gurgles and shrieks of excitement, because somebody has burned down parts of the building the previous night.

'But they only burnt the East Wing,' Helen says, claiming a monopoly on the experience. 'That's where my classroom is. Aggie's hasn't been affected.' Then she says, 'Nutty, our class hamster, got burnt to death in the fire.' She says this with what sounds like self-importance rather than regret. 'I'm on the Hamster Committee,' she adds, 'so I'll be involved in choosing a new one.'

'Dear me,' Pen says. 'Poor old Nutty.'

'*And* I'll be involved in choosing a new cage as well,' Helen says. 'It's all going to be such hard work.'

'And how was the fire for you, Aggie?' Pen says.

'*Her* classroom was not affected,' Helen says, jumping in before Agatha can speak. '*Her* classroom isn't in the East Wing.'

After a while the Samurai warrior has carried us beyond the suburbs. It travels on past hedges and stone walls and ditches full of wild flowers. Everything is bathed in brilliant sunlight. Then the warrior enters a stretch of woodland, at first so densely shaded that, until my eyes adjust, it is like being in a railway tunnel – except that here and there dappled elliptical discs of light penetrate to dance and flicker. I close my eyes against the optical disturbance, which has been known, in earlier times, to make me pass out, and when I open them again it is to see the odd squashed bunny and pheasant lying on the road ahead. Pen occupies the girls, asking them about their ponies and their roller-blades until we reach the house. He is like one of those favourite, jolly uncles to his own sisters.

Pen's house, though some distance from the road, is visible from it because the land rises. It has two tall grey stone gateposts with cast-iron gates that now stand open. From the drive, I see that the house is large, grey and forbiddingly plain. It has tall chimneys and, to the right of the main house, an octagonal stone dovecot and a long L-shaped stable area with a hayloft above and rows of doors that open onto a cobbled courtyard. The Old Thing parks the Samurai warrior in the courtyard alongside a couple of shiny cars. I know nothing about cars, but one of them is long, streamlined and black, and the other is snub-nosed, short and brown. There is evidence of building in the courtyard. There is a concrete mixer and a thing like a small tractor, along with some planks and bags of sand.

We get out and walk through an arch made in a tall hedge, onto a lawn with broad, flowery borders. I realize, at this point, that the house has its back to its gateposts, and that we are now at the front, which is newer and more ornate. It has what look like added-on Victorian baronial twiddles and wide, leaded bay windows. There are tall shrubs at the far end of the lawn beyond which I glimpse a sweep of landscaped, wooded park. To the left, I see sections of a high stone wall that, I imagine, runs all around the estate.

The hall we enter is beautiful. It is darkly panelled in oak and is something like seven metres square. It has a large Turkish carpet on grey flagstones and one enormous chunky dark table with heavy old legs and stretchers. Otherwise the hall is empty but for a throne-like, ornately carved chair with barley-sugar legs that has *Gott mit uns* carved in gothic lettering across the top. There are stone fireplaces to left and right and, at the far right, a wide, shallow staircase that leads to the floor above. To the left is a passage – presumably to the kitchen and the back stairs.

The Old Thing suggests that Pen show me to my room and that I settle in and come down for lunch in twenty minutes. My room is at the end of a passage. It has two casement windows that overlook the park, and a double bed with dark wooden endboards. Above it, on the wall, is a gnarled wooden crucifix with a skinny, Izzy-like Jesus. I have my own little bathroom and a bookcase full of yellow-backed detective stories – a genre which I never read because I can't seem to follow the plots. The bedside cabinet has an art deco lamp and a candle in a pretty silver candlestick that comes with a cone-shaped silver snuffer.

'The electricity supply can be wobbly,' Pen says, seeing me look at it. 'We're very high up here, but it does ensure good views.'

This is true. From my windows I observe that, after the Cotswolds, there is an almost alarming drama in the landscape. I also see that Pen's park contains a sizeable lake on which ducks are floating their young, and that, at the far end of it, there is a little sandy beach and a charming wooden boathouse with a veranda, like a small, clapboard-gothic cricket pavilion.

Downstairs I find the family large and gruesome. Ironically, it is just like the family I dreamed up for myself in childhood – ranks of fantasy siblings with poncy names like Jocelyn and Georgiana. Yet in the event, the reality is a turn-off. Lunch, which we eat in the kitchen, is a simple matter of potato soup and bread, but I am faced, throughout, with something like nine pairs of eyes. The eyes all stare out from under blond hair, some of it fine and wavy, and some of it thick and straight. I can hardly believe my ears when there is reference to two additional persons who are still away at school. And Pen's father, too, is mercifully absent since he is off doing boss-work in his factory in Newcastle.

It is a curious family, its members being either pushy and overconfident, or polite and amiable to a fault. The children come off one or other of two conveyor belts, I note. Conveyor belt A makes Old Thing people, like Pen and little Agatha whom I got to know in the car. These have high foreheads, prominent cheekbones, small features and thin, slightly wafty blond hair. Conveyor belt B makes more fleshy-faced, chunkier people with lower brows, bigger eyes and thicker, straighter blond hair. Of the latter, there is one male person called Ambrose who impinges in particular. He is an odious smart-arse and rugger hearty who has just done his A levels at Ampleforth and is clearly confident of having done brilliantly. He is one of those handsome, robust, loud-voiced men who doesn't realize that his good looks make him physically repulsive. Ambrose, who presumes to give me his biographical details, is off to read divinity at Oxford, he says, and he talks importantly about his 'vocation' – by which he means the priesthood. While I find this both embarrassing and repellent, the rest of the company, including Pen and the Old Thing, appear to take it on board as simple fact. There is a pleasant sort of boy of about my age, who is currently lobbying the Old Thing for the go-ahead to breed barn owls in the hayloft and says couldn't 'Dominic' and 'Joseph' please be made to move their drumkits and amplifiers elsewhere.

It is when the Old Thing rises from the table to replenish our soup bowls from her outsize cauldron on the Aga that I realize she is not pot-bellied but pregnant. The bulge is too high for middle-aged spread. I wonder for a moment if the woman is mad. Am I being fed and watered, I wonder, by a haggard, floaty mad-woman who smiles at me too often and with far too much visible top gum?

I feel more strongly repelled by her pregnancy when I finally encounter Pen's father, who appears in time for dinner – an event which takes place in the dining-room, with Mrs Ball to assist. Mrs Ball lives on the premises with her husband, who oversees things to do with the fabric and the garden. Pen's father hails from conveyor belt B. He is of medium height, shorter than Pen and the Old Thing. He looks a lot like Ambrose, but with a thirty-year head start for putting on extra weight. He is plumply cushioned, pebble-smooth, ruddy of complexion, and pin-striped. He is clever, scary and self-important. He has Ambrose's hair gone silver, without any sign of thinning, so that its thickness has the effect of making it look like a toupee, even though it grows from his head. It is that horrible hair that you see on men of power in American daytime soaps. He wears it rigorously parted and brushed backwards off the brow. He oozes a menacing good humour and he has smug, right-wing views. These he airs with a smoothie confidence, assuming he has consensus – and certainly no one contradicts him. No one can, because he pauses in the middle of all his sentences rather than at the end, to ensure no gap for interjection. Five minutes into watching him and I'm thinking, 'Opus Dei'.

I get this from my father, who gets it from *his* father – though both of them married out – this Jewish lefty paranoia about right-wing Catholic intrigue. So I'm watching him and envisaging a scenario of secret handshakes and plots to stamp on liberation theologists and Third World peasants. I'm thinking undercover educational projects and gravel in the shoes.

Occasionally, to underline a point, the Opus Dei wafts a smooth plump hand over his plate. On his left hand he wears a broad gold wedding ring and, on the right, a ring with little silver balls the size of peppercorns. While the Old Thing sits at the lesser end of the table, the Opus Dei sits at the head under a huge, spooky oil painting of *The Last Supper* in which the Paschal lamb is placed before Jesus looking like a flayed cat with a greenish mould.

The Opus Dei starts to say grace in Latin, just as I commit the *faux pas* of raising my fork to my mouth, spiked with a tiger prawn. I hastily lower it to my plate and cast my eyes downwards. We eat without Helen and Agatha, who are attended to by Tiffany, their nanny, in the nursery – their presence, I deduce, being too lacking in grown-up-dom for the Opus Dei to tolerate after a hard day's toil.

The food is awful, yet Pen, who, in Edinburgh, night after night, concocted lovely cheap soups and risottos for us, says nothing. But I am a picky eater, and before me is the dread 'seafood cocktail' – a yukky pinkish mess of watery, thawed shellfish and supermarket mayonnaise dyed with ketchup. It's even got those shreddy bits of crab in it, that come like squashed-up sections of celery. I try not to look at the dead cat as I eat. I muse about why Jesus and the disciples are usually shown eating only dry bread and wine for their Passover feast – except in some of those Venetian paintings where they have lobsters and grapes and Afro serving maids and acrobats and foreign emissaries and monkeys and golden goblets and doggies chewing bones under the table.

In the interim between pudding and coffee, which is served in the drawing-room, the younger generation plays a terrifying form of table-tennis at the large table in the hall. This exercise, into which I have been incorporated, requires that we be constantly on the move around the table. We have to run to hitting position, grab the bat and hit the ball on the wing, then leave it for the next person to grab before the ball comes back. In my pathetic, crawly efforts not to miss the ball at every turn, I swipe out in panic, causing it to shy rightwards off the table onto the carpet and then bounce its way across the stone flags, ending with a dying fall of little demi-semi-quavers. This happens repeatedly, to the accompaniment of rude groans from a sixteenish, female Ambrose lookalike whose name I can't remember.

'Buck up, Stella,' Ambrose says, smirking at me in a manner intended to be masterful.

Throughout the duration of this torture-game the Opus Dei, who has changed his suit jacket for – I kid you not – a quilted black silk smoking-jacket with orange corded piping and orange lining – sits on the carved barley-sugar throne under *Gott mit uns* and swivels a goblet of brandy, at which he sniffs with his puggy little nose, in between observing us all with fatherly pride.

As we proceed to coffee, the Opus Dei pats the cushion of the ample forest-green sofa on which he sits, indicating that I should place myself beside him.

'Take a seat, young lady,' he says. 'Come and tell me all about yourself.' In my wimpishness, I squirm away, pleading that I am very tired.

'Poor old Stella was up all night on the train from Euston to Edinburgh,' Pen says, coming to my rescue.

'Pish,' says the Opus Dei. 'You people are young and strong.'

I almost burst into tears. I almost tell him that I am not young and strong. I am young and weak. Fragile Stella. Precious Girl. Daddy's Butter Melon. I want to snivel that I'm having a hard time; that I'm convulsive, asthmatic and dyslexic; that I've had grommets in my ears; that I've had my tonsils out; that I've had three lumbar punctures before I was two and a half, and a pirate patch over my eye to help me read. I want to tell him that I can't swim because the chlorine in the pool always gives me rashes and that I'm allergic to penicillin. I want to tell him that Nutrasweet in lemonade gives me migraine headaches and that my mother isn't accessible to write me a note. 'Please may Stella be excused.' Furthermore, I want to tell him that my boyfriend has cast me aside without being decent enough to tell me to my face, and that my father, too, is cheating on me. On my mother, admittedly, but also on me. Me, me, me. I, Stella. Best Girl. Melodious exponent of 'The Cherry Tree Carol'.

Meanwhile, I stand in the doorway dithering while the Opus Dei susses me for a total weed. 'Off with you then. Run along,' he says. 'Nothing that a good night's rest won't cure, eh? What?'

As I flee, I reflect, with loathing, that the Old Thing is With Child because the Opus Dei, in his deluded state of self-importance, will imagine that the deity gives two beans for whether or not he clothes his prick in bits of rubber before he presses his plumpness upon her. Then I think of the pregnancy testing kit that I will need to confront in the morning.

The sound of my foot upon a floorboard upstairs draws Helen and Agatha almost instantly to my door. They are both in pyjamas. Agatha is clutching a weird, knitted creature with long skinny legs. The thing is pink, with yellow wool hair like an albino golliwog, its face chain-stitched with a fixed, linear smile.

'Please can we jump on your bed?' Agatha says. 'Because it's bouncier than ours.'

'Well, just for a bit, if you're allowed,' I say. I suspect that Helen has coerced Agatha into playing spokesperson, since it is Helen who is first to board the white wafflecloth bedcover and she's making vigorous trampoline leaps before Agatha has managed to clamber up. I reach to rescue the contents of my Kenyan basket, causing the girls to collapse beside me with interest.

'Puh, Ruh, Eh, Guh,' Agatha is intoning.

'I say "Pee, Are, Ee, Gee,"' Helen says.

I realize that the pregnancy kit is in her hand. I take it from her at once and ask, as a diversionary tactic, who made the knitted creature.

'Grandma made it,' Helen says. 'But she's dead now. She collected lots of china. Mummy's got it.'

'Mice and china,' Aggie says. 'But I wish we still had the mice.'

There is a knock and, after almost no pause, in walks Pen's oldest sister. I've gleaned over dinner that she's home for the summer from medical school somewhere in London. It strikes me now that she'll make exactly the sort of doctor who loves to have your leg off and your womb out if possible.

'I thought as much,' she says, sounding just like the Dragon Lady. It takes me a moment to collect myself and realize that I'm not the object of her intervention. She is addressing herself to the little ones. 'It's the squeaking that gives you away,' she says and her eyes bore through each of them in turn.

'Sorry, Julia,' Helen says.

'Sorry, Julia,' says Agatha.

'Off you go,' she says. 'Chop chop. We don't pester visitors in their bedrooms.'

Some of us do, I think. And, after she and the little ones have departed, I debate with myself whether or not 'chop chop' is my most unfavourite expression.

In spite of my tiredness, I have difficulty falling asleep. The bed is huge and cushiony and I have grown accustomed to sharing a hard, three-foot divan with Izzy, who is all knees and elbows. Somewhere around eleven o'clock I wrench the bolster from under my pillows and arrange it parallel with my body so that I can embrace it and damp its feathery bulk with my tears. I think about telephoning my grandmother in the morning and fixing up to go and stay.

As my thoughts begin to disassemble, they touch down briefly on shelves of china. My Grandma, too, collects china. She has lots of Staffordshire salt-glaze. Then I picture the mice trapped under the tea-cups on the dresser of *The Tailor of Gloucester*; the mice that the tailor's cat Simpkin is saving for his supper. Mice and china . . .

In the morning, I notice that the emaciated wooden Jesus hanging on the cross over my bed has, at some time, made a break for freedom. One of his hands has wrested itself free from the nail that must have penetrated the palm, but somebody has tied it on again with string. The self-serving callousness of this gives me the creeps: you just keep hanging there and save us, all right?

I remember my mother once testing me on my European Geography. She was holding my school notes in her hand as she tried me on German manufacture.

'What is Nuremberg famous for?' she says.

'Wood carving,' I parrot. (See notes.) 'And wooden toys.' There is a pause before we both burst out laughing. We scream with laughter until we cry.

'Really,' Mum says, 'these notes are something else.'

It's Friday and Dad is home. At supper we say to him, 'What is Nuremberg famous for?' Then we both snort and choke. I spray Dad with gouts of mashed potato.

'Am I missing something?' he says, after a while.

'*Wood carving!*' we scream. 'And wooden toys! Nuremberg is famous for wood carving!' We laugh uncontrollably, though both of us know that, five decades earlier, my dad's grandfather went missing in Nazi Germany.

Right now I take out my pregnancy testing kit and I lock myself in my bathroom against a possible repeat invasion by the medical older sibling. I catch my early morning midstream urine in the plastic beaker provided, and stick in the tab designed to change colour, one way or the other. Then, frantic to find somewhere safe to leave it through the morning, I drag a chair to the huge old pedimented hanging cupboard and I stash it away on the roof.

When I finally go downstairs, I discover, to my horror, that Pen is gone. He has gone into the office with his father to start the first day of his new life as the boss's oldest son; the one who will step into the Opus Dei's nasty, perforated shoes. Helen and

Agatha are off at school. The Old Thing has gone off into town, first to drop them and then to visit the doctor.

'She'll be at the hospital,' says the medical sibling. 'It's Thursday.' She is helping herself to a hefty bowl of Jordan's Crunchy from the sideboard. Ambrose and two of the others are already seated at the table, munching. One of them is the groany girl and the other is the barn owl person whom I find distinctly less terrifying than the rest. He told me, the previous evening, that he has just come back from a post-A-level year out, mapping the Peruvian Andes. I sit beside him in suitably cowed fashion, and begin to spread a slice of bread with jam.

Meanwhile, the predatory majority have planned a morning of mixed doubles on the tennis court and they are in the process of coercing the barn owl person into taking part, though it materializes that he has an inclination to spend the day doing voluntary work in a local nature reserve.

'You play, do you, Stella?' Ambrose says, turning to me.

'What?' I say.

'But *she* can't even play table-tennis,' says the one whose name I can't remember, with one of her best groans.

Ambrose ignores her. He continues to address me. 'The point is,' he says, 'that Benedict here is longing to be off communing with his newts. He's making them sunbeds.'

'But I thought it was adders today,' says the medical sibling. 'Isn't it National Adder Week, Ben?'

'Whatever,' Ambrose says. He wafts a hand in a manner unnervingly reminiscent of the Opus Dei. 'He's longing to be off with some ungodly creeping thing that creepeth.'

I am in absolute terror of being drawn into a tennis game and horribly grateful that, right now, someone else is drawing their fire.

The newt man smiles sweetly at Ambrose. 'Our religion will have to cure itself of species bigotry,' he says. 'That's if it's not to become obsolete. Like Mithraism.'

The predators make eyebrows at each other. Ambrose quotes the chunk of Genesis about man having dominion.

'Thomas Aquinas,' says the newt man, 'interprets "having dominion" as having responsibility to nurture, not to abuse.'

'Well, *are* we going to play mixed doubles?' says the groany one. 'Yes or no? If *she* plays instead of Benedict, then it won't be mixed doubles, will it?'

'I don't play,' I say quickly.

'In that case,' says the odious Ambrose, putting down his spoon, 'I'll make the time to teach you.'

In the event, my tuition thankfully consists – after the most rudimentary instruction in serving – of Ambrose handing me a half-dozen tennis balls and a racquet and telling me to hit the balls against a brick wall. He places me so that I am visible to him from the tennis court. Every so often he calls out, 'Keep it up there, Stella.' Then he goes on with his game.

Suddenly I realize that I am spending the morning in too much sun, being patronized by a boy who has just done his A levels. Am I insane? I stop and stare at them all for a moment. I envisage them without their clothes. I hear the voice of my junior school Sex Ed films: 'The main difference between Ambrose and the medical sibling is between the legs.' I see their boobs and willies bobbing with every thwack. I see them growing speeded-up hips and breasts, their pubic hair burgeoning precipitously, like mustard and cress.

I throw down the racquet and move off towards the house.

'What's up with her?' I hear the groany one say.

Back in my room, the colour tab is telling me that I'm pregnant. I discover that the hand in which I hold the beaker has begun to shake violently. I clamber unsteadily off the chair, sloshing pee onto the floor. I watch it, morbidly, as it trickles slowly between two of the broad oak floorboards. Then I seat myself cross-legged on the rug, with my head in my hands. If 'the Pill' is reliable, as I know all too well that it is, then this condition could only have come upon me in my very first week with Izzy. This would make the pregnancy almost five months old. Oh, Jesus. And all this time, I think bitterly, I've been swallowing the bloody pill every night, which has been giving me nice, slight, fake monthly periods, just as regular as you please.

My first impulse is to grab the phone and cry all over Izzy. My second is to calm down, and go into town all by myself, and find a doctor. One thing is certain, I decide. I am not to be embroiled with any genuflecting family physician – a physician who, at this moment, will be clamping a stethoscope to the Old Thing's stretch-marked abdomen.

The Old Thing is back in time for lunch. She has been at 'the hospital' visiting the sick, not being examined herself. She has been engaged upon corporal works of mercy. Ambrose sits beside her, leaning his head on her shoulder and stroking her hair. The groany one does the same thing from the other side. They afflict themselves on her in stereo, calling her 'Mumsie'.

'Leave her alone, Anastasia,' Ambrose says. 'Stop pulling her about.' Once they have done with their Oedipal rivalries, Ambrose sits up briskly and addresses himself to me.

'Tomorrow we'll get you on a horse,' he says.

I spend the afternoon hiding in my room, where I stare out at the miles of grey stone wall and wonder what the hell I am doing there, until Helen calls me for tea.

'We're in *tempry* classrooms,' she says, as we proceed down the staircase. 'That's all of us from the East Wing. Nobody else.' The child is a total wanker, I reflect; a power-hungry obsessive.

At the kitchen table Aggie is sucking her thumb. She stops and comes to sit on my knee. Then she settles in to twiddle her hair and suck her thumb at once. The Old Thing serves us custard creams and chunky slices of bought banana cake. Her offspring promptly embark on a noisy calculation of the ratio of biscuit and cake to family members present, and squabble over who's had too much. I watch them with an only child's amazement and distaste, but the Old Thing pays it no attention. She serves tea from an enamel pot of such enormity that it needs a second handle over the spout to make it liftable. I reflect that, for her, every day is like being a helping parent at the annual school sports.

And finally, mercifully, Pen comes home. I see the car approach down the drive. It's the shiny black one and it contains Pen and his father. I see it turn right towards the cobbled courtyard by the stables, before it disappears from my vision, and then they are both in the hall.

Unlike his father, who is, once again, a pincushion, tightly got up in navy pinstripes, with choking shirt collar and scarlet tie, Pen is elegant and dressy. Clothes always hang well on him. He wears a loose-cut suit of gingery beige viscose. It has a large unbuttoned jacket and he wears it with a cream brushed-wool shirt and burgundy red tie, loosened at the neck. On his feet he has lovely, plain laced brogues the colour of hazelnut shells.

'Come for a walk with me,' he says, possibly noticing the look of desperation in my stare. 'I'll just change my clothes.'

I am so pathetically grateful to see him that, without thinking, I follow him all the way up the stairs and into his bedroom like an eager little dog. I watch him hang up his jacket and remove his tie. I watch him remove his shoes, before it dawns on me what I'm doing.

'Oh, my God,' I say, 'just look at me. I've followed you into your room.'

'That's perfectly all right, Stella dear,' he says, sounding as unfussed as ever. 'Now if you are unacquainted with the sight of boxer shorts, you may avert your eyes.' Then he removes his trousers with his back to me while I keep on staring. I note that he has a really nice bum and well-made legs. Then he pulls on his jeans and does them up. He slides his feet into loafer shoes before returning with me downstairs.

'Tell you what,' he says, making a detour via the larder, 'I'll just grab a beer to drink as we go along. How about you, Stella?'

'Oh, something soft, please,' I say, since I'm a total baby about alcoholic drinks. I've never lost my dislike of the taste and I'd always sooner be drinking ginger beer. Or Orangina. Or, best of all, Sarsaparilla.

He comes back with two cans, one of which he hands to me. It's melon-flavoured spring water. He gives me an arm and we head sedately for the shrubbery that borders the park. Were it not for us intermittently swigging from aluminium cans, I suppose we could be rehearsing a marriage proposal scene from one of Jane Austen's novels.

'Your father rang last night,' he says, 'after you'd gone to bed . . .'

I practically jump out of my skin as I say, 'Was Izzy there, do you know?'

'Stella,' Pen says, 'I really don't know that. Why don't you try telephoning Izzy yourself?'

'Because,' I say. I shrug childishly.

'He spoke very briefly to the Old Man,' Pen says. 'He sent you his love and he hoped you'd feel able to call. Now tell me, how was your day?'

I avoid the question. 'I ought to be asking you that,' I say.

'Oh,' he says, 'mine was nothing unfamiliar. I've worked for my father most of my holidays these last few years.'

I think to myself how weird it is that, for Pen, growing up does not mean going away, getting your parents off your back, launching out into something different and new.

'But don't you long to get away?' I say.

'Not particularly,' he says. 'I've travelled quite a bit in my time.'

When I stare at him, he says, 'I'm to move into my own apartment actually. It's in the old stables. I'll show you in a while, if you like. It's almost ready. I have some decisions to make about the fittings. But now you must tell me about yourself.'

'Oh,' I say. 'I had tennis lessons. Ambrose took me in hand.' I speak sarcastically, but Pen doesn't notice.

'Good,' he says. 'That's excellent.'

I glance at him suspiciously. Next, I say, 'Pen, is there any way I can get into town by myself? Like a bus or something?'

'There's one bus a week, on Wednesdays,' he says. 'Market day. Welcome to the country, Stella.'

My disappointment makes me irritable. 'I know about the country,' I say. 'I live in the country.'

'The Cotswolds?' he says. 'On the train line to Paddington? Isn't that commuter country?'

'Well, it's not *me* who's commuting to Newcastle,' I say, 'in Daddy's shiny black car. All dressed up in a smart suit and tie.' I am made irritable not only by the knowledge that I'm trapped, but by an alarming notion that maybe I don't live in the Cotswolds any more; that I've set my life upon a different caste. I tell myself not to be melodramatic, but I can't help envisaging Izzy usurping my place. I imagine him stretched out arrogantly on my bed, reading my copy of *Meg's Eggs*.

We have been walking towards the lake, and now we stop, having reached the water's edge.

'That particular shiny black car is mine,' Pen is saying. 'I've been driving my father, actually.' He picks up a pebble and skims it across the water, making it bounce twice. 'The Old Man has Ménière's disease,' he says. 'It affects both his hearing and his balance. At any rate, he doesn't drive any more – and right now his driver is on holiday.'

I'm hardly listening to him. I refuse to feel pity for the Opus Dei, and my brain is a muddle of emotions. I have moments of wanting Izzy so badly that my heart seems to contract. Then, suddenly, I want to kill him.

'Shit,' I say out loud.

'Fortnum's, eh?' Pen says. 'Poor old Stella.' And he skims another pebble. 'Would you care for a swim?' he says.

'Me?' I say, and I shudder. 'Not me, but how about you?'

'Oh, that's all right,' he says. 'I swam this morning.'

'But not before work?' I say.

'I swim every morning,' Pen says. 'Every morning of my life. Two hundred metres before breakfast, or I don't feel alive.'

'But not in Edinburgh,' I say. 'I never saw you.'

'That's because I was always back before you got up,' Pen says, and he laughs, realizing perhaps that he sounds not unlike the most directed of the Three Little Pigs. 'Survival strategy,' he says, 'that's all. Gets one focused on the day.' After a while he says, 'I spoke to Ellen today. She's desperate not to have her sister cremated, poor girl.'

We don't speak for a while. Suddenly, I say, 'Are you in love with Ellen?'

There is a pause. 'Just friends,' Pen says and he skims another pebble. This one bounces three times. 'Ellen doesn't like blond men,' he says. Then he laughs again. 'She must surely have told you that?'

In the evening, before supper, I compromise myself before the assembled company. Even the two extras are there, home for the weekend, from school. We are about to eat al fresco and are relaxing in garden chairs with drinks. Aggie has, as usual, attached herself to me. She and I are sharing the delights of a wonderful old handmade toy – a wooden drum with arrow slits. The drum rotates when spun round on a wooden spindle that I hold in my hand. Aggie turns the drum, making it whizz like anything.

'But we have to be very careful, because it's precious,' Aggie says, parroting what's been told to her. 'Heinrich made it,' she says.

'Who's Heinrich?' I say.

Agatha giggles. 'Don't know,' she says.

'He was a German POW who worked on the estate,' Pen says. 'A woodcarver. Rather before our time. He made the chair in the hall and some of the wooden crucifixes. There's one in your bedroom, Stella. He was deported after the war – though I believe he was keen to stay on.'

The toy comes with ageing strips of paper that make sort of hatbands around the inside of the drum; strips of paper that have been delicately sketched and hand-coloured with repeating forms of men and horses and windmills; trees and birds and circuses. For the viewer – in this case Aggie and me – who holds his eye to the arrow slits, these sketches turn into moving pictures when the drum is rotated. They are early animated cartoons. She and I are excited by their cleverness.

We spin and spin. Aggie sits on my knee, rotating the drum. I continue to gawp, even though the pictures start to disturb my eyes.

'One more, one more,' Aggie says. She slots more and more paper hatbands into the drum, each with its own row of beautiful little pictures. The hatbands go on and on forever and I have had a hard day – too long outdoors in the sun with Ambrose; too long indoors, moping over a urine sample. Then Aggie jiggles unexpectedly and her head crashes into my jaw. Something happens inside my head that hasn't happened for years – a strange, zigzag electric current begins to suffuse my head; a charged, spacey feeling that in childhood I described as 'bizzy'. I have loud vibrations and shell noises right inside my ears. For an instant the visual effects are marvellous and extraordinary. Catherine wheels swirl before my eyes; Van Gogh skies with citric ammonite stars. The garden chairs bloom vivid abalone and orange behind my eyes. Then I fall to the floor, sending Aggie and the toy drum sprawling.

When I come round, someone has placed a cushion under my head, and the medical sibling is queening it over me as if she has just acquired the lead part in *Doctor Finlay's Casebook*. I have the strong impression that there has been a modicum of interference with my person.

'She ought to be on phenobarb,' Julia is saying, 'but the sticky bit—' she stops. 'On second thoughts I'll pass on the sticky bit,' she says.

Aggie is standing beside me, biting her lip and staring into my face. In her hand she is holding Heinrich's wooden drum, which must have been propelled from its spindle with my fall. It looks like a broken coconut shell. The thing is cracked open all along the line of one of its arrow slits and right down through the base.

Once I am tucked up in bed, Aggie brings the albino golliwog and clambers in alongside me. At my pleading, she is allowed to stay.

'Sorry, Stella,' she says in her little, slightly Geordie voice, as I drink a cup of weak tea. I can tell that she's been crying and I start crying too. 'Sorry I made you fall over.'

'It wasn't you. It was me,' I say. Dafty Stella. Dafty brain. 'Silly us. We banged heads. I'm really sorry about Heinrich's toy.'

'I think you look like a princess,' Aggie says. 'Because you've got lovely hair. Does Pen think you look like a princess?'

'I think you look like a fairy,' I say. 'You look like a fairy with a missing front tooth.'

'If I was the tooth fairy,' Aggie says, 'then I'd have to bring my own money.' Then she says, 'I've got another wobbly one. Look.'

She is dispatched when the doctor arrives. He and I are left alone. The door is closed behind us. The doctor is a dark rotund man with devil eyebrows at angles of forty-five degrees. He has a small black villain's beard and a black moustache. He is the Inquisitor, the genuflecting doctor himself.

'Evening, Stella,' he says. I endure his long and thorough examination, thinking it will never end. He takes my pulse. He takes my body temperature. He checks my blood pressure. He feels my armpits. He draws down my eyelids. He taps my knees and the soles of my feet. He makes me stand up and pick up a dropped fountain pen from the floor, first to left and then to right. He makes me follow his finger with my eyes. He puts a lolly stick in my mouth and looks down my throat. He takes a steel torch from what looks like a piccolo case and stares down both of my ears. He invades my crotch with a gloved right hand, while rotating the flesh of my abdomen with his left. He ties a rubber rope around my upper arm and takes a blood sample from the vein in the inner hinge of my elbow. He asks me my height, my age, my weight. He questions me at length about my medical history. He asks me about my family. He asks me what I do with myself.

I tell him what he wants to know. I tell him I play the cello and sing, and that I'm a music student at Edinburgh University, which is where I met Pen. I answer his questions mechanically, like a person condemned to death. Then I turn aside to sneeze.

On the bedside table the Inquisitor has left the piccolo case open and, on the velvety insides of its lid, there is an ivory nameplate with his name. Dr Joel Sachs. I almost pass out all over again with relief. Suddenly the beard and the eyebrows are no longer demonic. He is not a man of the Inquisition. Portly Dr Sachs is a Jew. I want to hug him and cry tears into his cushiony paunch.

'I want a termination,' I blurt out. 'Please. I've got to. Please. Say I can.'

Dr Sachs is evidently making a calculation in his head. 'You've left it a little bit late,' he says. 'Are you here for any length of time?'

'Oh, for ages,' I say promptly. 'All summer, anyway.'

He is cautious. 'Naturally, if I treat you,' he says, 'I will need to get your notes. This is really something for your GP.' Then he takes my GP's name and address.

'Leave it with me,' he says. 'I'll get back to you. Take it easy now, Stella, all right? No tennis and horse-riding.'

'No,' I say, grinning smugly.

Then he pats my thigh through the quilt. 'And if you really are here to stay a while,' he says, 'the wife and I could do with a decent cellist.'

He and the wife are amateur violinists and their daughter Lorraine plays the viola. Any evening I feel disposed to join them in their little house in Jesmond, he says, we could make up a string quartet. Dr Sachs, my wonderman; Dr Sachs, my hero.

Next morning I wake to brilliant sunshine and manic bird chatter. While I have always imagined that birds are engaging in a fine nuance of conversation in a language sadly unknown to me, Benedict, just before my humiliating collapse, has assured me that what the birds are really saying is, 'I'd like to be your stud and I've got the biggest perch in the area.'

On the bedside table I see that Pen has thoughtfully left me a small battery-operated twenty-band radio, that comes the size of a family bar of Bourneville, and a mobile phone. He has also left me a note: 'S,' it says. 'Schubt is Comp of Wk. + plus Hdn cello 11:15. Call if you like – P.' Then it gives his number and extension. I don't phone Pen, but three times I dial the number to my parents' house, and three times I change my mind before it starts to ring. I will phone, I decide, but only when I'm strong; only once I've heard from Dr Sachs. That will be my turning point.

At nine, Mrs Ball enters with a tray of breakfast. She calls me 'a little old-fashioned 'un' for reasons I can't fathom. The house is really quiet. 'The youngsters', she tells me, are all off horse-riding and 'Mrs M' is seeing to 'her prisoners'. For a moment, I stupidly assume these to be the youngsters, but then Mrs Ball elucidates.

'She always goes up the prison Fridays,' she says. She adds, 'Homeless Wednesdays, hospital Thursdays.' Then she goes away.

I eat some breakfast, after which I use up half the ivory watermark writing paper in my desk drawer, composing hopeless letters to Izzy which I screw up and scatter round the floor. Then I get up, wash, dress and sally forth, feeling a rush of freedom in having the house so much to myself. I fancy that it's a bit like being mistress of Balmoral.

I emerge on the front lawn and take the verdant archway through to the stable courtyard, where I observe that, along with one of the shiny black cars, the Samurai warrior is at home but not the little snub-nosed brown car, which must be the Old Thing's prison-visiting receptacle. And the builders' truck is there too. So is the sound of sawing and hammering, which is coming from the far end of the stables. I take these as signs that Pen's workmen are busy on his apartment and I decide to pass the time snooping.

The door opens directly onto a huge, light room on two levels, something like twenty foot high. The lower level is floored with pale hardwood, and the higher with nobbly oatmeal carpeting. There is no ceiling. Light streams from a row of roof-windows and from large glass doors at the far end that give onto a slightly sunken paved garden with old stone retaining walls. Beyond these walls are miles of open moorland.

There is a balustraded upper floor like a gallery, approachable via an open spiral staircase made of wood. This has been fitted out like a home office with a large desk and ranks of wall cupboards with panelled bookcases above them. Two doors lead from this gallery. One reveals a small bathroom with a white enamel hip-bath and the other leads into a bedroom under the roof. The whole place is fitted with translucent, fan-shaped wall lights.

I make my way back down the spiral staircase, staring into the great empty well of space and light below, and, as I do so, I try to beat down the fantasy that this is a wonderful new studio I have just uncovered for Izzy. I place myself and my cello against the tallest stretch of white wall and I envisage Izzy at the empty centre with his easel, grinding his paints into the beautiful, unmarked floor. Across the floor are another two doors. One leads to a downstairs bedroom with a little lavatory and shower and its own door onto the paved garden. The other leads into the kitchen, where three workmen are taking a break.

The kitchen has the same bleached hardwood floor and lots of industrial-looking stainless steel – steel hobs, steel oven, steel cooker hood, steel work surfaces. A steel-fronted fridge and dishwasher are standing out of position on runners with polystyrene packaging around their edges. But, mainly, I notice the men. I find it quite a relief, amidst this breathtaking evidence of Pen's wealth and good taste, that the cast of *Auf Wiedersehen Pet* should be lolling about in the kitchen with roll-your-own ciggies and mugs of instant coffee – and that their coffee mugs should have Batchelor's soup logos on them. Also that they should be listening to advertising jingles that are distorting from a dusty-looking tranny on the floor.

The builders seem pleased enough to see me. They make up a fourth mug of Kenco Instant and offer me one of their cigarettes. They invite me to take a seat with them on the floor, which I do, planting myself cautiously beside a pile of wood shavings topped with an electric drill. Talking above the tranny, they tell me about their package holidays in Spain and about each other's love lives.

'Jim here's getting engaged to a Gateshead virgin next week,' one of them says.

'Isn't any such thing,' says another. One of them wears a T-shirt that says 'Go on, admit it, you're after my body'. When I admire it, he offers to give it to me, while his mates make bullish noises. I demur, but he strips it off anyway and hands it to me pronto, all rolled up, sweaty armpits and all.

'Wear it and think of me, pet,' he says. 'Go on. Take it.'

I take it, but I feel myself compromised, as if he will now demand my hand in marriage. I stare at the black hair round his nipples and listen to the builders' banter, which is interspersed with an occasional, sneery undertone intended to belittle Pen.

One of them pushes up his nose with an index finger, in a gesture commonly used to indicate snootiness. 'I say, this is awfully what-ho not-so?' he says, making a Geordie effort at posh-speak. They stop quickly and look at me looking embarrassed. 'Mind, you're a proper little old-fashioned 'un,' the T-shirt says, rather to my surprise. 'You're a bit of all right, then, aren't you?'

'Ah, well,' says one of the others, 'back to the old grindstone, eh?' He pitches his cigarette butt out of the window into the courtyard and turns to invert the dregs of his coffee down the pristine sink.

'Ay,' say the others, 'back to the old grindstone.'

I return to my bedroom to find the phone is ringing. It's Pen, to ask how I am. I tell him that I'm much better. I don't tell him this is because I've been flirting with his builders who have given me a saucy T-shirt impregnated with bodily fluids which I have stashed under my bed.

Then, at lunchtime, the Old Thing returns and tells me about her prisoners. They are maximum security prisoners in Durham jail to whom she refers as 'all my lovely men'.

'All so handsome, so tall,' she says. She sounds like Mrs Bennet assessing Mr Darcy. 'They're great big gorgeous chaps. Very charming and very bright. You'd be proud to walk out with any one of them, Stella.'

I'm charmed by the idea of 'walking out' with anybody. I wonder whether she thinks that I'm currently 'walking out' with Pen. I ask her what crimes her gorgeous chaps have committed and she answers rather casually while searching for a saucepan.

'Oh, murdering police informers,' she says. 'Armed robbery, extortion, serious fraud. That sort of thing. The odd terrorist. Charming Palestinian fellow. And the drug people are terribly nice, you know. Especially the Caribbeans. Lovely smiles. There's one young man who simply won't stop murdering people. Can't control his temper. He's managed to murder two while he's been inside. Stabs people to death over which TV channel to watch. Such a pity, Stella. Such a waste.'

I blink at her, feeling the limitations of my own puny life experience, with a girlish self-consciousness.

'For big crime, you need to think big, on the whole,' the Old Thing says. 'You need ambition. You need brains. You need panache. These men are not run-of-the-mill, Stella dear.'

I wonder, for a moment, what the hunky extortionists and armed robbers make of her in her little dirndl skirts and cardigans. I decide that they probably love her. I begin to think of her as quite amazing.

Meanwhile, she's holding up two tins of Campbell's soup and she's asking me to choose which one we should share for lunch. Cream of Tomato or Cream of Chicken? I choose Cream of Tomato, so she opens it with a wall can-opener and chucks it into a saucepan which she slaps down on the Aga. Then we take our bowls and chunks of bread into the garden. The Old Thing has made the bread herself. Edward 'prefers' it, she says.

She makes me begin to wonder about what it could have been that my mother was doing all those years while Pen's mother was having nine children and making bread and visiting prisoners Fridays and the homeless Wednesdays. She was giving me her quality time, I suppose; practising a form of domestic monotheism; playing the omnipresent Ideal Mother and pretending not to notice that my dad was off in London messing around.

The Old Thing talks about her husband a lot – far more so than she talks about her children. Edward this, Edward that; Edward's dedication to a certain brand of petrol-operated lawnmower, Edward's passion for kedgeree, etcetera. It is as if the Opus Dei is her major project. She appears to have no idea that the man is an overweight creep with soap opera hair and roll-on roll-off opinions. Or perhaps she does? Perhaps she sees it and forgives?

'We are all of us sinners, Stella,' as she observes to me with reference to her prisoners. And, as she says it, I'm thinking quietly to myself, but we don't all bury our wives in concrete and blow the heads off security guards, do we? Please can I be allowed just a few small Brownie points for that?

When the little girls come home from school, Aggie once again attaches herself to me. I am fast becoming her adopted older sister and role model. And, that evening, when Pen takes me to see his new apartment, Aggie comes too on her roller-blades, which require her to clutch at my hand across the cobbles. She has her hair in minuscule bunches like two tiny paintbrushes, with most of the hair hanging out in a fringe at the nape of her neck.

'I'm growing my hair to be long like yours,' she says.

In the courtyard, the builders' truck has gone, but the two shiny black cars are now standing side by side. I do not tell Pen that I have already seen his place. He gets Aggie to remove the roller-blades before she enters, though I am allowed to keep on my sneakers. He talks through his plans for the garden and shows me little books of fabric samples for the soft furnishings. They are all of them natural fibres in twelve shades of sand.

'I think you should have pink,' Aggie says. 'Pink, pink, pink. Pink is my favourite colour.'

‘Mine too,’ I say, merely for reasons of solidarity. ‘Aggie and I think you should have pink.’ I tell them about the pink flouncy B and B in Edinburgh where I stayed with my dad and where he left a silly message in the visitors’ book.

‘You’re fond of him, Stella,’ is all Pen says, which plunges us into a silence.

All the while I’m thinking what a weirdo Pen is, to be giving his mind to questions of gardening and loose covers just as if we were proper grown-ups. Why doesn’t he think about dope and socialism and sex and fighting with his parents, like normal people?

‘So, why do you drive a car that is exactly like your dad’s?’ I say.

‘It’s not the same at all,’ Pen says. ‘Mine’s a Rover. My father’s car is a Jaguar.’

‘Well, they’re both black,’ I say, pathetically.

‘I like pink motorcars,’ Aggie says.

‘Me too,’ I say. ‘We like pink motorcars.’

‘Pink, pink, pink,’ Aggie says.

‘You are a strange girl, Stella,’ Pen says.

‘I’m not strange,’ I say.

‘She’s not strange,’ Aggie says. ‘She’s got lovely hair.’

My big advantage is that I can now play fragile Stella, unwell Stella, and lurk in my bedroom whenever I want, especially at supper time and breakfast. I much prefer it this way, with visits from Aggie and Pen, and Mrs Ball, who brings me things on trays.

On Sunday morning the family leaves for mass without me. I watch them go from my window – the boys shaved and spruce in sports jackets and ties and polished shoes; the girls with freshly washed hair and summer frocks, laundered and pressed. Some of them are clutching missals. The Opus Dei wears one of his nasty suits. You can tell that he doesn’t always wear the same suit, because the distance between the pinstripes varies by a few millimetres from one day to another, as does the slight shift in shade of navy. The Old Thing wears one of her skirts with a jaunty green blazer to dress it up. She has her hair out of the headscarf and instead has a small army of hairgrips running down each side and a girlish scrunchy band at the nape.

Just before Ambrose takes his turn to drive them off in the Samurai warrior, I reflect upon them with grudging amazement, thinking two pews' worth of well-scrubbed children, and among them not one with dreadlocks; not one a druggie or a drop-out; not one, as far as I know, who has ever been rusticated for swiping booze from the off-licence, or knocking off CDs from HMV. Not one who refuses to get out of bed on Sunday mornings and run a comb through his or her hair. I shrink back into bed and wish these vices upon the Old Thing's unborn embryo, before, with a shudder, I reflect that I have one of my own.

At lunch, where I feel obliged to put in an appearance, the Opus Dei picks on Benedict to carve, which he does, though he is the family's only vegetarian. In place of roast leg of lamb and gravy, Benedict eats a mound of coarsely grated, oily looking Cheddar along with his roast potatoes and two veg and a little slosh of mint sauce. This is Mrs Ball's idea of vegetarian cuisine. Then I take note of the china. Sunday best china, with a broad border of blackberry fool, interrupted, here and there, with white medallions and lots of gilt. Meissen china, I think. Click! Mice and china.

'Pretty plates,' I say.

The Old Thing smiles at me. 'They ought to be with my dear sister,' she says and she sighs. Her sister, she tells me – her much older sister – left home very suddenly, soon after the end of the war, after which her portrait had its face turned to the wall. 'A matter of the heart I believe,' she says. 'I was a very small girl at the time. Do you have a sister, Stella?'

I never think about the Italian half-sister, the cot death person, but right now I feel the stigma of being an only child. And perhaps I feel the need to compete?

'I had a sister who died,' I say and then I feel cheap, remembering Ellen.

'I'm so sorry,' says the Old Thing, touching my arm.

Mid-morning, on Monday, there is a telephone call for me from Dr Sachs's receptionist. She says will I hold, because the doctor would like a word with me.

'Stella,' says the voice of my saviour, my Jewish medicine man, 'I would like you to come and see me tomorrow morning. Eleven o'clock?' he says. 'Can you come up to the hospital?' He has a colleague he would like to have see me as well, he says. He gives me the address. I'm just to go to reception and ask for him, he says.

I spend the day feeling light in the head. My burden is lifted. Dr Sachs will see me, not at his surgery in the city, but at the hospital. Things are moving for me. They are really moving fast. By supper time the next day my problem will be over. That is to say, my most immediate problem. And once that is over, I will feel strong and sorted. I will phone my grandmother and arrange to stay with her in Hampstead. I will even be brave and confront Izzy, who will be at my parents' house until Wednesday, I'm pretty sure. He will have nowhere else to go till he starts Inter-railing, since he knows nobody south of the Scottish Borders.

I will speak to my parents with a sort of distant adult dignity. Izzy will tell me that he longs for me, that he needs me, that he tosses at night without me, that he knows I know about Grania and that he's terribly sorry – but Grania is nothing to him and it will never happen again. And shall he and I go Inter-railing after all? Yes? And shall we start from the week after next? Yes?

I go into Newcastle with Pen and his father early in the morning. I say that I have some shopping to do. I sit in the back while we drive in almost complete silence. Pen drops me off at the shops and arranges to pick me up at the railway station because that is a place I know. He says they will return for me at exactly six o'clock. He asks if I'm sure that I will find enough things to do all day. If not, he will arrange for his mother to collect me, along with Helen and Agatha. I tell him it's no problem. I will have lots to do.

The Opus Dei follows this up with some predictably bigoted witticism about women, time and shopping. I wonder when it is that the Old Thing spends time shopping – other than to buy up half of Tesco's to stuff down the family's throat.

'I'll get my legs waxed if time hangs heavy,' I say. I feel pleased with my repartee as I step out of the Rover. Only after I have waved them off does it occur to me that the old boy won't have heard. He never hears a single word that I say.

When they have gone, I take a taxi to the hospital, where I find Dr Sachs. Instead of directing me to a chair, he suggests that we go for a walk. We walk away from the building and down a grassed slope towards a wooden bench, where he directs me to sit down. All the while I have babbled at him about how good it is of him to see me so soon, and how much better I am feeling about everything, all thanks to him.

'Stella,' he says finally, once we are seated. 'Prepare yourself. I have the results of your blood test.' I turn sharply and stare at him. 'You've tested HIV positive,' he says.

My heart drops eight centimetres in my chest. My lungs have no air. After a moment I recover myself. I speak with confidence. 'But that's impossible,' I say. 'There's a mistake.' Then I start to cry – Dragon Lady's tears. No sound or movement, just a well of water that brims over and splashes onto my jeans. I do not cry because I believe Dr Sachs, but merely because I am deflated by the indignity and muddle of it. I cry for reasons of anticlimax.

'It can't be me because I've only ever slept with my boyfriend,' I say.

'Tell me about him,' says Dr Sachs quietly.

'He's Scottish,' I say, 'from Dundee. But his father was Lebanese. He's an art student in Edinburgh. He's just graduated. He's very good. He's—' I stop and look at him. Suddenly I'm quite angry. 'Just because he's Scottish,' I say. 'Just because everyone's seen *Trainspotting*—' Then I start shaking. After quite a long time, I say, 'This isn't happening to me, is it? Tell me it's a mistake. Well, I know it's a mistake.'

'Either of you ever use drugs intravenously?' he says.

'No,' I say, perhaps too quickly. Then I say, 'Well, not me anyway. And – well – I'm pretty sure not him. Certainly not ever while I've known him. I mean, why should he? He's so good. He's brilliant. All he does is paint and—' And what, Stella? Paint and what? And fuck? I wince. My voice begins to lose its certainty. 'He smokes,' I say. 'He drinks lager, that's all.'

'Unprotected sex?' says Dr Sachs.

'Only with him,' I say.

'Could the boy be promiscuous?' Dr Sachs says. 'Was he sexually active before you met him?'

There is an ant busy with a crumb in the grass at my feet. We are sitting not far from a litter bin and there is a small hoard of rubbish that has missed its target. I watch the ant as it staggers over a mountainous tussock.

'Yes,' I say eventually. 'Yes, he could have been.' Then I say, 'I didn't know you got ants as far north as this.'

We sit for a while, saying nothing. Then he says, 'Stella, I'm so sorry.' I watch the ant till it begins to wobble in the distortions caused by my tears.

'I'd like to explain to you, if I may, what this means,' he says. 'I don't know how you envisage it, Stella, but it may not be anything like as bad as you imagine.'

I shrug. 'So it means that I'm one of the living dead,' I say. My mind's eye is staring hard at those shuffling, emaciated young men with hollow eyes and facial sores who haunt Waverley Station at night, usually hobbling on steel crutches.

You'll see the same one for a few weeks, then he's thinner, then he's gone.

'Oh Christ,' I say, 'I'm not even the right sex.'

'Point A,' says Dr Sachs. 'This is a heterosexual condition, Stella.'

'Oh yeah,' I say. 'Well, I'll try telling that to the buddy boys. At least they sometimes have each other. They won't want me. Nobody will want me, will they? Nobody will want to wipe up after me. They won't be swabbing up my diarrhoea. They won't be helping me to bring up phlegm.'

Dr Sachs waits to make sure that I have finished. 'Point B,' he says quietly. 'Stella, you don't have AIDS. Please. You do know there's a difference?'

'I know that one of them leads to the other,' I say.

'Not necessarily,' he says. 'Not if you're careful. Not if you're lucky. It may be you could feel no ill-effects for over twenty years. It's not unknown. You will, in all likelihood, feel quite well enough for something like ten to twelve. In that time there will almost certainly be a significant breakthrough in research. It's very likely to be before you're too much affected.'

Too much affected. For just a moment on our walk back to the building, my mind blossoms into a self-important fervour, as I see myself as the heroine of my own operatic tragedy. But then, just as suddenly, I feel alone and frightened and sordid, and I shudder uncontrollably and say, 'No!' fairly quietly, but out loud. Dr Sachs takes my arm. Then we are in the vestibule. 'Your GP has faxed your notes to me, by the way,' he says. 'I'll arrange for you to be admitted as soon as possible, Stella. Naturally, in the circumstances, there is no problem about terminating the pregnancy.'

By now I have almost forgotten that this is why I came. It has become something of a sub-plot, overtaken by the greater crisis. When I say nothing, he says, 'Now I'm going to hand you over to the medical social worker. But come back to me when she's finished with you. We'll have a talk about drug therapy. And Stella, you must feel free to contact me whenever you want to talk. Absolutely whenever. All right? The next few days are going to be extremely difficult for you.'

I feel as though I am already on one of those automatic airport walkways, being drawn inexorably away from him. Away from all the nice, normal people who laugh and work and play and go to parties and concerts and have sex. I am a part of the leper colony. I know now that I can never, of course, confront Izzy. Or speak to my grandmother. Or to my parents. Never. Easier the people that mean nothing to me. Easier by a mile.

Dr Sachs stretches out a hand and puts it on my shoulder. He says, 'Don't let this stop you playing the cello, Stella. That's very important. And really, this needn't affect your career as a music student, you know. Let us try taking this one day at a time.' He looks at his watch. 'Come back to my room when Mrs Jarvis is finished with you,' he says. 'We'll talk about drug therapy.'

I nod. I don't even tell him that I no longer have my cello. Aunt Rosie's beautiful cello; the cello that my dad buried in the woods and then dug up again. So what? There is a weevil in my cello case. Gall and wormwood. Everything I love will turn to ash.

'Meanwhile I'll get on to the boy,' he says and he pulls out a pad. 'I'll need a contact address, Stella, and a phone number if possible.' I gawp at him with renewed horror which he reads as incomprehension. 'Your young man,' he says. 'He'll need help.'

'Yes,' I say and I hesitate. I can almost not bear to yield up my parents' telephone number. 'This will be completely confidential?' I say. Then I give it to him, along with that of the university administration. 'And then there's Grania,' I say. I explain. He writes it down.

'Good,' he says. 'I'll see you in half an hour.'

The medical social worker is a disaster. First, she asks me how I feel about myself, which causes me one response only and that is to grab great handfuls of Kleenex from the box on her table and say, 'I hope the hospital gets these discount price.'

'Feel free,' says the disaster. I tell her, unpleasantly, that I have never felt so free.

She tells me, first, that she has a duty to inform me that there is now a test available to me which can detect antibodies in the offspring of an infected mother but, unfortunately, not yet *in utero*. The test can be done at two months after birth, she says, and – in a case such as mine, where the infection is recent – the odds are extremely good. There's a seventy per cent chance, she says, that the baby will not be infected. It has also recently been estimated that this chance is dramatically increased if the pregnant mother takes AZT. I stare at her as if she is a mad-woman.

'These are options,' she tells me, 'just in case you should wish to proceed with the pregnancy.' I blow my nose extremely loud, as a sort of fuck-you gesture. Then I try counting down in fives from one hundred in my head. This is an area where, unlike my friend Michelle, I have never quite achieved fluency. This time I falter on sixty-five.

'Is your partner HIV?' says the medical social worker.

I tell her I don't have one. 'The conception was immaculate,' I say.

She ignores this. She says that she mentions it merely to warn me, lest my situation strike me as 'liberating'. It is highly dangerous for me to risk re-infection with the virus from any infected person, she says. It's absolutely not on. I decide she could do a good double act with Pen's sister Julia.

Then she tells me the good news. I may have regular sexual relations with my partner, she says, just so long as I do so in a 'responsible' manner – that is to say, no mouth-to-mouth kissing, no contact with saliva or menstrual blood, no oral, anal or penetrative sex without heavy-duty condoms, ever.

After a while she gets quite skittish. 'And no accidentally shared toothbrushes,' she says. Do I imagine it, or does she wag a finger at me? I begin to wonder if the woman has been at the bottle. Finally, she dispatches me with a bundle of leaflets.

'Good luck,' she says.

By the time I leave Mrs Jarvis, I see no point in returning to Dr Sachs. My mind is quite made up. I am resolved. That which hath made her drunk hath made me bold. I dump the leaflets in a hospital litter-bin in the forecourt. Pregnancy or no, I have concluded, the whole thing is quite obviously unacceptable. I take a taxi into the town centre and play with the testers at the make-up counter in Fenwick's. I spray myself with something called 'Ananya' and I paint my mouth to look like Maureen O'Hara's in *The Quiet Man*. This is one of my dad's favourite films. Then I treat myself to lunch in a crowded café. I leave a sexy lipstick mouth on the edge of my espresso cup. I feel high. I feel powerful. I imagine that I am insinuating myself among the revelling populace like the Mask of the Red Death.

Then I dawdle from one chemist's shop to another, buying packets of pills. I buy packs of heavy-duty Panadol in several branches of Boots. I buy a range of own-brand paracetamol that comes, sometimes in red and white, sometimes in turquoise and white capsules. I buy some of the economy range, which comes either in circular white tablets or in dull biscuit-coloured lozenges.

By the time I look at my watch and realize that it is 5.45 p.m., I have twenty-five packs of own-brand paracetamol, twelve packs of Panadol, eight packs of Migraleve in chrome yellow and six packs in bright pink. I have five packs of Nurofen and nine of ibuprofen. Along the way, I have bought a large zip-up sponge bag into which I have cast the whole hoard, and the sponge bag is in the Kenyan basket. It is at this point that I buy a bottle of brandy, for the first time in my life, with which to wash the whole lot down. I dismiss the idea of buying a bargain five-pair pack of knickers from a street trader that I pass on my way to the taxi rank, since, as I tell myself gaily, I am not going to need any knickers where I'm going.

The plan is to keep myself awake until the small hours and then to down the cocktail on the veranda of Pen's boathouse before falling slowly sideways into the lake.

I make a dash for a taxi, which takes me to the railway station, though I end up seven minutes late for Pen and the Opus Dei. The latter is slightly champing at the bit, but he manages a toxic smile.

'So where are all the bags and boxes, young lady?' he says.

'Sorry?' I say.

'Where are your purchases?' he says.

'Oh,' I say, 'actually I bought jewellery.' And so I did. In the sponge bag I have stashed my rainbow-bright dragon hoard. I have treated myself, at last, to my own necklace of boiled sweets and I don't plan to share them with anyone.

At supper I am in jaunty mood. I sit beside Benedict and ask him all about ants and bees. I banter with Ambrose about whether or not priests are required to confess acts of masturbation. I volunteer, over coffee, to coiff the Old Thing's hair – an offer to which she submits with surprising eagerness. After that, I sit on the forest-green sofa beside the Opus Dei and I tell him that, in my opinion, he needs a larger collar size. Then I get up and sing.

I sing '*Gott soll allein, mein Herze haben*' and, when it transpires that Julia can play the piano, she becomes my willing accompanist. I am so high that I almost give the game away when I sing Dido's lament. It seems so divinely suitable to my situation that I sing it fantastically well. I know that I am a complete and total knockout.

'When I am laid in earth, may my wrongs create no trouble . . .' By the time I get up to go to bed I have become quite fond of them all, especially Julia, who is now my sidekick.

When the clock strikes 3.45 a.m., I'm fully dressed and sitting cross-legged on my bed. I get up and check my basket. I pee without flushing the lavatory. Then I make my way downstairs. The front door lock is more of a struggle than I'd anticipated, but I manage it without too much noise, and then I'm away – over the grass and through the shrubbery and down the ably landscaped slope, towards the lake.

I have no torch, but I've brought with me the candle in the silver candlestick and the box of matches. I place this on the little table on the boathouse veranda. I light the candle, which blows out repeatedly, until I submerge it in an old jam jar I find in a dark corner. Then I begin to arrange my pills into colour-coded heaps. It takes me quite a while to get them out of their fiddly foil packaging, by which time I realize, to my slight alarm, that there is already a tiny glimmer of light on the horizon. I stuff five turquoise and white capsules into my mouth, uncap the bottle of brandy and take a hefty swig.

Bulk swallowing is harder than I anticipate, and only three of the capsules go down. It crosses my mind to regret that I've left the builder's sexy T-shirt under my bed and that I haven't ripped up all the stupid, abortive letters to Izzy. Also that poor little Aggie will be all too aware of the corpse dredged from the lake. Suddenly, there is a beam of light shining in my face. Then it moves to expose the colour-coded dragon's hoard on the table.

'May I ask what on earth you think you're doing?' Pen says. For answer, I snatch up the entire handful of pink Migraleve, but Pen springs forward and knocks the pills out of my hand. He is wearing the dressing-gown that I saw him pack in Edinburgh, and he has flip-flops on his feet. 'Are you insane?' he says. 'Stella, are you completely bloody round the bend?'

I drop my hands into my lap, close my eyes with resignation and sigh heavily. Oh shit, I think. Better luck next time, Stella; all-thumbs Stella; bodged again.

Pen is already scooping up my hoard and pushing it into his dressing-gown pocket. But the Third Little Pig, I think sarcastically, got up at three o'clock and he went into the field to gather turnips . . .

'Have you actually swallowed any of these?' he says. I tell him I've swallowed three. 'Jesus, Stella,' he says, still scooping away. 'This lot must have cost you a pound or two. There's enough stuff here to sink a battleship.'

I say nothing. Once he has scooped up all the pills, he sits down beside me. He switches off the torch, he snuffs out the candle, which is leaning against the side of the jam jar, guttering pathetically.

'Stella, why?' he says.

After a while I say, 'I'm pregnant, that's why.'

I hear Pen whistling quietly through his teeth. 'You really are a terrible, wicked, stupid girl,' he says. 'You're pregnant. So what, Stella? So absolutely bloody what?' I say nothing. 'You're pregnant,' he says again. 'Is that any reason to go killing yourself? Why are you always so extreme?' Again I say nothing. 'Izzy's baby,' he says. 'For one, have you thought of telling the wretched boy? Does he know?' When I say nothing, he says, 'Tell him, Stella. It might be the making of him.'

'Oh, fuck off,' I say. 'You really are a pompous twerp, aren't you?'

After a bit, Pen says, sounding just moderately aggrieved, 'I'm sorry, Stella, but I don't think I'm pompous. I really don't accept that.'

Then we sit in silence. 'Do you realize how extraordinary you are?' he says after a while. 'You sing beautifully. You play the cello. You must, of course, know that you are stunningly beautiful. Here you are, a beautiful, talented, unusual girl and the heavens shine down upon you.'

'Oh yeah?' I say.

'Well, let's think about this baby,' Pen says. 'Let's think about its gene package for a start. Here's a child with the potential for your musical talent and Izzy's draughtsmanship. Then there's your father's much fêted literary ability—'

'And let's think,' I say, through clenched teeth, 'that if I were to bite your leg off – well, I might just infect you with The Virus, Peregrine Massingham, and wouldn't that be nice for you?' Then, damn it, I start to cry.

Pen says absolutely nothing. I can tell that I've knocked him back. His whole body has sunk a bit, like a slowly deflating air mattress.

Eventually I speak. 'So what were you doing, prowling about at a quarter to four in the morning? It's just stupid.'

'I'm always up by four o'clock in the morning,' he says. 'I usually get up and swim at about this time. I'm afraid I heard you leave the house, Stella. I don't like to spy on you, but I thought it rather odd. Are you sure about the virus?'

'Oh sure, I'm sure,' I say. 'I got the blood test result today.' Then I say, 'But it's perfectly all right, really. I might even feel well for a whole ten years. It might be ten years before I start to get sores and phlegm and fungus in my lungs. I can even have plenty of sex, just so long as I don't kiss anyone. Just so long as I don't cause them to have contact with my spittle or blood or breast milk or vaginal fluids, etcetera.'

Pen just sits there beside me and says nothing. Finally, he says, 'Oh dear girl, it's utterly dire. Try not to hate me.' Then, eventually, he says, 'Shall I divert you for a while, Stella? Shall I tell you why I'm always up at four o'clock? Are you in the mood for a story?'

I nod. I don't really care. So Pen tells me that for five years between the ages of eight and twelve, he attended a Catholic prep school where he was a boarder. Two or three mornings a week, at 4 a.m., year in and year out, he was plucked from his bed in the dark by a tall, black-frocked monk who carried him in strong, muscular arms, slowly, silently, ritually, in horizontal position like a human sacrifice, from the dark dormitory, down the dimly lit corridor and into a small anteroom, where he always locked the door. There, summer and winter, he would strip Pen naked and keep him shivering on the rug, his bladder about to burst, his little pre-pubertal penis erect from desperate urge to pee.

But he was not permitted to pee. When the monk stood in front of him, Pen came just about level with the man's crotch, though by the time he was eleven he was having to kneel on a stool. The monk was always clothed. He would bury Pen's naked upright person under his black skirts, the skirts making an impenetrable tent around the boy's body. The monk's equipment was always at the ready. Pen could not see anything under the skirts, but he was aware of gigantic rubbery appendages emerging from a thicket of coarse hair. The appendages were always scrupulously washed. They smelt and tasted of Imperial Leather.

Pen was required to place his hands on the man's muscly buttocks and his mouth over the man's penis. His head was held in position by the guiding hands of the monk from the outer surface of the black tent. The hands moved in caressing gestures, even as they were coercive, and the monk recited, gently. There was a sort of mantra: 'There now, quiet now, nearly there, my pretty.'

On the first occasion, Pen choked on semen and peed all over the monk's legs, which he found utterly humiliating. After that, he learnt to swallow. He also learnt to wake up fifteen minutes early and tiptoe out to the lavatory to empty his bladder and return to his bed and close his eyes before the man came for him.

When the sessions were over, the monk would dress him, slap him affectionately on the rump, unlock the door and tell him to run along back to bed and get his 'beauty sleep'. Pen would stumble back along the half-dark corridor and lie awake until the bell went, waiting for the daylight to dawn. He has woken early ever since.

'These days I don't hang about,' Pen says. 'I always get up and swim.'

During the daytime the monk taught history. 'Spellbinding teacher,' Pen says. 'Absolute turn-on. He did tend to pick on me a bit. He used to like taunting me in public about having a "weak bladder". I don't in fact have a weak bladder. But the business has left me impotent. One of the many agreeable things about swimming is its tendency to encourage erectile tissue.'

'So you swim to get erections,' I say.

'I swim,' Pen says, 'for all sorts of reasons.' But then he adds, in that chronic, slightly humorous way, 'but I must admit that diving is pretty effective. I'm sorry about all that, sweetheart. I'm utterly appalled by your predicament. Let's talk about it later. Oughtn't you to go back to bed now and get yourself some sleep?'

My beauty sleep. 'All right,' I say, but instead I watch him as he walks towards the diving-board, where he strips off the gown and kicks off the flip-flops. He walks naked onto the diving-board, holds out his hands, rises onto his toes and dives superbly, making a brief swallow shape in the air before his body glides smoothly downwards and into the water. I've never seen anything so beautiful. He swims under the water and emerges finally at the boathouse end. Then he swims back to the diving-board. I watch him do this three times, four times. Then I join him, but not in the water. I begin to cartwheel round the lake. It's something I haven't done for years. I cartwheel faster and faster. Pen pauses and watches me. His naked body is lovely; his penis erect.

'Don't stop,' I call to him. 'Keep going. Keep doing it. Don't stop.'

'Don't stop, Stella,' he calls back to me, 'don't stop.' We begin to work it so that each time he reaches the beach end just before I get there, and he turns and heads back. Then, as I pass him at the opposite end, he mounts the diving-board and plunges in.

'Keep going,' we call out to each other wildly. 'Keep going. Don't stop.'

Finally, we collapse, exhausted, onto the little stretch of beach alongside the boathouse. I flop down with my head onto his wet, naked chest. Once I have recovered my breath a little, I raise my head to lick water out of his navel and off his chest. I am so turned on by his body that I can hardly keep my hands off his crotch. Instead, I kiss his pretty, gaunt cheekbone.

'So how was it for you?' I say.

'Oh, sweetie,' Pen says. He's stroking my hair. 'Lovely Stella. Mad, bad, crazy Stella – please, please don't die. Stay alive, Stella. Please. Stay alive for me. Will you marry me?'

I start to giggle. I giggle and keep on giggling. I can't stop. I try to envisage myself dashing out at four every morning to mount a diving-board and unroll heavy-duty condoms onto Pen's precariously erect prick. But I am phobic about diving-boards. There is absolutely no way I could ever get onto one. So what are we going to do? No mouth-to-mouth kissing, no anal, oral or penetrative sex, no shared toothbrushes.

'You're completely, absolutely bonkers,' I say, and I keep on giggling. 'Do you know that I can't even swim?'

The next day, when Dr Sachs telephones her, Stella surprises him by saying she's decided to risk having the baby and can she please come and talk to him about AZT and the test for foetal antibodies. Then she telephones Pen at work and tells him what she's done. Pen downs tools, seizes his jacket and breaks the speed limit to come home and catch her in his arms and dance her round the floor. That evening he tells the family that Stella has agreed to marry him and that she is four months pregnant. Everyone is delighted. Especially Aggie.

Stella seems delighted too. She is floating in some curious neverland of commitment and denial. She is like a creature who has emerged from a chrysalis and taken on a new, winged form. She cannot, will not, contact her family. She cannot contact Izzy. She refuses point-blank. She knows that to do so will mean the end of an illusion. She knows that the wings will melt. She knows, from somewhere inside her brain, that she is living in the middle of a lie, but it is also a new kind of truth. It has to do with form. It's a survival strategy. It has grace, commitment, structure. It offers her a kind of moral high ground. It is a way of living with disease.

Because she knows it is important to Pen, she takes instruction from a conveniently lax priest and professes herself burning with desire for Catholic baptism. When he asks her for how long she has felt this urge, she answers calmly.

'For all of my life,' she says.

At the altar, the priests dress her in a floor-length white robe, which she dons, accidentally, back to front, and moves forward to have them douse her head with consecrated water from a large silver scallop shell, which they dip into a font. At the altar, she renounces the devil and all his works in a cool, clear, confident voice, with her fingers crossed behind her back. She recites the Litany of the Blessed Virgin, marvelling at its moving beauty, and at the same time wondering if this impossible gobbledygook can go on forever. It astonishes her afterwards to see that the Opus Dei and the Old Thing both have tears in their eyes.

Then Pen, to avoid complications with regard to her family, arranges for them to get married in a church in Venice, where, afterwards, they will spend their honeymoon. Stella is not unaffected by her own nuptial mass, where she has Tintoretto to the right of her and Bellini to the left. And Venice is like a sort of analogy for her own life: it is an airy veneer, a trick of the light, an elegant poetical stylizing of dark, inadmissible undercurrents.

The streets are a teasing labyrinth that always lead to picturesque dead-ends on canal fronts. It always takes her ninety minutes in the mornings to make her way the three hundred yards from the hotel room to where she meets Pen in the appointed bar for breakfast – Pen who has already been up for hours and hours. On the way she passes churches with names that make her blink. San Samuela, San Moishe – but *is* there a Saint Samuel? *Is* there a Saint Moses?

'Jewish saints?' she says to Pen, and she laughs. One day she passes the church of San Pantalon.

'I *don't* believe it,' she says. She loves it that the fire engines are boats. She thinks that the duckboards, stacked in the streets, must be trestle tables for very small people to use during street parties.

And all the time, Pen is charming, witty, knowledgeable, diplomatic, courteous and attentive. Upon their return, he visits her parents and comes back with her cello. Everything is enchanting. Everything, except that Stella is crazy to have sex with him, and Pen is completely, intractably untouchable. Any attempt at groin contact, even when he is asleep, causes Pen to leap, shaking, from under the duvet in the beautiful white and sand-coloured apartment in the old stables.

'No, Stella,' he says, 'absolutely, definitely not. Those are the ground rules. No.'

He goes into work all day while Stella plays the cello. He cooks and tidies while Stella plays the cello. When the baby comes, he bathes her and changes her and sees to her in the night. Later, he reads to her, or he invents bedtime stories for her, while Stella plays the cello. He hires half shares in Tiffany to undertake all the little girl's daytime care, so that Stella can play the cello. She plays the cello all alone in the pale, gleaming, pristine space where once she envisaged Izzy's crushed tubes of paint on the floor. She plays in beautiful clothes. She adores clothes and Stella always has the prettiest things.

Once a week, in the evenings, she visits Dr Sachs with her cello; Dr Sachs and his wife and Lorraine, their viola-playing daughter. She loves Mrs Sachs, who bleaches her hair and has it set every week. She keeps china figurines on the sideboard and lays down quality bed linen and sexy undies in a cedarwood blanket box for the day that Lorraine finds a husband. She visits a shop called 'Trousseau Fayre' for all her own and Lorraine's lingerie requirements.

'You know, Stella,' she says, during one of her moments of intimate girl-talk, 'I think I must be losing my sex appeal.'

'Nev-er,' Stella says, who longs to be like Mrs Sachs.

'Well, all my life I've taken a D cup,' says Mrs Sachs, 'and now I'm taking a C.' Stella laughs. Her own measurement has never exceeded 32 AA.

The child is called Holly. Holly Valentine Massingham; born on Bonfire Night, otherwise known as Guy Fawkes Day – an awkward birthday for a Catholic child – but at two months she is tested for antibodies and, mercifully, all is well. Holly is wholly unlike Stella to look at and neither does she look like Izzy. She is a blue-eyed blonde like Stella's mother, which makes people – none of whom know Katherine – say that she looks like Pen.

Unlike Stella in childhood, Holly is a serene, self-contained, easy child, who shows every sign of becoming the sort of little girl who will make her own papier mâché Christmas tree decorations at six, and knit matinée jackets for all the neighbours' babies. Stella, unlike her own devoted mum, is not a hands-on mother. She feels no urge to play with Holly. She has learned to play on her own. She feels no need for quality time and very little for physical contact. Perhaps it is a habit that she now finds hard to break? No mouth-to-mouth kissing, no contact with spittle and bodily fluids, no shared toothbrushes.

5. Tränenregen

Jonathan

WHEN LYDIA COMES to see me a second time, the moment is not of the best. It is, in general, not a good time for me. The Sonia experience, I begin to sense, has almost run its course. I hang on in there for the sex, but here's the paradox. That which was sex is not sex. I have found myself, of late, warming and softening to Sonia. I have begun not to be provoked to dislike by the sight of her narrow shoulders, or by the sound of her slight, blurry lisp; I have even, occasionally, found myself respecting her mind. I give quarter, increasingly, to her opinions and the more I do so, the less I feel impelled to assault her flesh.

This is puzzling to me, because I have always found Katherine's cleverness to be a turn-on. If Katie produces one of her pithily couched observations about – about God knows what – about pretty well anything: Sophie Grigson; Legoland; the Nation of Islam – my response is to feel my sap rising. Yet Sonia's cleverness deflates me. I must despise her or keep my hands to myself.

I suspect the same thing is happening for Sonia, in that I have begun to notice a certain mellowing. She has stopped winding me up. She has suddenly stopped making theatre of Fortnum's and 'the girlie'. I have noticed, for example, that I have begun to feature as a likeable walk-on character in one of her more personal by-lines, where she parades me as 'Josh' – an amiable bit of rough who washes from the waist up at the kitchen sink and quaffs PG Tips from enamelled mugs, in between committing gruffly executed acts of sex.

While this is naturally flattering to me, as a middle-aged bourgeois pen pusher, with my roots in the German-Jewish intelligentsia and the Anglo-Irish landed gentry, it is also clear to me that I have become one of Sonia's dubious accessories. I belong in there with all that pricey furniture banged up from railway sleepers and salvaged driftwood. I am one of her items of fake rough.

Added to this, my own work isn't going terribly well. It stares at me from the printouts, as if set in concrete.

'Here I am,' it says, 'and if you don't happen to like me very much, there's sweet fuck-all you can do about it.'

The result is that I leave the bedsit far too often to replenish my supplies of Wotsits and Mini-Cheddars and, once out, I discover a tendency to malinger. I visit the launderette and the newsagent's and the bookie's. I find myself staring through Dixons' windows at those multiple TV screens depicting postprandial mind destroyers of the *Going for Gold* variety. I begin to brood on the fact that it's a long time since I've done the things I really love to do. It's an age since I've camped out on a river bank with my clasp knife and my Tranja Stove. It's forever since I've screwed Katherine out of doors. Truth to tell, it's some weeks since I've had any sex with her at all.

Which brings me to Katherine and the Nuisance Chip: Katherine has gone a bit remote of late and the Nuisance Chip, who is now ensconced in Edinburgh, has managed to be as preoccupying as ever, through a system of remote control.

I had, I confess, been looking forward to an upturn in my domestic existence with dear Stella's relocation. I foolishly envisaged that Katie's intensive, Suzuki-parent performance would be accomplished once, between them, they had got the child through her A levels and into the Music Department of Edinburgh University. I fancied that I would move back into the gap and kiss goodbye to Stella's grade-A support person and syllabus expert. I would reclaim my Rosie O'Grady.

But, from the first, it is clear that Stella is not happy in Edinburgh. She cannot find a niche among her peers. This ought not to surprise me, given that the Precious Girl is by now honed for exclusive minority taste. She is not only formidably articulate and intellectually intimidating, but she is of intimidating appearance. This is thanks partly to her own, mirage-like beauty, and partly to Katherine's ridiculous indulgence towards her in matters of dress.

Little dyslexic Stella is now a tall, pale, translucent vision with two foot of silk crêpe hair and a wardrobe that upstages undergraduates everywhere. Added to this, her curious combination of insecurity and arrogance makes her unable to engage in eye-contact. The flecked pussycat eyes always veer sideways; always slightly off target. It takes far more confidence than most undergraduates can summon in a month of Sundays, merely to greet her in the library. Most will simply pretend she isn't there.

All this is troubling to Stella, who – thanks to Katherine's two decades of four-star quality time – has extremely high expectations of the input she can expect from those around her. She anticipates, for example, that undergraduate conversation will be all about Kodály and Kierkegaard. Instead, of course, it centres round whether or not to install a luminous condom machine in the ladies' lavatory.

Furthermore, Stella has become driven. She is single-minded and scholarly. She practises the cello six and seven hours a day. She seems quite unable to recognize the signs of her own physical and emotional exhaustion when Katherine isn't there to punctuate her day with nutrients, diversions and treats – and exhaustion heightens her unhappiness. In short, Stella, who has always been fragile, complex and demanding, continues to be fragile, complex and demanding from a distance of two hundred miles.

Katherine, once Stella is ensconced in her student room in Edinburgh, goes off and gets herself a part-time job, but she soon gives it up again, since she decides it is necessary for her to make frequent trips to Edinburgh for the purpose of buoying up the child's flagging spirits. If she does not do so, she says – and probably quite rightly – Stella will simply drop out before she has given the place a chance.

This means that Katherine now spends approximately one-third of her time north of the border, going through money that I'm not earning while the aforesaid bloody book is busy setting itself in concrete. She spends it, not only on the rail fare and the sleeping car, but on a form of comfort psychology for the Nuisance Chip that necessitates constant treats – visits to restaurants, theatres, shoe shops and beauticians' counters. The result is that the Precious Girl's running costs don't come cheap.

Yet I cannot deny that we are rewarded, at the end of Stella's first year, by the knowledge that – fingers crossed, eyes crossed, toes crossed – the child has stayed the course.

As the summer term comes to a close, Stella suddenly makes a forceful case for living out, *à deux*, in a rented flat with a girl she has met called Grania. Such a move, Stella asserts, will dramatically change her life. Yet Katherine discovers, through tearful disclosures on the eve of the vacation, that the girls have failed to secure the flat in question and by now there's nothing else. Each blames the other and, in short, they have screwed up.

Katherine possesses a dire, female instinct to play rescuer – though, in this case, both I and my mother try to stop her.

'Rescuers, Katherine dear,' my mother tells her, 'always become victims.' But Katie has the bit between her teeth.

Having made a comprehensive one-day survey of letting agencies in the city, she finds, of course, that the student pigsties have all been taken and that no commercial letting agency of sane mind will submit its property to the husbandry of students. Katherine's solution is to take the lease herself on a well-equipped, newly appointed flat and to masquerade as Madame Tenant. She supplies a bank reference, a character reference and a hefty cheque as deposit. In signing the contract, she submits herself not only to a rigorous inventory, but to the prospect of twice-termly inspections by the landlord's agent – a clause which requires her to make even more trips up to Edinburgh, these last at twenty-four hours' notice.

In preparation for these inspections, she will arrive off the sleeper at Waverley Station and make her way at dawn to the apartment, armed with rubber gloves, bin-bags, steel wool, cleaning cloths, Windolene, stain remover, several litres of Mr Muscle and a can of spray-on oven cleaner.

She lets herself in while both girls sleep, dons the gloves and wades knee-deep through discarded wine bottles and stinking milk cartons, her feet sticking to the floor through patches of spilt beer. She confronts, at high speed, the half-dozen pots containing encrusted bolognese sauce and the indeterminate dried gunk that coats all the hobs and the pedal bin. She cleans out the prodigious supply of pudding bowls, tumblers, teacups and violated storage jar lids that the inmates and their friends have pressed into service as ashtrays. She clears the grate and chisels red candlewax off the chimneypiece. She attacks windows, ledges and work surfaces. She squares up the sprawl of undergraduate books and papers, and tidies away the CDs. Having vacuumed, cleaned and dusted, she sprays the ground floor woodwork with polish and buffs it up, leaving on the air the reassuring whiff of beeswax.

Then she gathers up the potted dead geraniums and walks the hundred yards to the corner plant shop to replace them with new ones. At the same time, she buys cut flowers, which she places in a jug. She carts out six large bin-bags of debris and distributes these equitably amongst the neighbours' wheelie-bins.

At this point Katherine pauses for a cup of instant coffee, before making her way through to the bedrooms, where she wakes the girls with some difficulty and urges them into their clothes. She makes them cups of coffee and, when they have drunk it, dispatches them to the library with instructions not to return until after 4.30. Then she confronts the bathroom. She repairs the broken shower head, sorts their various oozing pots, tubes and jars, removes tidemarks and human hairs from the fixtures, polishes the taps, cleans the glass and confronts a lavatory bowl whose condition, she is convinced, threatens the Athens of the North with a second cholera epidemic.

In the girls' separate bedrooms, Katherine bags up their quantities of strewn, unwashed knickers along with their tights and jeans. She folds and stores jumpers. She stacks shoes in the cupboard. She flings open windows. She hangs up shirts and jackets. She changes bed linen and, once again, she hoovers and dusts. She takes down the girls' telling, age-determining posters and re-hangs the landlord's vacuous pastel-framed Athena reproductions of *fin de siècle* fashion prints on all the requisite hooks.

Finally, she bathes and changes her clothes. With a Mozart horn concerto on the CD player and with quantities of blusher on her cheeks to cover the signs of her exhaustion, Katherine then sits down *tête-à-tête* with the landlord's agent over a pot of Darjeeling and a plate of Brontë biscuits; Mrs Middle-aged Tenant with her sober and impeccable domestic habits.

Afterwards, perhaps to apologize for her intrusion into their squalor, Katherine sees fit to treat the girls to an evening out in a restaurant – even though she is left speechless by Stella's choice of flatmate. Grania, her black hair close-cropped to her fine, shapely cranium, raises a plucked eyebrow as she lights up Sobranies in the no-smoke section of the restaurant.

'Frankly,' she says, 'I fail to understand why you don't tell the landlord's agent to fuck off. It's none of his bloody business who's living in his pathetic little Do-It-All flat.' Katherine endeavours to grit her teeth in a smile as Grania continues. 'Still,' she says, 'it doesn't have patterned carpets. There is *that* to be grateful for.'

In the event the project is of no use to Stella, who becomes progressively more depressed. By the beginning of the second term she has fled from the apartment, which results in my bearing incredulous witness as Katie not only continues to pay Stella's half of the rent, thus subsidizing the flat-sharer who is now in sole occupation, but continues to make her twice-termly visits for the purpose of cleaning up after somebody else's daughter.

'Well, I can't evict the girl before her exams,' Katherine says. 'And if I do, we'll only be stuck with having to pay all the rent on the place ourselves until the end of June.'

True. This is true. But it is also true, as I point out, that to do so would save Katherine from the ignominy of having to prostrate herself before someone else's adolescent filthpacket. Yet, all the while, as I mock her and plead with her and score points off her, I know that both Katherine and I would put our heads on the railway line to see our beloved Stella happy. This, as they say in media speak, is the bottom line.

And then the Precious Girl obliges us. Her life turns around. She falls in love. She becomes visibly happy and, in doing so, she does herself proud. She plays, she sings, she wins golden opinions. And, appropriately perhaps, given her name, Stella falls in love with a star – because it does not take Katherine and me long at the School of Art degree show to deduce that Ishmael Valentine Tench is no ordinary under-sized, inarticulate, chain-smoking prole. Izzy Tench is a star and his star is surely rising. But I anticipate a little.

When Lydia telephones from the end of my street, the time is early May, and the School of Art degree show is still almost two months away. I am, in truth, all too ready to take a break from thoughts of my domestic life; and of Sonia; and of the concrete novel. I am also, for the moment, wishing to avoid thoughts of Sheila, my niece – of all people – who has recently, and most awkwardly, thrown a spanner into our lives. But more of this later.

This time I arrange to meet Lydia in the greasy spoon two steps down the street. Once again, she wears a mini-skirt and Doc Martens. Once again, though the hour is ten thirty in the morning, we order tea and cakes; tea that comes the colour of Newcastle Brown and wedges of sawdust cake.

'Oh yum,' Lydia says. She likes the sawdust cake and almost immediately gets crumbs of it in her buoyant, curly brown hair. 'These are the best,' she says. 'Oh yum.'

The draft she pulls out of a small leather backpack is singlespaced and printed with a cartridge suffering signs of chronic anaemia. The combination threatens death to my myopic mid-life eyesight.

'I expect it's crap,' she says, sounding remarkably untroubled.

'I'm sure it's not,' I say.

But I speak too soon. Perhaps a degree of romanticism in me about Lydia – sweet Lydia, nut-brown country maid of fruit and flowers – makes it inevitable that the draft will be a disappointment to me. I will not say that it is unbelievably bad, but the truth is, it is quite bad. It is nothing but slightly off-beam lumps of my own improvised spoutings – none of these elaborated, or properly integrated – interspersed with unnecessarily long sequences of quotation. The essay lacks shape.

It is not so much an essay as a pile of not-very-wonderful notes towards an essay.

For an hour over tea, I attempt the pedagogical mode, while Lydia bites her lip, blushes, shrugs, giggles, smiles and yawns. Mainly smiles and yawns. To correct the thing on the page, close printed as it is and with practically no margins, becomes increasingly impossible.

'Told you,' Lydia says cheerfully. 'Told you it'd be wrong from beginning to end.'

I laugh. 'It's not "wrong",' I say. 'That's not the point.'

Since Lydia has sensibly brought her disk, I suggest that we return with it to my place and sit down with it at the keyboard, improving it as we go along.

This is not a good move. When two people are at the word processor, one will seize the initiative. The other will become passive. Inevitably, because of my superior experience and knowledge, not to say intellect, it is I who seize the initiative. Before long, Lydia disengages completely. She begins to look around the room.

'Is that your wife?' she says. She screws her head backwards towards the framed photograph of Katherine on the bedside table.

'Yes,' I say. Then I ask her to tell me the difference between image and metaphor.

Lydia yawns. She is full of yawns this morning. 'She's pretty, isn't she?' she says. Then she says, 'Gosh, um. Sorry. I really am quite thick about poetry, aren't I?'

I suspect her of having come to me direct from an all-night party, which turns out to be the case. One of her school friends' parents has a house in Belsize Park where adolescents have been carousing till the second cock. This explains her early appearance in my street.

When the telephone rings, Lydia moves gratefully from her little hard stool to the adjacent armchair.

'Jonathan,' Sally says.

'Sally,' I say. Sally is sounding terrible; intense and tragic, but she discloses nothing except to say that she's got to see me – has got to – and can we please, *please* have lunch that very day. Same time, same place. It's important. I look at my watch and hesitate.

'Jon,' Sally says, 'Please.' We arrange for half past two, before I abruptly effect closure.

'Sorry,' I say, turning back to Lydia.

'Is Sally your wife?' Lydia says, trying to vamp up her exhausted slouch as I find myself registering that, unlike the two women I sleep with, Lydia has proper breasts; breasts that rise and fall with her breathing. Katherine has very small breasts, and Sonia has none at all.

Just then the telephone rings. 'Sonia,' I say.

'Is Sonia your wife?' Lydia says, out loud, and she giggles.

'You have company,' Sonia says. 'Oh, I say.'

We exchange some words about Puccini. Sonia is diversifying and has been to the opera two nights running. Plus she is going to see *Norma* on Thursday. All expenses paid. She comes over terrifically sociological about the Wild West and the Left Bank and Colonialism, etcetera. There is an attractive purity about the newness of her responses here – because, for some reason, it surprises her that Puccini should be taking on the contemporary scene.

'And then schmaltzing it up,' I say. 'And playing it oh so safe.'

'Spoilsport,' Sonia says, but her mood is remarkably sanguine.

'There's a man-eating woman waiting for you in Thursday's production,' I say.

'Oh goodie,' Sonia says. 'Goodie' is one of those words that Katherine and Stella use a lot when they're together, but it's fairly new to Sonia. 'Goodie' is, I believe, entirely gender-specific. By the time Sonia's off my telephone, Lydia is asleep in my armchair.

Oh shit, I think. Oh shit. Having now got the bit between my teeth, with regard to Wilhelm Müller and his mooching mill man, I find this latest development somewhat frustrating. I've begun to enjoy Lydia's essay as an escape from my own stuff. I have made the discovery that A level essays are a lot nicer and easier for grown-ups to write. They offer a quick-fix illusion of facility and cleverness. So, I think, what the hell. Let's get the kid off my back. I've got two hours. Who gives a bugger if she's awake or asleep? Let's abandon all pretence of collaboration here. Let's just keep on going.

I speed up, shorten, re-phrase, nip and tuck. I tidy the links. I define the hypothesis. I clarify the conclusion. Without Lydia to hold me back, it takes me precisely ninety-eight minutes to polish off the essay. I press the button to save it. Then I print it out. I read it through and shove it into her backpack along with her disk. I grab my jacket and make myself ready for lunch with Sally. Then I shake sweet Lydia from her rosy sleep. I lead her, yawning and rumpled, to the front door.

'I'm *so* sorry,' she says. 'Oh God. How could I? What happened?' She stumbles down the stairs, leaning heavily on my arm. 'Where are we going?' she says. She's still yawning. 'How long have I been asleep?'

'About two hours,' I say and I laugh. 'Further suggested revisions to your essay are in your backpack. *You* are going that way to the tube station, Lydia, OK?' I point her across the street to where the road runs uphill alongside a small park with a man-made lake; pond, more like. 'I'm going for the bus,' I say. 'Don't leave your backpack on the train, all right?'

'Thanks, Jonathan,' she says. We part just beyond the greasy spoon. 'You're a star,' she says. From across the street she waves both hands at me and blows kisses which I blow back. She calls out and does a funny little dance. I am much diverted by her, but I can't hear a word she says.

'What's that?' I say, cupping my ear.

'I'm singing, *die Sterne stehn zu hoch*,' she says. 'Look at me. I'm tap-dancing to Schubert.' Then she crosses her eyes and pulls gargoyle faces at me. I watch her until she's through. Then I wave her off and turn right. Next stop, unhappy Sally. My spirits slump abruptly. My hope is merely that she has no wish to discuss her daughter Sheila, who has been billeted, none too successfully, in my outhouse – mine and Katherine's.

The outhouse. A boring topic; a Home Improvement; a minor but preoccupying property owner's headache. I eschew all talk of dampcourse and soakaway, but the question of its occupancy has some bearing upon events.

To be brief, Katherine and I have, recently, upgraded what was referred to in the particulars pertaining to the Cottage-on-the-Green as 'potential for development as granny flat or studio'. In plain language, the house has a slate-roofed single-storey stone outhouse, like a row of three superior sheds joined together, and it comes with planning permission to convert this into a dwelling. We have no sooner done so, now, in Stella's second year of university – and with a view to renting it out as a way of recouping on some of her costs – than we use it, in emergency, to house my brother's daughter Sheila.

The future for poor old sparky Sheila is not looking good. I run into her in a shop doorway and cart her off to the burger dump to stuff her with instant food – after which she declares herself in need of my help in weaning herself off the druggy boyfriend who is also, of course, her supplier. She will no longer speak to either of her parents.

'My dad's scared stiff of me,' she says, 'and my mum just rabbits on about body piercing.'

After consultation with Katherine, and after a morning spent wrestling with the medical bureaucracy, we fix her up with a sojourn in a clinic to be followed up by a spell of rehab in our outhouse, but billeting Sheila soon materializes as a pretty terrible idea. All my formidably laid ground rules nothwithstanding, Sheila discharges herself almost immediately from the clinic and the boyfriend is in there within the week, along with several friends and a pair of indeterminate wolflike dogs, neither of whom have collars.

The party comes and goes in a noisy, clapped-out Vauxhall Astra fitted with giant speakers and sporting one door painted matt oxblood. Intellectual consistency not being a major side-effect of addiction, Sheila now appears to welcome this development with enthusiasm and is instantly re-assimilated so that, within twelve hours, Katie and I are The Enemy; the landlord and the landlord's moll; the bad custodians. That's us.

The twerp and the bikist immediately lobby us over the Vauxhall Astra, which they consider lowering to the tone of the green and, further to that, the canines' prodigious crapping habits bring the fraggle-haired sociologist to a state of understandable frenzy. By day three, the Telephone Cascade has transformed itself into an avalanche, as the party embarks upon its day job, which is, of course, breaking and entering. Then the police come along and take the matter out of our hands.

But the business not only leaves a bad taste. It draws us into proximity with the fraggle-haired sociologist, who clearly fears the possibility of having alienated my wife, and comes to make her peace. By the next day, in my absence, she has offered Katherine an olive branch in the form of an ideal tenant for us: a lady academic from London, a colleague, she says, who is taking up a job at Oxford in October. During that summer for two to three months, this paragon will need somewhere to live while her own place is being made ready. Market rates, cash on the nail, rent in advance, the works. Katie meets the tenant during the following week and declares her utterly charming. The deal is struck in the week preceding my meeting with

Lydia in the greasy spoon, and Katherine banks the money with relief.

And I, too, am soon to be on the move. Having succumbed to the idea of the three-year writer's fellowship, I have finally informed my dear Quaker landlady of my intention to give up the bedsit from the end of July. It is no longer really working for me. Plus our house is now empty of the Nuisance Chip and the fellowship, due to start in October, comes with a college room overlooking cobbled lanes and Christchurch Meadow. The hope, too, is that to move back home will bring me closer to Katherine.

Katherine has once again got herself a job, this time working in the art bookshop in Oxford. The sight of my sweet Katie kitted out in her working clothes of a Monday morning never fails to inflame me – though there is, of course, something utterly perverse about propositioning a person who is about to fly out for the train.

Katherine's new clothes bring back to me what a glossy, dressy girl she always was when I first met her; what flair she invariably displayed in getting her kit together – before I sank her in the Irish idyll and forced her into hiking jumpers and thermal vests; before she embarked upon the vicarious activity of glamming up the Nuisance Chip. In addition, Katherine has resumed the habit of reading books. Proper books. Not Casebook-Studies-in-English-Literature-for-A-Level sort of books. Yet Katherine, as I say, has become inexplicably remote.

When I get home, she is either bubbly-remote, or clapped-out-remote. She is tired from gadding with 'friends'. Or she is just about to go out to meet up with 'friends'. Sometimes she goes out, like Little Red Riding Hood, with a basket over her arm. She has plastic tubs of food in the basket and a folded pinny on the top. She is helping out 'friends', she says.

So, unsurprisingly, Katherine is not in the house on the

evening when I return home two days early. It is a Wednesday. It is the evening in late June on which my daughter is due home with Izzy Tench. It is the evening of the day on which, four hours earlier, I have met with Sonia and have finally taken her to Fortnum's. It is the evening upon which, all unbeknown to me, poor, sweet Lydia Dent comes to see me in my absence, and dies on my doorstep.

Let us imagine for a moment that I do not know of Lydia's accident; that I do not know that I have seen her for the last time – or that, when I next 'see' her, I do not, in fact, see her. What I see is a plain cardboard coffin set at the front of a chapel which is full of red-eyed schoolgirls. Let us imagine that I have licence, still, to dwell upon other matters which converge with that appalling occurrence. There is the matter of Sonia and Fortnum's.

Sonia has been so busy since the Amsterdam TV interview that I have not seen all that much of her. And I have not – until this very day – seen her at all since the middle of May; not since the week after her opera week. She has been out of town quite a bit – here and there – and has telephoned to cancel twice. But today, midweek, mid-afternoon, Sonia appears in excellent form. She has a sort of smiley glow that ought to put me on my guard, and her fine sensitive skin is looking good. She enters with a bottle of Veuve Clicquot and with a bunch of those new-fangled, up-market, politically incorrect flowers that look as though they've been taking lessons from one of Katie's Jocasta Innes manuals. She kisses me on the cheek.

'What are we celebrating?' I say, once I've closed the door behind her and smooched her mouth clean of her lipstick that today comes Jane Russell red.

'Oh,' she says, 'this and that. Let's just call it your fellowship, Jonathan.' Having handed me the flowers, she places the palm of her hand four-square on my trouser zip and she sighs a little sigh.

I find that Sonia is, right now, a pleasing presence. Not only is she remarkably unspiky, but, for once, I really like her clothes. She is wearing a sage-green linen sheath dress with a Chinese collar and little slits up the sides. A vertical row of off-white buttons runs the length of the front from throat to hem. It's exactly the sort of dress that Katherine might choose. She has white button earrings and white high-heeled slingbacks on her feet. Her hair has been newly dealt with in the style of a post-war Coke ad and it gives off a faint whiff of shellac. She looks like a fifties movie star. I am so busy admiring the hair and the skin and the dress that it takes me a while to realize that there is something different about Sonia because, today, Sonia has boobs.

Meanwhile, she draws two plastic champagne flutes from her white beadwork handbag and sets them on my work table. One has a lime-green barley-sugar stem and the other has a vertical row of blue sparkly balls, each ball standing on the north pole of the ball below it.

'Open it,' Sonia says. 'Come on. Hurry up.' While I do so, she dumps the flowers carelessly on the table, leaving them constricted by their wrapping. 'Who gives a bugger for flowers?' she says. 'Bimbos, all of them. Cunts where their brains ought to be. Isn't that right? They do sex with their heads, don't they? Why do their lives have to be so easy?' And Sonia sighs another little sigh.

I hand her the barley-sugar glass and I take the bauble one for myself. 'Is something the matter?' I say.

'Oh no,' she says and she raises her glass. 'Jonathan, here's to us.'

After a bit she kicks off her shoes and presses her pelvis into mine. In response, I plant my free hand on her bum. In doing so, I discover her to be a woman devoid of buttocks. She is encased, under the slim, Chinese sheath dress, in some sort of tubular carapace with hard vertical spines spaced at eight-centimetre intervals. This apparatus doubtless accounts for why she has boobs.

'Jesus Christ, Sonia,' I say, 'what the hell are you wearing?' I make a start on the buttons of the sheath dress. I keep going until she is divested of it and is then standing before me in this copious, severely elasticated item, flesh-coloured and punctuated with awesome seams of whalebone. The central panel is made of nasty, tarnished satin. The thing looks like a peculiarly punitive exhibit from a surgical appliance museum. It sports a 'modesty panel' which runs in a straight horizontal line across the top of Sonia's thighs, and flesh-coloured suspenders, three to a side, emerge from below this panel to clamp Sonia's stocking-tops in horrible scoops and swags.

The conical boob compartments, shaped like coolies' hats – and completely hollow in Sonia's case – are made from satin-covered milliner's buckram backed with perishing flesh-coloured foam rubber. The rubber smells like old school erasers and it gives off granules at a touch.

'My mother wore this on the day I was conceived,' Sonia says. 'I have a fancy to be ravished in it.'

'Get it off, for God's sake,' I say, before I realize that Sonia is quite serious. For reasons that I cannot quite fathom, getting laid in the carapace seems to signify – though I know Sonia admires her mother; her mother and her grandmother. They are, including herself, three generations of strong, non-marrying women, she asserts. They have always made their own way.

So I steer her towards the bed and make efforts to oblige her, but the carapace defeats me. It's like trying to commit sex with an armadillo. The suspender clamps bother my aesthetic sense, as do the rotting boob compartments, which instantly turn concave with the pressure of my body. Having discovered the thing to be fixed along its left side seam with a hundred hooks and eyes, I endeavour, then, to wrench the hooks towards me – thus displacing its panelled sections and causing the right false boob compartment to lodge itself under Sonia's right arm, while the left is now four-square over her sternum. The thing looks ever more repellent to me.

I give up on the hooks and turn to loosening the suspenders, though their obduracy makes me irritable and I promptly wrench one suspender entirely free of the carapace.

'Temper, temper,' Sonia says, letting slip some of her old gladiatorial style.

Even with loosened suspenders, the modesty panel operates effectively to keep me from Sonia's treasures. It rolls itself into a stubborn wadded ring that clamps itself tight around Sonia's thighs. By now I am ready to rip the bloody thing off her with a breadknife, but instead I return to wrestle with the hooks and eyes. These are now aligned, off centre, down Sonia's left front.

When I have got the thing off her, I fling it angrily into a corner, where, for a moment, it stands up on its own, looking like an object one might use to saddle a malformed horse. The ultrasensitive skin of Sonia's chest has begun to get one of its nasty rashes from the rubbery granules, plus her body is by now vertically indented, at eight-centimetre intervals, with a brutal pattern of whalebone. I find that my desire has entirely left me.

'Oh, dear,' Sonia says, eyeing my shrunken crotch somewhat gloatingly. 'Oh, dear. Is that impotence or detumescence?'

Perhaps I am too defensive in response. 'Let's forget it,' I say quickly. 'Let's just get bloody dressed and go to bloody Fortnum's.'

Sonia sits up and smiles at me. She employs the goodie word with additions. 'Oh, goodie gumdrops,' she says and she climbs back into the carapace.

All the way to the tea-room Sonia is merry and skittish. She drapes herself over me, taking on a slightly ironic role as besotted honeymoon wife. She has made repairs to her hair and her lipstick and the high Chinese collar is obscuring the rash across her chest. There is no doubt that Sonia is looking great.

'I'm so glad we're "going out",' she says. In the tea-room, she insists on a table bang near the door. She plays footsie with me. She plants a kiss on my cheek, she picks food from my plate. She frequently touches my sleeve.

'I really like you, Jonathan,' she says, suddenly. 'You jammy bastard.' And she kicks me under the table.

'What's that supposed to mean?' I say, but Sonia will only smile; the radiant Jane Russell smile.

Once I have paid the bill and we have got up to go, Sonia turns to me, her arm linked with mine. 'Do you often "go out" with women?' she says. 'Or only when you can't get it up?' But when I turn and look at her, she adds, 'Ignore that, Jonathan. Consider it sour grapes.'

Once in the street, she detaches herself from me with a suddenness that momentarily confuses me, and she hails herself a cab. She makes it clear that I am to get my own. 'No hard feelings,' she says. 'It's been great, but I think you will agree with me that the time has come.'

I stand and watch her go. As I do so I feel decisively outwitted. Bloody women, I think and, though it is only Wednesday, I am sufficiently pissed off not to wish to return to the bedsit and face the lone, flesh-pink suspender. Instead I decide to make my way direct to Paddington, with the intention of returning home to my wife.

On the train I seek out a nice un-peopled nook, but I am joined, just as the whistle blows, by a casually clothed lager man of enormous dimensions, who seats himself opposite me and places two steel crutches, as a barrier, across the aisle. He possesses, aside from his encroaching girth, a can of Stella Dry, a mobile telephone and a broken leg encased in plaster from groin to instep, which emerges from a sawn-off trouser leg.

He heaves the leg onto the seat beside me, his naked toes invading my personal space. The toes are unpleasantly cheesy, since the lager man has evidently been obliged to perform somewhat restricted ablutions from the advent of the plaster cast. Quite a while, I decide, from the doggy look of it and from the mass of idiot scrawlings thereon. On the shin, directly in my line of vision, a female person has written 'Bad luck Ucle Perce love Nina.' A small heart-shape deputizes for the dot over the 'i' in Nina. This is what my Stella refers to as 'Sharon writing'.

Somewhere near Slough, Ucle Perce sees fit to make a call on the mobile phone. 'I'm sat here on the train with me can of Stella and me broken leg, and I'm just coming into Slough,' he says. Then he says, 'Cheers, mate,' and he signs off. Sometime later, when nearing Maidenhead, he makes another call: 'I'm sat here on the train with me can of Stella and me broken leg,' he says, 'and I'm just coming into Maidenhead.' Then he says, 'Cheers, mate,' and signs off.

I find myself loathing and despising this man. I loathe his phone. I loathe his niece with her moron spelling and her Holly Hobbit calligraphy. By Reading, I am fit to sever Ucle Perce's head. Fascistic and élitist. I know. Think I own the world. I know. But I am out of sorts with human kind.

Sonia is a shining light and I have managed to lose her. Bloody Sally has been on my telephone again, but, for the moment, I have stalled her. She has 'things to tell me', she says. The last time she also had 'things to tell me' – things which right now rise to knock me sideways as they bang me over the head.

Roger, Sally has told me, has decisively shipped out. Without her managerial assistance, he has risen from his bed, packed his clothes, his papers, his desktop and his laptop, and he has moved it all, along with himself, into his rooms in college. She assumes he is also eating his meals in the college dining-hall, where alcohol, dairy produce, sugar, fruit juice, mushrooms, tea, coffee, chocolate, yeast and wheat flour are presumably no longer an issue, she remarks.

'I think,' Sally says – and it's the afternoon of the day, in early May, on which I've polished off Lydia's essay – 'I think, Jonathan, that Roger is having an affair.'

'Oh, for God's sake, Sal,' I say. 'An affair? My brother?' At the time, the idea strikes me as utterly ludicrous. Now, in a flash, it is all too alarmingly credible.

Time for me to come clean. My brother Roger – scourge of Sally's pressure cooker and demon offal-eater; maths nerd and inexplicable heart-throb – was Katie's first great love, just as she, gorgeous creature, was mine. I had no sooner caught a distant glimpse, from my schoolboy bike saddle, of this exquisite female creature stepping from – of all things – a white Alfa Romeo in my parents' drive; a creature all legs and strappy shoes and pale, shampoo ad hair, than I discovered her, half an hour later, in the family kitchen, with her eyes fixed upon my brother. I was sixteen and Roger, like Katherine, was eighteen. At the time it made all the difference in the world.

Katherine was a philosophy student, a pupil of my dear, late father, who had been brought to the house, through a series of coincidences, by an old friend of the family. That day she fell instantly and heavily for Roger, who promptly annexed her, only to sharpen his insecurities and his snobberies on her. He determinedly read her interest in clothes as evidence of her frivolity, and her origins as a north London greengrocer's daughter as evidence of her intellectual inferiority. I suppose, looking back, that poor old Roger, his beauty notwithstanding, simply thought that any woman who agreed to append herself to him couldn't be worth the having. But there it was.

Over most of their time at university, Roger managed simultaneously to monopolize her and to make her miserable, until at last he dumped her for Sally's somewhat short-lived predecessor – a lank-haired, posh-voiced music student whose father owned a publishing house – while rejection drove Katherine precipitously to Rome, at a time when my back was turned. I met her again ten years later. Her Roman love life had come to grief and her very young baby had been found dead in its cot. Perhaps I can be said to have 'rescued' her?

It is always lowering to hear one's mother's maxims reverberating in one's head – and, right now, whilst sitting opposite the odious Ucle Perce, I hear that penetrating, maternal RP voice. It burns a hole in my brain. 'Rescuers, Katherine dear, always become victims.'

I am not temperamentally given to perceiving myself as victim. 'Cocky' is what my dear mother is habitually pleased to call me. But right now, I don't feel quite the king of the farmyard. Not two hours ago, I have shed Sonia Middleton – and in circumstances denting to the male ego. Right now, and far more dreadfully, the fact confronts me that I have once again lost Katherine to my brother.

I have for a while been staring glumly at my own reflection in the carriage window as a means of avoiding Ucle Perce's toes along with Nina's inscription. I stare hard, understanding, at last, why it is that Katherine and I have been passing, of late, like the weatherhouse man and the weatherhouse lady, never quite coinciding. I understand why it is that Katherine shies away from my embraces. I understand the new swing she has in her step and the new interest she takes in her appearance. I understand how it is that Katherine comes in so late from her job and how it is that she is constantly helping 'friends' with their interiors, or 'friends' with their catering requirements. It is precisely because Roger cannot make a bed, or hang a curtain. It is because Roger cannot cook. And I, of all people, should know the lingering power of a person's first love.

'Cheer up, mate,' says Ucle Perce, clanking his crutches as he struggles to make his exit at Reading. 'It may never happen.' He leaves his crushed lager can on the seat beside me.

I do something then that I have never done before. With my index finger I write in the steam of the carriage windowpane. I write, 'Nina is a slag.' I do it deftly in mirror-writing, hoping that Ucle Perce will see it as he heaves himself down the platform. I hope that he will twirl his crutches madly about his head in rage. 'Crippled passenger found prostrated on Platform 8.' '"Disabled customer" is more proper,' I say, but I mumble the words unintelligibly to myself.

By the time I reach home, I am in a state of high agitation. Katherine is not in the house, but I find her, eventually, in the outhouse, where I succeed in stoking a row. She is piling up stacks of matching bath towels and duvet covers, playing chambermaid for the new tenant who plans to take up residence in ten days' time. It seems to me that there is nothing Katherine likes better, now that she is finally shot of skivvying for Stella, than to place herself under somebody's feet. It's a habit she cannot break.

'That isn't necessary,' I say. She ignores me and carries on stacking. 'You don't have to do that,' I say. After a pause, I say, pathetically, 'You're never in the house when I get home.'

'What?' Katherine says.

I admit that this is a pretty lame form of attack, no less so because it is true. Katherine is forever on the gad these days. She has even become rather matey with the prospective tenant. She has told me so on the phone. They have tried on dresses in Whistles together. They have visited an outlet called Stella Mannering together, where they pick over Tricia Guild soft furnishings. Then they drink cappuccinos and banana milk-shakes – milkshakes! – in Brown's Restaurant across the road.

'That's rich,' Katherine says, 'coming from you.' She goes on bustling with her items of household linen.

'Katherine,' I say, 'we have to talk.'

She makes a great show of counting pillowcases. 'Personally,' she says, 'I'd rather watch the Channel Four News.'

'Katie,' I say. 'I don't happen to walk around with a white stick. Not yet.'

'Sorry?' Katherine says. Her hair, newly bobbed, swings divinely as she turns her head. What an utter sweetheart she is.

'What I'm saying,' I say, 'is that you don't have to pretend to me that there's nothing going on.'

At this point she dumps the pile of stuff on the bed. 'Between whom?' she says. 'Just what exactly are you saying to me, Jonathan?'

Oh Christ. 'Come on, Katherine,' I say, bulldozing on. '(a) You're never at home any more. (b) When you are, you're walking on air and it's sure as hell not for me. (c) Your clothes are all different. (d) You scurry off like Little bloody Red Riding Hood with your basket full of treats—'

'Oh I see,' she says. 'Is that what I do? And I do it in enumerated subsections (a) to (d). Well, well. Are you saying that you'd prefer me to be at home in my undies waiting for you with parted lips and my KY Jelly at the ready?'

This last is very Katie. She has never used KY Jelly, but her rhetoric is pretty down-putting once her anger is up.

'Mrs Dishcloth Goldman,' she says, 'stirring the porridge pot for you in her frillies? Give me a break, Jonathan. For one thing, I have a job to go to these days. It requires me to climb out of my tracky bottoms. I go to work five mornings a week, though it's not surprising you haven't noticed. As for points (b) and (d), I'm really not prepared to talk to you about it. Not while you adopt this stupid, confrontational tone. Just go get lost, duckie. Just go into the house and calm down. Maybe you're hungry? There's a seafood risotto I've made. It's on the stove. There's lots of it, so don't go eating it all.'

'It's interesting that you've made so much of it,' I say. 'Does Roger happen to like seafood risotto?'

Katherine gulps and swallows. She takes a deep breath. Then she lets it out again. She says nothing. She shuts her eyes and purses her lips. Finally, she deigns to speak.

'You'll notice if you look at it carefully,' she says, 'that it's full of the things that Roger can't eat. It has mushrooms, wine, butter, Parmesan cheese and God knows what—'

'So you're pretty clued up on his dietary fads, then,' I say.

Katie sits down on the bed. 'OK,' she says. 'I see your brother. I work about four minutes' walk from his college. And, OK, I cook for him occasionally. I make up batches of the food he can eat and I take it to the college chef who stores it for him in the freezer. Sometimes I even eat lunch with him, just the way you eat out with Sally. He's depressed, Jonathan. And he's ill. He's been ill for years. The man is rehabilitating himself. Do you ever think of what his life's been like, living with that woman? Plus the three King Lear daughters – all of them control freaks like Sally? And one of them turned serious druggie? Try thinking about it, if you can stop thinking about yourself for five minutes.'

'Oh please—' I say.

'He's lethargic, Jonathan,' Katherine says. 'You don't know what that means, you lucky bastard. You've always been tough as old boots. For two years he's hardly been able to get himself out of bed. He's found a doctor, at last, who's begun to make him better and all Sally has done meanwhile is sabotage and undermine – and gang up with those witch girls. If you don't believe me about your nieces, just try asking poor little Stella.'

'Katherine—' I say, but she rolls on.

'So finally Roger has made it to get up and leave the house. And, yes, I helped him pack up his stuff. And now, since he has no energy, I've helped him sort out his rooms. And now, because he's on a diet, I've helped him with some of his menus.

Look, Jonathan, he can't cook – but I'd have been afraid to touch the pots in that house. She'd have made me all thumbs. Even if nothing scares you, Jonno, I want you to understand that Sally *scares* me. She's got that place set up like the bloody Berkeley Homes Show House. Miss the perforations while tearing off a strip of bog paper and you'd be breaking the house rules. She's been out to kill his creativity for years. She's had no wish to nurture his talent. Well, he *is* very able, Jonathan. And women like her are two a penny—'

'Oh, give the poor girl a break,' I say. 'So she's not your type. She's not mine either. She's a decent, conventional Englishwoman – and cohabiting with a loony like Roger has totally blown her mind. Besides, she has an honest job to get on with. She's a competent, busy professional woman. She's been going out to work all these years while Roger's been lying in bed lobbing apple cores into the grate and pissing into old jam jars.'

Katie looks absolute daggers at me. 'If all this "competent professional woman" stuff is another swipe at my underachievement, Jonathan, I'd like to ask you where you think Stella would be if I had gone gadding off to London with a briefcase and a bunch of files like Sally these twenty years. I'd also like to ask you what you actually know about Sally's job.'

I'm on dodgy ground here, but I brazen it out as is my wont. 'She's an educational consultant,' I say. 'Something boring; something worthy. Who cares? And can we please stop talking about Sally? I came home to talk about us.'

'She's a spy,' Katherine says, which slightly knocks the breath out of me. 'Her job is to sniff out illegal immigrants. Sure, she worked as an "educational consultant" – something like a hundred years ago.' I stare at her in blank disbelief. 'Oh, she's not the person who bashes down people's doors and drags them away from their families,' she says. 'She has underlings who do that for her.' After a pause, she says, 'You can go pretty far in the Civil Service these days with that Home-Counties-

and-Oxbridge air that Sally has. So long as you're right-wing enough and xenophobic enough and stuffed with enough pathetic outmoded notions of what England ought to be. But, as you say, Sally is a conventional English Rose.'

Then, as I gawp at her, Katherine says, 'Izzy Tench's father was a Lebanese engineer, by the way. Stella told me. He was deported when Izzy was two. So the boy grew up with one of those evil single mothers who scrounge off us all on benefits. He's never met his father.'

Before I can observe that this is hardly Sally's fault, Katherine drops her bombshell. 'Sonia's grandfather too,' she says casually. 'He was a German POW; a woodcarver who wanted nothing more than to settle down and marry his pregnant girlfriend in Northumberland.'

I say nothing. I watch her pause to savour her impact before squaring up the bedcover.

'There are always enough school prefects around, like Sally,' she says, 'to ensure that people can't simply be happy together.' Then she says, 'You don't really drink PG Tips, do you, Jonathan? I do hope not. They're the people who abuse chimpanzees in their advertisements. Anyway, I always thought you were a Twinings man, myself.' Oh goodie.

When I say nothing for long enough, Katherine invites me to sit down with her on the bed. 'She's our tenant, by the way,' Katherine says. 'And I really like her a lot. And I must say that, to her credit, she came clean about you right away – the moment she made the connection. Well, the moment she'd sussed that Sally had made the connection too and would be onto me without delay. She tells me that it's over and I would like to believe her.'

But, before I can say a word, Katie says, 'Sonia met Sally through her recent efforts to trace her German grandfather. Apparently, after he'd been deported, Sonia's pregnant grandmother walked out on her somewhat grand family and tried several times to find him, but she always drew a blank. Naturally, Sally has access to all sorts of interesting files.' Then she says, 'Sonia stayed with me last week, by the way, while we got our heads together over refurbishing the Master's Lodgings.'

The Master's Lodgings. Sonia. Right. I do not damage my already disadvantaged position by supplicating for an explanation at this point, but I begin to realize what exactly it was Sonia and I were celebrating.

'All I will say,' Katherine says, 'is, you touch her under my roof, Jonathan, and I'm out of here. Do you understand me?'

I maintain my silence for so long that she adds, 'You do know who I'm talking about, of course? I'm talking about Sonia Middleton. Professor Sonia Middleton. Newly appointed Master of St Austin's College, Oxford – the college which is honouring you from October with a temporary writer's fellowship.' Ouch. 'The college where your brother is a distinguished and much valued maths fellow; the fourth most cited mathematician in the world, incidentally.' Ouch. 'I looked him up on the Internet,' Katie says.

'"The Internet?"' I say, finally finding my voice. I'm thinking what the hell has my Rosie O'Grady got to do with the Internet.

'And, yes,' Katherine says, 'I can use the Internet even if you can't. My job requires it of me. I've been promoted, by the way. And little wonder, when most of my colleagues can't tell Jacob Epstein from Brian "Ep*steen*". All they know is Klimt and other such undergraduate fads. Now, if you'll excuse me, my daughter is coming home this evening with her boyfriend, and – though I may not be young and sweet any more – I would still like to primp a bit and try my best to look nice. Plus, I'm tired of this conversation. If you think I've got the time and energy for sexual adventure, why don't you first try checking out my libido and what twenty years of family life has done for it?'

Then my sweet, lovely Katherine starts to cry. And I have done this. I have made her cry. I move to comfort her, but she backs off and aborts the tears with a quick, proud sniff.

'Kath,' I say, 'what can I say to you? I'm abject and contrite. I don't deserve you. I worship you. I always have. In that sense there has never been anyone else.'

'Yes,' Katherine says. 'I know that. But I think I've also always known that you screw around. It doesn't seem to cross your mind that it's not only hurtful to me, but it's dangerous. And I won't have it. Not any more. These are the nineties, Jonathan.' She pats the same bloody cushion for the umpteenth time. Then she says, 'I've had an AIDS test, by the way, and I want you to have one too. Why do you think I've stopped having sex with you?'

I stare at her hard. 'Are you being serious?' I say.

'Well, if you imagine it's because I'm lusting after your brother,' Katherine says, 'let me reassure you. I wouldn't care to have him in my bed. Not these days. OK, so he has the sort of pin-up good looks that adolescent girls go mad for. And tomorrow is my fiftieth birthday. And, thank you, I don't want any presents. Not from you. Nor any facile compliments either.'

It is at this point that we both become aware that Izzy Valentine Tench, the boy genius, is standing in the doorway and that he is carrying two backpacks and a James Thin carrier bag, along with Stella's cello.

'Sorry,' he says, 'but have you seen Stella? I lost her in a café.'

And that was three years ago. Neither Katie nor I has seen Stella for over a thousand days. She will neither speak to us, nor write to us, nor grant us an audience. We know that in that time she has given birth to a daughter, called Holly, who was born on Bonfire Night, two and a half years ago. This makes her eight hundred and seventy days old.

Izzy Tench stayed with us through that first week, but he would not elaborate nor speculate on the circumstances of their getting separated. Izzy's medium is visual, not verbal. 'I lost her in a café' was all he could come up with. After that, he moved on to roam the Middle East.

Thanks to another of Stella's Edinburgh housemates, one Peregrine Massingham, we were not kept in doubt of her whereabouts beyond one dreadful night. He told us that, for reasons he could not disclose, she had returned promptly to Edinburgh and would then accompany him home to Northumberland. She subsequently dropped out of her degree course. She has never honoured us with an explanation.

We know that Stella is still there with the Massingham family in Northumberland, and we conjecture, between the lines, that she has most likely had a serious nervous breakdown. We know that she has married Peregrine and I take this to be a marriage of convenience.

We know this, in the first instance, thanks to Sally, who telephones, hot-foot, one morning as Katherine and I are about to have our breakfast. 'If you haven't read the personal columns of today's *Times*,' she says, 'then I suggest you do so right away.'

The *Times* in question carries a notice of the wedding, which has taken place in Venice. And, to Peregrine's credit, we receive, by post that morning, a brief three-line communication telling us of the marriage. Peregrine, who is somewhat proper, not to say stuffed-shirt, in these matters, refers to Stella as 'frail', or 'unwell'. His is a family of wealthy Catholic industrialists, and his parents have ten children. He and Stella live, independently, in the grounds of a country estate. At our most emotionally low, it cuts us deeply, Katherine and me, that among such an excess of progeny these people should have inherited not only our precious only daughter, but also our only grandchild.

The message that comes at regular intervals is that Stella, whether rightly or wrongly, feels that, for her own emotional health, she can neither see us nor communicate with us.

Peregrine, I have had to deduce, has behaved fairly well. A part of me holds him suspect, but Katherine urges me not to, because that way madness lies. He came to see us once, two years ago, and has volunteered to come again.

Remembering that occasion, I suppose I did not behave terribly well. Something about being telephoned by a young Ampleforth snot who has become the custodian of one's daughter and one's grandchild. He is staying overnight in the Randolph Hotel, he says, having been in London on business. He has come up in the hopes of meeting with us. He suggests that we join him at his hotel for dinner, but I insist, cussedly, that he come to us instead, which he does, poor boy, in a hastily hired car and at no small inconvenience to himself.

The food is inappropriately un-special and poor Katie drops gollops of tears into her plate. She finds it impossible not to weep almost non-stop throughout the evening, while I all but freeze him out. I suspect him and his family of laying claim to Stella's mind. They do, after all, belong to what I regard as a highly sinister and authoritarian religious organization.

When Peregrine asks us, as he takes his leave, whether he might carry with him Stella's cello, both Katherine and I stiffen, but then, of course, we agree. If the Precious Girl has want of her cello – well, when have we ever denied her anything? Peregrine, on that occasion, comes with photographs for us, both of Stella and of the child – and he has been true to his word in sending photographs with regularity, ever since. The child is a little blonde sweetheart and looks quite excruciatingly like Katherine.

For the first year after Stella's defection, Katherine's spirit almost entirely leaves her body. She goes into work, she comes home, and that's it. Nothing in life interests her. Nothing amuses her. It becomes a series of grim survival routines. There are times when we think it might be easier for us had Stella, like Lydia, simply died that night – or had we died ourselves.

'If Stella was dead, then I could kill myself,' as Katherine says to me one day. 'The only reason I want to be alive is in case my daughter comes back.' If anything positive comes of the business, it is that Katherine and I cling together. We move from shipwreck to mutual support.

Sally, Sonia, Roger – all of them recede, though Sonia proves herself a model tenant during that summer, and evolves into a valued family friend. She leaves us alone when we need it, and becomes a source of strength and conviction to Katherine. Knowing Sonia for the provoking and mercurial creature that I do, I was inclined, initially, to hold her suspect in her role as ideal tenant, but the letting arrangement had been the result of genuine and innocent coincidence. I had never given Sonia my home address and I had always refused to discuss my wife with her, even to the point of withholding Katherine's name.

Having travelled up to meet Katherine in my absence, Sonia, of course, instantly recognized her from the photograph in the London bedsit. Not only that, but her eyes lit upon a second photograph on the bureau in our sitting-room – one, taken by my mother, of Katherine and me walking, arm in arm, on Hampstead Heath. At this stage, she tells me, she was all set to turn down the tenancy, though a combination of curiousity and attraction to Katherine held her in the house long enough for them to become firm friends.

And what clinched the thing was that, the previous day, Sonia had left the phone number of her prospective landlady with Sally's assistant as a place where she could be reached during a part of the afternoon. And Sally, who had rumbled me, likes, of course, to know everything about everybody. At that point, Sonia decided to jump the gun and come clean with Katherine.

According to Katherine, both of them, having drunk in what had happened, burst into tears; then they flung their arms around each other; then they had supper together in our kitchen. They drank a lot and it got late. Sonia stayed over and, the next day, in Katie's lunch hour, they looked over the Master's Lodgings together, which are large enough to house a small school. The day after that was Tuesday. They lunched together in the Ashmolean café, after which they flew upstairs, passing through the exhibition room, to the bust of Sir Christopher Wren. They agreed that he was a gorgeous bloke and just their type.

'The problem is,' Katherine tells me, 'that we both like brainy men. And you can tell by his face that he's brainy.'

Sonia's response was to say she'd like to kill me. And so it went.

A couple of weeks later, on yet another of her visits to Oxford, Sonia roped Katherine into visiting a dress shop with her, where Katherine bought a jacket and Sonia bought a sage-green linen dress with a Chinese collar and a row of white buttons down the front. After that, she returned promptly to London and touched down on her flat where she donned the carapace and sallied forth to ply me with champagne and bring me flowers, before denting my ego and aiming a blow at my shin in Fortnum's tea-room.

In the event, these matters pale into insignificance in the face of our grief – mine and Katherine's – over our precious daughter's defection. Were anyone at that time to have found us sexy people, I would have judged them seriously warped in the brain.

Dear Sonia, in her new role as college head, quickly puts a stop to Katherine's incessant catering for Roger and insists that this be undertaken by the college chef as part of his routine duties. And I may say that it is entirely thanks to Sonia's encouragement that Katherine begins to write. She writes children's stories. Katie sits all alone in the pristine, un-let outhouse –

un-let since Sonia's departure for the Master's Lodgings. She sits, every evening after work, for hours and weeks and months and, without making her intention known to me – without quite making it known to herself – she addresses five books of stories to a little girl called Holly whom she has never met. She teaches herself Japanese book-binding and acquires sheaves of beautiful handmade paper from Falkiner Fine Papers Ltd in Southampton Row. She transcribes the stories, elegantly spaced, in her beautiful italic handwriting, leaving alternate pages empty for the pictures.

Finally, she makes contact with Izzy Tench through information about his whereabouts she finds in one of the art magazines in her shop, and she arranges to go and see him. She meets him in his new studio off the Mile End Road and takes along not only the books and photocopies to leave with him, but also a sheaf of photographs taken of Holly and Stella. One of the stories is called 'Holly Finds the Butter Melon'.

Izzy is making sketches for a portrait of the Poet Laureate at the time, but the boy genius breaks off to give her books his whole attention.

'But these are great, Katherine,' he says at last. 'These books are really superb.' It is, perhaps, the longest and most committed utterance she has ever heard from him. To her joy, he expresses an eagerness to illustrate them and he produces, in time, a series of exquisite drawings in soft brown pencil which have – as do Katie's texts – the quality of messages in bottles. Four of the books are published at six-monthly intervals over two years, and a fifth is due out next Christmas. They become, while not quite a mass-market event, a sustained cultish success – and Izzy's illustrations are ultimately exhibited as a series in the exhibition room of the Ashmolean Museum, through which Sonia and Katherine once passed on their way to the bust of Sir Christopher Wren.

* * *

Sonia, having moved into the Master's Lodgings in the September of that horrible year, appears in October in her new role as Master, just as I take up the three-year writer's fellowship. She has got the job, Roger tells me, as the inevitable compromise candidate. It seems that, before either she or I get to putting in our appearance, there has been something of a civil war in the college over the Master's appointment. The outgoing incumbent is a surprisingly downmarket character, with a cad's gap between his two front teeth, a penchant for dog-racing tweeds, and a tendency to fart in public.

This brashly self-publicist male person has alienated almost everybody in the college by his blatant manoeuvrings on behalf of a somewhat limply undistinguished male acolyte who is afflicted with a nervous eye-blink. Yet – naturally – the serious outside contender, being a brilliant and somewhat abrasive scholar, is found to be possessed of a personality sufficiently forceful to strike fear into the faint-hearted, not to say the mediocre, among the fellows. The resulting compromise is Sonia.

In the event, Sonia turns out to be more of a force than the feebler dons have reckoned with. For a start, she sweeps into her first college meeting clothed, from shoulder to knee, in chamois leather and wearing her *Annie Get Your Gun* boots. She seats herself at the head of the table and addresses the company as 'ladies'. I turn and grin at Roger, who grins back – Roger who, I would have to admit, has improved beyond belief since his severance from Sally.

There is, in fact, only one lady present at the meeting, other than Sonia herself. This is an erudite but curiously androgynous person who always wears a waxed hat indoors. After the meeting, we go for lunch, where Sonia seats herself beside the senior tutor and adopts her favourite, winding-up style.

'The role of college head more often goes to women these days,' she says, 'not because women are coming up in the world, but because the job has been downgraded. It's not about scholarship. It's all about touting for funds. My situation is comparable with that of all those black mayors in American cities – as in, "Who is there sucker enough to want to govern a pile of trash cans?"'

Who, precisely, the trash cans are is not quite clear to me, but Sonia's words cause a detectable vibration of annoyance around the table.

Naturally, it does not help us that, within a week of Stella's defection, I have my mother on the telephone with the appalling news that her old friend Vanessa's god-daughter has been knocked down by a motorcar and killed, right outside my London landlady's house. Lydia's death is a horrible blow. True, I hardly knew the child, but I have a firm impression of her as a young person possessing a robust and resilient spirit. I think of her as the last person in the world who ought to have died young. I consider her to have been temperamentally unsuited.

Furthermore, though I speak with the tall, sad man who is Lydia's father and find him utterly decent and quite devoid of any implication of accusation, I cannot shift from my mind the idea that, in some way, Lydia's death is my fault. He ventures the speculation that Lydia had merely wanted to share with me her pleasure in the A-grade mark. And he thanks me for my help to her.

Thus, had I not responded to her letter, Lydia would not have died. Had I not obliged her with my time and expertise; had I not treated her to tea and cream cakes; had I not subsequently rewritten the essay – thus ensuring its A-grade mark – Lydia would not have died. Had I not left London two days early, on that fateful evening in late June, in order to exorcize the effects upon my ego of Sonia's mercurial brush-off; had I not headed home to accuse my wife of infidelity with my brother; had I only not been absent from the bedsit, Lydia would not have died.

And is there, I wonder morbidly, some dreadful, malign connection in the fact that Lydia dies on the night that we lose our daughter?

'It was an accident,' Katie says. 'Dear Jonathan, it's too horrible. It's unspeakable. But it was absolutely not your fault.'

My mother is not so consolatory. She wants to know, in no uncertain terms, what precisely has 'gone on' between me and her friend's poor god-daughter. Though she does not say so, she has clearly come to me with Sally's take on my affair with Sonia Middleton. When I tell her that we held discussions on German Romanticism, she tells me, abruptly, that she was not 'born yesterday'. This is true, since my mother is seventy-three.

She takes the moral high ground – and well she might, I concede – given that she and my late father were faithful, monogamous and true throughout the forty years of their marriage. They behaved extremely well. Looking at the roads taken by each of their six children will tell a different and, in the main, less uplifting story, but I draw a veil over this particular area for scrutiny.

Once my mother's pep talk has wound down, and we have, as usual, flung mud at each other, I embrace her with tears in my eyes and I tell her – moving on from poor little Lydia – that I wish to Christ the Old Man hadn't gone and bloody died so unnecessarily, at sixty-six. Given that this is something we can always agree on, she cries on my shoulder and wipes her eyes on my shirt.

'If only the old fool hadn't smoked so much, Jonathan,' she says. 'Just you keep doing Katherine that favour, at least. Don't you ever start smoking.' Since I am now forty-eight, and I gave up smoking at sixteen, I make her this promise with confidence.

I attend Lydia's funeral and seat myself at the back. I listen uncomfortably, during the oration, to chunks of my own prose, as the priest reads an extract from Lydia's A level essay from the lectern. *Love and Death at the Mill.* The effect is to leave me feeling cheap. I make no move when the throng files out into the churchyard and I keep my head down. For a while I sit there, registering that the day is fine but breezy. Branches scrape against the windows and the buttresses. The odd leaf has blown into the aisle.

When finally I get up to go, I see something that startles me. Beyond the dark little porch, in the arched segment of light that floods the doorway, Lydia crosses from right to left; Lydia transformed into *Diana of the Uplands.* Lydia dressed, not in mini-skirt and Doc Martens but in a long, dark skirt and jumper, and a billowing scarf. She is striding towards the lych-gate, preceded by two greyhounds, who are straining at the leash.

I blink and shake myself and she is gone. I sit down for a moment in the porch. Then I make my way briskly into the village and telephone Katherine from outside a pub.

'Jon,' Katherine says, 'didn't the girl have a sister?'

A sister. Yes, of course. There was the sister with the Bad Experience in Vienna; the sister who didn't like blond men.

'She had a sister,' I say. 'Thanks, Katie.'

'Have you eaten anything?' Katherine says. 'I'm worried about you, lovey.' I tell her that I'll buy myself a pasty. I tell her that I'm just outside a pub. Then, just as I become aware of a disturbance, Katherine says, 'What on earth is that noise?'

Across the road, Lydia's sister has begun to scream hysterically. 'He's taking my dog,' she's yelling. 'Help me. He's taking my dog.'

I see then that a boozy-looking street person is making off in the direction of a small single-decker bus and that one of the two greyhounds is trotting happily at his side. So I sprint for all I'm worth and rugby-tackle the dog, meeting the pavement in horizontal position and encircling the greyhound's collarless neck with both my hands.

'Good dog. Good dog,' I say, rising to kneeling position. The dog is utterly gentle, as greyhounds, of course, are – unless you happen to be a rabbit. Meanwhile the girl comes up, red-eyed and sniffling. She has a ferocious rash down one side of her face – the side that was turned away from me in the graveyard – and she is shaking too much to talk intelligibly. She keeps sobbing, 'Oh Dilly,' as she struggles to replace the dog's collar – but she can't, because of the shakes. So I take the collar from her and I do up the buckle. Then I stand up. Meanwhile we're neither of us taking any notice of the old man, who is mumbling something mumbly in a mumblish sort of way. A drunken old fool talking to himself. It is only once I'm driving home that I wonder, idly, why the dog was going along so readily with the old boozer.

And that is all there is to say, except perhaps that, one year later, Katherine finds me slumped at my desk with my head upon my ledger and she senses that I am close to tears. I have been working at my accounts and a receipt has come along to distress me. I have at some point written over its hopelessly faded printout. What I have written says, 'cello £595'. Though I stare at it for a good long while, I have no memory of this particular outgoing – but it serves to remind me that I no longer have the privilege of spending my money on my daughter.

'It says "Sellotape",' Katherine says. 'It'll be "Sellotape, five pounds ninety-five." You've abbreviated it, that's all. And you've omitted the decimal point. And misspelt it, by the way. You don't spell Sellotape with a "c", Jonathan. You spell it with an "s".'

'Oh Christ,' I say. 'Oh Katie. What on earth would I do without you?' Then I cart her off to bed. 'I love you,' I say, because, through all the pain and ageing, Katherine's kindness and cleverness has never ceased to assault my juices. 'I love you,' I say. 'I love you.' I say it again and again. And again.

6. Die liebe Farbe

Ellen

MY INTERVIEW WAS due to take place with the Conrad Scholar at twelve that day. After Edinburgh, I had applied to Oxford in the hope of becoming one of his D.Phil. students and I was consequently planning to write a fat book with footnotes, such as Lydia had envisaged Martin Luther nailing to the church door in Wittenberg, multiplied by ninety-five.

Having returned to begin my second year in Edinburgh after the summer of Lydia's death, I had picked up Stella's copy of *Heart of Darkness* and had read it, non-stop, through the first night back. When I had finished – and it isn't, of course, particularly long – I began it all over again. Over the next few months, I read my way through all of Conrad's writings. Nobody had offered me tenpence pieces in order to make me do so. Nobody had been required to tie labels to the books, recommending them to me as NOT literature. I read them, and I read them again, simply because the books had laid siege to my mind.

Beautiful, terrible, gloomy books – Boys' Books, if you like – and all of them, of course, a far cry from the sexy French *comtes* and fairytale *châteaux*, the butch lacrosse teachers and horse-mad schoolgirls in which Lydia and I had once taken such delight. At the time – and ever since – they have suited me very much better. Perhaps this is called growing up.

But the pull of *Heart of Darkness* lay not only in the book's unblinking stare into the dark channel that gapes before us when we forget to close our eyes to it. I responded readily to the story's brooding implication of the ghostly *doppelgänger*, the other self; the 'hypocrite lecteur'. Somewhere, in my darkest places, I suppose I felt myself to be incomplete. The bleakness that had come upon me with the death of my sister, the introspective tendency, had found its secret sharer.

Lydia's death had left me with a legacy of insomnia, or, at least, a habit of wakefulness in the small hours. This is something I now share with Pen, the great friend of my first year. Like him, I am inclined to wake at four in the morning and shake off the dark and begin upon the routines of the day. But where Pen always got up and took himself swimming, I go to my desk. It accounts for how I ended up doing so well in finals. It accounts, as Lydia and I would once have put it, for how I became such a boring swot. I had more hours in my day.

So there I was, before 6 a.m., on the morning that I had seen my dead sister. I was washed, dressed and ready in my navy schoolmarm clothes, waiting to take the train to Oxford. I had already dabbed twice at my face with my tobacco-brown lotion that smelt of tar, because – as always before important events – the whole of my right cheek was afflicted with an unscenic case of psoriasis. I could depend upon it, by then, to snatch away my looks at moments of challenge.

I wondered, as I glanced to left and right in the glass, whether I could realistically present the Conrad Scholar with a constant left profile throughout the duration of the interview – a profile like that of a painted figure on the wall of an Egyptian tomb. Then I thought, what the hell, warts and all, Ellen. Your face is as God made it. I have inherited from my father not only my height and my colouring, but a distinctly Protestant ethic – or so I am assured by dearest Peter, my half-brother.

Having carefully replaced in the box file the draft of my sister's letter to The Novelist, I tiptoed to the kitchen and made myself some coffee. The two greyhounds, after they had slapped their tails twice each on the kitchen floor in token acknowledgement of my entry, kept their eyes shut and continued with their sleep. Neither was as early a riser as I. Then, at around 6.30, I heard stirrings from the two little girls, my half-sisters, who slept together in the bedroom directly above the kitchen – a bedroom that had once been Lydia's and my nursery. And, when the stirrings had turned to grumblings, I heard the sound of the Stepmother's size two feet on the floorboards, as she crossed the room to her daughters.

The little girls were aged two and a half and eighteen months. Born within a year of each other, they seemed, like Lydia and me, to be each other's closest friend – a trait that I have come to observe with a killjoy degree of caution. Any day now, I thought, as I sipped my coffee, they would be blowing their little noses on the cornflower-sprigged curtains, just as we had done when our parents were not looking. And perhaps they were already sticking their bogeys onto the back of the captain's chest between the beds? The chest that held their little vests and tights, just as it had once held ours.

The girls even looked almost exactly like Lydia and me, from which I can conclude that my father has formidably dominant genes. Any photograph taken of us, aged eighteen months and two, is pretty well interchangeable with any one taken of them.

Lizzie and Phoebe – these were the two little girls who had been born to the Stepmother during my time in Edinburgh. They had taken the place of the stillborn male twins who had fetched up, one under the oak tree, and one in a hospital incinerator. And my father, I have noticed, is inclined to treat Lizzie and Phoebe as if they were two halves of the same pantomime horse. Neither little girl has thus far exhibited any interest in model aeroplanes or cricket.

The Stepmother has continued with her teaching job in 'the Smoke', and will not countenance the idea of a live-in nanny. She rises an hour earlier than of old, and drops the girls at a child-minder on her way into work. The Stepmother is head of department and is on the way to becoming school deputy. On the previous evening she had offered to drop me off as well – at the railway station in Worcester – so that I could take the train to Oxford and be there 'in good time'.

The Stepmother is big on punctuality. She is an efficient, restless, energetic little person who, strangely enough, seems to suit my father well. In her concern to get me to my interview on time, I think she may have been confusing the journey to Oxford with the one she sometimes makes to Cambridge, where she visits an old friend. Cambridge is, of course, much further from Worcester, as I know only too well, since not only did Lydia and I get sent to school near there, aged twelve and thirteen – once our mother had shipped out in that direction – but these days I go to Cambridge to pay regular visits of my own.

My mother; our mother; Lydia's and my once so imposing, elegant, grey-eyed mother – always so composed, so collected – is not quite what she was. The Stepmother has confided to me that, years back, she thought of our mother as the 'Mermaid Woman', for her cool grey eyes and her cool grey clothes, and her apparently cool unfeelingness. But, since her accident, my mother has more frequently been referred to as 'poor Gentille'.

I hope that I do not visit her merely out of duty, nor out of guilt, though I am quite tedious, these days, as Peter tells me, in the way that I take on burdens.

'You're doing penance again, Ellie,' he says, 'penance for being alive.' He warns me that I am no longer particularly good company – that is, for anyone but himself and his motley hounds.

What happened ensued from what my father once hinted at to my unreceptive ear; what happened was that, when Lydia died, my mother went to pieces. This was the last thing that anyone would have expected since, as my father had observed to me on the Spanish Steps in Rome, she was always 'so controlled'. Besides, my mother was accustomed to having people die around her. It had become a way of life. Her own antecedents had proved themselves extremely capable in this area.

She had been living in Paris when my father met her – a young French photo-journalist – but her grandmother had been from a Polish Jewish family, the only survivor of the Nazi occupation; a woman who had managed, almost literally, to walk to France with her very small, fragile baby. Once there, she had made a marriage of convenience with an ageing shopkeeper who had soon thereafter died. The baby had grown up to marry a man who was carried off, within twenty-four hours, by a bout of viral pneumonia. His little daughter, my mother, was six months old at the time. My mother had then, in her turn, married an Italian racing driver, who had duly died, aged thirty-two, at the wheel of a burning car. The racing driver, who was Peter's father, was dead before Peter was two.

'Death,' as Peter once observed to me, 'is a serial killer in our family.' After the racing driver, our mother had then met and married Father, who has thus far stubbornly refused to die. She had fallen for him while undertaking an assignment on an English beach one summer. And this was the woman who, after Lydia's death, had become alarmingly unhinged with grief – far more so, I think, than even my father had realized at the time.

I am fairly certain that the languid Hugo Campbell, my mother's third husband, had not expected to find himself suddenly married to a ball of raging emotions. He had married the Mermaid Woman, after all. He had not married Phèdre. He had always struck Lydia and me as a man much inclined towards recumbency and he exhibited, like Madame Récamier, a great partiality for the *chaise-longue*.

Yet his origins in the Scottish landowning class were enough to make him rise from the aforesaid *chaise-longue* once a year and take the train to Berwick-on-Tweed for his annual bird-shooting spree. For this purpose he kept a twelve-bore shotgun on the floor of his hanging cupboard, where it proved to be a most unsuitable object for a desperate, unhappy, bereaved woman to encounter in his absence.

Having, as I understand it, managed to balance the gun more or less upright on the floor, while she herself leaned over it with the barrel gripped in her left hand, my mother had then made the mistake that I have been told novices make. That is to say, she put the barrel to her forehead instead of in her mouth. Even taking into account the difficulty of managing the trigger – given the gun's length – had she done the latter, she might have achieved her object and blown herself to oblivion. As it was, she made a mess of her head and impaired parts of her brain.

At this point, it is my impression that Hugo Campbell simply copped out. Having returned to the house, he had seen her from the bedroom doorway and had retreated at once to summon the doctor, who in turn had summoned the ambulance. Within the month Hugo had sold the house and had moved into a top floor flat in a building that had no lift – presumably to ensure that my mother would never again be capable of joining him – and all contact with her ceased.

I visit my mother in a residential nursing-home, roughly every eight weeks. I have done so for over two years. Perhaps, as Peter suggests, I do it in an attitude of penance for not having done so when my father first suggested it. At the time I had, of course, turned him down with an unambiguous vehemence. My mother's mobility is limited and her vision is somewhat blurred.

She oozes water continually from her eyes – though the nurses have assured me that this apparently chronic distress is merely tear-duct malfunction. Nonetheless, it is difficult for me not to associate the constant tears with grief.

Neither is it gratifying to visit her, since my mother, even now, appears incapable of acknowledging me. I tell her that I am Ellen and she tells me, as if it were coincidence, that she has a daughter called Ellen – and another daughter called Lydia.

'Do you know my daughters?' she says. Now that she is accustomed to my visits, she will say, 'You are the other Ellen,' and perhaps I am. The other Ellen; the *doppelgänger*; the secret sharer, the 'hypocrite lecteur'.

Sometimes she will tell me that her husband is a headmaster – and, naturally, I have never told her that her husband is a Cambridge don called Hugo Campbell who lives in mortal fear of having any involvement with her. *Noli me tangere.* It is my father's and the Stepmother's earnings, or perhaps more realistically the Stepmother's trust fund, that pays for the high quality of my mother's residential care.

Whenever I can, I visit with Peter and the Übermensch, both of whom manage a more upbeat attitude and have a greater capacity for good cheer. For example, I have never taken the greyhounds to visit my mother, since she is not – was never – an 'animal' person. But Peter and the Übermensch will always take along one or other of their current canine puffballs and plonk it right in her lap. They unwrap beribboned sweetie boxes and push French bonbons into her mouth. They take her for manic wheelchair rides around the nursing-home grounds, until they and she are exhausted. Then they linger in the TV room, drinking tea, making small talk with the inmates, watching Aussie soaps and stuffing themselves with a miscellany of eagerly proffered chocolates.

'Life's a bitch,' Peter said to me, the last time we drove off together, 'and then we die. Cheer up, Ellen. Please do.'

'Life. She is a beach,' said the Übermensch, who likes to polish his accent along with his very special syntax. 'And Ellen she 'ave always the mange.'

'Psoriasis,' I said crossly, 'and I only get it when I'm visiting my mother. Or you.'

'My dearest,' Peter said. 'Gaiety, song and dance. Come on, try it. You're far too much like your father, Ellen. Do you realize that? Buttoned-up old ramrod. Perhaps we ought to find you a nice boyfriend?'

'Oh, piss off, Peter,' I said.

'Whatever happened to those cute boys you shared with in Edinburgh?' he said. 'The Catholic engineer was very nice.'

'Peregrine Massingham and the Guttersnipe,' I said. 'Peregrine has gone on to be somebody's husband, and the Guttersnipe has gone on to be somebody famous. You'd know that if ever you read the papers. He's off making his mark for Cool Britannia.' And at that point the puffball was sick into my lap. The nursing-home's inmates were always inclined to stuff Peter's dogs with most unsuitable, sugary biscuits – and the ensuing mess in this instance looked predominantly like half-masticated bourbon creams.

The 'cute boys' I'd shared with in Edinburgh. Oh dear. Of the two, Pen had remained a sort of friend – though I hadn't actually seen him in years. He had become what I might punningly call a pen friend, but life, I suppose, moves on. In Edinburgh he had taught me how to cook, and this is something that has made me quite useful at home. I make up batches of soups and stews, and store them in the Stepmother's fridge. Without me – who knows? – my father and my half-sisters might be reduced to living off the 'serving suggestions' on the sides of cracker boxes and off tins of Kashmiri Lamb Curry.

Pen taught me all the most basic things: how to cook rice and pasta without making glue; how to hard-boil eggs without getting black rings around the yolk; how to 'melt' onions, not frazzle them; how to glaze vegetables, or stir-fry them, or boil them, without destroying their bite. He taught me how to make a decent salad dressing. He taught me how to make stock. Pen taught me a half-dozen pasta sauces, and how to make risotto and biryani. He taught me not to be afraid to cook fish. He taught me how to make a béchamel sauce without getting lumps. He taught me how to make shortcrust pastry, using lashings of butter and lard.

We had always cooked the evening meal together, at first for three, and then for four, to include Izzy and also Stella, but Pen would banish the two of them, like children, from 'our' kitchen – and they were always completely willing to be excluded. Looking back, those culinary sessions were some of the nicest times I've had. The only thing that marred them was my sense that Pen was keen on me. But perhaps this was simply a misplaced hunch. That is to say, he never acted upon it, but it caused me a constant, attendant fear that Pen would one day spoil our friendship by grabbing me in a smoochy embrace, and declaring his passion for me.

In the event, this never happened. Perhaps because I had thrown out once too often that I did not go for blond men. Or, perhaps, because our friendship itself had simply got in the way. Pen would kiss me in public, but always on the cheek. He took an interest in the boys that I dated, but he never invaded my privacy. In short he was an absolute sweetie and was probably the nicest man I'll ever get to meet.

On the night that Lydia died, Pen came with me to the airport and he sat with me at the departure gate while I wept into his shirt. After that, until I left for Fiesole and Rome, he telephoned me every day in an effort to help me through. Then, on my return, he wrote. Though his marriage to Stella some months later came as a big surprise, it did not altogether trouble me beyond a small twinge of possessiveness, which very soon fell away.

And Pen has continued to write. He writes to me roughly every five weeks – always briefly – always on plain white postcards. He writes from his place of work, and it is to his place of work that I therefore reply. He calls this correspondence our 'Soup of the Month Club' – and one side of his postcard always contains a recipe. It can be anything from parsnip soup, to paella, to peperonata. Because the Stepmother is vegetarian, Pen concentrates on veg. Invariably, I try out the recipes before I sit down to reply.

On the reverse side of his card Pen will tell me, briefly, about all sorts of ordinary things – that the rocket he has been growing in his vegetable garden has been beset by early summer frosts; that Holly, his little girl, has learnt to speak in sentences; that he is travelling on business to Tokyo or to Budapest; that he has taken his family to the West Highland coast for five days of bucket-and-spade holiday; that Stella is 'frail' and often 'unwell', but that she nonetheless manages her weekly string quartet; that Stella sings solo with her choir and has recently sung a Handel aria at his sister Julia's wedding. He tells me whether she is rehearsing Mussorgsky, or Schubert, or Bartók. He tells me that his sister Anastasia has had impacted wisdom teeth.

From Izzy, by contrast, I have heard nothing, though I concede, now, that he was completely right in assuming the worth of his drawing to be in excess of the fuel bill. To my shame, I had kept the drawing for two months in a plastic bag under my bed in my student bedroom. Then I stuck it to the back of my door with hefty gobs of Blu-Tack pressed to its four corners. One day, finding that it had grown on me and feeling a little spendthrift on my way back from a morning lecture, I had lashed out on a cheapo perspex clip-frame, and had hung Izzy's drawing on the wall.

In my final year I had been surprised to get a letter from Izzy's agent, asking if the drawing was still in my possession and, if so, whether I would consider lending it for exhibition in Jerusalem and Vienna. Naturally, I said that I would. A local gallery representative came for it, as arranged, and clearly could not disguise his disdain that the drawing had not been properly mounted and framed. Contact with the perspex could be damaging, he said.

'Sorry,' was all that I said.

'This sort of frame,' he said, indicating the perspex with a slight shudder, '*this* sort of frame is best kept for high street poster art – and for Happy Snaps.' Then he asked me whether I had thought to have the drawing insured. The annual premium on the sum he suggested would have cleaned out two months' living allowance.

Thanks to the Stepmother, I was in Oxford far too early. I had made my way from the station on foot to New College Lane, where I'd had in mind to pass time in New College garden – having remembered it as particularly beautiful. Then I planned to take a walk around the college cloisters. Having done these things, I entered the chapel. From my position beside the Epstein statue of Lazarus, I saw that someone else was in the chapel, staring at the plaque containing the names of college members who had died in the two world wars. The person in question struck me as noteworthy because he was dressed in djellabah and Arab head-dress. But when he turned and came towards the statue, I saw that he was blond. We made brief, routine eye-contact and blinked and looked away. Then we both looked up again and stared.

'Excuse me,' said the blond Arab, and he bowed slightly from the waist. 'Is it Miss Ellen Dent?' He spoke English with a strong German accent.

'Why do I know you?' I said. 'I do know you, don't I?' Then, as I spoke, even before he could answer, the man's identity came flooding back to me. The lederhosen and the squeeze-box, the trumpet and the Easter Bunny. *Frau Mutti* White Mouse and the Infidel repulsed at the Siege of Vienna. Ellen doesn't like blond men.

'You're *Hubert-und-Norbert*,' I said, and I could not but hold out my hand. The blond man laughed. He took my hand for just a moment, then he gripped my shoulders in a brief, rather stiffly choreographed greeting ritual, before he released me and stepped back.

'I am Ahmed Hamman,' he said. 'Yes, I was once Hubert. Norbert is my brother, who is, since three years, dead from a motor accident.' We both of us fixed our eyes on the pale Hopwood stone; on the column of Lazarus rising. Then, staring at the loosening graveclothes, my heart pounding in my chest, I replied to him, hearing myself on some idiot impulse echo his un-English syntax.

'My sister Lydia is also three years dead,' I said, 'and also from a motor accident.'

The mood was one of passing strangeness. I looked at my watch. 'I thought I might get a cup of coffee,' I said. 'I have an interview in one hour.'

'Just nearby,' said Ahmed who was once Hubert, with another of his small bows, 'there finds itself the Vick-ham.' Then, because, involuntarily, I grinned, he said, 'You are laughing at my English. I am for much of my life now speaking Arabic.'

Hubert who is now Ahmed seats himself beside me in the window seat of the Wykeham and orders us coffee and toast. Then he tells his story. He and his brother had both become increasingly alienated from their parents' burgherish complacency, and had each chosen ways of life in reaction to it. Norbert had become a journalist and had followed a party of Turkish migrant workers to Ankara, where he was briefly and happily married to a local woman before he was killed by a goods lorry with faulty brakes, while riding his brand new motorcycle.

Hubert, who attended Norbert's funeral, had been charmed by Norbert's widow and by her welcoming extended family, which he'd found so different from his own. Having previously visited Israel half-way through his legal studies at university – a visit he had made as part of a progressive German's exercise in exorcism – it now came home to him what he had read, once, in a novel by Amos Oz: 'We,' says the Israeli-born anti-hero to his Polish Zionist father, 'we are the Cossacks now.'

Hubert had returned to his studies, after which he had gravitated towards the Arab community in West Jerusalem, where, like his brother Norbert, he had married a local woman; an older woman, a widow, with one young son called Mohamet. He is a lawyer now, who works on human rights abuses, and has become involved in the peace process. His wife Jamila is a paediatric doctor and a family friend of Hannan Ashrawi.

Having drained my coffee, I asked him a silly question, but I was feeling light-headed for the first time in quite a while. I was beginning to feel almost skittish. 'So was it you who played the accordion,' I said, 'or were you the trumpet player?'

Ahmed who was once Hubert responded by tinkling with laughter. 'I play always the horn,' he said. 'Excuse me. This instrument, Miss Dent. This is not a trumpet. This is such a *Jägerhorn*. This is a *Jagd-horn*. So. I am the hornplayer.'

'Oh gosh,' I said, feeling rather strange. 'So you are "the hornplayer". I see. Do you know, my sister, just before she died, wrote an essay for her school German. She'd called it *Twenty Poems from the Posthumous Papers of a Travelling Hornplayer*.'

'Ach so,' said Ahmed who was once Hubert, displaying a ready interest. 'This is *doch* from Wilhelm Müller, the poet. *Sieben und siebzig Gedichte aus dem hinterlassenen Papieren eines reisenden Waldhornisten*. Schubert is also, of course, using these poems, Miss Dent.' Then we were quiet for a moment. 'Hubert – *der Heilige* – is of hunting – the – er—' Hubert said.

'Patron saint?' I said.

'Of course,' Hubert said. 'The patron saint. So I, not Norbert, must play the hunting horn.'

'Of course,' I said.

'Saint Hubert,' he said, 'is hunting always on the Holy Days, when he is seeing, once, such a cross – a crucifix – between the horns of the deer. The same thing exactly is happening also to Saint Eustace, but he is seeing this vision many centuries earlier; this strange sight of the crucifix so in the animal's head. In this religion to which Norbert, and I also, are once belonging, the men are becoming often saints for hunting, so, on the Holy Days, and the women more often for being forced, so most unwilling *und ganz nackt* into the bordello. Then the suitor is cutting off usually the nipples, or the fingernails and he is then throwing the lady into such a huge pot—'

'A cauldron?' I said.

'A cauldron,' said Ahmed who was once Hubert. 'Right into such a cauldron of boiling water.' The torturer, Hubert went on to observe, was invariably a male person affected with lust for the poor young martyr whose hair, breasts, etcetera, had happened to turn him on.

Then, after a pause, he said, 'I played always so loud the horn under your window, Miss Dent, because my father is often entering your room.'

'What's that?' I said.

'While you sleep,' he said. What Ahmed told me confirmed what I had sensed rather too vaguely at the time – namely that his parents were quite seriously not-nice people. What I had not given any credit for, was that poor old Hubert and Norbert had all that time been struggling saboteurs where I, ungenerously, had read them as collaborators. Thus, had I made any serious effort to learn their language and to engage with them, I might have had a better time.

'Well, thank you,' I said. 'Look. I'm really so sorry about your brother.'

'I am having here a letter,' said Ahmed who was once Hubert. 'It is for you. Is this not strange? And now, I think, you must go.'

The letter which Hubert placed in my hands had been written by himself. It had been addressed to me via Izzy Tench's agent in London. He explained to me that he had written it just two days earlier in his Russell Square hotel room – sparked by the fact that, some months prior to his trip to Europe, he and his wife had attended the opening of an exhibition of Izzy's paintings in Jerusalem. And there, on the wall alongside one of the drawings, he had seen an attribution: 'Lent by Miss Ellen Dent.'

I kissed him as I rose to go. 'Look,' I said, 'can we swap addresses? Please – Ahmed – if I may – I'd love to see you again.'

Ahmed who was once Hubert pulled out a professional-looking card with writing on it in Roman and Arabic script. I scribbled my address for him on a slightly dog-eared sky-blue Post-It.

'I stay here just one night,' he said. 'This is in St Austin's College, where I am a guest, since I speak this afternoon in the students' hall.'

Then I left him to go and meet Mister Conrad – who materialized as one of that particular brand of Englishman who speaks, like a ventriloquist, without ever moving his mouth. Throughout the interview, I fancied that he kept his eyes fixed upon my afflicted right cheek and – to add further to my discomfort, his companion at the interview was a man who seemed just as troubled by my presence as I was by his.

'This is my colleague,' said Mister Conrad, once he had introduced himself. 'Mr Jonathan Goldman, who is our current Writing Fellow. Please take a seat, Miss Dent.'

'Oh, boy,' I thought, as the day turned macabre. 'Think Conrad, Ellen. Think clever. This is the man who saved your dog and probably killed your sister. Think ambivalence here. Think "hypocrite lecteur".'

But Conrad floated away from me. Mr Kurtz, he dead. The interview was a mess. The Conrad scholar was a turd. The Writing Fellow was edgy and, I thought, confrontational, a prodigiously well-read brainbox who quizzed me and found me wanting. He tied me up in knots over Conrad's politics and over the eastward spread of the political dimension of German Romanticism. He seemed surprised when I confessed myself without a good reading knowledge, either of German or of Polish.

'I read French,' I said stiffly. 'I'm far more interested in why Conrad didn't write in French.'

As I said it, something happened to me. It was as though my sister was once again crossing the room. I did not so much see her, as feel a subtle change in the light. I imagined that I saw the room, for one split second, become drained of its yellow. It became just slightly blue – like the change that occurs in a less than perfect colour photocopy – and, in this change, I sensed the passing whiff of laundered cotton. I thought to myself, Liddie was right about all this. This stuff; all this dwelling among footnotes and folios. This is the other Ellen. This is all the stuff that we were running away from when we'd made such joyful burlesque of our schoolwork. This is Hugo Campbell's cabbage patch. *Was hast du gern?* Had Lydia given me a moment of truth?

'Excuse me,' I said. I spoke quite sharply to Mister Conrad, who actually looked into my eyes at that point, and not into my rash. 'I think I'd rather be taking a cordon bleu cookery course,' I said.

'I beg your pardon?' he said, without once moving his mouth.

'I've changed my mind about coming here,' I said.

And then I left. I walked out and across the quad and back to the porter's lodge to ask where I could possibly find Mr Ahmed Hamman, who was currently occupying one of the guest rooms. I hoped that dear Hubert who was now Ahmed would be available for lunch.

What happens next is really most unexpected, but Ellen's day is, in general, taking on a somewhat floaty air. As she stands at the window watching the porter check out room numbers, a middle-aged man emerges from the Fellows' pigeon-holes within the porter's lodge. Though he is old enough to be her father, he is Ellen's idea of dreamboat. The man is slim and tall with straight black hair that falls, schoolboy-wise, into his beautiful, shadowy blue eyes. The hair is lightly touched with a few becoming strands of silver. He has a fine thin face and he wears a shapeless, ancient jacket made of what looks to Ellen like pool-table cloth. He is evidently a little on the scatty side.

With his arms full of jiffy-bags and assorted envelopes, he tries several of his jacket pockets, searching for some elusive item. Each time he investigates a pocket he draws out miscellaneous articles, some of which fall to the floor: crumpled tissues, halved cinema tickets, herb tea-bags in little sachets, loose change, a single cycle-clip trailing pocket fluff, a small pack of sugar-free chewing-gum and, eventually, a ten pound note creased around a half-dozen furry-looking pills.

'Shit,' says the Dreamboat. By now he has some of his letters between his teeth.

Ellen is enchanted. She has not seen such a beautiful man in all her life. She moves forward instinctively to play big sister to the Dreamboat.

'May I hold your post?' she says. 'That way you'll have your hands free.'

When the Dreamboat smiles at her, Ellen goes weak at the knees. He has the sweetest dimples that play around his mouth.

'Thank you,' he says, sounding shy. 'You're very kind.' And he unloads the mountain of jiffy-bags into her arms. She notices, at a brief glance, that the letters are all addressed to R. J. Goldman, Dr Roger Goldman, Professor R. J. Goldman, Roger Goldman, Richardson Professor of Mathematics, etcetera. R. J. Goldman is the name inscribed in Stella's much read copy of *Heart of Darkness*, but this fact, for the moment, passes her by. Calm down, Ellen, she tells herself. He'll be married. Anyone can see that this man is married. He is quite evidently harassed by too much domesticity. He'll have a wife and five young children. Else why are his clothes in such a mess?

Nonetheless, she is grateful that Dr R. J. Goldman has emerged from the porter's lodge to confront the unafflicted left side of her face. Viewed from the left, she knows that she is handsome.

'Hah!' says the Dreamboat triumphantly, and he holds up two small car keys, which are, of course, unattached and calculated to mingle easily with the loose change in his pockets. 'Thank you.' Then, as she hands him back his post, he catches the merest glimpse of her right cheek and his reaction is unusual.

Clutching his envelopes to his chest with his left hand, he reaches out his right to her face and takes hold of her chin. He turns her afflicted cheek towards him and stares at it hard and long, while Ellen suffers the scrutiny in a state of mortification.

'I have a doctor,' says the Dreamboat at last, 'who could treat that condition really well. But I'm afraid he practises in Basingstoke. Still, you ought to give him a try.'

'I have a lotion,' Ellen says, backing off. 'I get it from my GP. It's really—'

'Poison pedlars,' says the Dreamboat with contempt – the Dreamboat, who is Sally's ex-husband, diet freak and violator of bedroom carpets and Kilner jars – 'this doctor is special. I have an appointment with him myself at two o'clock. As a matter of fact, I'm on my way to him now and I strongly advise you to come with me.' As Ellen gawps, he continues. 'My car is just across the street. It's in the college car-park,' he says.

At this point they are interrupted by Mr Jonathan Goldman, who has sprinted across the quad. 'Excuse me,' he says to Ellen. He sounds puffed. 'Hi, Roger, excuse me. Look, I, er . . . things were getting pretty gruesome in there. Forgive me. This is the original bad hair day for me. No excuse, I know. Plus the old bugger is no sort of human being when measured on the Richter scale, I concede. But, from my observation, I would say he's a better supervisor than most and he really does know his stuff. Both of us think that you're great, Miss Dent. He wants you. He really does. So, in short, please come back.'

'Fuck off, will you, Jonathan,' says the Richardson Professor of Mathematics, somewhat to Ellen's surprise. 'The point is that I'm in a hurry. *We* are in a hurry. I and Miss erm . . .'

'Dent,' says Jonathan smugly. 'Look. You don't even bloody know her name, for Christ's sake, and you're helping her to chuck away her future.'

'Ellen,' says Ellen quickly to the Dreamboat. 'My name is Ellen, and I'd really like to come with you.' Ellen, in her wildest dreams, has never imagined that her facial affliction would give her this kind of entrée.

Jonathan looks from one to the other. Then he laughs. 'I see,' he says. 'I've barged into some kind of cute meet here. My apologies. Well, never mind about coming back, Miss Dent. Just tell me, what do I tell him? Will you be his graduate student? Is the answer yes or no?'

'You can tell him yes,' Ellen says. Then she says, 'And thank you.' It occurs to her that she'd be insane to be turning down this opportunity for more sustained proximity to Dr R. J. Goldman, dreamboat and proselytizer for alternative medical causes; a man divinely menaced by padded envelopes and wayward car keys; a man with an evident zeal for her flesh, albeit for the most eccentric of reasons. 'Tell him definitely yes,' she says. 'But tell him I really have to go now.'

Jonathan surprises her by kissing her lightly on the cheek. '*Gesundheit*, Miss Dent,' he says. 'And thank God for that. I'll tell him. And, forgive me, you may not know this. But I once knew your sister. I helped her with an A level essay.'

'Yes,' Ellen says. 'I know that.'

Jonathan hovers uncomfortably. 'In case that fact has ever given you cause to wonder—' he says.

'It hasn't,' Ellen says firmly.

'Good,' Jonathan says, 'because I hereby cross my heart.'

They stand as if suspended for a moment. Then Ellen speaks. 'There is a guest here in the college who calls himself the hornplayer,' she says. 'Isn't that a bit weird?'

Jonathan blinks. 'Right,' he says, catching on, after a second's delay. 'I see. As in "posthumous papers". Oh, Christ, Miss Dent, I'm so sorry.'

'Thank you, by the way,' Ellen says stiffly, 'for getting back my dog.' Then she turns to the Dreamboat. 'Please can we go?' she says.

In the car-park, Ellen slides into the passenger seat. She minds quite a bit that her right profile is facing the driver, but, short of procuring for the Dreamboat an instant left-hand drive, there is really nothing that she can do about it. She notes that the Dreamboat has a violin case on the back seat of his car, along with a hundred sub-sections of Sunday newspaper and several empty litre bottles of carbonated spring water. Onto this miscellany, he now throws all his bags and envelopes of unopened post.

'That man was at my interview,' she says.

'Jonathan,' says the Dreamboat. 'He's my brother.'

'He was a pig to me,' Ellen says. 'As it happens, I was at university with his daughter.'

'Stella,' says the Dreamboat. 'She's my niece.' Then they proceed for several miles in silence.

The Basingstoke doctor has slightly weird hair replacements and he relays evangelical clappy hymns over a tannoy, but he examines her for a full forty-five minutes in a most extraordinary fashion. After that, he puts her on a drip. Then he sends her away with strange infusions and tells her what not to eat. The bill comes to a hundred and sixty-five pounds, plus eighteen pounds sixty for the infusions, but Ellen signs the cheque just as merry as you please.

On the way back, the Richardson Professor lets drop that he and his wife have parted some three years earlier, and that he has three grown-up daughters from whom he is estranged. Also, that he lives a bachelor life in two rooms in the college. Then he says, inexplicably, 'Oh Christ. Is today the twenty-sixth?'

'That's right,' Ellen says. 'It is.'

In response he says, 'Oh shit.' Then they again proceed in silence. Finally, he stops and gets out and makes a phone-call. When he comes back he asks Ellen if she will accompany him, that evening, to the college feast. He's checked about bringing a guest, he says, and it's OK, because somebody else's guest has taken ill and cancelled.

'The chef is very obliging about special diets,' he says. But special diets are not uppermost on Ellen's mind.

'What on earth will I wear?' she says. This is not the sort of thing that Ellen usually says, but she's thinking in panic that her bank account is now minus one hundred and eighty-three pounds sixty, thanks to the Dreamboat's medicine man and that, in any case, the shops will soon be closed.

'Come as you are,' says the Dreamboat unexpectedly. 'I think you look terrific.'

Then he pulls off the road and stops the car with a jerk and he sits and says nothing. Finally he says, 'If I were to kiss you, would you call it molestation? What I mean is, may I?'

'Yes,' Ellen says. 'I mean no. That is, no, I wouldn't call it molestation.' So he kisses her with a certain clumsy intensity, and at great length, on the mouth. Ellen loves it. She wants it never to stop. Blood rushes to her nipples and to her groin in great, unfamiliar swoops. She starts to make involuntary, infant munching noises as the kiss goes on and on. Finally, when he stops, the Dreamboat sits straight up and does not look at her. He stares straight ahead. Then he dredges up three of the furry-looking pills from his bottom right jacket pocket and he swallows them, dry, in two bird-like gulps. Ellen watches the Adam's apple lurch in his throat. He leans, almost slumps, on the steering-wheel, still staring straight ahead. Slowly he begins to intone. What he intones is a thing that Ellen recognizes all too well. It is a love poem in which a wandering miller seeks to have his doubts allayed by the brook.

'"*Ich frage keine Blume,*"' he says, '"*Ich frage keinen Stern.*"'

'Oh God,' Ellen says. 'Must you?' Then she translates, out loud, a little haltingly. '"I do not ask a flower,"' she says, '"I do not ask a star." I know where this comes from, by the way, and, please, I'd really rather you didn't. I can hardly believe that this is happening to me. I came here to talk about Joseph Conrad.'

'"*Sie können mir alle nicht sagen,*"' says the Dreamboat, '"*Was ich erführ so gern.*"'

'"They can none of them tell me,"' Ellen says, with her heart in her mouth, '"what I . . . er . . . feel so . . . um . . . keenly?"'

'No,' says the Dreamboat, 'not "feel". What I "yearn to know".'

'Sorry,' Ellen says. 'This isn't my language you know, and I've already copped some flak for that today.'

'"*Ich bin ja auch kein Gärtner,*"' says the Dreamboat, undeflected.

' "I am no gardener," ' Ellen says, 'and the next bit is that bit about the stars – and don't say it, please, I beg you. Do not say it to me, do you hear?' Ellen is shaking slightly. She hasn't had any lunch. She is thinking that if the Dreamboat says the line – that line – out loud, then she and her life might cease to be. The Dreamboat turns and kisses her again. Then he strokes her right cheek, where she knows, without having to look, that the scaly rash is falling away like the graveclothes from the Epstein Lazarus.

' "*Die Sterne stehn zu hoch*," ' he says. He says it cautiously, sensing that it signifies and that he has no need to understand why. There is so much that neither of them understands – though among the miscellany of muddled thoughts that passes through the Dreamboat's mind is the thought that his mother, whom he loves, will love this woman.

'Are you fond of gardening?' he says.

Ellen isn't listening, because her mind is still on the poem. 'That line,' she says. 'My sister said it to me this morning. But the thing is, my sister is dead.' Then she starts to cry, though this is in itself strange, because Ellen seldom cries. 'My sister is dead,' she says, just as if it had happened yesterday, and her sobs gain momentum. 'My sister is dead.' She says it again and again. And again.

7.

Danksagung an den Bach

THE COLLEGE FEAST is no ordinary affair. This particular feast is an occasion that spreads itself beyond college members and their partners. It goes for the wider trawl. Sonia has read it as one for charming captains of industry into parting with their money, so the rich are present in force. She has also invited, as her special guests, two people whose achievements she admires. They flank her now to left and right at the high table, under a line of portraits that add up to six hundred years of all-male college head. Not for much longer, because to her left is Ishmael Valentine Tench, who has recently been commissioned by the college to undertake her portrait.

Artist and prospective sitter are getting on very well. Sonia is enlivened by Izzy's hint of rough, while Izzy goes for Sonia's get-up. He is intrigued by her dress as a feat of engineering, because she has taken advantage of her non-existent breasts to wear a neckline that plunges in a narrow ravine, almost to her waist – and yet it does not gape to reveal her nipples. Izzy has never much gone for female breasts. They don't attract him. He regards their absence as an asset and wonders, occasionally, what one is supposed to do with them during the act of sex – these inflated bovine obstructions. Stuff them sideways into the woman's armpits, or what? Most of all, Izzy goes for the Master's footwear. She has four-inch stiletto heels and lots of sequinned black straps that criss-cross her instep and ankle like the gateway to the seraglio.

Skinny Izzy is also pleased with his own appearance this evening. In the past, where evening dress has been unavoidable, he has always hired his kit, but for this occasion he has gone to the trouble of purchasing his own. He considers it theatrical costume and he enjoys the fact that his choice leans towards the vulgar, boasting too much newness. He likes it that the fabric has a trashy, all-over sheen and that his jacket lapels are made of polyester satin. He likes it that his non-iron shirt-front is not so much pleated as ruffled. He enjoys, though they are not visible, his grass-green Pocahontas braces.

Ahmed Hamman, to Sonia's right, has wisely ignored the dress code. He wears his robes, which give him a gravitas beyond that provided by a stiff shirt and what look to him like regulation postman's trousers. He finds it difficult to interact with the Master, and his conversation with her is thus characterized by a worthy, stiff sobriety – so different, he thinks, from the sparky dialectic, peppered with insular colloquialisms, which he perceives as taking place between the Master and her other guest of honour. Ahmed, who cannot decode the underlying rudeness of Izzy's staccato ripostes, can, therefore, not appreciate that Izzy is simply unable to construct a complex sentence.

Across the room he notes that one of those present is Ellen Dent, the handsome dark girl with the bold eyebrows and the scowl who was once his family's guest. But Ellen is not scowling now, and neither did she scowl at him that morning when he met her in the chapel. How strange that she should be always popping up like this, like the Cheshire cat in his boyhood copy of *Alice in Wonderland*.

Seated in the body of the dining-hall, at right angles to Ahmed, Sonia and Izzy, are Mr and Mrs Peregrine Massingham, who have been on the guest list for months. They have accepted the invitation in place of Mr and Mrs Edward Massingham, since the Opus Dei's ill health this last year has caused him to decline all such opportunities and obligations. And right now the old man is in hospital convalescing from minor abdominal surgery. Sonia has a particular interest in the family. Besides, she knows it is wealthy and that it may be disposed to endow a hall of residence or a nicely proportioned repository for the college's collection of Middle Eastern antiquities. She knows there is a Massingham daughter who is about to enter the first year to read Law. Anastasia. Peregrine and Anastasia. What idiotic, pompous names, Sonia thinks. Curiously, though she has grieved with the Goldmans over the estrangement of their daughter, she does not know that it is Peregrine Massingham who is Stella Goldman's husband.

Naturally, when Jonathan and Katherine accept the invitation they have no idea that this will bring them face to face with their only daughter for the first time in three years. Jonathan's writer's fellowship is about to end and the Feast will constitute his last social commitment to the college. His last academic commitment he has honoured that same morning, when the Conrad Scholar suggested that he sit in on a graduate interview.

'This might be up your street,' says the Conrad Scholar. 'Do join me, if you'd care to.' Jonathan, after three years on the premises, reads the Conrad Scholar's offer as strictly non-optional – and it is on the way to the Conrad Scholar's room that he passes through the senior common room, where he notices the seating plan for the evening's event.

Naturally, Jonathan's heart leaps straight into his mouth. He is due to appear in two minutes at the Conrad Scholar's door. He is quite unresolved about what to do. Will Stella be aware that her parents, too, are guests? He decides that this is highly unlikely, given that she will have no knowledge of his recent connection with the college. So what, then, ought he to do?

Should Katherine be forewarned of Stella's presence, or should he allow the confrontation to occur spontaneously, in a spirit of mutual astonishment?

He will see Katherine within the hour, since they plan, as they so often do, to meet for lunch in a pie-and-chips café much frequented by chain-smoking traffic wardens and members of the city police.

Jonathan likes to be there early and watch Katherine come in. Lovely, dressy Katherine, who is walking taller now – now that she has finally stared down the awful fact of severance from her daughter. Now that she has found a medium for her creative talent beyond that of dressing up the Nuisance Chip and crackle-painting the porch. It gives him joy to reflect upon the fact that Katherine and he have come through. They have survived. He likes to sit at the back of the café and take a long view of Katherine's entry through the smoke. He likes to imagine that he is seeing her for the first time.

'I did but see her passing by,
Yet will I love her till I die.'

With the end of the writer's fellowship, both Jonathan and Katherine have intermittent thoughts of returning to the west of Ireland, but both separately sense that there is one enormous obstacle. The obstacle is Stella. Ireland would put the sea between themselves and their only daughter. And, while they no longer expect it, no longer jump up to converge upon a ringing telephone, each separately thinks – or hopes – that, one day, when the telephone rings in the Cottage-on-the-Green, the caller will be Stella. At the end of the line, from somewhere outside Newcastle, will be the voice of Mrs Peregrine Massingham.

Jonathan reaches the Conrad Scholar's room in a state of heightened emotion and, naturally, it does not help that the prospective graduate student is Lydia's look-alike; Lydia's sister; *Diana of the Uplands*; the graveyard girl. And not only that. Lydia's sister is, in temperament, wholly unlike Lydia. She is better informed – this is not surprising – but she has none of Lydia's bubble. Miss Ellen Dent, God help him, is inclined to bring on the heavy guns. Miss Ellen Dent is earnest.

Jonathan reacts against her – and he reacts against the emotionally retracted style of the Conrad Scholar, who suffers from an irritating rigor mortis of the jaw. Pain and anger and confusion collide to produce in Jonathan a formidable mindset. His tone with the girl is challenging. 'Come on, come on,' he is thinking. 'Woman, you've read your stuff. Scintillate, lighten up, observe the etiquette here. When I throw a ball at you, for God's sake throw it back.'

And then he sees – just before the Conrad Scholar looks up at the girl in puzzlement – that Miss Dent has called his bluff. She sees that the Conrad Scholar is a drybones, meshed with veins of ink. She sees him, Jonathan, as a smart-arse, building a spurious house of cards, in the hope that she will blow it all to pieces.

'I've changed my mind,' she says, or words to that effect. 'I'd rather go and take a cordon bleu cookery course.'

Contrition speeds his steps as he makes a dash across the quad to stay her hand. And, after that, he goes to meet Katherine – and misses his moment, and says nothing.

So that evening, while Katherine is composed and ready in her new, chocolate-brown lace dress and her new, chocolate-brown lace party shoes, Jonathan cuts himself while shaving and loses a cuff-link down the back of the bedroom radiator.

'Oh, fuck,' he says and he pokes at it with a broom. He gets black Kiwi shoe polish stuck underneath his fingernails.

'Oh, fuck and buggery,' he says. He screams, 'Kath! I need a nail-brush. Where the fuck is the bloody nail-brush?'

'Sorry?' Katherine says, as she comes in. 'What is it you want?'

'Oh, forget it, all right?' he says. By now he is wrestling with his bow tie. 'Christ,' he says. 'I bloody hate these fucking things.'

Katherine starts to laugh. She pats him on the bum in a gesture of wifely affection, laced with a touch of come-on. But Jonathan twitches quite unnecessarily and loses the half-way point in his knot.

'Kate-ee!' he says. 'Now look what you've gone and made me do.'

He lets her do the tie. 'Jon,' she says, 'it's been nice having you around.'

'What?' he says, on the edge of paranoia. 'And what is that supposed to mean?'

'God, Jonathan,' she says. 'You tell me what it means. I mean that it's been nice having you around. You know. Having you not go into London all the time. What's the matter with you?'

'Nothing,' Jonathan says. 'Christ, but don't you hate these bloody dos?'

In the Bath Place Hotel – so conveniently close to the college – Peregrine, who has showered and shaved, dresses quickly and without incident. He has no problem with his cuff-links, nor with his bow tie. Somebody else has polished his beautiful, handmade shoes. His only source of wavering has to do with his mobile phone. Shall he, or shall he not, carry it? He knows his concern is unnecessary, but he worries about the Old Man. He slips the thing into his inside pocket and settles down to read the paper. After a while, he looks at his watch.

'Come on, sweetie,' he calls to Stella, raising his voice to carry through the bathroom door. 'We'll end up being late.'

Stella is dawdling in the bathtub, her mind ranging over her past. She feels the strangeness of being back on home ground, and she toys with the idea of telephoning Michelle. Dare she? Or will Michelle tell her parents that she's been in town? For a moment she almost wishes that she had brought her little daughter, so that she and Michelle could play at being mothers – storybook mothers, taking Max and Holly to feed the ducks in the University Parks. But Holly, of course, has ducks on the lake at home. Perhaps even nicer will be if she and Michelle can meet for lunch in a café, like two proper grown-up ladies.

Stella smiles to herself. She stares down at her slim white schoolgirl body, whiter and slimmer for being under the water. The Fairy Princess hair is wound up in a band to keep it out of her neck. She wiggles her long white toes. Stella's beauty is ever more extraordinary. It has, if anything, increased with illness, childbirth and frailty. It has the effect, as it always had, of setting her apart. It compounds her isolation. Brambles have wound themselves between her and other people. She has withdrawn almost completely into Pen's immediate family and she depends, especially, on Pen and Aggie and the Old Thing. And then, of course, there are Dr and Mrs Sachs, especially now that Lorraine has married and is living in Honolulu.

'Come on, sweetie,' Pen says again. He knocks and enters the bathroom. He takes her hands and coaxes her to her feet. Then he wraps her in a large white bath towel. 'We're about to be late,' he says.

'Does it matter?' Stella says. And then she says, 'I hate it when you make that mouth. Pen, I wish you'd stop it.' What Stella means is that she would dearly love to commit rape upon Pen's mouth. She would like to go at it with her tongue and her teeth and her spittle.

Stella is a quick dresser. She steps into her knickers, then feet-first into her dress, then into her shoes. She shakes her hair free from the band and brushes it in seven long strokes. She wears no bra, no stockings, no make-up. She carries no handbag. She pauses only to swallow four of the twenty-four pills that she is obliged to swallow every day.

'There,' she says. 'Look. I'm ready.'

Her unpainted eyelashes and eyebrows are gingery pale against her milk-white skin, her mouth is the colour of bruised violets. Her dress, which is Thai silk, is the colour of her mouth. The neckline is low and severely horizontal, the sleeves enormous, the bodice tight and elongated, the skirt full and rustling. In the dress, Stella is a romantic figure; a sixteenth-century oil portrait; a slim, white, orange-haired, wasted Virgin Queen.

They are, of course, within seconds of being seriously late. There is no time to linger in the anteroom over a drink. A college servant ushers them straight into the dining-hall and to their appointed places, where Stella finds herself seated between her husband and the Uncle Fiddle Anorak – since the Dreamboat's eleventh-hour lady guest has required his relocation from the high table. To Pen's right, Stella registers with shock, are her mother and then her father. And, to her uncle's left, most mercifully, is Ellen.

The convergence affects the company in several different ways. Pen and Ellen are overjoyed to see each other and lean sideways to embrace briefly behind the backs of Stella and the Dreamboat. Then Pen turns to his parents-in-law, where he mimes normality with a creditable suavity.

'What a very pleasant surprise,' he says. 'I hope you are well, Mrs Goldman.' But Katherine is silent and shaking. She is glancing anxiously beyond him towards her thin, white, ice-queen daughter who will not look at her. In the glances, and in the set of her wide blue eyes, Pen sees that she is the image of his beloved little Holly, and his heart goes out to her. It pains him that Stella's own particular method of coping is to pretend that her parents are not in the room.

Stella has closed in on Ellen and her uncle, and has turned her back to her husband. She is meanwhile buffing up her best Grania style. Stella bubbles and laughs and chats. Though she normally drinks no alcohol, she downs the contents of her wine glass quickly – and it is then quickly refilled.

'But isn't this just too wonderful?' Ellen says, being happily innocent of the subtext. 'And to think that even Izzy is here.'

'Where?' Stella says.

It is at Ellen's direction that Stella looks up towards the high table and, immediately, she laughs out loud. 'God in heaven,' she says, 'and what does he think he's wearing? Has the Liberace fan club been selling off the shirts?' Then she says, 'And there's a bloke up there who's wearing a drying-up cloth on his head.' Pen, who has picked up on the cause of her louder speech, has tried removing her wine glass. He hopes that she will not notice, but Stella observes it at once and reaches out across his plate to snatch up his, instead.

'All right. I'll have yours,' she says. 'Look. There's lots more in it.' She laughs, again, at her own wit. Then she turns back to Ellen.

'And, oh boy!' she says. 'Do I know that woman – *or do I know that woman*!'

'Which woman?' Ellen says.

'*That* woman,' Stella says.

'Sshh,' Ellen says, because Stella's volume is beginning to attract a bit of unwelcome attention.

Stella drinks deeply from her husband's wine glass. 'That woman flirting with Izzy,' she says. 'Lydia somebody. When I last saw her, she was in Fortnum's, kissing my father.'

'But she's not "Lydia",' Ellen says. 'Her name is Sonia Middleton. She's Master of the college. I got introduced to her – just before we came to sit down.'

'Master?' Stella says. 'Mistress, more like it. She leaves her suspenders in other people's beds.' Then the wine goes up her nose. Pen strokes her back. He is having no fun at all, poor man, wedged as he is between his silent mother-in-law and his suddenly garrulous wife.

Katherine, too, has turned away from him and is talking in anxious whispers to her husband.

'She's terribly thin,' she says. 'Jonathan, why is she so pale?'

'She was always pale, remember,' Jonathan whispers back.

But Katherine is not placated. 'Jonathan,' she says, 'for heaven's sake, take a look at her. Stella is as white as a sheet.'

The senior tutor has risen to his feet and he bangs on the table with a gavel.

'Will all the gentlemen please move two gentleman's places to the left?' he says.

'But I ought not to leave you,' Jonathan says.

'Go', Katherine says. 'Please. Talk to her, Jonathan. Try.'

The move brings Jonathan to Stella's left, and Pen to the left of Ellen. Stella is the first to speak.

'If I'd known you were going to be here, then I wouldn't have come,' she says.

'Strange meeting,' Jonathan says. 'Stella, we really had no idea—' Then they are silent for a good long while. 'All the same,' Jonathan says, eventually, 'for my part, I'm very glad.'

'That woman,' Stella says, ignoring him, 'that woman up there next to Izzy. Your girlfriend as was. Or is she still your girlfriend?'

'Stella—' Jonathan says.

'She told me her name was Lydia,' Stella says.

'Sonia?' Jonathan says. 'You've met her?'

'Oh, I haven't exactly "met" her,' Stella says. 'But I've had words with her on your intercom. You know. That speaky thing in your little place in London – the one you keep for screwing her in, I suppose. I found her suspenders in your bed that night – that night I ran away. So when she came round and rang the doorbell – well, I told her to get lost.'

Jonathan has turned rather cold. 'You told Lydia to get lost?' he says.

'Well, I *was* in a bit of a state,' Stella says. 'So I told her to piss off.' She drinks briefly from Pen's glass. Then she goes on. 'I told her she was wrecking your family. Something like that. Something corny. So then she must have pissed off. Well, I wasn't going to entertain her, then, was I? Izzy'd been getting off with Grania and, what with you and her in Fortnum's—'

'Her?' Jonathan says.

'Yes, her,' Stella says. 'That woman up there next to Izzy. Why do you ask? Are there lots of them? Gosh! And to think I always imagined that Fortnum's was just for you and me.'

Jonathan sits in silence as things click into place. Stella, who had been in a little bit of a state, had told Lydia to piss off – Lydia, whom she had assumed was Sonia, whom she had seen acting flirty that afternoon in Fortnum's, where she had happened to be falling out with Izzy, who had lost her in a café on account of her having taken flight to the Quaker landlady's bedsit, where she had let herself in with her key, having found him absent from the spot. And Lydia, poor sweet Lydia, lacerated by his distressed daughter's tongue, had run from the doorstep, straight into a passing car.

'Well, you've gone very quiet,' Stella says. 'Why do I remember you as a talkie sort of person?'

After quite a long time, Katherine overhears Jonathan speak to Stella. 'Your mother has begun to write children's books,' he says.

'I know,' Stella says. Her tone is completely deadpan. 'They're Holly's favourite books.'

'And do you like them?' Jonathan says. 'It's my hunch, Stella, that she writes them for you.'

'I've never read them,' Stella says. Her deadpan tone does not waver. 'Pen always reads Holly's bedtime stories. I'm not a very good reader – especially not out loud. I tend to stumble over words. But why should you remember?' Then she turns aside to address the stranger who is seated to her right. He is a man of middle age; a manufacturer of quality swimwear for ladies. Stella smiles at him, most charmingly, and affects great interest in his trade – though she is, of course, a lady who has never cared to swim.

When Pen is alerted to his mobile phone, he excuses himself from Ellen and makes his way from the hall, through the low Tudor doorway which requires him to bow his head. He takes the call in the barrel-vaulted corridor between the dining-hall and the kitchen. Then he returns at once.

'It's for you,' he says quietly, into Stella's ear, and he hands over the phone. 'It's Dr Sachs and he says it's good news. I suggest that you take it in the passage.'

There are many eyes in the dining-hall that follow Stella's departure; the rustling departure of the beautiful girl with the death-white skin and the mass of hair that spreads out like tongues of fire. Two of these eyes belong to Ishmael Valentine Tench who is beginning to itch for a smoke.

'Christ Almighty,' Izzy says, out loud. 'If that's not Stella, I'm an Arab.'

'But I thought you were,' Sonia says brightly. 'Well, on your father's side, that is.'

Izzy pays her no attention. He gets up quickly and crosses the floor. Unlike Pen and Stella, he passes easily under the low Tudor doorway, having no need to bow his head.

Stella is at the end of the passage with her back towards the doorway. She is listening to Dr Sachs, and what he is telling her is causing the carefully constructed artifice of her life – the careful sacrament of each and every day – to fall in pieces around her. What he is telling her is that, thanks to her new medication, the virus within her cells is no longer actually detectable.

'I'm not saying that it's eliminated,' he says, 'but Stella dear, there is now scope to envisage that it will be. The prognosis is really very good.'

In short, Dr Sachs is telling Stella that she is once more under sentence of real life. 'I had to let you know,' he says. 'I hope this is not a bad time? I wish you were right here beside me, Stella. Will you come and see me tomorrow – just as soon as you get back?'

Stella can hear the pleasure in his voice, but she, herself, feels only confusion and anticlimax, and an alarming drop in stature. She sees herself exposed and insecure in a field of dreams and choices. She stands there, trembling slightly and can think of nothing to say.

'Stella?' says Dr Sachs.

'But who am I?' Stella says, at last. And, to herself, she thinks, 'I am Mrs Nobody, that's who I am. I am a stupid, stupid girl who threw away her life to have a baby at nineteen and live in a nutshell fitted out in twelve shades of sand with a man who will not touch me.'

'Stella?' says Dr Sachs again. 'Stella, are you there?'

But Izzy has come up behind her and has disconnected the caller. He licks the white exposed skin of Stella's shoulder where it meets the base of her neck. 'D'ye fuck?' he says and he blows briefly at the spot, cooling his own glistening deposit of saliva.

Stella pulls herself up with a start and turns to confront him. Pale hairs have jumped to attention all along her forearms.

'Izzy don't,' she says. 'Please. Go away. Now. Izzy please. I want you to go.'

In response, Izzy extrudes his tongue, a gesture which she struggles to ignore. Then he kisses her mouth. He could be said to commit rape upon it, with his tongue and his teeth and his spittle. Tears have sprung to Stella's eyes. She wipes her mouth vigorously with the back of her hand.

'For God's sake,' she says. 'Izzy, you must know that we shouldn't. You must know that we're sick—'

'We're all sick,' Izzy says. 'What's your problem?'

'Izzy—' she says. 'That's just—'

'Life's a disease,' he says. 'You could choke on a sweetie. A wee rock could fall on my head.' Then he kisses her again. After that he leads her by the hand, down a narrow dark passageway that disappears to the left, and he tries a door at random.

Once within, where he switches on the light, Stella sees that they are inside the men's lavatory. She states uneasily at two urinals, knowing what they are only from the photographs she has seen in a book about Marcel Duchamp.

'I don't want to be in here,' she says. 'I don't like it. Izzy, I want us to go.'

By the time they are scuttling hand in hand across the quad, the thing has become a little adventure; a conspiracy to play hookey; a breath of air in a night almost stifled with *angst*. In the car-park directly across the road, Sonia Middleton has made available to her guest of honour her own private car space. It is there that Stella stops dead in her tracks.

'Well, I don't believe it,' she says. 'Izzy, I do not believe it. How can your car be so idiotically pink?'

Izzy's car is a pink, fifties Chevrolet, long as a goods truck and gleaming with chrome. The tart's teeth of its radiator are leering at her in welcome. Stella begins to turn cartwheels in her head. Her heart is dancing to the Cello Suite in D. She is suddenly high on the prospect of an act of unretractable daring. And hasn't Dr Sachs just set her free?

'Where to?' Izzy says. She directs him to Port Meadow, where he parks his car beyond the railway bridge, and they walk towards the river. It amuses her to realize, suddenly, that she still has, clutched in her left hand, her husband's mobile phone. On the low-lying damp of the meadow grass, Stella gets cow dung on her beautiful dress and goose turds in her hair. Izzy throws off the shiny jacket and rips open the constricting neckband of the non-iron, Liberace shirt.

'Oh, God, how I love those braces,' Stella says. 'Izzy, your clothes are something else.'

'Don't blather,' Izzy says, because his preference is for unprotected, penetrative sex without audial accompaniment. His medium has never been vocal. Before he is through, he has turned her over and got her onto her knees – the Allen Jones coffee table presenting from the rear. Varoom.

Back in the car she stares down at the mess that was once her dress. Izzy is smoking a cigarette.

'I've forgotten the phone,' Stella says. 'Never mind. Pen will buy another one.'

But Izzy has opened his door. 'Hold on,' he says. 'I'll get it.'

'No,' she says. 'Don't. Leave it, Izzy. You'll never find it. Not in the dark.'

'Can't take you back without the mobile,' he says. 'Your old man'll give you what for.'

'What?' Stella says. '*What?*' But Izzy has already moved off. She sits alone in the darkness, trying not to brood upon the implications of Izzy's latest quip. Because she knows that she cannot go back. Will not. Not now. Not ever.

Izzy returns remarkably quickly. He throws the phone into her lap. Then he starts up the engine.

'So where are you staying?' he says.

'Nowhere,' Stella says. 'Izzy, I can't go back. You know that. You'll have to take me with you.'

Izzy laughs. 'Still the same old Stella,' he says. 'One fuck and bingo. You start to dryclean my life.'

'But, Izzy—' Stella says.

'Coal in the grate. Teabags in the cupboard. That's what your husband is for.' Stella says nothing. She tries not to cry.

'Come on,' Izzy says. 'Where are you staying? Or I could drop you back at the party—'

Stella closes her eyes. She says nothing. She thinks maybe she'll sign up at the nunnery where Pen's family always goes for midnight mass. That's if the nuns will have her. *Gott soll allein mein Herze haben.* It is certainly crystal clear to her that Izzy does not want her heart.

Meanwhile Izzy reverses, at speed, back over the railway bridge, after which he swings backwards into a junction at the bottom of the hill. Then he heads purposefully back towards town. 'The phone was ringing, by the way,' he says. 'D'ye know a bloke called Ambrose?'

'Yes,' Stella says. 'Ambrose is Pen's brother.'

'He wants Pen to phone him,' Izzy says. 'Their dad's just died in hospital.' Meanwhile the diners have moved from a table of fruit and nuts and port, to an upstairs room for coffee and Belgian chocolates. Pen makes the first approach. He crosses to Jonathan and Katherine.

'You're worried about Stella,' he says, 'and, frankly, so am I.' He volunteers himself to telephone Izzy's room and to check the extension at the porter's lodge.

'I really think—' Jonathan says, uncertainly.

'Isn't it a bit—?' Katherine says, but Pen is adamant. In the event, the matter is academic, since there is no reply from Izzy's particular guest room. As the evening draws to a close the three of them retire to Pen's hotel. At one o'clock in the morning, Pen is running a hand through his hair.

'This may be a matter for the police,' he says and he sits down with a sigh.

'Oh, surely not,' Katherine says, but during the last ninety minutes she has become very fond of her son-in-law.

'Mrs Goldman,' Pen says firmly, 'I'm afraid this is not quite all that it seems. Stella is very ill and so is Izzy.' They both stop and stare at him. 'Stella is HIV positive,' he says. 'And Izzy is the source of her infection.'

Stella's parents say nothing. They absorb this disclosure in total silence, understanding, at last, how it is that their daughter is 'frail' and 'unwell'. Shortly afterwards, they leave Pen's hotel room and return home to wait by the telephone for him to call – just as soon as he has news.

When Stella enters the hotel room, Pen is standing, in his clothes, with his back to her. He is staring out of the window. 'Stella, call your parents,' he says, without turning round. 'They are worried half to death.'

I have been here before, Stella reflects. She pauses. This time she says, 'Yes. Yes, all right. I will.' Pen keeps on standing with his back to her.

'Pen,' she says. 'There is something I must tell you. But I need you to look at me.'

When Pen turns round, she sees him observe her with a flicker of distaste. 'I suggest you run a bath,' he says. 'You smell of cowpats and your hair is full of goose droppings.'

'Yes,' Stella says. 'Yes, I know that and I'm sorry. Pen, you must listen to me. Something awful. And my timing couldn't be worse.' She stretches out to him the hand in which she holds the mobile phone. 'You're to phone Ambrose at once,' she says.

There is a pause. 'It's my father,' Pen says.

'Yes,' Stella says. 'Oh Pen, I'm so sorry. How can it be, when he was getting on so well?'

While Pen phones home on the mobile, Stella phones her parents. She taps out the number with no hesitation since, in the event, she finds that it is carved into her brain.

'Hello, Mum, it's Stella,' she says. 'I've phoned to tell you I'm all right.' Stella finds that making the call is, after all, not difficult. It is as easy as talking to a stranger. The bonds are all dissolved; the shared past all erased. She thinks, I and this woman could meet; will meet. We will talk pleasant, superficial nothings. We may or may not like each other. That is not important. It no longer signifies. But Holly will discover new grandparents. My father will make her laugh. My mother will teach her how to knit. Holly is the sort of daughter that she should have had all along. But it gives me no offence. This is because I am no longer the Precious Girl and the Fairy Princess and Mummy's Angel-pie and Daddy's Butter Melon. I am myself and that is all.

'Stella,' Katherine is saying, perhaps a little too eagerly. 'Can we possibly meet? Can we have breakfast tomorrow? Late-ish? In Oxford? The Old Parsonage is very good, you know. You'll not have been there, I think.'

But the moment is not altogether appropriate. 'The thing is,' Stella says, 'we've had bad news. Pen's father has just died.'

'Oh,' Katherine says, 'Oh how dreadful. Oh, the poor boy. Tell him I'm so sorry.'

'The thing is,' Stella says, 'we'll have to go back right away.'

'Yes of course,' Katherine says. 'Another time, I hope?'

'Yes,' Stella says.

'Stella,' Katherine says cautiously. 'Can it be soon?'

After that Stella runs a bath. Then, having first sealed up the dress in a plastic hotel laundry bag and crammed it into her suitcase, she steps into the tub and washes her hair.

'What was it Dr Sachs had to tell you?' Pen asks her. He is brushing his teeth alongside her at the washbasin and has paused to spit toothpaste and rinse his mouth.

'Oh,' Stella says. 'He says the virus is much reduced. Still. It may be that, after this evening, I have put all that at risk.'

Pen stows his toiletries in a bag and draws the zip shut. 'Dearest,' he says, and he hands her a towel. 'We ought to hurry things up a bit. We'll need to get all that hair of yours dry before we can face the night air.'

* * *

'Pen,' she says, once they are headed north in the Rover. 'Who is Lydia?'

'Lydia?' Pen says. 'She was Ellen's younger sister. She died in a car crash, remember? Somewhere in London. On the night that you fled back to Edinburgh.'

'But where?' Stella says. 'Where exactly did she die?' She asks this because her mind has begun to flash an image at her, of bollards and police cars and plastic tape. The image runs, always to the left of her, just within the orbit of her left eye, as she heads out, from her father's bedsit, for Euston Station. She has the Kenyan basket over her shoulder.

'Where, exactly, did she die?' Stella says. And, although Pen does not know and cannot tell her, Stella finds that she knows already, because – while she tries repeatedly to blink it away – the image comes back to her again and again. And again.

Acknowledgements

To Margaret Alice Stewart-Liberty for the loan of her cello and to Sandra Dodson for making a helpful connection for me, between Joseph Conrad and the German Romantics; to my father, F. J. Schuddeboom – a mathematician wholly unlike the Dreamboat – for filling my childhood with the sound of his tenor voice singing *Die schöne Müllerin* and, finally, to 'dearest her, who lives, alas! away'.

A NOTE ON THE AUTHOR

BARBARA TRAPIDO was born in South Africa and is the author of six novels – *Brother of the More Famous Jack* (winner of a Whitbread special prize for fiction), *Noah's Ark*, *Temples of Delight* (shortlisted for the *Sunday Express* Book of the Year Award), *Juggling*, *The Travelling Hornplayer* (shortlisted for the 1998 Whitbread Novel Award), and *Frankie and Stankie*. She lives in Oxford.